Morgan,
I hope you [...]
Story as much as [...]
writing it.
Happy Reading!

Let Me Save You

Lindsey-Anne Pontes

LET ME SAVE YOU

Front and back cover design by Jasmine Keats (@jasminekeatstattoo)

ISBN: 978-1-9992421-0-7 (paperback)

ISBN: 978-1-9992421-1-4 (ebook)

Acknowledgements

Catherine Muss: With a hefty story, from a first-time author, thank you for putting up with me over our time working together. I always looked forward to receiving emails when they came from you. Each time another editing draft was completed, I couldn't wait to dive back in and read your thoughts and recommendations on how to make my story even better. Throughout this process, I was glad to hear I inspired you to pick up a manga in order for you to get a better understanding of the style and atmosphere of which I chose to tell my story. There are pages beyond pages I could write about how wonderful you have been, but unfortunately, I need to keep this short and sweet. Without you, I would not be where I am today. A million times, thank you!

Jasmine Keats: From the bottom of my heart, I cannot thank you enough for everything you have done. Through many online sessions, you put up with my criticism and feedback for the book's cover with a smile. You were able to create something I had envisioned for many years and presented me with a gorgeous piece of art. I have enjoyed both the work you have tattooed on my body, and the work you have created for something close to my heart. Again, thank you!

Telma Rocha: From start to finish, without your help, I would not be where I am today. With all the time and hard work you have put into making this story a success, I cannot thank you enough! I will never forget our regular meetings where you would sit down with me and go through each edit and revision, one-by-one. You are a lifesaver when it comes to knowledge about self-publishing a book and detailed editing—a true sensei.

Terry Rocha: Thanks to you, I have learned many things about documents, templates, and creating a cover. You easily explained where and how to find things and were always willing to help. Between you and Telma, I cannot thank you both enough when it comes to the success of publishing this book.

Samantha Lacey-Jennings: Thank you for pushing me to finish this story after several years of ongoing nonsense, with incomplete thoughts and poorly written sentences. You were reading each ugly, unrefined chapter just as I wrote it, with no rounds of editing. I hope you notice a change from when I started, to how I finished.

Melissa Frattolin: Thank you for offering to take the time and edit a story you knew little to nothing about, twice. I enjoyed hearing your thoughts and perspective of my story during our sit-down discussion at my favourite coffee place. It brought me joy when you could recite passages from the book, stating how it stuck out to you for different reasons. I also enjoyed hearing your take and explanation of the character's personalities and traits, as it is how I intended and hoped would easily transfer to the readers.

Tara Mondou: I am grateful for your honest feedback and suggestions when it came to certain characters and scenes. You were very thorough and gave comments throughout your edits, which I enjoyed reading, to better my story. Thank you for being one of my beta readers. I appreciate all the time you put into my novel.

James Pemberton: As someone who knows me well and has put up with me for many years, thank you for your general concepts and sketches corresponding with my ideas. Although I chose another path, I was very happy to have witnessed your enthusiasm to help.

Note from the Author

As an anime and manga lover, I've always dreamt about taking a manga and Americanizing the writing platform for others who are not a fan of the Japanese comic book reading style, but enjoy the stories told. Thus, leading to the story you are about to indulge in.

For those less experienced with Japanese formalities, I have kept the usages of traditional words and honorifics, such as senpai, sensei, -chan or -san, limited. There are traditional usages involving the way an unfamiliar individual is addressed out of respect; for instance, the last name of a person is usually used when speaking with someone whom you do not have a close relationship with, unless the person permits it openly when meeting. Typically, until a rapport is formed, only then will the first name be used in everyday conversation.

I have chosen to write in such a manner so I could incorporate a passion of mine while introducing a culture, other than my own, to those willing to read something different. In no way, shape or form, am I an expert on Japanese culture; therefore, I apologize if I have used anything incorrectly. The story written is fiction, and is to be treated as such.

Without further ado, please enjoy!

P.S.

I would love to get emails from whoever reads my story. No matter the context or type of feedback—I want to read it all!

letmesaveyou.petalpublishing@gmail.com

Part One

Chapter One

"DADDY, DADDY!" I tugged on his sleeve. "Can we use this piece for the front?"

Turning, he glanced at the small, wooden object in my hand and smiled. "I don't see why not. Give it a shot." He guided my hand. "Steady, steady, alllllmost. Now, firmly press it. There, you've got it!"

I smiled as he lifted me up and placed me on his hip. Together, we gazed proudly at the new door on the dollhouse.

"You're the best, Daddy!" I hugged his neck. Burying my face underneath his chin, I whispered, "Thanks for helping me build a house for my dolly, Daddy."

He kissed the top of my head, then whispered back as he tickled my side, "You're welcome, Peaches. I'm glad you like it. But I can't take all the credit, this little four-year-old did most of the work."

"Daddy! Stop it!" I laughed in between tickles.

"I know for a fact, your doll's going to like it just as much."

My head popped up. "Really? You think so?"

"Yep, sure do." He set me down and bent to my level. "It looks great now, but it will look even better when we're finished."

"YAY!" I squealed in excitement.

"When it's all done, your dolly can invite all her friends over to have a party. Maybe even her boyfriend," he winked playfully.

"Daaaddy! Gross." My face scrunched up. *"My dolly does NOT have a boyfriend."*

He ruffled my long, brown hair as he chuckled. "I'm only kidding, Peaches."

"Nila, what's taking so long?"

"Huh . . .?" I strained away from the window and spun around to see my best friend, Kida, standing outside the classroom door. She looked irritated as she spoke.

"Jeez, you're seriously the slowest person ever. Everybody's already gone home. You didn't even have cleanup duty today. What's the hold up?"

She'd chosen to curl her shoulder-length, brownish-red hair and hike up her school skirt higher than usual, meaning she had been trying to catch the attention of some guy. Kida kept up with the latest fashion trends and always had her makeup and hair done for school, even though it was against the school rules. To her, school meant boys and boys meant dates, a very complex life really. I, on the other hand, barely did anything to my plain, long, brown hair. I never came to school to impress others or stand out. I was fine with getting good grades and living quietly in the shadows of my classmates and friends; that's where I felt most comfortable.

"Sorry, I guess I zoned out," I explained, continuing to pack my schoolbag.

How strange, the last thing I remember was watching the leaves blow in the cold winter wind outside the classroom window. I wonder where that memory of my father came from?

"Holy shit! Why do you need all those books?" Kida asked as she watched me cram countless textbooks into my bag. "It's the start of winter break. I know we're third years and have exams when we get back, but are you sure you need every single one of those?"

I clipped my brown, leather, messenger bag shut and headed for the doorway to walk out with her.

Making our way down the spacious hallway, I answered, "I need to be well-rounded in each subject if I want to maintain my high marks. This time of year is not a joke, you know." *More like, my mom thinks it's a good idea to study harder during the break.*

"Nerd. How did I become best friends with such a lame person?" she teased, throwing her hands up in exasperation, and shaking her head back and forth in shame. "You sound like my mom, except she's over forty and you're only seventeen. See what I'm getting at?"

The winter break normally started right on December 25th, with only a half-day of school. For some odd reason, this year, our break started a few days before Christmas. I wasn't sure if this applied to all schools in our district or if it was an action mine decided on alone, since I didn't converse with anyone outside of my school. The break was supposed to be used for homework and to study for college entrance exams, along with regular exams, but many students spent the month planning and preparing for dates with their romantic partners, considering Christmas in Japan is a time for lovers. I, on the other hand, used my breaks in the way it was expected of me: studying until I became mindless. Ready or not, the dreadful exams would take place shortly after we got back.

Kida and I reached the shoe lockers and began exchanging our regulated indoor slippers for our outdoor shoes. The lockers in the school were all painted navy blue to colour coordinate with our school logo and uniforms, minus the girls' plaid skirts. They were very small, enough for two pairs of shoes if you squished them together, unlike the ones near the gymnasium which were triple the size. Those were reserved for students with extracurricular physical activities. Kida's locker was two down from mine, making things convenient for walking to and from classes together since her classroom was next door to mine. I was in class 3-1 and Kida was in 3-2.

Kida Nazuka, seventeen, had been my best friend since junior high. For as long as I could remember, she had always been the loud and outgoing type. She was able to make friends easily and didn't care if she made a scene in front of others. I had to say, even though she could sometimes be wild, she'd always been there for me. As time went on, Kida got me to come out of my tightly closed shell, allowing me to accept, and even welcome friendships with others at school; although, the extent of my friendships usually expired after the dismissal bell. Kida and I were polar opposites, so I wasn't sure how we got along so well. I was more of the shy and conservative type, preferring to stay home and watch a movie instead of going out to party. I guess it's like they say: opposites attract.

After returning from the winter holiday, I would be in my third and final semester of my third year at Ogawa Gakuen with Kida and other familiar classmates. I planned on attending the local college right after high school so that I could stay near my family and support my mother. Kida, on the other hand, had no plans on what she wanted to do after high school. All she cared about was the here and now, while I was trained to constantly prepare for the future. Over the break, she would most likely be partying with friends and working at her part-time job, not giving much thought to studying for exams. Even though I didn't approve of her carefree lifestyle, I sometimes wished I could forget about the pointless stuff I worried about and just have fun like she did. It's not as if she excluded me though, she always made sure to invite me to go out with her and her friends, but being from another class, I felt uncomfortable going out with people I didn't know well enough, especially crowds involving guys.

This past summer, Kida told me she had lost her virginity to a younger guy from another high school. She never told me the name of his school, his name or age, but I wouldn't have cared if she did. No doubt at the time of telling me, she could see I wasn't comfortable listening to her 'big news' by the off-putting expression on my face. To me, sex was something I had always heard to be special. It was something you decided to experience with your partner after marriage, or at least after some sort of commitment, not just a one-time thing with someone you hardly knew. I'd never been very good at easily accepting some of Kida's choices. I was honoured she trusted me with her secrets, as I trusted her with mine, but there were some things I wished she would keep to herself. Sometimes, I felt isolated, like she left me behind each time she experienced something new. In the end, it was like there was a huge maturity gap between us.

"Alright, well, I'm ready," Kida said, throwing her bag over her shoulder. "I'm not going straight home today, so I'll message you through Line later to let you know if there's a party happening tonight that might interest you. Probably not, but I'll message you anyway!" she said, walking backwards towards the exit as she faced me with a grin.

"Yeah, yeah. I'll talk to you later. Don't get your hopes up about any parties!" I shouted as I watched her exit the building ahead of me.

Closing the locker door, I exhaled a sigh of relief. Listening to the amount of energy in Kida's voice and watching her hop around, left me exhausted. Wrapping my scarf around my neck, I straightened my uniform jacket before placing the strap of my schoolbag over my shoulder. Once I had everything, I was ready to leave peacefully.

I walked down the school's sidewalk and onto the path that would eventually lead to my house. The route to my house from the school was about a twenty-minute walk. As I started my journey home, my mood changed as quickly as air filled my lungs. Kida enjoyed being at school, not because of the work but because of her friends and all the boys. When the bells chimed at the end of each day, she couldn't wait to go home or out somewhere with a group of people. I didn't have anything even remotely similar to that. Not at school, and definitely not at home. A sudden bleakness whisked through me; my whole body grew sluggish. My feet dragged against the plain concrete with each step as if weights had been inserted into the soles of my shoes. Lonesome, undesirable thoughts occupied my mind, robbing me of peace. I was dreading the idea of going home and occupying myself with textbooks and unnecessary work dictated by my mother. I repeatedly did the same thing day in and day out: school, study, eat, sleep. To me, it felt like my life lacked something, something I could see in other girls my age, but not in myself. I wondered if this is what some called jealousy?

A cold breeze penetrated my uniform jacket, sending a shiver down my spine as it blew my hair across my face, making the day seem much cooler than the forecast had predicted this morning. It was currently winter, but so far, it wasn't as cold as previous years. I lived off the coastline, southwest from Tokyo, where there are many small towns, but no major surrounding cities. Even though the ocean borders my town, my house and school were on the opposite end, away from the water. This was where I spent most of my time, staying around the parts of town that I knew and exploring as little as possible. It takes approximately an hour and a half to get to Tokyo by plane and more than double the time by bus or train. It snows almost every year during this time in my town, but right now, the ground was clear of white as all living things continued to hold onto their last bits of life, but still, it was easy to see that things were dying and wilting away, leaving everything dull and colourless.

I approached the sacred Pink Path, as I did every day. It was my favourite part of the walk to and from school during the spring, my secret safe haven. This beautiful path made going to school worth it each day because of the huge cherry blossom trees growing all along the sides of the road. Even though the trees were currently bare, they engulfed me with encouragement, lifting my spirits with their power and natural beauty. This glorious path was most beautiful when things were pink as could be, utterly breathtaking. The colour and grace of the falling petals were mesmerizing to the naked eye. Sadly, the trees only bloomed for a short period in the spring, which is when most Japanese people go cherry blossom viewing with their family and friends. The cherry blossom tree is my absolute favourite; likely because when it blooms, it symbolizes life. I took a moment to fill my lungs with fresh air as I watched the naked trees and branches bounce in the wind surrounding me. Unlike major sidewalks, which were painted yellow, the walkway through the Pink Path was embedded with patterned stones, scattered sparingly among the concrete. Taking one step onto the first embellished stone, a flame of hope sparked inside of me. Many different types of cherry blossom trees grew here in Japan, but this path was special. There were rumours of this path having the ability to bring people together. I first heard of this tale from my mother when I was young. With that in mind, I continued down the path.

I made my way to the halfway point between the school and my house. In the middle of my route was a tiny, unkept public park which had an old swing set, a worn-out jungle gym, two sandboxes, and a basketball court—if you could even call it that. The whole park looked aged from extensive use and lack of maintenance. The paint on the jungle gym was chipped and faded from the sun, and the basketball court only had one good hoop. I decided to stop at the park to avoid going home for as long as possible.

My eyes were drawn to the swing set near the sandboxes. I found myself heading towards it with determination and somewhat childish delight. I dropped my schoolbag in front of the swings and took a seat on one of them. Facing the pathetic basketball court, I pushed off the ground with my feet, slowly swaying back and forth.

I guess it's too cold for people to play basketball now. I wonder if the court will be covered in snow soon?

While observing my environment, I noticed a small group of boys playing on the jungle gym and one little girl playing by herself in the far sandbox, all of them bundled in winter clothing. The sand the little girl was holding seemed easy to manipulate with her ungloved hands, even though it must have been cold to handle. I decided to kill time by watching the children play and interact with each other, hoping to bring joy to my unstable disposition. Looking at the band of boys, who couldn't have been any older than six or seven, I saw one of them throw a small rock at the little girl, pinning her on the back of the head. My eyes widened in shock. These were the typical kids you knew were troublemakers just by looking at them. Anticipating what her reaction might be, I waited for her to start wailing or begin screaming—something! She didn't react to the rock at all; instead, she dropped her head and continued to play in the sand, quietly.

As I reflected upon the scenario happening in front of me, I immediately got upset. *Stupid kid! Who does that little punk think he is? Throwing rocks at girls—how dare he!* I gripped the chains of the swing tightly and started to haul myself out. As I did, the little boy began shouting.

"Why don't you do something? Stupid girl! I threw a rock at your big, dumb head. Don't pretend you didn't feel it! Why are you so weird?"

Right after the little boy spoke, he looked towards his friends who were standing behind him. The other boys synchronized in laughter while saying, *'Yeaaaaah!'* in snobbish, mocking voices.

He must be the leader of their group . . . .

At that point, I decided I was going to let those snot-nosed kids have it. Just as I was about to get involved, an older, masculine voice came from another direction of the park.

"You know, if you want to get a girl's attention, you don't throw a rock at her. You simply go up to her and compliment her while wearing a prince-like smile. Like this." The guy went over to the little girl and bent down beside her, demonstrating the described smile. "Hey there, sweetie."

The little girl looked up at him with what seemed like tears in her eyes. She must have been crying the entire time. The guy took a quick look at her face. "Did you know, you have the most beautiful eyes I've ever seen?" he said as he reached out his hand cautiously before wiping away her tears. The little girl smiled brightly at the older boy.

Silently, I stood by the swings and watched his every movement. He moved so gracefully and had a gentle vibe about him; I couldn't look away. He was probably one of the most beautiful people I had ever seen who was around my age and not some famous, teenaged idol. The way he acted with the little girl, and the words he spoke to her, were god-like. I was almost jealous of the preschooler for having the chance to be near him.

He was wearing a high school uniform, different from mine. Over his uniform, he wore an unregulated, army green winter jacket, making it impossible to see the school logo on his sweater, but his pants and necktie were definitely a different colour and pattern from mine. This gorgeous guy had light, almond-brown hair that was short at the sides, with a heavier top and bangs that grazed the middle of his forehead. I couldn't see his eyes from where I was standing, but I suddenly found myself wanting to know the colour—bad.

"Why would I EVER compliment or smile at a stupid girl?" exclaimed the little boy as he took a step back into a defensive stance.

"Because, you obviously like her. Don't you?" taunted the high schooler with a smirk.

The little boy turned beet red as he spoke. "NO, I DON'T! Mind your own business, weirdo!" Right after his comment, the little boy turned to his friends. "Come on guys, let's go play at my house. This park is lame."

Just like that, the group of boys stormed off together. The high school guy laughed as he watched the boys leave the park. He then turned towards the little girl and helped her up. "How's your head? Does it hurt?"

The little girl shook her head no and said, "Thank you for h-helping me. Those boys go to my school and pick on me every day . . .."

The mysterious high schooler bent over and whispered something into the little girl's ear. From where I was standing, I couldn't hear a single word, but the little girl had a delighted expression. A huge smile appeared on her face as the high school boy stood up straight. She hugged his long, slender legs; it was as high as she could stretch, and ran off. As she ran, she waved at him until she was out of sight. Once she had vanished, the high school boy went to get his schoolbag from where he left it. As he did this, our eyes met. Without realizing what I was doing, I kept looking at him intensively. I could feel my face burning from the awkward stare-down between us. After realizing how embarrassed I was, I held my breath and turned my gaze in another direction, pretending to look at something else—anything else. Peeking from the corner of my eye, I could see him walking towards me. My heart started pounding profoundly as I felt myself internally panicking.

Why's he coming over here? What do I do when he gets here? Is he going to say something to me? What would I even say back?

Chapter Two

*H*E WAS CLOSE enough for me to smell the strong fragrance of his cologne as he bent down and picked my schoolbag up off the ground. Standing in front of the swing set, he held the bag out in his hand.

"Here," he offered.

"Th-thanks . . .," I shyly replied. Reaching for it carefully, I stole a glance at his eyes. They were a startlingly beautiful shade of green, vivid, like an emerald. Another thing that caught my attention were the two, small beauty marks he had right underneath his left eye.

"That was a nice thing you did. For that little girl." *Jeez, why am I shaking and stuttering like a complete idiot!*

"Ah, that was nothing. Besides, I had to step in, since it didn't look like you were going to do anything," he smirked rudely.

". . .." *What did he just say?*

"You know it's true. All you did was stand there while a little girl had a rock thrown at her. I had to take action before something else happened."

"Excuse me?" *What happened to that 'prince' who was here only moments ago?* "Um, I was going to interfere, right before you showed up. I jumped off the swing and everything."

"Don't make me laugh," he clicked his tongue. "I observed the whole situation and knew what was going to happen before it actually did. Couldn't you see the boy plotting it with his group of friends?"

"Oh, really?" my face twisted. "Well then, why didn't you step in sooner? That way, the rock would've never been thrown in the first place!"

"Because," he began with a hateful grin, "I thought you were going to attempt to get involved, since you were already sitting there when I arrived. I decided to give you a chance to be the hero."

Taking a step closer to me, he was right in my face. I could think of no words to say in return; his closeness had me flustered. One thing was for sure; I highly disliked this person.

"Ugh! Boys. You're all stupidly infuriating! Whatever." I gripped the strap of my schoolbag tightly and started to walk off, then picked up speed.

"Hey, wait!" I heard him shout as I ran towards home, and away from him; I didn't dare look back.

No way am I going to stop for that stupid jerk! And to think, I thought he was some 'princely' guy with a 'gentle vibe.' Makes me want to barf.

By the time I reached my house, I was out of breath. I had run all the way from the park to my house in half the time it usually took me. Staring up at the place I called home always put an indescribable weight of sadness on my shoulders. Once I was inside my own room, everything was fine, it was getting there that posed a problem. My house was average, like many others on our street; nothing stood out or succeeded at catching a person's attention. The only thing someone might question was the fact that our household nameplate was completely scratched out. Taking a look at my driveway, I was puzzled to see my mother's car.

Why is Mom home? She can't be done work already. Crap, I could have sworn today was her late day!

Cautiously, I walked up the steps to my front door and attempted to enter the house as quietly as possible.

"Nila, is that you?" my mother's voice questioned from the kitchen. Quickly, she poked her head around the corner of the wall as I stood frozen in the entrance.

Guess I wasn't quiet enough. "I'm home," I answered with a thick sigh, taking off my shoes and replacing them with slippers.

She left the kitchen and began approaching me with a furious look. "Where have you been? School has been out for more than an hour already."

Here we go. "Sorry, Mom. I stopped by the park on my way home and got sidetracked."

"Nila, that was an unnecessary waste of time. You could've gotten an early start on studying for your exams."

It's the same damn thing every time. Why is studying so important when my grades are above average? "Sorry, I won't be as careless next—"

"Good. I already have one problematic child, I don't need another," she said with no room for discussion, disappearing into the kitchen.

I knew she was talking about my younger brother, Kenji. She always put pressure on me to succeed but accepted his failures as if they weren't worth addressing.

"How come the school let you out earlier this year?" she questioned from the kitchen. "Usually, you stay right until the 25th?"

"I'm not sure. I overheard some people in my class saying the board of directors wanted to try something new with some of the schools in the area, but I'm not sure if that information is correct."

"Ah, I see."

"Yeah," I replied in a whisper, trying to end the conversation and head upstairs.

"By the way, do you know where your brother is?"

"No. He wasn't at school today either . . .."

I heard my mother stressfully exhale as she slammed something on the counter. "What am I going to do with that boy? He brings shame to this family! I see the neighbours whispering about us and talking behind our backs. I will not allow us to be the laughing stock of this neighbourhood! A mother who can't control her own children is pathetic," she expressed dramatically. "By the way," she said, changing the subject, "dinner will be ready in about thirty minutes. Get some of your schoolwork out of the way so you can have the rest of the night to study. Also, don't forget chores tomorrow morning."

"Yes, Mom," I moaned, dragging myself, and my belongings, up the steep staircase leading to the bedrooms.

I opened the door to my room and tossed my bag onto the corner of my bed. Shutting the door behind me, I allowed my body to fall back against it, slowly sliding down the hard, wooden surface until I reached the floor.

I don't even want to look at my schoolbag anymore, let alone open any textbooks.

After taking a moment to breathe, I found the energy to pick myself up off the floor and sluggishly walk to my dresser. Stripping myself of my uniform, I selected something more casual and comfortable to wear. Knowing it was time to begin my basic studying routine for the night, I reached for my bag and unlatched the clips.

"What? Ah, crap." *One of the clips is broken. How did that happen?* I dug through my schoolbag in search of my English textbook. *Where is it? I remember . . . putting it into my bag before leaving school. Could it have fallen out on my way home? Shit!*

I started emptying everything out of the bag in desperation, in case it was hiding at the bottom.

Oh, no. PLEASE don't tell me I actually lost it! "Ugh . . . ." *This is entirely that stupid guy's fault for distracting me!*

Without hesitation, I took my cellphone out from one of the pockets in my bag and rushed out of my room. Stumbling down the stairs, I reached for my winter jacket and threw it on.

"Mom, I'll be back in a few minutes!" I shouted, getting ready to go back out. "I think I left my textbook at the park."

My mother poked her head around the corner. Rolling her eyes, she shook her head in disappointment. "Nila, you're so careless. Go, quickly. Dinner is almost ready. You better hope that book is still there and no one's taken it. Textbooks are expensive to replace, you know. The money won't be coming out of my pocket, that's for sure."

"Yes, Mom. I'll make sure to hurry," I said, bolting out the door.

Running as fast as I could back in the direction of the park, a puff of mist accumulated in front of my face each time I exhaled into the cold winter air. When I got to the park, I headed towards the swing set. Looking around, my book was nowhere to be found. I decided to check other areas of the park in case someone found it and placed it somewhere else, but nothing turned up.

Damn! Mom's going to kill me. I'm going to have to use my allowance to pay for the book when I get back to school. My teacher isn't going to be happy about this either.

Before making my way to the park exit, my cellphone rang. The caller ID displayed the name: *Kida*, so I stopped to answer it.

"Hello?"

"NILA! Come quick! I neeeeed you."

Shocked by how Kida answered the phone, I replied in a panic. "Kida, are you alright?"

"Nila, meet me at the karaoke bar in front of the train station as soon as possible—hurry!" she shouted before hanging up.

"Kida! Kida!" I shouted back into the phone, only hearing the disconnected tone in return.

OH MY GOSH! Is she hurt? Is she in trouble?

Wild thoughts ran through my mind as I stood in shock looking down at my cellphone. The time on the screen read: 4:43 p.m. *Holy crap! Where has the time gone? I'm going to be late for dinner. Kida said the karaoke bar in front of the station, right? That's at least fifteen minutes from my house by bus; I'll never make it back in time! Mom will kill me if I tell her I need to stay out even longer.*

In the spur of the moment, I made a split decision to go and help my friend and not inform my mother of where I was going.

She'll probably get worried and call my cellphone eventually. When she does, I'll tell her I'm still at the park looking for the textbook. I'm hoping that will dispel her suspicions.

Missing the bus, I was forced to run nonstop for about thirty or so minutes and arrived at the location looking like a sweaty mess, hair untidied and in knots. I started examining the outside of the building and its surroundings.

It doesn't look like anything suspicious is going on. Where could she be?

"Nila, you came!" shouted a familiar voice from the side of the building.

I quickly turned to my left and saw Kida coming out of a side door, happily waving in my direction. *She doesn't look like she's in any danger . . ..* "Kida, what's going on? Are you okay?"

"Yeah, I'm completely fine," she replied as she grabbed hold of my wrist. "Come this way. I'll explain as we go."

"Um?" was all I could muster as Kida dragged me into the karaoke bar.

"You see," she began, "we're short on girls tonight for the mixer. This time, we're having it with guys from West Oji Gakuen. There's one extra guy and we couldn't get another girl to come out last minute, so I thought of you. I know this isn't really your scene, but you're my last hope! Please say you'll stay," she begged, giving me her famous puppy dog eyes.

I knew this look all too well. She used it on the guys and teachers at school whenever she needed or wanted to get out of something, but it never worked on me—and I wasn't going to let it start now. "Kida, you know how strict my mom is when it comes to staying out late. Plus, I didn't even tell her I was coming here, so she's going to freak out if I'm not home soon," I said in frustration. "Isn't there anyone else from our school who could—"

Before I could finish my sentence, we had arrived at the karaoke room where the rest of the group was waiting.

"Hey, guys! I found our last girl. Sorry she's late, she got the times mixed up," Kida excused, shoving me further into the room and steering me towards an empty seat beside one of the guys.

"Kiiida, why did you bring Nila Izawa?" complained one of the girls from Kida's class.

"Yeah, Kida, I thought she was the 'brainy type' who didn't come out to places like this?" asked another girl who was also from Kida's class.

"Are you kidding? Nila and I go out all the time. Just not with you losers! Right, Nila?" she asked, giving me a signal with her eyes to agree.

"Uh . . . yeah, sure."

"See, told y'all," she winked playfully. "Now, it's winter holidays, so let's get this party started!"

"Yeah!" shouted the group as they held their drinks in the air.

I sat quietly on the end of the sofa as the music blared, still trying to catch my breath and straighten out my messy hair. Next to me was a guy I had never met before. He had short black hair which was buzzed on both sides, with a longer top that was slicked back and dyed blonde. He never paused his conversation with the girl sitting on the other side of him to acknowledge my presence. Ignoring him, I took a look at the room as a whole. It was a standard karaoke room, large enough to hold approximately ten people. It had built-in, connecting seats which wrapped around a portion of the room's perimeter, a long table that ran through the middle, dimmed lighting, and a TV with a touchscreen karaoke machine in the corner where you could select songs to sing. I had been here once before with Kida, after the opening ceremony of our first year, but avoided coming back ever since Kida made friends with the popular girls in her class.

I can't believe I fell for another one of Kida's schemes. This better not be like the time she tried to set me up with that guy from class 3-3 by ditching me so he could be alone with me. Sometimes, I don't know whose side she's on. I'm definitely going to let her have it later! Mom's going to murder me. Asking for forgiveness is WAY easier than asking for permission with her, so I'll worry about Mom later.

Not knowing what else to do, or why I even bothered to sit down and stay, I decided to take another look around, but this time, at all the different faces surrounding me. The girls from my school were all over the guys from West Oji, causally placing their hands on the guys' shoulders and playfully hitting their arms when the guys made jokes I could barely understand—disgusting. Kida was chatting away in the corner with a guy, not paying attention to my existence at all. *If I snuck out, would she even notice?*

While glancing over everyone, I noticed someone staring at me from across the table.

"No way . . .." My eyes cracked open as I shied away. *IT'S HIM! The same guy from the park! Why is he here?*

Looking up, our eyes met in exchange once again. Staring at me intensely, he smirked, then stood from where he was sitting.

An instant panic overcame me as I sat frozen in my seat. *Oh, man . . . what's he doing now?*

He got closer and was now standing right in front of me. A smile beamed from the corner of his mouth, the same way it did earlier with the little girl at the park.

"Well, well, we meet again," he said, just like a villain from a cheesy movie. "We didn't get a chance to properly introduce ourselves the last time. I'm Kai Kento, and you're Nila . . . Izawa, was it? Nice to meet you." He reached his hand out to shake mine.

"I beg to differ," I sarcastically replied while crossing my arms. Unwilling to shake the hand of someone who was extremely rude to me earlier, I rolled my eyes.

He started to laugh while retracting his hand. Looking directly at me, he placed both hands down onto the table in front of me. Slightly bending over the corner of the table, he got really close to my ear and whispered, "This just keeps getting interesting."

Backing away, I noticed a devilish look burning in his eyes.

Interesting . . .? What the hell does he mean by that?

Chapter Three

"HEY, TAKI, SWITCH with me," Kai said to the guy sitting beside me.

"Yeah, sure thing, bro. I'm up next anyway. Found your next prey?" the boy named Taki said, grinning suggestively.

"Funny," Kai snarled, smacking the back of Taki's head as Taki passed him.

When Taki stood up to cross over me, I realized he was slightly shorter than Kai. With one hand, Taki held his drink, which I assumed was a soft beverage as we are too young for alcohol, while receiving a karaoke mic from one of the girls in his other.

Kai sat down next to me, forcing me to scoot over into Taki's old spot and out of my seat that was conveniently close to the exit. Now I felt even more uncomfortable, sandwiched between Kai and the other girls made me somewhat claustrophobic. Kai's eyes never wavered as he changed places, focusing all of his attention on me. His stare was extremely intense and a bit irritating. His eyes settled on mine like a hawk closing in on a mouse. I felt almost annoyed as I kept asking myself why he was sitting so close. My heart was beating harder and faster than a drum—I wished he would just back off. I started to get angry and nervous all at the same time.

Just my luck. I got tricked into coming to a mixer and then, out of all the guys in the world, I'm reunited with this jerk.

"What? Do you have a problem? Why do you keep staring at me?"

"I'm just analyzing you," he said calmly. He was almost too calm for my liking.

"You're . . . what?"

"Analyzing you, you know, like observing and taking mental notes? Jeez, I thought you were the 'brainy' one."

Every word coming out of this fool's mouth is beyond infuriating. "I understand what it means, idiot. I just want to know WHY you're doing it?"

"Because, you're interesting to me," he said sharply.

His response startled me. "W-why do I interest you?"

"Well . . .," he said, smiling, "when we met earlier today, I assumed you were stuck-up because of the way you presented yourself. Then, after talking to you, I realized that's how you actually are," he said, bursting into laughter. "Now, here you are, at a mixer with a bunch of girls who seem nothing like you. It's all so fascinating."

"I'm not stuck-up!" I growled.

"I know."

He knows? Then why did he say I was. "Then why . . .," I started to ask, but was interrupted.

"Kaaai!" one of the girls whined. "Come sing a song with me!"

The girl flaunted the cup in her hand, making it seem like she had been drinking more than soda.

Kai looked over, giving her what seemed to be a forced smile. "Maybe later." He then turned back towards me; the forced smile disappeared from his face. "The girls here are all stuck-up and full of themselves, every single one of them—except you," he stated. Propping his elbow onto the table, he leaned on it while resting his chin in his palm.

His answer threw me off guard. I could feel my face getting hot and turning red as I clutched the edges of the jacket I never took off. *This is ridiculous. He thinks he knows all about me based on my appearance and the few words we've exchanged.*

"I don't have to explain myself to someone who judges others by the way they seem on the outside! For your information, I wasn't supposed to be here tonight. I got called here by mistake," I stated before urgently standing. "And what a big mistake it was," I muttered under my breath, crossing over him to head for the door.

"Hey! Wait a minute," Kai exclaimed, grabbing my hand.

"Let go!" I shouted as I turned to face him. "What do you want from me? To pick on the outcast, huh? You 'popular' people are all the same. Now, let go of me!" I tried pulling away, but he was much stronger than I was.

When I raised my voice, the whole group stopped what they were doing and looked directly at us. Immediately, Kai let go of my hand. I could hear the girls from Kida's class whispering about the scene I was making.

"What's your problem? You're interrupting the fun with whatever meltdown you're having," said one of the girls.

Kida stopped her one-on-one conversation and looked at me with narrow eyes. "Nila, you okay?"

"Yeah, she's fine," Kai answered for me. "I told her a joke and took it too far."

"Leave it to Kai to piss a girl off," said another one of the guys as they laughed.

The whole group joined in on the laughter and then carried on with whatever they were doing, brushing off the disturbance.

Kai looked back towards me with a bitter look on his face. "Now, who's judging who, hmm?"

I rolled my eyes at his snarky comment.

"Can you calm down for a second and listen. I need to tell you something, but it's a bit crowded in here. Let's step outside," he suggested.

"Fine. I guess I also have something to ask you. Let's make this quick. I'm running extremely late," I demanded.

"Yes, Ma'am."

He grabbed his coat before we headed out of the room. When we reached the front door, he held it open for me.

Hmph. What's his game . . . ?

"Okay, we're outside and it's cold. Hurry up and tell me what you want," I said, crossing my arms and rubbing them up and down to keep warm.

"It's straight to the point with you, huh?" he teased. "Well, okay then. I just wanted to let you know you dropped a textbook when we were at the park."

My eyes lit up with a joy like no other as I heard those beautiful words spill from his idiotic mouth.

"I tried to give it back to—"

"Where's the book now?" I interrupted excitedly.

"Relax," he placed his hands up in front of his chest in self-defence. "It's at my house. I wasn't expecting to see you, tonight of all nights, so obviously, I didn't bring it."

"Right," I agreed. "I didn't even know I was coming myself." *Let alone staying for as long as I have.*

"I was going to ask the girls from the mixer if they knew you. I realized they went to the same school as you when I saw the school stamp in your textbook. I was planning on returning it to you in person."

Oh, that was surprisingly thoughtful of him. To go through the trouble of returning a textbook to someone he just met.

"I see. So, when can I get it back?"

"Well, we can head to my house now if you want it that bad? I live kinda far from here though," he said, checking the time on his phone.

I don't even know him, but I really need that book . . .. "Um, how far is it?"

"About two bus rides, sooo, half an hour-ish—maybe more."

There's no way. "That's too far for me to go tonight. I'm already super late, so I have to head home."

"I figured as much."

I can't believe what I'm about to suggest . . .. With a deep sigh, I couldn't help but ask, "Can I possibly pick it up another day? Maybe tomorrow?"

"Yeah, that's not a problem. I don't think I have any plans tomorrow, so anytime of the day works."

My heart lifted. "Perfect. I will pass by after lunch. Thank you for taking care of my schoolbook." I bowed to Kai in gratitude and turned to head home.

"Um, Izawa."

"Yeah?" I said, turning around.

"What were you going to ask me?"

"Oh, I was going to ask if you found a book at the park after I left, but I guess you did," I chuckled.

"She laughs!" he joked. "We're on the same page then," Kai said, smiling.

"I guess we are," I smiled back politely. *What is this awkward feeling in the pit of my stomach?* "Well, I'll be going now. See you tomorrow," I said nervously, turning my back once more to walk away.

"Aren't you forgetting something else?" he hinted again.

I whipped around with concern. "Like what?"

"I don't know, maybe my address?"

"You have a point. I guess I should ask where you live. How else am I expecting to get there?" I asked rhetorically.

"Here," Kai said, plugging away at his phone. "Do you use Line? Give me your Line ID and I'll message you my address. You can save my number to your contacts and message me when you're on your way over tomorrow."

"Yeah, I do. Good idea."

"I know, I'm full of them," he said, arrogantly.

He's quickwitted. "Ha, ha, verrry funny. Like, SUPER funny."

"Whatever, you're just jealous because I'm hilarious."

"Hardly," I joked while showing him my phone inquiry so he could see my Line contact information. I watched as he entered it into his phone. *His fingers are long . . ..*

"There, done. Now, we're set."

"Yep . . .," I replied. Somehow, it started to feel even more awkward than it had moments ago, so I decided it was best to finally leave. "Well, thanks again, bye," I waved while walking away from him once more.

"Wait!" he hollered. "Let me walk you home. It's getting dark out, and these streets can get pretty sketchy for a girl on her own."

"It's okay, you don't have to do that. Really, I'm fine. Plus, you have to get back to everyone inside."

"Right . . . I completely forgot about them. Oh, well," he shrugged his shoulders. "They'll be fine without me."

Just then, Kida came out of the karaoke bar with her jacket on top of her shoulders.

"Nila! Ohhh, damn, it's getting cold out here," she said, rubbing her hands together. "Are you okay, girl? You've been missing for some time now, so I came looking for you." Kida looked over and saw Kai standing beside me. "Ouu, am I interrupting anything?" she said, winking at me.

"No! I was just about to leave and Kento was . . .."

"I was about to take her home," Kai slickly interrupted. "It's late and this area is pretty dangerous at night, so I don't want her walking home alone. Let the others know I won't be coming back, okay?"

"Uh . . . yeah, sure, no problem," Kida said with a dumbfounded expression. "Thanks for taking care of her. I leave her in your hands." She smiled mischievously, as if she planned for this to have happened. "Nila, I'm sorry for dragging you out tonight. If your mom gives you shit, you can totally blame it on me. She doesn't like me much anyway. Goodnight!" Kida waved as she went back into the bar.

That's it? Kida! What the hell?

"Alright, so off we go then. Lead the way," Kai initiated.

"Hey, I never agreed to you walking me home! Don't just decide things on your own, idiot."

Kai started laughing. "Alright, alright. Man, you crack me up. I am truly sorry, 'Oh, Great One'!" he teased, repeatedly bowing towards me as if I were royalty.

"Pffft, idiot." *Why am I playing along with this? This game of his is suspicious, but truthfully, I don't hate it.* "Whatever, let's just go."

"Alright! We're off on an adventure. To the Izawa's house we go!" he sang obnoxiously loud in the middle of the street.

"You're so weird."

As we walked along the street, I checked my phone to get the time. It was already close to 6:00 p.m., and my mother had called twelve times and left four voicemail messages.

"OH MY GOD!" I shouted and instantly stopped walking.

"What is it?"

"NOO! It's almost 6:00 p.m. I am so dead! PLUS, my mom called me like a hundred times and I never answered because my phone was on silent."

"Oh, phew. I thought you were hurt or something. Just explain the situation to your mom; it'll be fine."

"No. You don't understand. I will be grounded for an eternity! You don't know my mom. She's going to chew me up and spit me out." At that exact moment, my mother was trying to call my phone once again. "AH!" I shouted at the screen.

Do I answer it? She's just going to talk over me and I won't even be able to get a single word in. Tonight is going to suck when I get home. She's going to yell at me until my ears start bleeding.

"Aren't you going to answer it?" Kai questioned. "It's your mom, right? Didn't you just say she's going to be upset?"

"Yeah, that's the reason why I'm so hesitant." I looked at Kai in fear of what was going to happen next, as if he could help me in a situation completely unrelated to him. Impulsively, I picked up. "Hell—"

"WHERE ARE YOU? WHY AREN'T YOU HOME YET?"

"I was—"

"What reason could you possibly have to STILL be out this late? What are you doing right now? Why aren't you through this door yet?" my mother demanded furiously.

Holy crap, she's sooo pissed. "I went to look for the book and—" I tried to respond to her questions, but couldn't complete a single sentence.

"You better not come home empty-handed! Don't tell me you were out this entire time and STILL haven't found it! If that book is not IN YOUR HANDS when you enter THIS house, then you better kiss your whole winter break goodbye and say hello to cleaning supplies! You're going to spend your whole holiday cleaning this house from top to bottom!"

My eyes started watering up; I couldn't hold my tears back. *I hate it when she yells at me like this. It makes me feel worthless. Kento can obviously hear her through the phone because of how loud she is. How embarrassing.* A tear fell from my cheek and onto my shoe as I held my head low to hide my tears from Kai.

Just then, Kai took the phone from my hand. "Hello, Mrs. Izawa?"

"Wha— who is this? A BOY! What have you done to my daughter?" I could hear my mother yelling into the phone at Kai as if he had placed her on speaker.

"Mrs. Izawa, your daughter is fine. I'm sorry, I am the reason she is late, so please don't blame her. She bumped into me and I distracted her. I will have her home in ten minutes. Thank you and sorry once again."

"WAIT!" I heard my mother shout as Kai hung up the phone before handing it back to me.

I can't believe he did that! I can't believe how easily he spoke to my mom. He put all the blame on himself when it wasn't even his fault.

"Why did you do that?" I asked sincerely. "You aren't to blame for this."

"Yeah, but neither are you. I didn't like the way your mom was yelling at you. She went too far."

Those words from Kai impacted my heart greatly. My eyes instantly welled up, and I began crying joyously. For so long, I have wanted to stand up to my mother. Whenever she started yelling, I was never able to build up the courage to confront her about my feelings. But this person, he's the total opposite. His voice didn't waver once while he was on the phone with her, someone he has never met before. He was still polite and managed to get his message across quickly. I admired him for doing something I could never do.

Kai got closer to me and wrapped his arms around me. "It's okay. Cry as much as you need to before we get to your house. I don't mind."

Kai's embrace was warm and comforting. *So, this is what a hug from a boy feels like . . .*

I soon came to realize the situation I was in. I was in the arms of a guy! A guy I had just met was hugging me, and I was allowing it to happen so casually! I immediately pulled away from his embrace in embarrassment, my heart pounding uncontrollably.

"Sorry! I got carried away. I saw you crying, so I . . . I tried to comfort you without thinking!" he admitted, backing away from me quickly.

"Um, no, uh, it's okay." I quickly tried changing the subject. "I'm very sorry for ruining your night and dragging you into my personal affairs. This is humiliating," I confessed.

"No, not at all! Izawa, trust me, you didn't ruin anything. In fact, you saved me," Kai said with a smile as he wiped the last tear from my cheek.

His smile is something powerful; it's scary. "Thank you," I said, cheering up.

"Don't worry about it," he said, placing his hands into his pockets. "Now, let's get going because it's almost been five minutes and we haven't even moved. I can't break a promise to such an important woman."

"Yeah," I giggled, not really knowing what he meant by 'important woman.'

When we arrived at my house, my mother was waiting outside of our gate with her coat and boots on.

"Crap . . .," I whispered quietly.

"Don't worry," Kai whispered back as he jogged towards my mother. "Mrs. Izawa!" he shouted as he approached her, then bowed. "I am very sorry to have kept your daughter out this late."

"And who might you be, young man?" my mother questioned, looking Kai up and down, trying to read him. "You better not tell me you're my daughter's boyfriend, because I certainly won't allow that!"

"Mom, he's . . .," I tried to explain, but Kai shook his head in my direction as he stood tall, indicating I should keep quiet.

"Mrs. Izawa, my name is Kaichi Kento and I'm in my senior year at West Oji Gakuen. I had met your daughter earlier today at the park and realized she dropped a textbook from her schoolbag. I picked it up and took it home with me in hopes of finding her to return it. I did not expect to run into your daughter twice in one day, so I did not have the book with me at the time of our second encounter. We got carried away and started talking about school, classes, and interests in future colleges. I am very sorry for the inconvenience I have caused your family tonight. Please apologize to Mr. Izawa as well for me. Thank you, have a good night." Kai bowed to my mother once more, then turned to walk away.

When did he become so proper? That was amazing.

My mother looked flustered and was unable to find the words to respond to Kai's formal introduction.

"Um Kento," I spoke up as he walked past me.

Kai turned around with a gentle smile. "Have a good night. Sorry for getting you in trouble." Just before he turned away a second time, another thought seemed to have crossed his mind. "Oh, and one more thing, Mrs.

Izawa. I would appreciate it if you could allow your daughter to pass by my house tomorrow after lunch, in order to retrieve her textbook."

"We shall see," my mother replied, crossing her arms.

"Of course, Ma'am. Good night." Kai placed both hands into the pockets of his coat and continued making his way down my street.

I subconsciously watched him until my mother called my name. "Nila!"

Jerking around, I answered fearfully. "Yes!"

"Come inside. It's cold and we have things to discuss."

"Yes . . .," I replied once more, quivering where I stood.

My mother was first to go through the gate and walk up the pathway to the front door of the house as I quickly scurried behind.

Chapter Four

I TOOK EVERYTHING OFF by the door and followed my mother into the kitchen, noticing the rise of tension in the air.

"Sit," my mother demanded with a stern look, pulling out a chair for me at the table. As I sat in silence, she hunched over me and gripped onto the back of my chair with one hand as she rested the other flat on the table. "What were you thinking? Lying to your mother and staying out this late—with a boy no less! You were raised better than that," she expressed with disappointment. "That boy must not know you very well if he believes 'Mr. Izawa' still lives here."

"Mom! I didn't lie about going to the park to look for my textbook. I'm sorry about everything that happened, and he . . . just happened to be there." My lips quivered as I relived the comfort of being wrapped in his strong arms.

"Nila, this is . . .," she started, but got interrupted by the front door opening. Standing up, she headed towards the hallway. "Kenji!" she exclaimed. "Where have you been? I got a call from your homeroom teacher today saying you didn't attend any of your classes! It was the last day before the winter holiday, what is this all about?"

From inside the kitchen, I could clearly hear my mother yelling at my brother as if she were still standing next to me. The walls in this house were thin as paper, so it wouldn't surprise me if people could hear her from outside.

The front door slammed shut. Being nosy, I peeked from around the corner of the kitchen wall. Standing at the doorway was Kenji, wearing a black jacket, purposing ripped black jeans, scuffed up running shoes, and a baseball cap pulled down far enough to cover his eyes. His brown hair shyly poked out from all sides of the hat, as if he carelessly put it on. My brother didn't make eye contact with our mother as she lectured him. All he did was stare at the floor the entire time before taking off his hat, shoes, and jacket.

"Kenji, it's rude to ignore your mother. Answer my question, now!"

"Which one?" Kenji replied coldly, under his breath.

"Pardon me?"

He shook his bangs to the side, uncovering his eyes, staring straight at her. "You asked me to answer your question, but you asked more than one. So, which one do you want me to answer?"

Still peeking around the corner, I could see my mother's face change into an enraged shade of red. "Don't you DARE get smart with me, young man! I am your mother, not some friend you hang out with."

"Whatever," he mumbled as he brushed past her, heading upstairs.

"Kenji, get back here! We are not done with this conversation!" She watched him continue up the stairs without glancing back. "UGHHH! I don't know how to get through to him anymore!" she exclaimed, her face blood-red from the confrontation. "Why . . .? Why has he changed so much?" The tension from her body finally released in one huge, exaggerated breath as she tried to calm herself down. "From that sweet, little boy he used to be." She turned and saw me standing against the wall in the hallway. "Hmm," was all she muttered as she walked past me, heading down the hallway before plopping herself down on the couch in the living room. "Nila, we will continue our conversation later. There's too much on my mind right now to deal with tonight's incident," she said, massaging her temples. "Plus, tomorrow is an early shift for me. Go to your room and start whatever homework you were assigned for the break."

"Alright . . ."

It pained me to climb back up that awful staircase. My room was the first door on the right, the second was Kenji's, and the third belonged to my mother. Across the hall from all of our rooms was the only bathroom in the entire house and a small closet. I walked past my door until I reached Kenji's; nothing but a dead silence emanated from it.

My brother and I used to be fairly close until about two years ago when my father left. We haven't seen or heard from him since that day. No phone calls, no visits, nothing. Our father's absence has affected my brother greatly because they were extremely close. Kenji looked up to our father, like he was a hero and a best friend. Whenever something broke or wasn't working properly, our father knew exactly how to fix it. My brother really admired him and said he wanted to grow up and become just like him. They always spent time together either playing sports, building things, or fixing whatever needed to be repaired around the house.

The final year my parents spent together was tremendously stressful on our family. My parents fought constantly, and my father spent many nights away from home. My mother used to be a very understanding, warm-hearted person, but during that last year, she turned into a really strict and tough woman—especially with me. It was as if she was already preparing herself for the worst. She always kept a positive face around the neighbourhood because she didn't want the neighbours to gossip about our family crumbling. It was as if she wore a mask to hide what she was feeling and what was really going on.

Last year, rumours spread around the neighbourhood about my father having a second family somewhere in town. Having had no contact with him for over a year at the time, curiosity got the better of me. I had discovered the unforgivable truth one day when returning from school, where I overheard one of our neighbours conversing with another neighbour that my father and his new family had indeed been living close, almost too close for comfort. My heart yearned to visit him, yet I couldn't bring myself to do it. Who in their right mind could abandon their children without even a second thought?

Ever since he left, my mother continuously picked up extra shifts at work and constantly asked for more overtime hours. We needed the money, but I'm sure it was also to keep her occupied so she wouldn't have to think about him. My mother was a nurse at the hospital in town and did a bit of work at the senior home attached to the building. Her shifts were all over the place and she was always on call. Lately, she had become extremely strict with me when it came to school and getting good grades, but she didn't push my brother nearly as hard, even though we were only a year apart.

My mother and brother butted heads a lot when it came to rules and expectations. Sometimes Kenji didn't even come home at night and often we'd be unable to get in contact with him. Talking to him about anything was out of the question, considering all he ever did was push us away.

Faced with Kenji's door, I decided to knock on it gently. "Kenji . . .." I waited a couple of seconds for a reply, but didn't receive one. "Ken—"

Before calling his name a second time, the door cracked open, wide enough to see only half of his face.

"What is it?"

"Um . . . I just wanted to make sure you were okay. You know we . . .."

"I'm fine. Is that all?"

"Oh, uh, yeah, I guess . . .."

"Okay, good night then," he answered sharply, shutting the door in my face.

"Yeah," I whispered under my breath, staring at the closed door. "Why can't things be the way they were before?" I asked Kenji's door rhetorically before walking back towards my room.

Entering my prison with a bleeding heart, invisible shackles tight and heavy around my soul, I tried to remember the last time I shared a pleasant moment with my brother but was unable to find the lost memory. Shutting the door behind me, I silently cried. Leaning up against it, I grasped the handle for dear life, as if it were the only thing holding me up. It felt like I was chained to this house, cursed if I stayed, but forbidden to leave.

Falling back onto my bed, the tears continued rolling down my face. The plain, white ceiling stared at me. To calm myself, I counted the small imperfections the ceiling had obtained over the years, like I had done many times before. Mid-count, my phone vibrated—it was a message.

The screen was so bright that it blinded me; I'd received a Line from Kai. I opened the message and read:

[Line Kai]: Hey, Izawa, it's Kento. Are you free to talk?

Well, I can't be too loud because of Mom, so talking on the phone is out of the question. Plus, I don't think I could handle talking on the phone with him right now, crying like this.

[Line Nila]: Hey, I can't talk on the phone right now. How about messaging like this?

[Line Kai]: That's fine. Is everything okay over there? Tonight, was pretty intense.

[Line Nila]: Um, things are not too great right now. My mom and I started having a serious talk, but then my brother came home and things got more complicated.

[Line Kai]: Oh shit, really? Are you okay?

[Line Nila]: Yeah, I'm fine. She didn't yell at me—so that's a plus. She's put our conversation 'on hold' for now.

[Line Kai]: I'm glad she didn't tear you apart. I would have felt really bad if she got even more upset with you for something I did.

[Line Nila]: No, it's not your fault at all. Technically, it's Kida's for dragging me to the stupid karaoke bar in the first place.

[Line Kai]: Haha, I guess you're right. I'm really glad she did though.

What does that mean? Why is he glad she forced me to come?
A few seconds later, another message appeared on my screen.

[Line Kai]: Because I was able to get in contact with the owner of the book I picked up . . . .

Oh, that's what he meant . . . makes sense, I guess. I wonder why it's so easy to talk to Kento like this. I just met him and yet he makes it easy to continue a conversation.

[Line Nila]: I guess that's true.

[Line Kai]: Well, I'm going to let you go then. Just wanted to make sure everything was alright after I left.

That's it? He's ending the conversation? Why did my heart suddenly tighten up after reading his message? I couldn't possibly be feeling upset because the conversation is ending . . . What more was I expecting?

He seemed genuinely concerned for my wellbeing. It was comforting knowing someone actually cared enough to ask about the relationships within my family. At the bottom of the same message, he included his home address, followed by a *'good night.'*

I almost forgot, I have to go to his house tomorrow to pick up my textbook—if Mom let's me, that is. So, this isn't the end. My heart thumped deeply in my chest. *There it is again! Why am I reacting this way?*

With a lump in my throat, I tried to calm myself enough to send a reply.

[Line Nila]: Yeah, things are okay for now, thanks. See you tomorrow—hopefully.

Hopefully? Ugh, what an embarrassing reply! Did it make me sound too willing?

With that final message, our conversation ended.

I wonder what he's doing now. Maybe he's in his room lying on his bed just like I am. He said he wasn't going to go back to the karaoke bar with the others, but that could have been a lie. Seriously, why do I even care? I don't know him well enough to be concerned about what he does. If I end up going to his house tomorrow, I'll pick up my book and end this little game. After that, nothing will be connecting us and there will be no reason to talk to him anymore. That's right. This all started because of a textbook, and once it's back in my possession, it will surely end. Tomorrow, this will all be over . . ..

Chapter Five

*J*UST AFTER 1:00 p.m., I got ready, packed my bag, and headed downstairs. My mother had left for work earlier this morning; therefore, I was able to avoid confronting her or asking for permission before leaving the house. Putting on my outdoor attire, I couldn't help but think about Kenji and what happened last night.

I wonder if he's still here or if he's left already? "Kenji, I'm leaving!" I shouted, just in case, but received no reply.

Scurrying to leave, I left for the bus stop closest to my house. Along the way, I noticed a few skinny trees on the sides of the road, blowing harshly in the strong wind.

It really is getting colder.

Reaching the bus stop, I waited for the bus to arrive. Digging deep into my purse, I pulled out a piece of paper with directions to Kai's house. *For some strange reason, I feel like I've read these street names somewhere before.*

The bus arrived shortly, eventually taking me to the terminal at which I made two transfers before getting on the bus leading to Kai's house.

I should message Kento and let him know I'm almost at his house.

Minutes after pushing send on my phone, I received a reply.

[Line Kai]: Awesome! I'll be waiting outside of my house so that it's easier to find.

[Line Nila]: Okay, thanks.

After about two blocks of walking around like a lost puppy, I spotted a person standing on the side of the road waving in my direction. Heading towards him, I realized it was Kai.

"Did you find the place okay?"

"More or less. I got directions from the internet, so I wasn't sure if they'd be right."

"Sorry, I guess I should have written out proper directions for you. It completely slipped my mind."

"It's okay. So," I said, quickly changing the topic, "do you have my English book?"

"Yeah, it's inside, come with me." Kai took my hand and led me towards his house.

This is awkward. His neighbours will probably think we're dating or something. Would pulling my hand away offend him? All he's really doing is leading the way. This sort of thing doesn't seem to bother him, so why does it bother me?

Instinctively, I pulled my hand from his grasp and Kai immediately stopped walking. He turned around with a puzzled look on his face.

"Uh . . . sorry . . . um, it's just . . . ." I didn't want to tell him that holding hands made me uncomfortable. It made me seem sort of pathetic.

"No, no, it's my fault!" he apologized. "Sorry, ha . . . ha, I forgot you're different."

Different? What's that supposed to mean?

Before asking any more questions, out of nowhere, a baseball flew right by my face and landed on the road.

"Whoa! Where did that come from?" I blurted out.

"Hey, Kai! Can you get my ball?" a little boy in a winter suit shouted over a short fence. Like most, the fence gated his entire property from the road and surrounding neighbours.

"Yeah, no problem, Yano. But be more careful next time, you almost hit us! A baseball is pretty hard, y'know," Kai warned as he grabbed the ball and tossed it back to the boy.

"Sorryyy! It was Kiro's fault. Yell at him," he whined.

"Yeah, yeah, whatever you say." Kai laughed at Yano's upset

expression, then glanced at me. "Are you okay?" he asked in concern before pointing at Yano. "This is my neighbour's kid. He's always playing ball and hitting things like cars, windows—you name it."

Yano's mouth dropped. "Nuh-uh!" he pouted, putting his hands on his hips. "Stop telling your girlfriend that or she's gonna think I'm a bad kid."

"She already knows you're a bad kid," Kai said playfully, sticking out his tongue.

"Don't lie to him, Idiot!" I replied, placing my hands onto my hips.

Wait a minute. Yano said 'girlfriend' and Kento just laughed it off. Did he not hear what Yano said?

"Yeah, idiot!" Yano repeated, devilishly giggling. "I like her. She also thinks you're an idiot."

"Shut up, you little brat! Why are you even playing ball outside? It's frickin' cold!" Kai retaliated.

"'Cause I can!"

Watching the two of them go at it made me laugh. For some reason, it was nice to see Kai getting along with little kids. Just like the time at the park.

"Bet she thinks we're both idiots," Kai expressed jokingly.

"Don't lump me with you," Yano stuck his tongue back out at Kai.

I couldn't help but laugh even more because it was like watching a comedy duo. As I watched them bicker, I happened to glance over at Yano's family nameplate. It was engraved with the last name: *Izawa.*

"Kai, you're . . .," Yano started, but didn't get a chance to finish before I butted in.

"Um, Yano . . .."

"Yes, lady?"

"How rude. Her name is Nila," Kai stated.

"You never told me her name, stupid. How am I supposed to know?"

The two of them continued to bicker, overlooking the fact I called out Yano's name for a reason. "YANO!" I raised my voice without realizing.

Yano's eyes widened as he answered shyly. "Y-yes?"

"What's . . . your dad's name?" I asked, holding my breath and clenching the strap to my purse.

"Izawa."

"I mean his first name . . . ."

"Oh, it's Youji. Why?" he asked, tilting his head in confusion.

My heart dropped as the name *Youji* left Yano's small lips. I could feel my throat closing up, leaving me unable to breathe normally.

"YAAANO!" Another small boy from behind the fence called out. "Hurry up and throw the ball already! I'm gonna turn five from waiting so looong."

"Coming, Kiro!" Yano shouted back as he looked over at Kai. "Thanks for getting my ball, stupid." He then faced me and bowed. "Nice meeting you, lady." He straightened up and ran back towards his friend to continue playing.

"Why, you!" Kai shouted, watching Yano run back to his friend. "It's Nila!"

My ears were playing tricks on me. The air around me felt polluted, slowly choking me like I was inhaling poison. My heart was a block of heavy ice and the world around me started to spin. *There's no way. It can't be . . . it just can't.*

"Izawa, you okay?" Kai's voice kept asking me in the distance, even though we were standing side-by-side. At that moment in time, Kai felt miles away. "You don't look so good," he paused, placing his hand on my shoulder, almost shaking me back into reality. "Why did you ask Yano for his dad's name? Do you know him or something? I just realized when Yano said it, but you both have the same surname."

There was no way I could properly answer Kai. My mind had stopped working, everything was blank.

"Izawa?" he placed his hands on my cheeks.

"My dad . . . ."

"What?" Kai stopped, slowly removing his hands from my face. "Your dad . . .? What about him?"

Tears trickled down my face as I encountered Kai's gaze.

"Izawa, I don't understand?"

Kai quickly grabbed my hand and finished leading me to his house. His gated property was much larger than mine as it was on a corner lot. In the front yard, slightly off to the side of the house, stood an enormous tree with a wooden bench underneath. Kai guided me to the bench, directing me to sit down. He took the purse from my shoulder and placed it down on the ground beside me, then bent down to my level. Holding my hands tightly, he rested them upon my lap.

"Nila, I don't understand what you mean?"

Nila...? When did we get so comfortable? "Yano's dad...."

"Huh? Yano's dad? I don't get it, what about his dad?"

"He's . . . my dad."

Kai's expression hardened. "What do you mean? Isn't your dad living at home with you? Yano's family has lived beside me for a couple of years now. I'm pretty sure his dad is married to a younger woman who is expecting their second child. Are you sure you're not mistaking him for someone else?"

The only words that caught my attention were *'expecting their second child.'* Inside, I was freaking out. *He's having ANOTHER baby? BUT HOW? He's only been gone for two years!*

At this point, the tears had stopped. I felt something warm embrace my upper body, tempting me to snap back into that awful reality. I found myself deep in Kai's embrace as he forcefully hugged me, almost like nothing could tear us apart.

"Nila, I have no idea on what's goin' on, or why you were crying, but I want you to know that I'm here. No matter what, I won't go anywhere."

This was all too much to process: my father, Yano's existence, and Kai's overwhelming kindness; all of it left me mentally and emotionally defeated. My body decided to act on its own and all of a sudden, I pushed Kai away from me.

"STOP!" I pleaded. "I can't take this! I just need—"

Before I could finish my sentence, the front door to Yano's house opened and a man came out onto the porch. His voice left me speechless.

"Yano! Kiro! A rerun of last season's championship baseball game is starting on TV. There's also some warm hot chocolate inside for you boys."

I looked to Yano's house next door and saw an older man standing at the front door. That man was indeed my father, the one I hadn't seen in over two years. The father, who abandoned his loving wife and family with no explanation. The father, with whom I used to share meals and drink hot chocolate in the winter. The father who was no longer mine.

"Yeah, woohoo! Baseball, baseball, baseball!" Yano and Kiro chanted all the way inside.

The man held the door open as both boys entered safely before shutting it.

I slid off the bench and fell to the cold ground in disbelief. My whole body began shaking uncontrollably.

"NILA!" Kai rushed back to my aid. "I want to put my arms around you, but . . . I don't know what I should do."

Without responding to his concern, I pushed Kai away once more as I rose to my feet. "I have to go!" I got my purse and ran as fast as I could out through the gate and down the street without looking back.

"NILA, WAIT! Hold on a sec!" I heard Kai shout in the distance.

My body was reacting on its own; it was unstoppable. I kept running until my legs gave out. Even though it was winter, it felt like summer due to the adrenaline rushing through my body and the sweat seeping into my jacket.

I was able to get on the next bus before it departed and found a seat in the back. The phone in my pocket kept vibrating, so I pulled it out to see five messages from Kai and a couple of missed calls.

I knew those directions seemed familiar; it was because HE lived in this area.

Remembering back to when I searched for my father's rumoured whereabouts online, I had forgotten the names of the nearby streets. Today, I was so focused on meeting up with Kai, my father's new home slipped my mind.

Kento must think I'm crazy. He asked me so many questions, but I couldn't answer at all. I have another brother . . . and a sibling on the way. What do I do now? Should Mom and Kenji know? How would I even go about telling them? No, they definitely can't know. This will completely destroy them. I don't want to complicate the lives of my family any more than they already are. We're already broken as a whole; I don't want us to break individually.

Leaning my forehead against the cold, frosted window of the bus, I couldn't control the thoughts running through my mind.

Dad, if I came to you with questions . . . would you answer them, or would you toss me aside?

Chapter Six

I GOT OFF THE bus and stood beside the sign indicating the numbered bus route. Taking a minute to reflect, I remembered the textbook.

After everything, I didn't even get that stupid book!

Letting out an anguished sigh, I pressed forward on my journey back home. Turning onto my street, my hands started to quiver as I stepped closer to my house. Already knowing I wasn't going to tell my mother or brother about what happened today, a rush of panic washed over me. Still in thought, I continued with my head down as I approached the front gate. Pushing the gate open, I raised my head to find a person I wasn't expecting to see, sitting on my doorstep.

"Kai . . .? What? How did you . . .."

Oh! I just called him by his first name so casually . . . Why did I do that?

With slightly frostbitten cheeks, he raised his head. "I rode my bike as fast as I could, in hopes of getting here before the bus. I didn't want you to go inside before I could figure out what's goin' on."

Looking at the side of my house, Kai's bike was leaning up against it.

"Why did you come? You shouldn't have come here. I—"

"Enough, alright!" Kai raised his voice as he stood.

Standing quietly, shocked that he had raised his voice to me, my shoulders tightened. *He should be mad at me. I left without an explanation.*

The front door to my house started to unlock; someone was coming out. Kai quickly grabbed my hand and yanked me over to the side of the house where his bike was. We were around the corner from the front, where no one could see us if they stood near the door. Kai pinned me against the wall and covered my mouth with his icy hand. Holding me close, my nose was engraved with his scent.

"Shh," he whispered.

"I could have sworn . . . Hmm . . .."

By the voice, I could tell it was my mother who came out. Not seeing anyone, she went back inside as I heard the door shut.

Mom's back from work? I didn't even pay attention to her car sitting in the driveway . . ..

"Holy crap, that was close!" he exclaimed in relief, removing his hand from my mouth. "I thought she was gonna catch us for sure."

I gazed up at Kai as he peeked around the corner to make sure everything was clear. *This is weird. Why is my heart pounding this fast? Standing so close, he must be able to hear it.*

"You okay, Nila? Your heart is beating so fast. Look, feel." Kai took my hand and placed it on his chest. "Mine is, too," he said with a dorky smile.

My body was getting exceedingly hot because of where my hand was placed. It was true; his heart was beating just as fast as mine. "Um . . . why are we hiding from my mom?" I questioned, curious by his response.

"Because she can't have you yet. I'm not finished with you."

My eyes widened. *What does he mean by that? What does he plan on doing?*

"Hey! Don't get the wrong idea, pervert," he said jokingly. "I just want you to tell me what happened back at my place."

Oh, I see. That's what he meant.

"You seemed like a completely different person compared to the Nila I've gotten to know."

"What do YOU know about ME?" I tested, raising my voice. *That's not what I wanted to say. Why am I yelling at him?*

"Huh? Nila, I—"

"Just stop. I can't deal with this right now. Not with school, not with a dumb textbook, and most certainly not with you. Just leave me alone!"

That very moment, I broke down and the tears exploded from my eyes again.

All I ever do is cry around him. Why can't I tell him? Why can't I just answer his simple questions? Is it because I don't even know the true answers to those questions myself? Either way, he doesn't need to get involved. I can take care of this on my own.

The humble and understanding Kai, let out a long stressful sigh. "That's it," he said, picking me up and throwing me over his shoulder.

"What are you doing? Put me down, idiot!"

"Shh! You're getting too rowdy; your mom will hear us. We have to go somewhere else to talk. I don't care what you say, or how much you hate me right now, but I'm not going to leave you like this. Not when you're crying."

His words hit me hard; they made me extremely happy. After that, I didn't struggle anymore. "You can let go of me. I can walk by myself. I promise I won't run off."

Kai gently placed me back on the ground, one foot at a time, then placed his hands on my shoulders. "Are you sure?"

"Yeah, I'm sure. But I can't promise all of your questions will be answered."

"Good enough for me," he said with a comforting smile as he removed his hands.

Without realizing it, I was already smiling back. "Where do you want to go?"

"I was thinking we'd go to the park where we first met. That way, I can try to understand you at the place where I first met you," he responded, looking directly into my eyes. I noticed a glimmer in Kai's eyes as I stared back at them. It was amazing how this guy could use his expressions to get me to tell him things I haven't told anyone.

"Okay," I said, though I found myself puzzled with another question. "Hey . . .."

"What is it?"

"Why were you at the park yesterday? It's far from your school, and even your house, so why go there?"

"Hmm . . . I wonder," he said, looking up to the sky. "Yesterday, I skipped last period and homeroom. I had a few things on my mind, so I went for a walk to clear my head before going home." Turning his gaze back to me, he smiled distantly. "I'm glad I ended up there."

Curious as to what had him bothered, I wasn't sure if it was my place to ask. His distant smile seemed guarded and gave off the vibe like he didn't want to talk about it, so for now, I left things alone. "Oh, I see . . .."

We walked off my property and down the street, making small talk as we headed for the park. For the most part, our walk was quite silent.

Is he waiting until we get to the park to ask me something? I would have been okay with him asking me questions along the way. Now, it's getting awkward . . ..

"Nila."

Finally. "Yeah?"

"Can I hold your hand?"

My heart flipped inside my chest. His question threw me off guard. I started slowing down without realizing it, as he continued walking ahead. My eyes were wide, in awe of his request.

"Uh," he muttered, looking back. "You can say no, it's fine. I just thought it would be a more comforting walk—for you, if we did . . .," Kai explained, turning away from me.

Is he embarrassed about what he asked? Is that why he won't look at me? "If we hold hands . . . people will assume we're dating."

"Is that a bad thing?" he responded immediately, looking at me as if waiting for a reply.

What? What is he saying? IS HE CRAZY?

At this point, we stopped walking completely. We had less than ten steps until we reached the park, but somehow, it felt like we would never arrive.

"Um . . .." *How do I answer? He's so direct; it's scary. My guard is always low around him. He doesn't even give me a chance to reinforce my wall before barging through it again.*

"We're almost there. Let's keep going," I said, darting past him, completely avoiding the question.

"Yeah . . . sure."

45

We reached the empty park and headed towards the swing set, taking a seat.

It's funny, I was here just yesterday, but today, the park feels like a completely different place.

"This is where I first saw you," Kai said, breaking the silence. "Oh, what an interesting day yesterday turned out to be."

"Yeah," I giggled. "It sure was. You know, I decided right then and there that I couldn't stand you."

"Oh, yeah?" he said, intrigued. "What about now?"

"You're growing on me," I teased as we both laughed. It felt good to laugh after all the crying. *When did I start feeling better?*

Things went quiet for a moment as we swung back and forth slowly, digging our shoes into the sand.

"Is my neighbour, Youji Izawa, really your father?"

I couldn't answer his question right away, but I kept repeating it over and over in my head until I formulated an answer. "Yeah, he is. He's my dad."

"By your reaction today, I assume you didn't know he lived there?"

"No, I didn't. I was so focused on getting my textbook from your house; it completely slipped my mind. I had heard he possibly lived in your area; I just never went to check it out for myself."

"I see. I'm sorry," he said, looking down at his shoes as he dug them further into the sand. "I caused you heartache by showing you something you weren't ready to face."

"It's not your fault," I reassured. "You obviously couldn't have known. It's been over two years . . . something like this was bound to happen eventually."

Kai stopped swinging and pulled my swing, by the chains, close to his. "TWO YEARS! Two whole years since you last saw him?"

When he pulled my swing close to his, it startled me. It took a moment to process my answer as my swing jerked sideways. "Uh, yeah. One night, he just . . . left . . . and never came back."

"Did you guys move after he left?"

"No, we're still in the same house as before."

Kai let go of my swing, launching me back in the other direction before he jumped out of his seat. He started pacing back and forth in front of the swing set, pondering the situation.

"Wait! Okay, hold on. So, you're telling me he knows exactly where you live and never came back to see you?"

"Pretty much . . .."

"WOW! That's messed up. That's just—wow," Kai said as he stumbled back into the seat of the swing. "I can't believe a father would pick up and leave his family like that. His wife—his kids!" With his face already in a state of uncertainty, another point of realization crossed it. "Wait . . . Nila, you said two years ago, right?"

"Yeah?"

"Yano's about four or five, I think. So, that means . . .."

I already knew where he was going with his question. "Yeah, it means he had an affair," I swung sharply.

"Wow. I never pinned Mr. Izawa to be THAT kinda man . . .," he said, taken aback by everything he was hearing.

We both sat in silence for a few moments. When I looked over at Kai, he seemed to be having a hard time soaking in all the information. Just when I thought the silence would go on forever, he finally opened his mouth.

"I'm sorry, Nila. I'm sorry I can't fully understand what you're going through. I've never been in this kind of situation before, so I don't know the type of conflicting feelings you're currently having. What I do know is that this isn't right. It's frustrating because I can't do anything about your past or anything to help fix this," he replied in a dejected tone, as if he were giving up.

He looked like a sulking child. I somehow found comfort in knowing that he truly wished he could have helped.

"Actually, you've done a lot already."

He perked back up and looked at me. "How?"

It was hard to explain my exact feelings to him in words, but inside my heart, I knew he had helped me greatly. "By listening."

"Really?"

"Really. You're the first person, besides Kida, who I've told. Technically, you know more than she does."

"I feel kinda special," Kai said with a gentle smile.

"Oh, yeah?" I playfully smiled back. "How so?"

Kai let go of the swing and reached for my hand and held it, interlocking his fingers with mine. He peered into my eyes, lighting a fire within my heart.

"Kai . . .."

"I know you don't want people to think we're dating, Nila, but that's not why . . .."

All of a sudden, a familiar, upbeat tune began to play out loud.

"Sorry, that's my phone!"

Nervously untangling my fingers from his, I jumped up and pulled out my phone. The caller display read: *Mom*.

Dammit! If I answer it, then Mom will start yelling and freaking out. But, if I don't, she'll keep calling until I pick up. Either way I lose and eventually, I'll have to answer.

After hearing the tune play for a few seconds, I decided to answer. "Hello . . .?"

"WHERE ARE YOU?" my mother shouted through the phone. "I'm assuming you went to get your textbook back from that boy's house. You've had plenty of time to get it and return home. What are you doing? I came back from a day's worth of work and you're STILL not home. How is that possible? Do you realize it's the dead of winter and it's cold outside?"

Mom's as loud as ever. "Um, I . . . didn't end up going."

"What? Why not?" she asked, confusion tangled in her voice.

"Uh . . . because . . . he wasn't home." *Liar.*

I began mentally panicking at the thought of her finding out I was with Kai this whole time.

"Hey! Now, she's gonna think I'm a jerk," Kai whispered loudly, getting up from the swing defensively.

"He wasn't home? He arranges for you to go to his house to pick up a book, and then he forgets to be there?" she mocked through the phone.

"Mom, he didn't forget! He um . . .." I had to come up with something quick. "Something came up last minute . . . regarding his family, so we had to reschedule."

"I see . . .," she said suspiciously. "Well, next time, HE will be the one to go out of his way to deliver that book to our house instead. No more of this back and forth nonsense. Understood?"

"Yes, Mom."

"So, when are you coming home?"

"Um . . .." Not wanting to separate from Kai just yet, I made a quick decision. "I've decided to stay at Kida's tonight," I said impulsively.

"Kida's? You've decided . . .? Pardon me? What, so now you think you're old enough to make whatever decisions you want? I don't think so. Nila, come home this—"

Without a second thought, I hung up.

"Whoa! I can't believe you hung up on your mom. She's gonna flip!" Kai smiled mischievously.

Oh. My. Gosh. What have I done? She's probably going to send the police out to drag me home! My hands and legs started shaking like crazy. "I can't believe I did that . . .." Coming to a quick realization, I blurted out, "Kida!" *Shit! She'll definitely call the Nazukas to make sure I'm actually going there. I'm going to have to call Kida and tell her to lie to my mom for me.*

"Ohhh damn, Nila's turning into a badass!" Kai said as he burst out laughing.

"Shut up!" I waved at him to be quiet. I quickly called Kida's cellphone while Kai continued to make jokes and laugh behind me.

Pick up! Pick up! Pick—

"Hey, Nila. What's—"

"KIDA! I need your help!" I pleaded desperately, disregarding her greeting.

"Huh? Is everything okay?" she asked, alarmed.

"If my mom calls your house, asking if I'm there, just say I am and I'm staying over tonight. Got it?"

"Uh . . . yeah, sure, but what's going on?" she asked, confusion lingered in her voice.

"No time—I'll explain later!"

"Oooh-kay . . . but you know you can actually stay over, right? You don't have to lie about it."

"Well, if she calls, just say I'm with you, okay?"

"Yeah, yeah," she said, brushing off my worry.

"Thanks! Plus, you owe me for last night."

"Okay, okay, I get it already. I said I'd do it, jeez. Rub it in some more why don'tcha."

"Thanks! I'll see you later. Bye!"

"Sooo, 'Miss Badass,' does that mean we are hanging out longer?" Kai looked at me with a satisfied grin as I put my phone away.

"Well, I wasn't sure if you were finished with your questions yet, so . . .." Pausing, I crossed my arms, gently biting my bottom lip.

"Ah, I see. So, this was all for my benefit then?"

"Precisely."

"I think you've had enough for today."

"Huh?" *Does he mean it's over? Our time together has ended? After I hung up on my mom and lied!* "Well, I guess I'll just head to Kida's like planned then . . .." I looked at the park exit and started walking slowly away from him.

"Nila."

I rapidly turned around to face him. "Yeah?"

"Wanna go somewhere else with me?"

My heart tightened. "Where?"

"My favourite place. I'll tell you a little more about me . . . to make things even," he uttered sincerely with sharp eyes, demanding my attention.

Without second-guessing my actions, I obligingly accepted. "Yeah, I really do."

His eyes softened, compared to the way they looked at me a moment ago. They were gentle and inviting, making it seem like it would have been alright even if I had said no.

A dorky smile appeared on Kai's face. "It's a bit of a walk from here though."

"That's fine. I don't have a set time to be at Kida's anyway."

"Perfect. There is one condition before I take you though."

"What is it?"

"We have to hold hands."

What's with him and always wanting to hold hands? Is this a game to him? Why can't I ever take control of the situation? In fact, it seems like he's always in control . . ..

Although I was rolling my eyes at his ridiculous request, and my mind said, *'Don't do it,'* my heart said otherwise. In the end, I pushed my thoughts out of the way and sided with my heart. The next thing I knew, we were holding hands and heading out of the park. I followed his every step as he led the way on a new path.

Who have I become? Even though I know a world of pain is heading my way after hanging up on my mom, I don't have time to care. My mind is busy with other thoughts, mostly of him. I feel more relaxed around him than I do with Kida. Why is that? Could it be, I'm more comfortable around a guy than I am with my best friend?

There aren't many people I confide in because they tend to let you down. At school, people always judge others for what they see, not what they know. But Kai, he absorbed what I told him like a sponge. Why does being with him right now seem more important than anything else? What is it that attracts me to him?

Chapter Seven

"**W**E'RE HERE. SORRY about the long walk in the cold," Kai said as he rubbed our hands together to keep them warm.

After a chilly walk, which didn't feel all that long, we came across a dirt path hidden between a few trees. The path led to a secluded spot on a riverbank running through a small field broken into two parts. The river was narrow, seeming to carry on forever, while a sturdy, wooden bridge linked both sides of the field together. On the one side of the river, the land was larger and seemingly untouched as it was dusted in a winter's mist, while the smaller side had a few benches and connected with the path we walked. The larger side was engulfed by tall, lifeless grass, each strand frozen solid like sparkling shards of glass.

"Wow, it's gorgeous!"

"I'm glad you like it. It looks even better in the spring when the flowers and greenery are in bloom," Kai said passionately. From his smile alone, I could tell this place held importance to him.

"How did you come across something so beautiful?"

"My best friend showed me this place about a year and a half ago, and I've been coming ever since."

"He definitely found a lovely spot for the both of you to share. Is it alright for me to intrude on such a place?"

"Yeah, it's fine. It's not like he owns it or anything," Kai chuckled.

"I know, but won't he get mad if he finds out you bring people here? Seems like the place itself wants to stay hidden." *I bet Kai brings girls here all the time . . ..*

"Nah, he's not like that. Besides, you're the first person I've brought here," he grinned.

"Really?" I said, my excitement shining through.

"Yep," he confirmed, looking at me with a devilish grin. "I bet you thought I brought people here all the time—like girls, perhaps?"

Continuing to stare with an outrageously sly grin on his face, he waited for my facial reaction to shift.

It's like he can read my mind. "Maybe," I said, looking away from him. I could feel my cheeks turning crimson from embarrassment.

"Nila, you're too funny," he burst out laughing. "You're so easy to read."

Scolding him for making fun of me seemed like the proper punishment. "Hey! No, I'm . . .."

"You look really cute when you blush," he said, with that famous smile of his.

Hearing Kai say the words 'you' and 'cute' in the same sentence left me speechless. Now, scolding him didn't seem like an appropriate response at all. Instead, I tried covering my blushing face.

"Don't cover your face. I want to see those rosy cheeks," he teased.

Kai grabbed both of my hands with one of his and pulled them down away from my face. My long hair became tangled in front of my face in the struggle to set myself free from his grasp. Kai realized how embarrassed I was and used his free hand to brush away the loose strands I was hiding behind. His hands were much bigger than mine, but unbelievably soft as he readjusted the fine strands of hair, tucking them behind my ear.

"You have beautiful hair, Nila."

My heart was thumping nonstop from the slight touch of his hand against my face and left me unable to say anything in return. Rather, I continued to blush as I stood motionless in front of him. The hand he used to run through my hair, was now placed on top of both my hands. His other hand rested underneath, clasping mine in between his.

"Your hands are freezing!" he said in shock.

Attempting to warm my hands for a short minute, he slowly opened his hands to set mine free. Before I could remove them, he reached for my hand again. Holding it comfortably, he guided me towards one of the benches along the river's edge.

"Let's sit for a while," he suggested, hovering over the bench before taking a seat. As he sat down, he released my hand.

Sitting side-by-side, we took a moment to admire the beautiful scenery around us. The wind was gentle, as it jumped through the branches of the naked trees. In the spots that weren't completely frozen over, the river splashed as the breeze passed.

"Every now and then, I like to come here to sit and think," he confessed.

"What do you come to think about?"

"Important things."

"What would you consider to be 'important things'?"

"Things to do with my family, friends . . . the future. Not just my future though, but also the ones of those who matter to me. The one question I tend to ask the most is 'What does the future have in store for me?'"

He usually seems so carefree and sure of himself; I never would have pegged him to be the type to concern himself with others in such detail. I can't believe I judged him before getting to know him. People who do that anger me, but somehow, I have become the type of person I hate the most.

"I'm sorry, Kai."

"What are you sorry for?"

"I misjudged you. This entire time, I have thought you to be someone you aren't. Being such a harsh critic is unlike me. I feel ashamed."

Again, Kai reached for my hand. Squeezing it tightly, he gazed across the water. "Everyone does it, no matter how hard they try not to. Judging people is natural, no matter how unpleasant. Don't beat yourself up about it." Kai shifted his gaze back to me. "Remember, I also judged you, too."

"Really? When?"

"When we first met, and again when we met at the karaoke bar."

"Oh, yeah. You thought I was the 'brainy type' or something," I giggled.

"Ha, ha, yeah," he confirmed, laughing under his breath.

"You are kind of right, though. Studying hard, getting good grades, and spending all of my free time reading is true to my nature. Going out with friends doesn't happen often," I admitted, staring at the ground so that Kai wouldn't see how depressed and pathetic I looked.

"So, you're saying you don't want to be the person you are now?"

"I don't follow . . . ?"

"Are you unhappy with the 'current' you?" he reworded, with a gaze powerful enough to pierce my soul. His eyes seemed unstable.

My mind searched for an answer as I sat thinking. "I'm . . . not sure."

Kai patted me on the head, just like you would to a small child. "There's nothing wrong with that answer," he advised. "I believe the person you are now is not the person you will be for the rest of your life. My grandpa told me that once, and it's stuck with me ever since."

Wow, that was unexpectedly insightful. I'm sure he has his own reasons for thinking this way, though I wonder what they are. This side of Kai seems so far out of my reach . . . .

"Kai, you amaze me," I said, looking up at him.

"How?"

"You just do."

He smiled back as we both laughed under our breath.

"So, what's your best friend's name?" I asked.

"Hatori."

"Do you guys go to the same school?"

"No. We attended the same elementary and junior high school, but ended up going to different high schools. Back in junior high, we were on the basketball team and used to go to that park a lot to practice—the one where you and I met. The court is bigger than the ones closer to our places, but it's pretty rundown now. I don't see many people playing ball there anymore."

So, that's why he was at the park. "I agree. I also noticed that the park is needing an extreme makeover. And that must suck; attending a different high school than your best friend must be hard."

"Yeah, it was . . . ." He paused as he got up from the bench, freeing his hand. "Especially when your girlfriend and best friend attend the same school and start seeing each other, secretly behind your back."

"Your girlfriend . . . cheated on you? With your best friend?" I repeated in awe.

"Ex-girlfriend, as you can probably guess." He laughed dryly before glancing away, perhaps eager to end the conversation.

"How could they do that to you? And you STILL consider Hatori your best friend?"

"Yeah, that's what I thought, too," he answered quietly. "It's been over a year now since it's all happened. Hatori's still my best friend; I forgave him, but her, let's just say it didn't work out."

"You're an amazingly strong person, Kai. If Kida did that to me, I don't know if I could ever forgive her," I confessed honestly.

"Yeah, well, there is more to life than holding grudges. I learned that the hard way." Kai walked slowly towards the bridge. As he did, I could see a hidden sadness lurking in each step he took away from me.

Talking about this must've brought up unpleasant memories. But . . . I want to know more. "Kai!" I called, rising from the bench. Walking closer, I confronted him. "Did I say something to upset you?"

Smiling gently, he answered, "No, sorry, you didn't say anything to upset me. I think the moment just got to my head. I guess it's still a touchy subject for me. I'm sorry if I made you uncomfortable."

"Good. We're in the same boat now."

"How so?"

"Today, you learned about an issue I'm not ready to deal with, and I also learned about one of yours."

Kai paused for a second as he thought about what I said. "Hmm, I guess you're right," he smirked. "You're also the only person I've ever talked to about this. That's two things we have in common," he said, reaching out for a high-five.

I raised my hand to connect with his. As I did, he interlocked his fingers with mine, clasping our hands together. With blushing cheeks, we both gazed at each other, then turned towards the water, peering at it once more with our hands down at our sides, still bound together. I wanted this moment to last forever.

"Thank you for sharing that with me. It made me feel a lot better knowing you chose to talk to me about it instead of someone else."

"Yeah, it just felt easier to talk to you about it for some reason. I should technically be thanking you," he joked as we both smiled at each other.

A harsh gust of wind came bursting through the trees and blew over the field of grass, forcing the top layer of snow into a sparkling dance. The cold breeze reached the bridge where Kai and I stood, making its way through us and every bone in our bodies. The wind whisked my long hair into a hurricane disaster, flinging it in every direction.

I turned to see my hair blowing in Kai's face. "Sorry! I can't control it."

With his eyes closed, he laughed. "No worries." Easing away from the bridge's railing, he looked at me. "Well, enough of this depressing crap. I promised you some information about myself, so that's exactly what you're gonna get."

"But, you've already told me so much. So, it's fine; you don't have to share anything else."

"I don't mind. Like I said, I like talking to you. I want you to know the positive parts about my life, too, not just the depressing and negative stuff," he smiled brightly.

He's right. How does he make our conversations so effortless and natural? I'm able to share my thoughts and feelings out loud like it's nothing. What's happening to me?

"Well then, how . . .," I started, but got interrupted by the vibrating phone in my pocket. Letting go of Kai's hand, I pulled out my phone and saw a new Line message. "It's a message from Kida. Sorry, I'm just going to reply to it really quick."

"No problem."

[Line Kida]: Make sure you message me before you come, okay? I'll meet you outside.

[Line Nila]: Yeah, sure thing.

"Everything alright?"

"Yeah, she just wants me to message her before I head over."

"Oh, right. So, you've decided to stay at your friend's place tonight?"

"Yeah, I really don't want to go home and face my mom . . .."

"That's understandable. We should start heading out then." Kai looked at his watch for the time. "I know it's only 5:45 p.m., but it will be dark soon. Plus, I still have to get my bike from your place."

"That's right! I completely forgot." Feeling the need to adjust my purse, I reached for the side of my waist where it usually sat. "Um, where's my purse?"

"Uh," Kai paused, searching with his eyes. "Honestly, I think the last time I saw you with it was back at your house."

"You could be right. I probably dropped it when you picked me up."

"Sorry, that makes it my fault you lost it then."

"No, it's okay. It's fine. As long as it's still there, everything will be fine," I declared, trying to reassure myself.

We decided the bus would be the quickest way for our long trip back. Since I didn't have my purse, Kai kindly paid for my fare. On the bus, we started off holding hands, but as Kai started telling me a little about his family, he became energetic and soon let go in order to talk with his hands. He told me he lived with both of his parents and his little brother, then went on to explain he actually had two brothers. His older brother, Sosuke, was twenty-six, and his younger brother, Ryu, was thirteen. The eldest lived in a neighbouring town with his wife and their new baby. Kai shared the excitement of being a first-time uncle to a little baby girl of about five months. He continued to tell me that he was fairly close with his older brother, but not particularly close with his younger one.

As he spoke of his younger brother, it reminded me a lot of my own. The whole time Kai talked about his family, his face lit up with an over-powering amount of energy and passion. Listening to, and watching him tell his stories, made my heart melt. Afterwards, he shared funny moments he had with his little niece, and other side stories about a couple of pranks he pulled on the teachers with his friends at school.

"During the closing ceremony of our second year, me and the guys played the ultimate prank—we really outdid ourselves. Close to our school was a construction site where a new store was being built. While all the students and faculty were attending the ceremony in the gym, we stole some of the spare tires from those huge machines used to haul dirt, and placed them against each one of the exits." Kai couldn't control his laughter as he tried to continue the story. "Everyone was freaking out because they couldn't figure out why the doors wouldn't open. The guys and I stood and watched in the distance, laughing our asses off."

"How did they get out then?" I asked, inching towards the edge of my seat, intrigued to hear the result.

"There was a student teacher who didn't attend the ceremony, so one of the teachers trapped inside called him on his cellphone to come and see what was wrong with the doors. Man, you should have seen the look on the student teacher's face when he arrived at the gym and saw these huge tires leaning against the doors."

Trying to keep myself from laughing, I needed to know what happened next. "What happened after that? Did you guys get caught?"

"Yes and no. The student teacher called the police in panic, so we gave ourselves up before things got too serious. We wanted to play a joke, not get arrested."

"The police? That's a bit extreme!"

With dim laughter, Kai answered, "I guess he was scared."

"Oh my God, you guys are a bunch of delinquents! You must have gotten into serious trouble after pulling a stunt like that."

"We had to write an apology to the school and read it out loud in front of the entire student body. Plus, we each got detention and grounded by our parents for the whole summer break," Kai finished, laughing subtly at a memory he didn't seem to regret. Resting his head for a split second against the back of his seat, he jolted forward with excitement. "Oh! There was also this one time when . . . ." Kai attempted to start another story, but stopped as we reached our destination. The bus ride seemed extremely short because of all the joyful stories he kept sharing. "Oh man, we're here already," Kai expressed in amazement, looking down at his watch. "It felt like we just got on the bus, but it's already close to 7:00 p.m. I don't even remember it stopping for transfers."

"I know," I replied, slightly disappointed.

Kai reached his arm up and over his shoulder to stretch. "Sorry, I talked so much. I didn't get a chance to learn anything about you or your family. When I get going, sometimes it's hard for me to stop," he chuckled with embarrassment.

"No, honestly, that's alright. I enjoyed listening to the stories about your family and friends. I learned a lot about you. It felt like we were getting a bit closer." *Closer . . . is that what I want?*

"Really?" he asked, surprised by my response. "I hope you're right."

Folding my hands down in front of me, I answered with a silent smile.

Kai, I actually DID learn a lot about you today. Not just about where you come from or what you've been through, but also how you think. You've opened my eyes, allowing me to see things in another perspective. You're actually . . . amazing. Lately, you make my heart race like a fiend. It can't be . . . I don't actually like Kai—do I?

Kai grabbed my hand and started running. "Come on! We gotta get our stuff from your house before your mom realizes it's there."

When we got closer, I could see my mother's car still parked on the driveway. Approaching my house with caution, the front door unexpectedly opened and my mother walked out in her work uniform. Kai, who was now running slightly behind me, grabbed my waist and jumped into some bushes on the edge of my neighbour's property. We peeked through the bushes and watched my mother walk down the driveway in a hurry towards her car.

Shit, I didn't know Mom had another shift tonight. But at least she won't be coming after me. It doesn't look like she called the police to come and find me either, like she always threatened when it came to Kenji's disappearances.

Terrified by the thought of my mother catching us, I automatically held my breath. Taking off, she didn't notice us in the bushes, or Kai's bike leaning against the side of the house.

Exhaling loudly, Kai escaped the bush gracefully before helping me. "Man, that was another close call with your mom. We gotta stop getting into these situations."

"I agree. I assumed she didn't work tonight, since she left extremely early for a shift this morning. I guess she's doing a double."

"Either way, let's get our stuff and get the hell outta here!" he said panting, as he marched up to my house.

Heading through the gate, Kai immediately went for his bike while something more important caught my attention.

"Yes!" I shouted with relief.

"What? What is it?"

I spotted my purse on the ground near Kai's bike and ran to pick it up. "My purse is here like we thought."

"That's great."

"Yeah," I said with a relieved smile.

Now that we both have our stuff, will this finally be the end of our time together?

"I'll walk you to Kida's house. It's way too dark for you to walk there alone."

"It's not that late yet; I should be fine. Plus, her house is in the opposite direction from yours." *Why am I disagreeing with him when I know I want to spend more time with him?*

"Well, at least, let me walk you halfway, okay? Just until I know you'll be safe the rest of the way on your own."

He really is sweet. "Alright. There's a fork in the road on the route to her house. It will be the easiest way for you to get back on track to your side of town."

"Perfect. Let's head that way then," he said with an illuminating smile.

As we were about to leave, my brother strolled out the front door.

"Kenji?"

"Oh . . . hey," Kenji answered with a blank expression. Peering over at Kai, Kenji looked him up and down. "Who's this? A boyfriend?"

"Oh, um, this is—"

"I'm Kaichi Kento," Kai cut in, bowing as he introduced himself.

Kenji quickly rejected Kai's formal introduction by looking away. "Whatever."

Kenji then turned his back towards us as he walked off the property. Lifting his head, Kai seemed a bit thrown off by Kenji's rude reaction to his kind gesture.

"Hey, wait! That was rude! Where are you even going this late?"

"Out," Kenji replied bluntly, continuing without looking back.

"Hey!" I shouted, watching Kenji walk off. *I don't know why I even bothered. I knew he wouldn't tell me where he was going.* "Sorry about my stupid brother," I excused, turning back to Kai.

"Brother, huh?" Kai said, as he watched Kenji walk further into the distance.

"Let's just go."

"Right . . .."

Heading towards our destination, we walked side-by-side while Kai guided his bike, talking the entire way. This time, I chose to share some stories about my family. I ended up talking about the past and how things used to be versus how they were now. I explained how my brother and I used to have a pretty tight-knit relationship, but after my father left, it weakened.

On our way, we passed a gas station, a local bakery, and a small library where I used to borrow books with my father and Kenji. The library was small and privately owned, so it didn't get new books until months after they were released, but it held many wonderful books, especially for children. Before I knew it, the fork in the road was upon us, patiently waiting to split us up.

"Well, I guess this is it then. Thank you so much for everything you've done, Kai. You spent your entire day taking care of me. I'm very sorry for dragging you into all this. First, the encounter with my mom last night, and now, this. You probably think I'm a problematic girl."

"Seriously, don't worry about it. I kinda think it was fate, us meeting the way we did and all."

"Fate?"

"Yeah. We found out your dad is my neighbour, which still boggles my mind, so technically, I've known a part of your family for a while now," Kai said, trying to lighten the mood.

"You might be right," I brushed off his comment. "I should get going to Kida's now. I don't want to waste any more of your time."

"Nah, it's fine. If you need anything, like someone to talk to, you have my number," Kai said as he turned down the opposite path. Holding onto the handlebars of his bike with one hand, he waved goodbye with the other.

"Thank you!" I shouted.

I continued down the road leading to Kida's. When I approached her street, I heard Kida's voice mumbling loudly in the distance with someone outside of her house. Curious to know what was going on, I got a bit closer to see if I knew who it was she was conversing with without getting detected.

A boy? Is this one of her 'temporary boyfriends' I don't know about?

Kida had multiple boyfriends. Not all at once, but too many to count. She didn't cheat on any of them, to my knowledge, but her relationships never lasted very long.

I hid behind one of the thick light poles across the street from her house. I peeked around the pole to see if I could recognize the boy's face. I did.

What's my brother doing here? And why is he talking to Kida? I've never seen them talk to each other alone before . . . not even when Kida comes over to our house.

From where I was, no matter how hard I tried, I couldn't hear a single word exchanged between them.

Should I go over there and ask them what's going on? I think I should. He's my brother and she's my best friend after all. There shouldn't be any secrets.

I was about to reveal myself when all of a sudden Kida slapped Kenji across the face. The slap was so loud that it echoed down the street. I decided it was best to remain hidden and out of sight to watch what would happen next. After the slap, Kida stormed back into her house as Kenji stood on the side of the road, alone. Holding his head down, Kenji walked past Kida's house, making his way down the slope on the other end of the steep street.

What the hell! Why did Kida slap my brother?

Without thinking, I decided to spy on Kenji a bit longer to find out where he was going from here.

Actually, though . . . what the HELL is going on?

Chapter Eight

"*Y*O MAN, OVER here!"

"Hey, guys."

Passing a few silent streets and a small park, I ended up following Kenji for a couple of blocks until he stopped to meet up with two older looking college guys. The strange guys were hanging around a beat-up car in the abandoned parking lot of an old minimart. One of the guys had a leather jacket on while the other wore a long, black trench coat. I kept my distance so they wouldn't see me spying.

"What's happening? You alright, man?" asked the guy in the leather jacket.

"Yeah, I'm good."

"Whatever you say, bro. Want one?" The guy in the leather jacket offered Kenji a cigarette.

Kenji took the cigarette, placed it between his lips, and had it lit by the guy who offered it to him.

Smoking? Kenji! What the HELL are you doing?

The guy in the leather jacket snorted a laugh at Kenji. "Better?"

"Yeah," Kenji replied after exhaling smoke from his mouth.

"Alright, let's go then. We still got that one place to hit up tonight," said the guy with the trench coat.

I watched as Kenji entered the car, followed by the two sketchy guys, before driving off.

First, Kida and Kenji together, and now this! What is with all these secrets? What place are they 'hitting' up?

Without thinking, I'd pulled out my phone and was staring at Kai's number in my contacts. *What am I doing? I can't bother him again. Why was he my first thought?*

This was something I needed to deal with myself. I came out of hiding and started walking back in the direction of Kida's house. *What do I say to her when I get there? Should I pretend like I didn't see anything? Ugh! It's eating away at me!* All I wanted to do now was corner Kida and demand an answer from her.

Just then, my phone vibrated.

[Line Kida]: Hey, you okay? Still coming over?

That's right; I was supposed to message her when I was on my way.

[Line Nila]: Mhm.

[Line Kida]: Everything okay?

Well, not really.

[Line Nila]: Yep, on my way.

[Line Kida:] Perfect! See you soon!

I slipped my phone back into my pocket and decided to take the longest way possible back to Kida's. I needed time to rethink what I witnessed and prepare what to say.

I passed through the downtown area where shops I had never seen before appeared. My head kept turning both left and right as I passed by curiously looking in the dark windows. I was so busy window-shopping that I forgot to pay attention to what was going on in front of me. I bumped into someone head-on, fell backwards, and crash-landed onto the hard sidewalk.

"I'm so sorry," I said, rubbing my head to soothe it. "I wasn't watching where I was . . .." Looking up at the person I bumped into, I realized it was someone I knew.

"Hey, you're—" We both started our sentences at the same time.

"I know you! You're that girl from last night at karaoke. Damn, what was it again . . .? Izawa or something, right?"

It was Taki, Kai's friend with the delinquent hairstyle from the mixer. He was wearing a thick, navy-blue jacket with blue jeans, white worn-out running shoes, and a hat that read: *Adachi's.*

"Yeah, and you're, Taki? Sorry for seeming so familiar, I didn't get a chance to hear your surname."

"You remembered! Don't worry about that. It's Takinishi Fujiwara, but Taki is fine. Sorry for bumping into you, I was looking down at my phone."

"No, no, that's okay. It was also my fault; I wasn't paying attention to where I was going."

"I didn't hurt you though, did I?" Taki asked in concern, reaching out his hand to help me up.

"No, I'm fine," I answered, accepting his hand.

"Good, good. Don't wanna scuff up Kai's girl," he joked.

Kai's girl? Does he think I'm Kai's girlfriend? "Um, I'm not 'Kai's girl.'"

"Oh? I thought you guys were going out. My bad."

"We're not," I corrected.

"Alright . . .," Taki paused. "Anyway, what are you doing out this late by yourself? It's pretty cold out, not to mention dark." He made that obvious by blowing warm air into his hands and rubbing them together.

"Oh, um . . . I'm on my way to a friend's house."

"I see. I have some time, so, I'll take you."

"Oh, no!" I said, shaking my head, scared of being alone with some-one I barely knew. "I couldn't ask you to do that. I'm fine; it's close by."

"I know you didn't ask," he said sternly. "I offered. I was on my way home from work anyway, so taking a detour is no big deal. Come on."

"If you say so . . . ."

He was already leading the way, even though he had no idea where he was going. It was kind of him to offer to take me, but it was uncomfort-able being with a guy other than Kai. Taki insisted on making small talk on our way to Kida's, and we ended up having an awkward conversation with closed-ended questions and one-word answers.

Taki spoke up after another dead-end question. "So, uh, are you always this quiet?"

"Sorry, I'm not really sure on what to say."

He started to laugh, then looked at me with a straight face. "You're actually pretty cute. The stuff the girls from your school said about you doesn't seem to fit at all."

"Huh?" I was shocked by the fact that he called me cute. *First, Kai— now him? This is weird.* "What . . . did they say about me?"

"Well, you know. They said you were stuck-up and stuff, but you don't seem that way at all."

"I see." *Again, with the 'stuck-up' comment. It's nice to know he doesn't believe them. I can't believe those girls!*

"How come you came to the mixer in the first place? It didn't seem like you wanted to be there."

"I didn't. My friend tricked me into going."

Taki's eyebrow raised. "The same friend whose house you're going to tonight?"

"Mhm."

"So, you guys are still okay after that incident then?"

"Well . . . I guess. She often does stupid things, but I still believe her to be my friend." *Depending on how tonight goes though, but he doesn't need to know that.*

"That's good."

"Yeah . . .."

Arriving at Kida's house, I stopped. "This is my stop," I pointed to the house with the nameplate: *Nazuka.* "Thanks again for going out of your way to bring me here."

"No problem. Well, later," Taki said, waving goodbye as he walked away. A couple of seconds after he waved, he spun around and started walking backwards while facing me. "If Kai doesn't claim you, I just might!"

By the time I understood what he had said, he was already too far for my words to reach him. Standing there like an idiot, the words 'claim me' uneasily settled inside my head. Not having any more time to concentrate on Taki, I shook off what he said and walked up to Kida's front door.

I rang the bell once and waited. Suddenly, it flung open and there was Kida, ready to chew my head off.

"SHH!" she hissed with a finger pressed up against her lips. "Are you crazy? It's already after 9:00 p.m.—my parents will freak!"

"Sorry . . .."

"I was expecting you to message me when you were on your way so I could've met you outside. Come on," she sighed, as she yanked my arm and dragged me inside, locking the door behind me.

We walked up the stairs to her room where I made my way to her bed. Her room was bigger than mine, but the layout was fairly similar. Closing the door behind us, she took a seat at her computer desk.

"Alright, missy," Kida started. "I haven't talked to you in, like, FOR-EVER! Spill! What have you been doing that you needed the excuse to come over? Why is it a secret from your mom? And what's going on with that hot guy from the karaoke bar?"

"First of all, you're exaggerating. You saw me yesterday."

"Whatever! That's a minor detail. What about the guy?" she whispered excitedly.

"His name is Kai Kento."

"That's right! I remember someone calling out his name. To tell you the truth, I don't remember last night's details very well," Kida said, giggling. "One of the guys snuck in some alcohol after you left."

Of course . . ..

"There's nothing to tell. He found my textbook and wanted to return it."

"Oooh-kay, but he ended up ditching us to walk you home . . .?" she said with a raised eyebrow. "That's gotta mean something! Oh my God! Were you with him today as well? Also, when do YOU ever lose a textbook?"

So many questions . . .. "It really doesn't. He was just being nice. And yesterday on my walk home from school."

"Yeah, right, come on! Guys aren't that nice for no reason, Nila. There is ALWAYS an ulterior motive. You can be so naive."

She was starting to frustrate me with her annoying persistence. "Kida, nothing happened! End of discussion. I'm extremely tired and just want this day to end, okay? So, if you don't mind, I'm going to get ready for bed," I said, taking off my jacket.

"Um, excuse me? What's up with you? I knew something was bothering you from the moment you got here. Whatever it is, you don't have to take it out on me, alright?"

At that point, something snapped inside of me; I couldn't keep myself calm any longer. "Taking it out on you? Kida, are you serious? Why don't you share what you've been up to with my brother?"

Kida's eyes shot open as she looked at me, frozen with fear. After raising my voice, we could hear Kida's parents rustling around in their room down the hall.

"Shh, my parents will wake up with all the yelling! And what . . . do you mean?"

"Don't play dumb with me!" I said in a loud whisper. "You're hiding things behind my back, too! So, excuse me for not being willing to share what I've been dealing with!"

"I-I'm not . . . hiding things from you," she said with a shaky voice.

"Oh, yeah? So, what were you doing with Kenji tonight?"

"Nila, I don't . . . ."

"Just stop! Please! No more secrets, no more lies. I can't take it anymore. Just . . . tell me the truth." I broke down and cried in front of her.

I couldn't look at Kida any longer as she sat there lying to my face. I was getting tired and felt weak from the long day I had.

Did I even eat anything today . . . ?

"Nila, Nila . . . Niiila!"

My body swayed back and forth as I lost control. I could hear Kida shouting my name, but her voice seemed to be getting further and further away from me.

Chapter Nine

"MMM . . .," I MOANED, getting up slowly to commence morning stretches. *Hmm? Where am I?* Half asleep, I woke up to find myself in a bed other than my own. Looking around the room, I started to remember where I was. *Right, I'm at Kida's.*

There was no one else in the room with me, which was strange considering I always woke up before Kida after a sleepover. I looked over at the alarm clock positioned on Kida's nightstand.

"What? It's almost 12:30 p.m.!"

The next thing I knew, someone came flying into the room.

"NILA! My God! Thank goodness you're alright!" Kida exclaimed, running in with her arms flaring out. She jumped onto the bed and tackled me.

"Uh, yeah, I'm fine? What's going on?" I asked in a daze.

"What do you mean, 'what's going on'? You almost gave me a heart attack! THAT'S WHAT'S GOING ON! Don't you remember anything?"

"Uh . . .," I said with a blank expression. Finally recalling last night's events, I lowered my head. "Yeah, I remember a couple of things. I don't really know what happened after we started talking though."

"Nila . . . you passed out on my bed. We were talking and then you . . . just fainted. When I was calling out to you, you couldn't hold a conversation. You kept fading in and out."

Tears were filling Kida's eyes as she spoke. "I was so scared; I didn't know what to do. I woke my parents up, calling out for help. They called your mom, then quickly called a doctor who does house calls. The doctor said you passed out from exhaustion due to stress. He asked me if I knew why you might have been stressed and . . . Nila . . . I didn't know what to tell him. I had no idea you were even stressing about something! My own best friend! I couldn't . . . do anything to help. I-I'm sorry, Nila! I'm so sorry." Kida explained all in one breath. She attempted to hide her face from me as she wiped the tears trickling down her cheeks. I couldn't help but want to comfort her, so I sat up and embraced her.

"Kida, I'm sorry for last night. A lot happened to me yesterday and I guess it was too much for me to handle all at once. I want to tell you everything!" I admitted as I let her go and backed away to see her face.

"Yeah, I really want you to. I also have some stuff I need to tell you. Something I shouldn't have kept from you for this long, but we'll have to talk about it later."

"What, why?" I countered. "Why not now?"

"Your mom is on her way over to come pick you up."

Forgetting she had already mentioned contacting my mother, my eyes shot open and caught fire after the realization. "YOU CALLED MY MOM! WHY WOULD YOU DO THAT?"

"Nila, you FAINTED, and a DOCTOR had to come to my house and see you. We were all freaking out! Obviously, we called your mom!"

"Ugh, I can't believe you did that! This is terrible. She's going to yell at me and ask me so many questions. Kida, you shouldn't have called her. There was a reason I stayed at your place instead of going home last night." I jumped out of bed to gather my stuff. I looked down at my clothes to find myself in a pair of Kida's pyjamas. "Who put these on me?" I asked, tugging on the pyjama shirt.

"I did. Take them home; I don't need them right now. Just make sure you bring them back."

"Yeah, whatever."

Just then, the doorbell rang.

Great, she's here . . ..

We ran downstairs to find both our mothers' having a conversation by the door.

"Nila!" my mother shouted as she saw me coming down. "Oh, dear God—how are you feeling?" she asked in a panic, rushing to my side.

"I'm fine, Mom."

"I was so worried when I got the call from Mrs. Nazuka last night during my shift! The doctor had said not to come and get you because you were finally resting. The Nazukas promised to call me first thing in the morning. Are you sure you're okay, hun?"

"Yes, Mom; I'm fine," I reassured.

Just wait, when we get in the car, she'll let me have it.

My mother and I thanked the Nazukas and said our goodbyes before leaving their house. She bowed to Mr. and Mrs. Nazuka and continued to thank them repeatedly before approaching the car. I got in on the passenger side and waited for my mother to enter. She didn't say a single word the whole ride home. When we reached our house, she pulled the car into the driveway, put it in park, and cried.

"Mom . . . what's wrong?"

My mother turned her head and stared at me for a few seconds before responding. "Nila, I'm sorry. I'm so, so sorry."

Huh? She's apologizing . . . to me? But why? "Mom, why are you . . . apologizing?"

"I've been a failure as a mother, to you and Kenji. Your father leaving . . . can no longer be my excuse for everything. I've used that excuse for far too long. It's been more than two years for heaven's sake—I have to pull myself together! I will not let this family break apart any further!" my mother declared. She turned her gaze towards her lap, where her hands rested. I watched quietly as each teardrop fell gently against the backs of her hands. "It's just so hard. So unbelievably . . . hard."

I couldn't watch my mother beat herself up any longer. I ripped my seatbelt off and put my arms around her shoulders. "Mom, it's okay! We don't blame you at all! Kenji and I don't blame you for Dad leaving or for any of it! We know you've been trying your hardest to stay strong for us.

We're okay, honest. You can stop trying so hard to fix something that isn't even broken. Our family will be fine . . . We're all fine."

My mother lifted her head, glanced into my stern eyes, and started crying harder. I watched as her struggling eyes softened, expressing signs of relief and comfort. She pulled me in closer towards her chest, leaving watermarks on my jacket as I felt her tears seeping through. We stayed in that position for a while, just holding each other. When I felt my mother loosening her grip, I released her, knowing she would now be okay.

We got out of the car and walked up to the house arm-in-arm. It felt like the relationship between my mother and I would be different from here on out. She didn't ask me why I chose to stay at Kida's instead of coming home last night, nor did she yell at me for going above her and making my own decisions. All we did that afternoon was sit on the couch and look at old photo albums of when Kenji and I were little. My mother spoke of times when Kenji and I would fight about pointless things, but as soon as I got hurt, Kenji would apologize, even if it wasn't his fault. We laughed as we flipped through each album, until we got to a picture of my father.

"We can skip this one," I suggested, quickly attempting to turn the page.

"It's okay," she insisted as she gracefully touched the page with her finger. "Do you remember this day?" She pointed to a photo of my father and I playing in the sand at the beach.

"Not too well. All I remember was that I built a sandcastle with Dad."

"Ah, I see. I guess you were really young here, huh? In this picture, you must have been around five or six years old. So, Kenji would have been," she pondered, "about four. He was so mad that day because he didn't want to wear sunscreen. He said he didn't want to look like a ghost." My mother chuckled sadly, muttering the words 'silly boy' under her breath.

I looked at her face and saw tears swelling up in her eyes once again. *This is too much for her. She's not ready for all this yet.*

"I think it's time we stop looking at these," I acknowledged, as I took the album off her lap and closed it. I got up from the couch and placed it back into the box we pulled it out from. "I don't want to see you cry anymore, Mom."

She looked up at me and wiped the tears away with her fingertips. An empty smile appeared upon her face. "You're a good kid, Nila. I'm glad I did something right." My mother stood up and patted me on the head. "Being older doesn't always make you wiser." She made her way to the stairs, then announced, "I'm going to lie down in my room for a bit. I'm on-call again tonight so I should prepare myself, just in case."

I watched my mother walk up the stairs with a looming sadness that grew with each step.

I crawled back onto the couch and reached for the remote to turn on the TV, then elevated my head with a pillow. Sadly, there was nothing good on. Honestly, with everything that had been happening, I was too tired and sluggish to get up and do anything else.

"What day is it today?" I questioned out loud. *I feel like the days are flying by and we'll miss Christmas.* After some time, I got up and went to the kitchen to check the fridge where the calendar was hung. "December 22nd," I read out loud. "Holy crap!" *Three days until Christmas and we don't even have our tree up! And, I still have to go Christmas shopping! What the hell have I been waiting for?*

I ran out of the kitchen and went outside to the storage shed in the back where we kept all of our Christmas decorations. I found three boxes with the word 'Christmas' written on them and lugged them inside. Once all the boxes were in the living room, I began digging through them efficiently.

It was a little over an hour later when I finished putting up the tree and decorations. Proud of my simple accomplishment, I was excited to show my mother. Walking to the edge of the stairs, I looked up at the dark, empty staircase. I could tell my mother wasn't coming down anytime soon, so I decided to send Kida a message as I waited.

[Line Nila]: Hey, we still need to talk. When are you free to meet up?

I waited for a reply but didn't get it as quickly as I had hoped. I laid back on the couch and started channel surfing to kill time until Kida replied. It wasn't until half an hour later that she messaged me back.

[Line Kida]: Hey! Sorry I took so long to respond. I'm at work. I can

74

swing by your place afterwards, if that's alright? By the way, how are you feeling?

Oh, she's at work. I thought she was purposely avoiding me.

[Line Nila]: No worries, sorry to bother you at work. That should be fine. What time will you be done? And I'm doing better, thanks.

[Line Kida]: Nah, don't worry about it, girl. I'm only on break though, so I don't have much time to chat. I have a short shift today, which is kinda cool. I'll be done in like two hours. And, that's good to hear! I'm glad you're feeling better!

[Line Nila]: Yeah, that's fine. I'll see you then.

[Line Kida]: See you soon!

She seems pretty happy in her messages. Hmm . . ..
Just after closing Kida's message, my phone buzzed again.
Another reply? I thought she had to get back to work?

[Line Kai]: Hey, Nila, how'd last night go?

Whoa! It's Kai! He's asking how my night went . . . Should I tell him? I shouldn't, he'll probably worry if I tell him I passed out from exhaustion.

[Line Nila]: Hey, it was fine. How did you make out on your way back?

[Line Kai]: It was good. I hung out with some friends afterwards.

Oh . . . I was probably keeping him from plans he had with his friends. Getting a book from someone usually doesn't take all day, and in the end, I didn't even get it.

[Line Nila]: Sorry! I kept you away from your other plans yesterday. I probably messed everything up.

[Line Kai]: Don't worry about any of that. I was only asked after we parted ways.

I let out a sigh of relief.

[Line Nila]: That makes me feel a lot better. I would have felt guilty if I made your friends wait for you.

[Line Kai]: Nah, it's fine. Even if you did, they'd be okay with waiting, haha.

[Line Nila]: Haha, I doubt that but okay.

[Line Kai]: By any chance, did you happen to bump into Taki last night?

How does he know? Was Taki one of the friends he hung out with last night? Did Taki mention me?

[Line Nila]: Um, yeah, when I was downtown. He had just finished work.

[Line Kai]: Isn't downtown closer to the exit I took when we went our separate ways? If I knew you were gonna take that way, I would have walked you all the way to your friend's.

Shit, he's right. I can't tell him about my brother and Kida. Mostly because I haven't even figured it out for myself yet. Plus, he doesn't need to know everything I do. He's not my boyfriend or anything . . ..

[Line Nila]: I decided to take the long way to my friend's house. I needed more time to clear my head.

That technically isn't a lie.

[Line Kai]: You okay? Did something else happen? You can tell me if you want; I'll try my best to help.

No, you can't! Ugh, why is he being so nice?

[Line Nila]: Everything is fine. I'm figuring out things as I go and working through them. I'm okay.

[Line Kai]: Are you free around 6:00 p.m.?

What? He dodged my reply. Does he mean 6:00 p.m. today? Why does he want to meet up? We spent all day together yesterday; isn't he sick of me? I was a huge burden to him, so why does he want to hang out again?

"But, Kida is coming over soon," I stated mindlessly to the screen on my phone.

[Line Nila]: Sorry, I can't today. I have plans.

[Line Kai]: Oh, too bad. Sorry, that was pretty last minute. Um, when's the next day you're free?

He's actually trying to work out a day to make plans with me, but why?

[Line Nila]: I'm not sure. Things are pretty chaotic around home right now, even though I didn't get grounded. Plus, Christmas is coming up . . . so, yeah. Why?

[Line Kai]: That's true. Sorry, I just wanted to know when it would be a good time for me to drop off your book.

Oh, so that's why he wants to meet up . . ..
Not even a second later, I received another message from him.

[Line Kai]: Also, I want to see you.

My heart thumped fiercely after speed reading the message. *Really, he wants to see me? Not just because of the book, but because of me?*

I wasn't sure if what I was feeling was excitement or nervousness. *Does he want to talk about something? What will we do? Is this considered a 'date'? No, it can't be!* Countless ideas were fluttering around in my head as I asked myself those questions. *These feelings couldn't possibly be a sign of wanting to be something more than friends, could they . . .? I mean, Kai seems to be popular, so why would he be interested in someone like me?*

Chapter Ten

*I*T WAS PAST 5:30 p.m. and I hadn't heard a single word from Kida. Kenji wasn't home yet and I was hoping he'd stay away until after Kida left, that is, if she ever decided to show up. My mother also hadn't made an appearance in a while, making me a bit worried.

I made my way upstairs and peeked into my mother's bedroom. Cracking the door open, I found her sleeping soundly in bed. *Maybe I shouldn't wake her. She hasn't had a decent night's sleep in a while. If work calls for her, then I'll wake her.*

Back downstairs, I made my way into the kitchen and prepared for dinner.

If I make dinner, it will be one less thing Mom has to worry about when she wakes up.

An amazing cook, I was not, but I knew enough to get by. To start, I brought out the ingredients and a large pot, attempting to make the least amount of noise possible. As I worked, Kai's last message kept repeating over and over in my head: *'Also, I want to see you.'* I never ended up replying to his message, nor did he send another one after that. *If only he would stop saying those things. I don't want my heart to take it the wrong way.*

The soup was simmering when my phone vibrated.

[Line Kida]: Hey, girl, sorry I'm late! I'll be there in five!

My head ached and my hands became clammy; butterflies were spreading in my stomach like a virus. It wasn't until then that I registered why she was coming over in the first place.

[Line Nila]: Alright.

Moments later, there was a knock at the front door. Leaving the stove unattended, I went to answer it. Reaching for the handle, I took a deep breath, mentally preparing myself for the person I called my 'best friend.' The door creaked as I opened it cautiously. Kida stood in the doorway holding a plastic grocery bag.

"Hey, I brought ice cream," she said, lifting the bag up to show me.

"Thanks. You can put it in the freezer. I'm making dinner, so we can have that for dessert. You can have dinner here if you haven't eaten yet," I explained as I went back into the kitchen to continue cooking, leaving Kida behind to remove her outerwear at the entrance.

"That would be amazing, thank you. I'm starving!" Kida walked into the kitchen shortly after, placing the ice cream into the freezer. After shutting the freezer door, she went to the kitchen table and took a seat. "Think we'll get snow before Christmas?"

I looked over at the table where she sat. "It's sad when your best friend starts a conversation off with the weather. That's when you know things have gotten bad. To answer your question, no," I replied before turning around towards the stove to continue stirring the pot, "I don't think we will."

"Ha ... ha ... yeah. Sorry, that was pretty lame, huh?"

"Just a bit," I said over my shoulder.

"So, whatcha making?" she asked, slightly lifting off her seat.

"Just a simple vegetable soup."

"Sounds great."

After a lengthy silence, and a stiff feeling of not knowing how to speak to each other, the soup was ready. I poured some into a bowl and placed it in front of Kida. "Here you go."

"Thanks for the food," she said, reaching for the bowl and bringing it up to her lips to take a sip. "It's good."

Turning off the stove, I poured some into a bowl for myself and made my way to the table, sitting across from her. "So, who's going first?" I asked, getting straight to the point.

"You can!" she eagerly replied, choking on some vegetable chunks.

"Okay, well . . . yesterday, I found out where my dad lives."

Kida spat out a sip of soup at my revelation. The soup landed everywhere, except for in the bowl. "YOUR DAD! YOU FOUND HIM! Holy shit, where?"

"Shh! My mom's asleep upstairs!" I warned.

"Sorry, sorry!" she quieted down.

"You're not going to believe this, but . . . he's Kai's neighbour."

"NO WAY!" Kida said in shock. Dropping her hands slowly, she rested the bowl on the table before leaning back against the chair.

"I said SHH! You're going to wake her up! Kenji and my mom don't know. I haven't told them."

"Nila," she looked at me sternly. "You have to tell them."

"I don't have to tell them anything," I said, slamming my hand down on the table. "The relationship between me and my mom just got better, so I'm not going to screw it up now. Besides, my mom isn't ready to know yet."

"Well, what about Kenji? I think he wants to know."

"How would you know?" I questioned in suspicion.

"Well, you see . . . ."

"I saw him at your house, you know . . .," I cut her off. "I saw both of you talking, right before you slapped him across the face. Explain that to me. I've never heard about you guys talking or hanging out without me around. So, what's going on?" I demanded, my voice rising.

"Fine. You want to know? You want to know so badly that you're willing to ruin our friendship?" she said with eyes full of tears, standing up quickly.

"Just tell me, dammit!"

"I slept with him."

Dropping my bowl on the table, I froze.

Gazing up at Kida, tears were streaming from both her eyes as she opened her mouth again to speak. "He was my first. The guy I told you about . . . from last summer."

My brain couldn't process her words, or more like it didn't want to. It was as if a shield immediately went up in my head, blocking out everything Kida was saying. I could tell my body wasn't allowing my brain to process what she had said. Deep down inside, I knew if it did, I wouldn't be able to erase it. I was disturbed by this person across from me. All I could do was stare.

"Nila, I . . .," she started, but couldn't finish.

I looked down at my bowl on the table. My body was stiff. A loss of appetite came over me, not allowing my stomach to enjoy the meal I had prepared. My blood boiled. Kida's words had attacked my shield, destroying it, then engraved themselves into my mind forever. I was left with this indescribable rage that my best friend, and my brother, went behind my back and hooked up. That alone, was enough to push me over the edge. But, to hide it from me, too? For almost half a year? That's where I drew the line. I didn't want to think about it any longer. I wanted everything I had just heard to be erased from my memory and buried into the depths of the earth. How could they do this to me?

"Ni—"

"Get out," I demanded without moving an inch. My fingernails gouged my palms as I squeezed my hands into tight fists.

"But, Nila—"

"I SAID GET OUT! GET THE HELL OUT OF MY GOD DAMN HOUSE RIGHT NOW!"

Kida's eyes widened. Her teeth parted at my outraged appearance. She wiped the tears on her face with her sleeve and ran out of the kitchen towards the front door.

I remained seated, paralyzed, concentrating on a scratch I just noticed in our wooden kitchen table. A scratch so insignificant somehow became of huge importance to my distracted eyes.

In the background, I could hear Kida rustling to put on her jacket and tripping over herself as she threw on her boots. Right after, I heard her messing with the doorknob.

"Kida?"

I rose from the table and dashed to the hallway at the sound of my brother's voice.

"Ken . . . ji," Kida muttered.

Kenji stood outside the door looking down at her in confusion. "What happened? Why are you crying?" He stepped inside and reached over to wipe her tears, but she quickly slapped his hand away.

"D-don't!" she stuttered. "Nila knows . . .."

Kenji grabbed hold of Kida's shoulders, shaking her. "What do you mean SHE knows? You didn't . . .," he questioned as his grip on her shoulders lightened. His hands slowly slipped off as he made eye contact with me.

"I'm so sorry, Kenji. She saw us last night, in front of my house. She asked and I . . . I couldn't keep it to myself any longer," Kida placed her face into the palms of her hands. "I have to go!"

Pushing Kenji out of the way, she ran out the door.

Kenji watched as Kida ran past him and down the walkway. He grabbed the wooden door and slammed it shut. Placing a hand on each side of the frame, he repeatedly smashed his head into the door with all his might. Stopping his aggressive action, he rested the top of his head against the door and looked down at the floor.

He fell silent. "Fuck . . .."

"Kenji! Stop!" I shouted.

With all the noise, our mother came running down the stairs. She was out of breath by the time she reached the bottom.

"What's going on here?" she asked as she saw Kenji against the door.

The door now had a huge split in the middle, and sharp, wooden slivers stuck out in multiple directions. My brother's face remained hidden.

"KENJI!" my mother screamed as she ran to him, tugging on his shoulder. "ARE YOU OKAY?"

He spun around quickly, trying to release his body from her grasp. Within seconds, a loud slap pierced through the entire house. My mother dropped to the ground with her right hand covering her cheek. Her bangs swept in front of her eyes as she hung her head.

"MOM!" I yelled.

Shaking, Kenji stood with eyes wide in front of us as he stared at the mess he created. Blood trickled down the side of his face and onto his shoulder from where he had smashed his head. Everyone froze, as if time itself had frozen. All three of us were just there, for what felt like an eternity, not knowing what to do.

"Mom, I'm . . .," he tried to explain.

"It's okay; I'm fine," my mother said sharply, continuing to look away from him.

I rushed to my mother's aid. "MOM!" I shouted again, bending down beside her. A huge red print was traced on her cheek. Right away, I glared up at Kenji. "WHAT DID YOU DO TO HER? Did you . . . hit her?"

My mother grabbed my hand. "Nila, I'm fine. Just help me up."

I helped my mother get to her feet, then looked directly at Kenji. "Tell me! Did-you-hit-her?"

"I didn't mean . . . ."

"GET OUT!" I yelled uncontrollably as I got up into Kenji's face. "GET THE HELL OUT OF HERE!"

"Nila!" my mother shouted, pulling me away from him. "Stop this! It was an accident!"

I looked into my brother's eyes and saw an overwhelming amount of regret trapped within them. Turning around, he fumbled the damaged door open, then rushed out. My mother chased after him. She chased him all the way into the middle of the street without a coat or a pair of shoes. I took a couple of steps forward and stood in between the doorway, watching her pathetically run after him.

"KENJI, COME BACK! IT'S OKAY!" she cried at the top of her lungs as she tripped and collapsed on the road. Her desperate shouts fell on deaf ears.

I put on my shoes and walked out to aid her once more.

"Nila," she said, staring at me in anguish. "What happened? I don't understand what just happened . . . ."

I looked down at my mother, wanting to tell her how sorry I was, but no words came out. I couldn't imagine the amount of confusion she must have been going through. The deep emotion she had demonstrated for my brother and his faulty actions, was enough to concern anyone who witnessed what happened inside. She had absolutely no idea what went on moments before she ran down that set of stairs. All I could do was help my mother up and guide her back into the house before she caught a cold. I knew that if she were in her right mind, she would have wanted to get inside as soon as possible before any of the neighbours saw.

That night, Kenji didn't come home, and Kida never contacted me. My mother sat on the couch with a blanket around her shoulders like a zombie, continuously repeating the same questions to me while I stood in front of her. Not a single answer was able to slip through my lips.

"Where is my son? What has happened to my boy?"

My mother's frustration was building. Her shoulders were tensing up as she sat, traumatized. Without saying a word, I left the living room, never looking back to check on her. I went up to my bedroom, where I knew I could manage some peace before another storm hit. In my room, I slumped down onto my bed face first, not bothering to change my clothes. Eventually, exhaustion got the better of me. I felt my eyes flutter as I prayed for this nightmare I was living to end.

Chapter Eleven

*T*HE FRONT DOOR slammed shut and all I could hear was my mother shouting.

"Where have you been? You're two hours later than usual!"

"Shh! You're going to wake the kids," he hissed.

"Stop avoiding the question! Where were you?"

He let out a heavy sigh. "After work, some of my co-workers and I went out for drinks, okay?"

"I tried calling your cellphone, but it kept sending me straight to voice-mail. Was it off?" she interrogated.

"Must've died during the night . . .."

"Oh, really? Just like that?" she questioned suspiciously. "Why do you smell like perfume?"

"I don't! Why are you always on my case?"

I had gotten out of bed, put my slippers on, and tiptoed out of my room. Stopping at the stairs, I'd sat on the top step to watch and listen.

"You've been seeing some whore, haven't you?" my mother attacked, shoving my father into what sounded like the closet door. "Don't deny it! The neighbours have been gossiping about it for weeks!"

"Stop talking nonsense! Do you even understand what you're saying?"

My mother fell silent. "I saw you, Youji. I saw you . . . drive to her house."

Using everything she had within her, she confronted him. "I SAW YOU KISS HER WITH THE SAME FUCKING LIPS YOU KISS ME!"

The amount of yelling frightened me. An unidentifiable noise started to escape my mouth, but I quickly covered it with my hands.

"Stop this," he said, attempting to embrace her.

"No!" she said firmly, slapping him across the face. "You stop! Stop pretending to be a part of this family!"

I couldn't see everything from where I sat, but I heard the familiar squeakiness from the closet door open and shut. The sound of heavy bags slamming to the ground shortly followed.

"Shino, what is this . . . ?"

"Your stuff. You're not welcome here."

"You're . . . kicking me out? What about the kids?" he asked desperately.

"Don't pretend to be worried about them now. They don't need the likes of you in their lives."

The front door opened, and cold, winter air blew through the entire house. Forgetting I was in hiding, I ran down the stairs.

"Dad! No! Don't go!" Shouting with everything I had, he glanced back at me.

Despair and sorrow consumed his face, but he flashed me a fleeting smile. My mother rushed to my side and grabbed my arms as I tried my hardest to reach him.

"Nila! Leave him!" she demanded, holding me back.

"No! I don't want him to go!" I cried, struggling in her arms, pleading for her to reconsider her decision.

"Nila . . .," he spoke softly, "this isn't goodbye. I'll be back soon. Promise."

With those final words, he walked out.

I woke up in the middle of the night, panting and drenched in sweat. I knew I should have been forcing myself out of bed to change my shirt, but I laid there looking up at the ceiling instead. Tears trickled down the sides of my face, soaking into the pillow. I thought about the memory I had just relived in my dream—the night my father left.

You promised . . . Liar. That's all people do around here. They lie and then they leave.

Chapter Twelve

ANOTHER DAY WENT by, but nothing changed. It was now Christmas Eve and my brother was still nowhere to be found. My mother was feeling 'under the weather,' so couldn't make it into work for her shifts. There wasn't a single present under our tree or a single snowflake on the ground. I knew this year was going to be a terrible Christmas, just like last year and the year before that. I was counting down the days until the winter break was over so I could go back to school and get out of this shithole.

I'd spent the last two days with minimal movement outside of my room. With a ridiculous amount of time to myself, I'd thought long and hard about Kenji and Kida ... together. Nasty, disgusting thoughts swept my mind and anger bubbled deep within me.

Were there any feelings involved, or did they decide to have sex just for the hell of it?

This thought, plus many others, kept popping in and out of my head. Trying to come up with all the answers, I couldn't grasp the truth. The crisp, white walls of my room started to close in on me, even though I was safe in a familiar space, I was scared of what was to come.

In between the thoughts of Kenji and Kida, I angrily stared at my dollhouse from my bed. Positioned on the floor in the opposite corner of my room, was the dollhouse my father and I built together when I was a kid. I hadn't played with dolls in years, but I was never able to throw it away. Growing up, I was so excited to play with it that I never fully paid attention to its unique features. The house was bright yellow, just like the sun. It had a white door with white windows, and a white wraparound porch that I had begged my father to incorporate. It had three storeys, the inside of which you were able to see by pulling apart both sides of the house, just like opening a storybook.

My father's hidden passion was carpentry, so he was fairly good with wood. Instead of taking it up as a career, he used to say: *'Keeping your hobbies separate from your day-to-day work, gives a person greater fulfillment when completing a project for fun.'*

The parts he created for the dollhouse looked amazing compared to mine, of course, especially considering I was only four at the time. I always admired his work and thought what he did with wood was magic. As a kid, I would watch him for hours as he worked away in his workshop. His workshop was actually our tiny storage shed in the backyard, but to him, it was probably so much more.

I continued glaring at the dollhouse until my vision became blurry from not blinking. "I hate you."

As I laid on my bed, deep in thought, the doorbell rang. I perked up as I heard the sound. Checking the clock on my nightstand, it read 1:20 p.m. *It can't be Kenji? He wouldn't ring the doorbell when he has a key. And, isn't Mom downstairs? I'll just let her get it.*

A minute passed, then it rang again.

"Is she really not going to answer it?" I asked under my breath as I sat up on my bed, staring at the closed bedroom door.

The doorbell rang for a third time.

Well, whoever it is, they sure are persistent.

I made my way downstairs and looked down the hall towards the living room before answering the door. I saw my mother lying on the couch with a blanket over her, her back towards the front door.

She must be in a pretty deep sleep for her not to hear the doorbell.

The doorbell rang for a fourth time as I quickly turned to answer it. To my amazement, standing at the door was Kai.

"Finally! Not gonna lie, I was about to leave."

"Kai! What are you doing here? It's Christmas Eve!" I asked, alarmed.

"You never answered my question about the book, and you haven't been replying to my other messages or phone calls either, so I was getting worried . . .."

Crap! I forgot; I turned my phone off. "Sorry . . . my phone's been off."

"Oh, why?"

"No reason. So, why are you here? Is it to return my book?" I asked, changing the topic of concern.

"Weeell, not exactly. I actually forgot it at home."

I gave Kai a displeased look. "Of course, you did."

"Are you free right now?"

"Free? Free for what?"

"Let's go out." Kai grabbed my wrist and pulled me towards him.

"Wait! I can't go outside without shoes!" I said, looking down at my feet.

"Oh, right, sorry," he said with a childish grin and gently let go of my wrist.

"I also look terrible right now! I can't go out looking like this," I said, pointing to my comfy stay-at-home outfit.

"Nila, don't be dumb, you look fine. Come on."

Dumb? Who does this idiot think he's talking to?

Irritated, I looked back at my mother and saw that she hadn't changed her position on the couch since I opened the door. Without much thought, I got my stuff and ran out of the house. Kai caught my hand and started pulling me along.

Stop doing these things dammit—you're so confusing!

We ran all the way down the street before I stopped to ask questions. "Where are we going?"

"Downtown."

"Why?"

"I need to get a few things."

"So, let me get this straight. You're taking me with you . . . to do errands?" I said, puzzled.

"Uh, I guess you could say that," he chuckled.

Doesn't he have anything better to do on Christmas Eve than to go shopping with me?

Reaching downtown, we went into a clothing and accessories shop called: *Itch & Stitch Fashion*. I drifted off towards the women's clothing section and began flipping through the clearance racks in the back, while Kai headed to men's accessories.

Hmm, I wonder if Mom would like this sweater for Christmas . . ..

Still flipping through the racks, Kai snuck up behind me. "I think that purple sweater would look good on you."

Startled, I turned around and saw Kai hovering over me. "Jeez!" I shouted. "You almost gave me a heart attack!"

"Sorry," he said stepping back, grabbing his sides as he laughed.

"Idiot."

"Classic Nila. Just when I thought you were getting nicer," he continued to tease.

"I am nice," I said, slightly insulted.

"It's just, you haven't called me an 'idiot' in a while."

I didn't realize it, but he was right. I hadn't called him any names recently because we hadn't been in contact. Guilt swept over me. "I'm sorry, I didn't know that it bothered you so much."

"I didn't mean it like that. To be honest, I kinda like it when you call me names," he said, sticking his tongue out playfully. "Plus, saying it like that makes me seem like a little kid who got his feelings hurt." He furrowed his eyebrows as if wanting to demonstrate how tough he was. "I want to be seen as a cool, young adult."

The people shopping around us stared, but somehow, I didn't care. An uncontrollable laugh came flying out of me.

"Hey! Don't laugh, I'm serious!" he said as he crossed his arms and tapped his foot.

I hadn't laughed so hard in what felt like ages. The feeling was overwhelming, but in a pleasant way. With everything going on lately, it was hard to imagine I would be laughing so soon.

The laughing started to ease and break down into choppy, gasps of air as I tried to speak. "Sorry, sorr—" The laughter continued; I couldn't keep a straight face with him looking at me the way he was.

Kai's face flushed red as he attempted to turn the focus back to clothing. "Anyway, you should get that sweater."

I was finally able to settle down and control myself. "I'm not shopping for myself today. I need to use my money wisely for Christmas presents since I haven't bought anything for anyone yet. I don't have a job, so I rely on the allowance my mom gives me."

"Oh, I didn't know that. I thought you would've had a part-time job or something."

"Is it bad that I don't?"

"No, it's completely fine. For some reason I just assumed you'd have one."

"Well, I don't. Do you?"

"Yeah," he replied proudly.

"Really? Where?"

"Just at my family's flower shop, nothing special."

"Wow," I said in amazement. I could never picture Kai knowing anything about flowers, let alone selling and arranging them.

"Surprised?" he chuckled. "From the look on your face, I'm guessing it's hard for you to imagine me as a florist?"

"Uh, well, yeah, it just doesn't seem like something you would take an interest in."

Kai smiled, almost sadly. "I'm not super into it, but I've been around flowers since I was a baby. The flower shop originates from my grandfather, who's practically retired, but works every now and then because he doesn't know how to let go. My dad's been managing it in the meantime. Someday, the shop will be passed onto me, so I gotta start learning the ropes now."

"That's awesome!" I said excitedly.

"It's alright," he answered, but not as enthusiastic as I was.

"I wish my family owned a business, then maybe I'd finally be allowed to work."

Kai looked confused. "You're not 'allowed' to work? Technically, it is against most schools' rules for students to have part-time jobs, but so many of us do anyway. So, why?"

With a deep sigh, I answered, "My mom won't let me. She said the reason she works a lot is for Kenji and I to focus on our studies. She gives us a decent amount of money as an allowance, so it's not like I really need a job. Besides, I hardly spend money, so I have a bunch saved up.

I want to be able to pay for at least half of my college tuition when the time comes."

"That's respectable; I get it. Your mom really pushes for you guys to do well in school, huh?"

"Yeah," I said softly as I continued shuffling through the next set of racks. "She apparently had a rough upbringing and my grandparents struggled financially. Because of that, she couldn't go to college like the rest of her friends from high school did and ended up working for a couple of years until she had enough to pay for it herself. Mom told me she doesn't want that to happen to us. She wants to be able to send her kids off to college right after high school."

Kai placed his hand on my head. "Your mom seems really caring. Even though she may be a bit strict and rough around the edges, she works hard to give you and your brother the best. I admire that," he smiled wistfully, then removed his hand from my head and turned away slightly.

He said that with sadness in his voice . . . why?

"Should we check out another store or are you getting hungry? There's a small restaurant called Tetsu's down the street that I've been to with some friends. Their food is pretty good, if you're interested."

"Oh, I haven't been. Food would be good about now," I said as I placed my hand on my stomach. "I haven't eaten yet today."

"What?" he shouted, checking his watch. "It's already past 2:30 p.m.! What were you doing all day?"

"A whole lot of nothing, to be honest," I said, remembering all the time I had wasted staring at the plain walls in my room.

"Jeez, let's go eat then. It scares me that you haven't eaten a single thing today." Kai shook his head, angrily.

"Alright, alright. Let me just pay for that purple sweater," I said as I walked back towards the first rack.

"I thought you weren't shopping for yourself?"

"It's not for me; it's a Christmas present for my mom. I think she'll really like it."

"I bet she will," Kai said with a gentle smile.

We walked to the register so I could pay for the sweater. I placed the item on the counter and waited for the shop attendant to appear. Kai was busy looking at the last-minute bargain items conveniently placed around the register. A young lady, wearing an orange apron with the shop's logo on it, came from the back room and approached the front counter.

"Hello!" she said in a friendly tone. "Did you find everything you were looking for?"

"Yep, I'm all set," I replied, reaching for the wallet in my purse as I waited for her to scan the sweater and read me the total. I looked at Kai and saw him playing around with the key chains.

Pffft, he's like a little kid.

"Your total is . . .," she began as she looked up at the two of us. Her sentence had started to fade as she refocused her attention. "Kai!"

Kai looked up at the shop attendant who spoke his name.

I first looked at her, then at Kai. I could see the colour drop from his face as he intensely stared at the girl behind the counter.

"Momiji . . .?"

Chapter Thirteen

KAI STOOD COMPLETELY still. His eyes were wide and glossy; pain lingered deep within, while his skin paled. I could not explain why, but it felt like the relationship between Kai and I had taken one step backwards.

"Wow, I can't believe it's you, Kai! It's been a while . . . Looks like you finally changed your hairstyle," the girl playfully joked. "Almost a whole year since—"

"Nila," Kai interrupted the shop attendant, "I'll wait for you outside." Looking at me with a fake smile, Kai then walked out of the shop, without further acknowledging the girl known as Momiji.

I had no idea what was going on, or how these two even knew each other, but I could feel myself getting jealous. Kai's fake smile made it look like he was seconds from breaking down.

I glanced back towards the girl. She visually sighed, looking down at the register with disappointment. "Sorry to delay your purchase. I'm glad the shop is dead today, ha . . . ha," she attempted to make light of the situation, avoiding the stiff awkwardness.

"It's okay," I replied, feeling uneasy. *There's something about her that doesn't sit well with me. What could it be? I keep saying I don't like to judge people but that's all I seem to be doing lately.*

The shop attendant, Momiji, read me my total, then continued to fold and bag the sweater. I opened my wallet, pulled out the money, and handed it to her. Carefully, she took the money from my hand, making sure not to drop any of the coins resting in my palm. She counted the money before typing the amount into the register. The register drawer opened and she calculated the change, then ripped off the receipt from the printer.

"Is the receipt okay in the bag?"

"That's fine," I said, wishing she would go faster so I could go meet up with Kai.

As I reached for my change, she quickly closed her hand, keeping the money hostage. "Are you his girlfriend?"

"What?" I said, astonished by her unrelated question. "No," I confirmed strictly.

"Oh," she said with some relief. "That's odd, he never goes out shopping with girls unless he . . .." She stopped her sentence and her eyes widened, as if shocked by her incomplete statement.

Puzzled, her grip on my change loosened, allowing me to finally receive it from her hand.

"Have a nice day," I snapped as I took the shopping bag with my left hand and gripped the change tightly in my right.

Walking to the exit, I opened the door and saw Kai leaning against the shop's window ledge with both hands in his pockets. He looked unsurprisingly cool as he stood there waiting for me.

"Sorry to keep you waiting," I apologized while shutting the door and putting my change into my wallet.

"You didn't," he said in a shaky voice without facing me, "I'm the one who left."

Continuing down the strip of the shopping district towards the restaurant, we walked silently side-by-side as thoughts raced through my mind.

Who is she to Kai? A friend? An ex-girlfriend? Should I ask him about her, or will he think I'm nosy? After all, his past is none of my business. But still, I want to know so badly.

"Um, back there . . . was that your . . .."

"Yeah. She's my ex-girlfriend—the one who cheated on me. Sorry, you had to be a part of such an awkward situation," he answered, still avoiding eye contact as we walked.

I shook my head, disagreeing with him. "No, it's alright. You did nothing wrong. It's just that you seemed really surprised to see her working there."

"Yeah, I was. Last I knew, she was working at a restaurant close to her school. Since we've broken up, I've avoided going to that restaurant so I wouldn't bump into her." Finally looking towards me, another sad smile appeared on his face. "Guess I don't have to worry about that anymore."

Looking at him, I tried to imagine what their relationship was like back then. *How long were they together for? Was he . . . happy?*

Clearing his throat, he pressed, "Hey, uh, did she say anything to you after I left?"

Watching Kai get agitated, I quickly recalled her asking me if Kai and I were dating. *For her to ask such a thing, could she still have feelings for him? Impossible. She's the one who cheated on HIM. Obviously, she stopped caring for him long ago.* "No, she didn't say anything," I lied.

Looking relieved, he let out a huge sigh. "Alright, cool."

We continued on our way and came across a store that sold hats. The shop's outer design was bright and attracted my attention, causing me to stop and peer into its window.

"Wanna go in?" Kai leaned over me to also peer into the window. "We can eat afterwards if you're okay to hold off a bit longer. Or we can come back?"

"I'm not sure," I replied, thinking of Kenji.

"Who would the hat be for?"

"My brother."

"Then we should go in," Kai insisted. "It would be his Christmas present, right?"

I looked down at the ground, afraid to answer. I wasn't sure if I should tell him what happened in the past couple of days with Kenji.

"Nila? Everything okay?"

"I don't know. I don't know if I want to get him a gift this year," I confessed.

"Why wouldn't you? He's your brother. You should get him something.

It doesn't have to be worth a whole lot, it's the thought that counts," Kai reassured.

"I know that. Money isn't the issue."

"Then . . . I don't get it."

"Yeah, I know, sorry. It's nothing, we don't have to go in," I said as I started to walk away from the shop window.

Just then, the chimes connected to the door of the hat shop jingled. Looking back, I saw the backside of Kai's jacket as he went into the shop. I quickly ran in to follow him. He stood right in the doorway and brushed off his shoes on the floor mat.

"What are you doing?" I asked as I tugged on his sleeve.

Kai turned around to face me. "I know you want to come in here and buy something for your brother. The only thing I can't figure out is what happened between the two of you to make you deny it. So, you're going to buy a hat you think your brother will like and give it to him for Christmas. End of story."

Slowly releasing the grip I had on Kai's sleeve, I stared up at his eyes. I could feel my throat closing up as my eyes filled with a layer of tears. I began sobbing in the store's entrance.

Kai took a couple of steps towards me and wrapped his one arm around my head to hide my tears. "It's okay," he comforted, holding me in close. "After we get the hat, let's go eat so you can tell me what happened."

I felt the glares coming from people in the store as they shopped around. They probably thought we were a stupid teenage couple fighting or making up.

Kai took his arm off me and smiled. "Come on, let's do this quickly so we can eat. I'm starving!" he announced, playfully rubbing his stomach as if he hadn't eaten in ages.

Knowing he was trying his best to cheer me up made me happy. I used my sleeve to wipe the tears away before smiling back. "Yeah."

Looking around at the different styles of hats, I decided to go with a simple baseball cap because I usually saw Kenji wearing those. *He seems to always wear darker colours, so maybe a black or navy blue one would be best.*

Kai was over by a bin sorting through some hats as he looked to me. Lifting up a hat from the bin, he asked, "Do you like this baseball cap?"

"Yeah, it's nice. Are you buying it for yourself?"

"Nah, I think I'll also get my little brother one for Christmas. He's a pretty big baseball fan."

"Kenji is, too . . .," I whispered under my breath.

Together, we went to the register with our selections and purchased gifts for our brothers. When we were done, we walked out of the shop with our bags.

I'm glad that shop attendant didn't know Kai; I'd hate to have a repeat of last time.

"How many more gifts do you have to buy?" Kai asked.

"I think I might be done."

"Oh, yeah?"

"Mhm."

"Alright, well, let's head to the restaurant to eat and then we can shop more if you think of anyone else."

"Sure."

We made our way to the cozy restaurant and took a seat at a booth. We sat across from each other and placed our shopping bags on the empty spaces beside us.

"Ughhh! It's a quarter past three and you're only eating breakfast now," he said, furious.

"I wouldn't call it 'breakfast' anymore. It's pretty much an early dinner now."

"That's even worse! It's only your first meal of the day. You better not get sick!" he scolded.

I laughed at his overprotectiveness. "Don't worry. It's not like I'm going to die on you or anything." *Although, I did pass out the other night at Kida's.*

Kai's face went from playfully stern, to extremely serious as his smile turned into a frown. "Don't say that."

"S-sorry." *Did I say something so terrible? I was only kidding.*

Just then, a server approached our table with a pen and pad of paper.

"Good evening, my name is Ume and I'll be your server today. Can I start you off with drinks?"

"Ume," Kai paused after repeating her name. "That's a very pretty name, but why aren't you presenting yourself with your surname?"

Suuure, flirt with her right in front of me. Jerk . . ..

The waitress giggled. "Thanks! It means 'plum.' And, the owner here wants the restaurant to have a family vibe with the customers. Most of us don't mind."

"Oh, I see," Kai stopped to think. "'Plum,' huh? Doesn't it mean 'Ocean' or 'Sea'?"

"That's *Umi*, with an 'I,' mine is *Ume*, with an 'E'; different Kanji."

"Ah, I see. Well, regardless, it's very cute," Kai replied, with his prince-like smile. "Ume, I think I'll start off with a Coca-Cola. What about you, Nila?" He looked at me.

"I'll just have water," I said assertively, as I opened the menu and propped it up onto the table to block my face. *Why am I getting so mad? He's not even my boyfriend . . ..*

"Alrighty then, I'll be back in a minute," Ume announced, placing the pen and pad of paper back into her apron before heading off.

"You okay, Nila?"

Without removing the menu from my face, I replied, "Yep, just fine."

"You don't seem 'fine'?"

I snapped the menu closed and slammed it onto the table. "I said I'm fine, so that means I'm fine. OKAY?"

Kai looked at me with widened eyes as he clenched his lips tight. "Yes, Ma'am!"

UGH! What am I doing? I shouldn't be upset with him for no reason. "I'm sorry," I said, ashamed, as I put my head down on the table and wrapped my arms around it. *Why am I acting like this? I'm so pitiful.*

"Here are your drinks. Oh, my! Is she alright?" Ume asked as she returned to our table. She took our drinks off the tray and placed them in front of us.

"Yeah, she's fine. She just has a bit of a headache," Kai said convincingly.

"Oh, okay, well, I hope she feels better soon. Do you need another moment to decide on your order then?"

"Yes, please," Kai answered for us again.

"No problem, I'll be back in a bit," Ume said as she jumped to the next table to take another order.

"So, what happened between you and your brother?"

As Kai asked that question, the jealousy of the waitress escaped my mind. *That's right. We're here to talk. How could I be concerned with something so petty as jealousy?*

I lifted my head from the table. "We should order first."

"Okay." Kai flipped through his menu. "I think I'll get something simple, like udon."

"Hmm, maybe I'll get the beef sukiyaki."

"Ohhh, that's also a good choice!" Kai replied, drooling over the mere idea of food.

Minutes later, the waitress came back.

"Have we decided?"

"Yes Ume, I think I'll go with the udon."

"That's our top choice!" Ume exclaimed as she wrote down Kai's order on her note pad. "And for you, Miss?"

"I'll get the same."

"The same?" Kai questioned.

"Yes," I answered selfishly. "I changed my mind."

"Excellent, I'll be back with your food shortly." Ume took our menus and darted off.

"She seems like she's always full of energy," Kai joked.

"Yeah."

"Now tell me," he demanded. "No more distractions."

"I don't even know where to start . . . ."

"How about with the reason for you turning off your cellphone?"

It took a while to get me going, but slowly, I spilled my guts to Kai about everything that had happened in the past couple of days. It was as if he was a diary that I couldn't stop writing in. It felt so good to tell someone about everything I had been keeping to myself—someone who wasn't related or involved in any of the drama. I felt like I was annoyingly ranting about my problems, but every time I glanced at Kai's face, he was attentively listening.

About fifteen minutes went by before Ume arrived with our food.

"Sorry for the wait. Here's the udon."

"Already?" Kai asked, looking surprised as Ume placed a bowl and a package of chopsticks in front of him. "That was quick."

"It only seemed quick because we were talking," I giggled.

"And here's yours, Miss." Ume also placed a bowl and chopsticks in front of me.

"Thank you," I replied.

"If you need anything else, just let me know. Enjoy!" she bowed, then left our booth.

"Will do," Kai answered, placing both hands together. "Thank you for the food." He ripped open the package and split his chopsticks in half.

We both tasted our dishes at the same time. The udon I ordered smelled and looked amazing. At home, my mother always put a lot of salt in her udon because she said it 'enhanced' the flavour. I wasn't a huge fan of excessive amounts of salt, so I always tried to avoid my mother's dish whenever she made it.

Using the chopsticks, I placed a big portion of noodles into my mouth. "How is it?"

"It's really good actually. Just the right amount of salt," I said, delighted. "How's yours?"

"Mine's perfect, but let's compare," he suggested as he reached into my bowl and stole some noodles with his chopsticks. "Mmm, you're right. Yours is good." He licked his lips and winked.

"Hey, that's mine!" I pouted, slightly embarrassed as I watched him eat from my bowl.

Kai laughed, attempting to keep the noodles in his mouth. After he'd finally swallowed, he spoke. "You're just too cute when you make that face."

I felt my face burn up by his comment. With a slight turn of my head, I replied, "Pffft, whatever."

He chuckled at my reaction. "So, where did we leave off?" He shut his eyes as if to think back on our conversation before our food had arrived. "Oh yeah," his eyes popped open, "you caught your brother smoking a cigarette before you headed to your friend's. That must have been a sight to witness."

"Yeah, I was surprised, but a little relieved," I admitted.

"What do you mean?"

"Well, a cigarette is better than drugs. I don't know what he's doing when he's out with his 'friends,' but I'm glad I didn't witness something more serious. If I did, I would worry about him even more," I confessed, as I took a chopstick and twirled the noodles around in my bowl.

"Hmm," Kai let out a small sigh. "I guess you're right. Drugs would be a lot worse than a cigarette. It's still sad to see him heading down that sort of path though. I know I'd kill Ryu if he started doing any of that shit. I wonder what your brother was doing with those kinda guys."

"I don't even want to think about that because I feel like it wasn't something good." I closed my eyes and took a deep breath. "To be honest, I kind of blocked that part from my memory because a lot happened afterwards."

"Like what?"

As we continued eating, I told Kai about the night I stayed at Kida's and how Kida and I had a tiny argument. I left out the part about me fainting at her house because I didn't want to further worry him. While I explained, Kai listened to everything I said without a look of judgment. Ume eventually came by, took our empty dishes, and cleared off the table. We didn't order any dessert. Instead, we sat at the table for an extra hour or so as I shared what I was currently dealing with.

"WHOA! She slept with your brother!" Kai burst out, jolting forward.

"SHH!" I exclaimed, jerking my head up to look around at the surrounding tables. "The whole world doesn't need to know!"

"Sorry, sorry! I'll keep my voice down, but WOW—that's insane! I can't believe you didn't start with that," he said in amazement, leaning back in his seat.

"That's the part that shocked me the most too, but . . . there's still more."

"Holy crap! There's more? How much worse can it get? That was already the icing on the cake!"

Reliving the night Kida told me about her secret relations with Kenji, I told Kai about the incident that happened a couple of nights ago. It felt good to get such a heavy topic off my chest because for the last couple of days, I felt completely alone.

Kai paused for a moment to blankly stare at me. "He . . . hit her?"

"Yeah."

He turned white as a sheet, his face overflowing with concern. "Is she okay?"

"I'm not sure. I haven't really spoken to my mother, even though we've both been home. Kenji hasn't come home at all since then, not even to sleep. I have no idea what he's been up to or where he's been staying."

Kai looked at me with sad eyes as he slowly pulled his wallet out and placed some money on top of the bill Ume left for us on the table.

"Let me pay for my meal," I said, reaching for the wallet in my purse.

"No, it's okay. Please, let me get it. It's my Christmas present to you."

Usually, I didn't allow people to pay for me, but his expression was extremely upsetting to look at; I couldn't say no. From his slumped shoulders, he seemed depressed. I couldn't help but think it was related to what I had just finished telling him about. "Thank you."

"Don't mention it."

We both stood and stepped out from the booth. We put on our jackets, grabbed our shopping bags, and headed to the exit. Kai held the door open for me.

"Thanks," I acknowledged.

Finding it strange that Kai didn't respond to my polite remark with one of his own, I turned around to look at him. With his head hung, Kai stood still without saying a word. We both moved off to the side and stood in front of the big restaurant window as the door shut behind us.

I'm a terrible person. Pushing all this onto him when he's not even involved . . . . "I'm sorry to have burdened you with my problems. I guess I just wanted someone to listen to me while I vented. It's one thing to think about something, but it's another to actually say it. I realized, saying it out loud made the situation feel even more real than it did in my head."

Without looking up, Kai walked closer to me and grabbed my wrist. I didn't say a single word as he pulled me into the narrow alleyway in between the restaurant and the shop beside it. Kai raised his head slowly as his stuff dropped to the ground. Where no one could see us, he reached over and placed both arms around me, forcing me to drop my bags as well.

"Nila, I'm so sorry. It's unbelievable that you had to deal with all this alone, and so close to Christmas. You couldn't have your family, or even your best friend, help you through any of this; you weren't able to rely on a single person. Nila, you are seriously a strong person, you honestly amaze me. It makes me extremely happy that you feel comfortable enough to confide in me."

It sounded like Kai was choking on his words. The way he held me was as if his body was telling me *I'm here.* I felt his grip on my body grow stronger and tighter as his fingers dug through my jacket, indenting my skin. His face was hidden from me because mine was pressed into his chest, while his rested atop my head. It felt as if we had known each other our entire lives. Even though Kai couldn't understand my situation from experience, it was like he truly understood my feelings.

I had longed for comfort like this from another person. Secretly, I knew he was right; I did feel alone. I couldn't talk to anyone. Kida was usually the one I turned to, but this time she wasn't the one I could rely on—Kai was. That moment, I realized something. Recently, a majority of my time had been consumed by Kai that when the break was over, and we were to return to school, what would our days look like? Would they continue to go on like this or go back to how they were before?

"Kai," I mumbled into his chest. "I just want to . . .."

"Nila." He cut through; his assertive tone forced me to stop mid-sentence. "Ever since I've met you, you've always had something going on. I could tell you were trying to be brave in front of others, even though you were scared—just like the time at karaoke." Taking a deep breath, he continued. "Tough, I soon realized you weren't trying to be strong; you actually were strong. Showing emotion is a sign of strength because it's very easy to hide how one feels. But," he paused, moving me away from his chest to look at me, "everyone has their limit and I can tell you're close to reaching yours. Your body seems strong and sturdy on the outside, but on the inside, you're crying and pleading for help. From the beginning, your eyes sucked me in; they were like nothing I had ever seen before. They were interesting because I knew there was a story behind them and

I wanted to discover what it was. In the end, I find myself wanting to get involved with you, wanting to save you." Kai raised one hand to my cheek. "It somehow became a goal of mine to make those sad, dark brown eyes shine with happiness whenever I could."

Tears overwhelmed my eyes, clouding my vision as they trickled down my cheeks. My chest pounded, as if someone was beating it with a hammer. My throat went dry like a desert while I gasped for air. I could feel myself getting overly emotional, so I moved back to cover my mouth with my hand, hiding an obnoxious cry from Kai. I placed the other hand over my stomach to prevent it from convulsing, but for some strange reason, this difficult breathing felt warm. My whole body burned with immense joy as I stood in front of Kai, ugly-crying, unable to say anything as sweet in return.

Kai touched my chin, tilting it upwards as he wiped the tears from my eyes. My vision was still a bit blurry, but I didn't need to see anything; I knew what was about to happen. Kai removed my hand from my mouth and brought his face closer to mine. I felt a humid air bouncing off my face as something warm brushed against my lips. My mind went blank. Kai's lips were tender against mine—that was my first kiss. Pinning me against the wall of the restaurant, he took my right hand with his left and brought them down to our sides, intertwining and locking our fingers together. Carefully, he took his other hand and ran his fingers once through my bangs before resting his arm against the wall above me.

As we kissed for the second time, the first snowfall of the season began.

Chapter Fourteen

THE SNOW FELL calmly, landing on everything exposed to the sky. Upon opening my eyes, I saw a tiny flake land onto Kai's cheek before quickly disappearing into his warm skin. Snowflakes floated down on top of our heads, dampening our hair. I could feel the heat from Kai's breath brisk across my face as he placed his forehead against mine. Outside the alleyway, I'm sure there were people passing by, but I was in a magical world, and didn't hear a single footstep. Standing in the snow, I became deaf to the world around me. The only thing I could hear was the sound of my heart beating monstrously. It was cold, but a comfortable warmth surrounded me. At that moment, I knew I had fallen for Kai, a boy who was still a stranger to me. Even though we kissed for less than a minute, it felt like it lasted an eternity. It was my first time kissing anyone, and there was a strong probability I sucked at it. With Kai having had a previous relationship, he automatically one-upped me in experience. A giddy, nervous teenager finally started to grow from within me. My world had changed; sweeping me far away into a new, mysterious place—I was enjoying it.

We stayed embraced in each other's arms for a short time after. Nothing was said; no words could express or explain the moment better than the kiss had. The snow continued to fall silently on top of us, covering the ground and buildings surrounding us in a fresh, white canvas.

Breaking eye contact, but never letting go of my hand, Kai bent down to pick up our stuff. Holding the bags in one hand, and my hand in the other, he led us out of the alley and back onto the road where we continued down the district in silence. As we were walking, Kai's phone rang. He hesitantly let go of my hand to pull out the cellphone from his pocket.

"Sorry, it's a call from my house. I should answer it."

"Yeah, sure," I said, my lips still tingling from the kiss.

After hanging up the phone, the expression on Kai's face seemed a bit defeated. "Sorry, Nila, I gotta go. My dad needs me to close the shop tonight, and for the next few nights, so my parents can go visit my grandparents for the holidays. Seems my grandma has the flu, so my grandparents can't come over this year."

My emotions synced with Kai's expression as I felt sad about our time coming to an end. "That's okay; I should head home, too. My mom was asleep when I left, so I didn't tell her I was heading out."

"That's true. I'm surprised she hasn't called yet to find out where you are," Kai said, a sense of sarcasm to his words. "I'd love to walk you home, but unfortunately, it's in the opposite direction of the shop and my dad wanted me to hurry. The most I can do is take you to the bus station. I'm really sorry," he apologized sincerely.

"No, it's fine. I'm a big girl; I can handle myself," I joked, flexing my arm.

Kai smiled with ease as he reached for my hand nonchalantly. "Let's go then."

This time, without making a fuss, I allowed Kai to hold my hand as we walked to the station.

"Well, there it is," Kai dragged his words as we arrived.

"Yeah."

We stood across the street from the station, trying to find a good time to cross in between the wave of traffic. While waiting, my eyes wandered up to a familiar sign on the building beside us.

That's right; the karaoke bar is across from this station. I almost forgot.

"Annnd, now!" Kai exclaimed, quickly tugging on my hand.

Taking me by surprise, I almost tripped over my feet, trying to keep up with him. Once we reached the other side of the street, Kai let go.

Taking a minute to catch his breath, Kai bent down, placing both hands on his knees before inhaling and exhaling dramatically. "Man, I'm outta shape. Here," he looked up at me. "You'll need these," he said, holding out my shopping bags.

"Thanks," I said shyly, reaching for the bags. His hands were red from the cold but as they grazed mine, I could feel a small amount of warmth emanating from them. After our sudden kiss, I couldn't muster a simple 'thank you' or 'goodbye.' Instead, I remained practically speechless.

Kai grinned. "Merry Christmas, Nila. I hope everything is okay with your family. I'll message you."

Before we parted ways, he snagged a quick kiss on my cheek, then jogged in the opposite direction, waving as he went. Watching him go, my chest thumped with loneliness.

He does everything so naturally. What am I to him? It's not like we're a couple . . . are we?

I remembered I still needed wrapping paper, so I dashed into the convenience store beside the bus station. I bought two rolls and made it back in time to see my bus arrive. When I got on the bus, all that played through my mind were the two kisses. Using the tip of my index finger, I traced the invisible prints Kai's lips had left. Each kiss felt like a dream; a distant memory of the past, already fading. In my heart, I prayed for this day to be real and not just a dream soon to be awoken from.

Pulling up to my stop, I gathered my bags and walked to the doors of the bus to exit. When the bus came to a complete stop, I jumped off and began speed walking towards my house. Heading through the metal gate and up the walkway, my knees trembled as soon as I saw my mother's car. The anticipation of what awaited me inside consumed my thoughts, and the wonderful day I had spent with Kai, vanished. Glancing over at the kitchen window, I saw that a light was on. Terrified to enter, I loitered at the bottom of the steps to the front door. My heart was pounding. The strings holding my heart in place were being ripped from my chest as I stared at the wooden door of my house. Looking closely, I could see a few hairline cracks in the wood, measuring from my fingertips to the edge of my palm. After inspecting the door, and remembering an unforgettable incident, I was scared to enter this place I called home and see the people I called family.

Persevering, I walked up the steps and turned the knob quietly to enter the house. Eyeing the shoes lined up at the entryway, I could see that Kenji's were still missing. Looking down the hall, I noticed my mother was no longer on the couch. The whole house was dark, not a single thing different from when I left, except for the one light in the kitchen. I dropped my bags by the door, took off my shoes and jacket, then made my way into the kitchen. The air in the kitchen was stale; not a single thing had been touched, including all the dirty dishes.

Mom's probably moved up to her room . . ..

The dishes needed to be washed and put away, so that task fell onto me by default. After tidying things up, I went to the table and noticed a couple of letters scattered on top.

These weren't here yesterday . . . were they?

I picked up one of the letters which read: *City Hall: Ministry of Marriage Licencing and Personal Affairs.* After reading the letter thoroughly, I came to the conclusion that my mother was in the process of changing her surname back to her maiden name. It seemed as if this action had been going on for quite some time because the document indicated that the process was in the final stages. Holding the paper in one hand, I reached for the second letter. The letterhead of the second document was the same, but its content was different. It was about a divorce proceeding.

Switching my focus back and forth between the two documents gave me a headache. My parents hadn't been together for over two years, but they technically never got a divorce; according to the law, they were only separated.

"Nila."

Startled, I dropped both sets of papers on the table and spun around to find my mother standing in the arch of the kitchen entrance in her nightgown.

"Mom!" I screamed with panic. "Sorry, I . . .."

"It's okay. I left them there on purpose," she stated as she walked towards me. "Here." She handed me a sealed envelope. "I want you to think carefully before giving me your answer."

When I reached for the envelope, she took another step forward, placing a kiss on my forehead. This was something she used to do when I was a child right before putting me to bed.

As my mother turned to walk away, she stopped with her back towards me. "I know it's fairly early, but I'm going to bed." Seemingly agitated, she sighed heavily. "I can't wait for this holiday season to be over. If Kenji happens to come home, please be kind to him and let him in. Alright, Nila?"

Without waiting for my reply, she left the kitchen.

Standing there in a daze, holding the envelope, hundreds of ideas began accumulating in my head. The letter could contain anything. The pressure of this new information consumed my thoughts as I held the envelope with trembling hands. I couldn't bring myself to open it. I didn't want another thing dancing around in the back of my mind before Christmas. I had such a wonderful time with Kai, I didn't want whatever was in this letter to ruin it.

I took the envelope and shoved it into my sweater pocket before heading back to the front door to retrieve my bags. I brought the bags into the living room to set up a small wrapping station for the presents I bought. After wrapping both gifts, I placed them under our gloomy tree in the corner of the living room.

I'll stay up and watch TV to see if Kenji comes home. For Mom's sake, I hope he does.

Soon enough, without realizing how tired I actually was, I fell asleep on the couch.

Chapter Fifteen

*W*HEN I AWOKE, Christmas Eve had turned into Christmas morning. Sitting up, I found myself on the couch covered with a blanket, wearing the same clothes from the day before.

"Dammit, I fell asleep!" I shouted, slapping my face. *Strange . . . I don't remember putting this blanket over me?*

Standing to stretch, a small package tumbled down my body and landed on the floor in front of me. Bending down, I picked up the box which resembled a small Christmas present. Stumbling backwards onto the couch, I noticed my name was on the tag, so I quickly opened it. Inside the box was a pair of mittens, tightly folded around a small box of chocolates, along with a note which read:

Nila,

I'm sorry for everything. I don't want to buy your forgiveness, so don't see the value of this gift in that sense.

Ps. We need to talk.

-Kenji

My eyes widened as I read who it was from. *He came home!*

I dropped the note and tossed the box aside, then immediately ran to the stairs so I could head to Kenji's room. Reaching his bedroom door, my heart raced profoundly, in fear of facing my brother. Hesitantly, I gripped the handle and turned it slowly; the door creaked as I peeked inside. My heart stopped as I saw Kenji lying on top of his sheets, sleeping soundly. Having Kenji at home was the best Christmas present I could have asked for.

I would have been lying to myself if I said I could put everything behind me in order to start fresh. No matter how happy I was to see him safe, an image of Kida kept popping into my head. Whenever I thought of Kenji, I saw the image of him and Kida together. Deep in my heart, I knew my brother and my best friend betrayed me and ruined the friendship I cherished most. It was hard to describe what was festering in my mind, but the feeling was unbearable.

I quietly backed away, shutting the door to Kenji's room. Before going back downstairs, I decided to also check in on my mother. Silently opening the door to her room, she was also sound asleep.

Downstairs, I tidied up the living room where I'd slept, folded the blanket, and straightened out the cushions on the couch. In placing the final cushion, my foot grazed something. When I looked down, the Christmas present from Kenji that I had tossed was on the floor. Picking up the contents and garbage to discard, I tried shoving them all into my sweater pocket.

"What the . . .." Holding onto the present, I reached into my pocket with my other hand and pulled out an unfamiliar object. Glaring down at my hand, I saw the forgotten envelope handed to me by my mother. Still not ready to deal with it, I shoved the envelope and present deep into my pocket and started to look for my cellphone. Remembering I hadn't used it since yesterday, I went to check my purse.

When I found my cellphone, I took a look around the room and noticed the empty shopping bags and scrap wrapping paper scattered across the floor from yesterday. After collecting everything, I headed up to my room and tossed all the garbage into the waste bin beside my desk, then pulled out the envelope and the gift from Kenji and placed them on the desk. Still avoiding the envelope, I dragged my feet towards the bed and slammed my body down onto it. Sluggishly pulling myself towards the other end of the mattress, I took in a deep breath before lifting my body to lean against the wall of my bed. Phone in hand, I decided to check Line. My eyes shot open when I noticed a message from Kai from late last night.

[Line Kai]: Merry Christmas, Nila! I know it's past midnight, and you're probably asleep, but I hope things are looking up. Also, I know it's not really your scene, but I wanted to invite you to a New Year's party my friend is hosting. Think of it as a date, haha!

"Idiot," I whispered with a tiny smile. *At this party, I won't know anyone except him. Plus, he said it was a date. This is all going so fast and it's so far outside my comfort zone. I'm getting nervous just thinking about such a thing. But, in all honesty, I really do want to go . . . I want to see him.*

[Line Nila]: Hey, Merry Christmas to you, too! As for the party, I think I will go.

Before I had a chance to drop my phone, a new message appeared.

[Line Kai]: Awesome! I'll let my friend know I'm bringing a date.

Looking at my screen, my cheeks grew hot when, again, I read the word 'date.'

[Line Kai]: How are things at your place?

I don't want to bother him with my family issues over Christmas, so I should stop texting him soon. Yet again, if I remember correctly, his parents did go away to visit his grandparents . . ..

[Line Nila]: Things are fine. Kenji came home last night, and he even got me a gift. I was really surprised.

[Line Kai]: That's awesome! Bet you're glad you got him that hat now.

[Line Nila]: Yeah, you're right.

[Line Kai]: Like always.

[Line Nila]: Whatever! Anyway, how's taking care of the shop without your dad?

[Line Kai]: Busy! I called Ryu about thirty minutes ago to come and help me, and do you know what that kid said? *'Sorry, can't bro. I have a date.'* The nerve of that kid! He's only in junior high! Who does he think he is?

I couldn't help but laugh out loud at the thought of Kai's face when his brother bailed on helping him for a date. *I can feel his rage through our Line conversation.*

[Line Nila]: It must be hard if it's only you working on such a busy day of the year. I can't believe the shop is open on Christmas.

[Line Kai]: Yeah, it's been insane! But flowers make great gifts, what can I say? I'd like to see you, but I have no free time. I have to get back to work now, so I'll talk to you later. See you on New Year's Eve!

My heart jumped. *He'd like to see me? I wish I could go and help him.*

[Line Nila]: Okay, good work today. I'll see you then.

Kenji's gift and my mother's envelope on the desk caught my eye again. After building up the courage and strength, I got off the bed and reached for the envelope. Pulling out the chair from my desk, I took a seat. Turning the envelope over, I ripped the top open and removed the papers inside. Holding my breath, I slowly unfolded the set of papers, finding an official document addressed to me. They were similar papers to those on the kitchen table and after reading the document carefully, I understood what my mother had meant earlier. The document asked me to confirm my name change by signing on the designated areas highlighted.

What? I never sent a request through to change my last name. Why did Mom prepare this paperwork without asking me? Did she prepare one for Kenji, too . . .?

Feeling frustrated, I took some time to consider the document's purpose.

Do I actually want to change my last name to Mom's maiden name, Kimura? If I do, it's like . . . I'll no longer be connected to the Izawa family.

She told me to think about this carefully before deciding on an answer. How much time is she giving me to decide?

As I re-read the document to find the submission date, I began eating the chocolate from Kenji's Christmas gift. *He still remembers my favourite chocolate, how sweet.*

Just then, there was a knock on my door.

"Come in," I answered, spinning to face the door.

The doorknob turned and standing at the doorway with a small package was Kenji. "Hi . . .."

"Oh . . . um, hey," I responded nervously. *I hope he doesn't want to talk about it already. I don't know what to say to him yet.*

"I just wanted to come by and drop this off. It's from Kida," he explained while holding out a decorative box.

"I don't want it. Take it with you and get out!" Turning in rage, I mumbled, "Is that where you've spent all your time away?"

"Nila, we need to talk about—"

"NO!" I blurted out, tears flooding my eyes. "I don't want to talk about it now! I'm not . . . ready," I whispered.

"Well, I don't really care if you're ready or not because I've been ready for more than six months," Kenji said.

I looked back at him and saw him turn to close the door to my room, trapping us both inside.

I stood up. "What are you doing?"

"We're not leaving this room until we discuss this and until you hear me out."

"Like hell we are! Kenji, seriously—get out."

"You always say we should talk more, well, here I am—talk to me!" Kenji moved closer, making his presence known.

Attempting to avoid his large frame, I tried gunning it to the door. Before I could come close to making it, he grabbed my hand and swung me around, shoving me against the empty wall beside the door and pinning me. He dropped the gift from Kida and held both my hands securely.

"Ow, Kenji, you're hurting me!"

"Then stop running from me, Nila, and just listen!"

"I don't want to hear about you and my best friend having sex, or how sorry you are!" I shouted into his face.

"Nila—I LOVE HER!"

Hearing those words leave my brother's mouth sent a shock like lightning through me. Everything stopped. I no longer attempted to struggle; my body hung still. Every bit of fight I had in me disappeared, simply washed away with those three little words. I was no longer in control of my body or actions. "You disgust me!" is what I thought and unconsciously blurted out.

With those hateful words, I pushed Kenji away and he stumbled backwards. He tripped over the gift from Kida and crashed onto something, causing a loud ruckus. I looked over to see what happened. Pieces of my dollhouse were scattered everywhere on the floor. I fell to my knees.

"WHAT HAVE YOU DONE?" I wailed. "WHAT THE HELL HAVE YOU DONE?"

Kenji got up and looked at the damage. "Nila, it . . . it was an accident."

"It's gone—He's gone! THERE'S NOTHING LEFT NOW!" Even though I was screaming at the top of my lungs, it felt like I wasn't screaming loud enough. There was no air left to breathe inside my tiny room. I could feel my throat closing up as if someone had their hands wringing my neck, choking me. I brought my hands up to my neck.

Kenji rushed to my side. "NILA! NILA! What's wrong?"

Curled up into the fetal position, I could sense his panic but was unable to tell him what was happening to my body. Every time I tried to form a word; I would choke. I tugged on the neckline of my shirt, wanting to rip it off. *Am I dying?*

"MOM! MOM! COME QUICK! Something's wrong with Nila!"

Distantly, I heard someone yelling and felt the vibration of footsteps stomping closer. The door to my room flung open and my mother barged in. She ran towards us and quickly knelt down beside Kenji.

"KENJI, WHAT HAPPENED?"

"W-we were arguing . . . and then the dollhouse . . . and then she fell and ended up like this!"

She glanced over his shoulder, taking note of the smashed dollhouse off to the side. After taking a moment, she grabbed me and cradled me in her arms as she sat cross-legged on the floor.

"MOM!" Kenji shouted, eager for an answer.

"Kenji, I need you to calm down. If you don't, you will make this worse for Nila. Listen carefully. I need you to go into the kitchen and get a paper bag from one of the drawers," she instructed. "Nila is hyperventilating—she's having a panic attack."

"A paper bag . . .?"

"Just do it!"

Kenji ran out of the room and down the stairs. Just as quickly as he left, he returned, holding a pile of paper bags in both hands.

"Here! Here!"

My mother took a single bag and placed it over my nose and mouth. "Nila, hun, I need you to focus and take deep breaths, okay?"

Listening to my mother's calm voice, grounded me back to reality. Immediately, I grabbed hold of her wrist and began inhaling and exhaling deeply into the bag. The speed of my breathing softened as I closed my eyes in order to concentrate.

"It's working!" Kenji exclaimed, hovering over me.

"Mhm, the bag helps her control her breathing by controlling the pH levels in her body. We often use this technique with patients at the hospital."

"Mom . . .," I whispered, removing the bag from my face.

Looking down at me, she tucked my hair behind my ear. "Yes, hun?"

"I love you."

Smiling, she replied, "I love you, too, Nila."

I woke up the next morning tucked into my warm bed with a pile of paper bags resting on my nightstand. I had slept through Christmas.

Chapter Sixteen

AFTER CHRISTMAS, EACH day seemed to drag on longer than the one before. My mother informed me about my panic attack and showed me how to use the paper bag technique if it were to ever happen again when she wasn't around. If she hadn't been home, I don't know what would have happened to me. In the moment of my attack, I was terrified. The feeling of being choked from the inside out is something I wouldn't wish upon anyone. Armed with a way to help combat an attack, I needed to figure out how to prevent future ones from occurring.

Kenji and I never finished our conversation and when we passed each other throughout the house, we didn't exchange a single word. The odd time I tried to talk to him, he'd brush me off, completely distancing himself. It felt as if he was afraid to talk to me, when usually it was the other way around. My mother told me how my brother reacted during my attack, and it seemed as if he couldn't shake the intensity of it. When I brought the concern up to her, she told me to give him some space.

'Nila—I LOVE HER!' was the only clear part I remembered from our conversation that day. Kenji never denied the accusation I made towards him about being with Kida during his absence from home, nor did I give him the chance to. I was too scared to hear him confirm it, so I chose to yell at him instead. The distance between my brother and I, I wondered, would it ever go away?

Those few days after Christmas, I received a couple of messages from school friends, all wishing me a great holiday, but none from Kida. Though I was upset with Kida, I wasn't sure what I would even say to her if she had messaged me. Still, I couldn't help but check my phone every so often. Loneliness crept up on me, and I began feeling insecure the more time I spent with myself.

My mother and Kenji opened their gifts from me the morning after Christmas. Kenji seemed to like the hat I picked out for him, since he put it on right away, but never really told me with words. My mother opened her sweater and started crying as she tried it on. It seemed to fit her perfectly as she modelled it around the living room. Kenji's gift to our mother was a long, wool scarf which she also decided to model for us. My mother apologized for her gifts to us because they were just envelopes of money. She's always been a last-minute shopper, but she usually went all out with our gifts. Since a lot had happened this holiday, neither Kenji nor I were upset about it.

I hadn't opened the gift from Kida. It continued to lay toppled over on my bedroom floor beside the broken dollhouse. Pieces of the colourful house remained scattered and I had not stepped one foot near that corner to clean it up. Those two items were left untouched only because I was too weak to face the meaning behind them. I hated myself.

My mother went back to work and things seemed to have returned to normal for her. I saw her broken confidence rebuild; the confidence I knew my mother never truly lost. Watching such a strong woman easily waver, had thrown our household off balance.

She confronted me about the name change and asked for my final decision. I told her I decided to keep the last name 'Izawa' and found out later on that Kenji did the same. My mother didn't seem too pleased with our answers, but she knew she had no right to be upset, considering it was her choice to change things in the first place, not ours.

Chapter Seventeen

*N*EW YEAR'S EVE; a holiday meant to be shared with family and friends. Normally, Kida would come and spend the night on New Year's Eve, then, in the morning, we would visit a shrine to pay our respects and pray for a good year. This year, being given the option to spend it with Kai and his friends made me extremely nervous.

What if his friends don't like me?

I spent most of the morning planning my outfit for the big night, leaving mountains of clothes piled on the floor and a bunch of combinations laid out on my bed.

What about this dress? "Hmm." I hung it up on the door. *No, it's way too dressy.*

Going back to select another option, I made a poor move. "OW!" I lifted up my foot to find a piece of the broken dollhouse underneath. My foot had a slight cut on it and had started to bleed. Looking around at the rest of the pieces scattered on the floor, I decided it was finally time. I went downstairs, got a garbage bag, then made my way back into my room. As I picked up each piece, an invisible fist clenched my heart tighter and tighter until, at last, the final piece of the dollhouse was tossed into the bag. My shoulders sagged, and I was surprised to find I could once again breathe normally.

A fresh start for a new year.

Tying up the garbage bag, a tear trickled down my cheek.

Why am I crying?

Not having the heart to throw out something so meaningful, I decided to put it in the shed. Lifting the heavy bag, I swung it over my shoulder and slowly made my way to the stairs. Looking down from the top, I saw Kenji.

Damnit, I didn't want to see him while doing this.

As I took my first step down, I wobbled from side to side, attempting to reach the next step without toppling over.

"Do you need help?" Kenji asked, coming up to meet me.

Breathing heavily, I replied, "It's okay; I got it."

Kenji made a hand gesture, indicating for me to give it to him.

"Well, I guess if you're offering." I handed the heavy black bag to him with caution.

As he took it from my hands, he judged it by its weight. "What's in this?"

Not able to look him in the eye, I quietly responded. "The dollhouse. I'm taking it to the shed."

For a moment, there was no answer. Deciding to steal a glance, I saw a look of confusion on his face.

"What for? It's broken, just throw it out."

"NO!" I shouted unintentionally. "I . . . can't."

I lowered my head and stared at Kenji's feet which rested a few steps below mine. Another moment of silence passed, but this time, I chose not to look up, fearing the expression painted on my brother's face. Watching his feet, I saw them turn around to head back downstairs.

"Kenji, wait!" I pleaded, reaching my hand towards his back.

"Don't worry, I'll put it in the shed," he announced before continuing his way down the stairs without looking back.

Should I trust him? I know how much he hated that I kept it these last two years. He offered to get rid of it for me at least a dozen times.

I watched him get to the bottom and turn the corner towards the living room.

I ran back upstairs and raced to the end of the hallway to a little window overlooking the backyard. Through the window, I watched my brother walk across the stone path leading to the shed. When he got to it, he stood in front of the shed's sliding door for about a minute with his hand on the handle. As I watched him stand there, I couldn't help but wonder what was going through his mind. When he finally decided to enter, he quickly shut the door behind him. From the window, I waited patiently for him to exit the shed. Minutes went by, but he never came out. Curiosity got the better of me, and before I knew it, I found myself making my way down to the back door.

Trampling across the yard, I reached the same path Kenji walked. Coming to a halt, I observed the shed's surroundings to see if any further movements from Kenji had been made. From the left side of the shed, I could see smoke coming out from the window and moving its way up through the air. I walked up to the shed, quietly lurking around its corner. With a clear shot of the opened window, I saw Kenji leaning on the windowsill, looking up at the sky while smoking a cigarette. Just as I was about to reveal myself to scold him, I saw a few tears trickle down his face. Keeping myself hidden, I backed away from the corner and made my way back to the sliding door at the front.

Kenji . . ..

I decided it would be best to leave him alone, so I went back inside the house. No matter how much I wanted to grab that cigarette out of his mouth and toss it on the ground, I couldn't do it, not after seeing such an empty expression on my brother's face. That was the first time I'd seen him cry since we realized our father wasn't coming back.

From the doorway of my room, I glanced at the bed full of clothes. *Right, I still have to decide on my outfit.*

Walking to my bed, I couldn't help but notice the light blinking on my phone. Running to get it, I checked the message.

[Line Kai]: Good evening, Nila.

My heart leaped inside my chest just from reading his name.

[Line Kai]: Is it alright if I come to pick you up around 8:00 p.m.?

He wants to pick me up? From my house!

With immense worry, I wasn't sure how to reply, but somehow, my fingers started typing.

[Line Nila]: Hey, yeah, that's fine. I can meet you at the station if you want though, it would probably be easier for you. I don't want to make you come all the way here since it's out of the way.

[Line Kai]: Don't worry about it. I want to pick you up. After all, you are my date.

That idiot! I can't even think of it that way without getting nervous. I don't ... know what to do on a date ....

[Line Nila]: If you insist ....

[Line Kai]: Yep, I do! I'll see you then.

After sending the last message, I fell back onto my bed, lying on top of my outfit choices. I caught myself smiling as I looked up at the ceiling. *Why am I so caught up in this, and with him of all people? Do I want this to go somewhere? I mean, we've already kissed ... but he hasn't said anything about it since then. UGH! I'm freaking out!*

Night quickly approached and it was already 7:30 p.m. I finally picked out an outfit after trying on almost everything I owned. I decided to wear a red laced shirt with a nice pair of dark blue, skinny jeans. Normally, wearing a skirt with tights was my go-to preference for occasions such as this, but I knew we had to walk in the snow, so a skirt would've been a poor decision.

As I finished the final details to my makeup, techniques learned from Kida and applied lightly, my phone vibrated.

[Line Kai]: Be there soon.

This is it, my first date! I'm starting to feel even more nervous than before. I don't want to make a fool of myself in front of his friends. Kai gave the impression that many people would attend.

Finally, I packed up the box of daifuku I had bought in advance for tonight's party, then sat on the bottom of the staircase facing the door, waiting for Kai to ring the bell. It was a couple of minutes past 8:00 p.m. when the doorbell rang at last.

"I got it!" I shouted, hoping that my mother wouldn't come running to the front door. I told her I would be spending New Year's with friends, but I didn't tell her *which* friends. I was afraid to mention Kai's name in case she didn't let me go. I wasn't sure if my mother approved of me being around Kai based on how they met. I got the feeling that she disliked him almost as much as she disliked the wild side of Kida.

Unlocking the door, I opened it to find Kai standing in the doorway. He wore a mid-length, black winter jacket, with grey jeans he cuffed at the bottom, and dark brown boots—he pulled the look off well.

"Hey! You look great!" he complimented eagerly.

Embarrassed by Kai's reaction, my cheeks started burning. "S-stop saying things like that! You're embarrassing . . .."

He laughed playfully before continuing, "Sorry, I'm late. Ready to go?"

"Ready as I'll ever be." Putting on my jacket, I took a step out the door, attempting to shut it quickly before my mother noticed me leaving.

"Nila!" My mother shouted from the small crack left open in between the doorway.

"Crap," I muttered under my breath.

Kai quickly turned around. "Everything okay?"

"Yeah, hold on, my mom's calling me. I was hoping to escape before she noticed."

I pushed the door open and found my mother pulling it at the exact same time from the other end. It opened dramatically, leaving us face-to-face.

"You planned on leaving without saying anything?" she asserted.

"No . . . I did say bye. I said it before walking out the door," I lied.

"I must not have heard you then. So, you'll be gone for the rest of the night? I'll be leaving shortly as well for my night shift at the hospital. I'll be home a little after 6:00 a.m. Did you tell Kenji to make some plans with his friends for tonight so he's not alone? I forgot to mention it to him myself."

"I didn't get around to it."

I could see my mother's gaze look past me, outside the door. I knew she was trying to see who rang the bell in order to find out who I was going out with. When she spotted Kai, her eyes turned into dangers. "I see," she barked, glaring at me. "You are to be home no later than 1:00 a.m. When you get home, I want you to call me from the house phone immediately, understood?"

Not wanting to pick a fight with her, I nodded.

"Good night then," my mother ended the conversation.

Turning away from her and back towards Kai, I saw him bowing.

"I'll have her home by 1:00 a.m., Ms. Izawa—no later."

Signalling with a head nod, my mother acknowledged Kai's mannered gesture. I'm sure she watched us head down the street until we turned the corner and disappeared out of sight.

Kai and I walked side-by-side, making small talk as we arrived at the bus stop.

"She's pretty intimidating. I don't think she likes me," Kai said, jokingly.

"She doesn't like anybody," I played along.

We stood and laughed together, our sides hurting from the amount of effort we put in.

I don't know why, but every time I'm with him, I end up laughing really hard. Lately, he seems to be the only happy part of my life. It's refreshing, but also terrifying.

Once the bus arrived, we got on. The bus was crowded; we only found one seat at the front close to the driver. Kai offered me the seat while he stood in front of me, holding onto the strap attached to the railing above. I placed my stuff down in between my feet.

"So . . .," Kai picked up the conversation, "how are you and Kida doing? Any progress?"

Looking up at him, I smiled politely. "No, I haven't spoken to her since that day."

"Not even through Line?"

"No, because I don't even know what to say to her. We've been best friends for so long, but I'm so mad to the point where I don't know if I even want to fix this," I answered truthfully. "She betrayed my trust with a huge lie; it can't be fixed by just saying 'sorry.' Even if we do make up, I don't know if I can ever trust her like I did before."

"Hatred is born from hatred. The longer it continues, the harder it will be to fix—trust me," Kai coached, breaking eye contact as he looked over me, then gazed out the bus's window. He let out an unsettled breath of air. "We call them 'best friends,' but the moment they do something we don't like, we demote them from their position." He tilted his head down at me. "Nila, don't be like me. Don't let things drag on longer than they should. Before you know it, it'll be too late and you'll be full of regret."

Before I could question the madness Kai spat out, the bus came to a stop and its doors opened from both ends.

"This is our stop," he said, smiling at me, as if the conversation we just had never happened. "Let's go."

What did Kai mean when he said 'Don't be like me'? There are so many questions I want to ask him, but not a single word wants to come out of my mouth.

After walking for a bit, Kai never continued the conversation from the bus, leaving me to wonder what he meant. We ended up talking aimlessly about the time we spent apart and he told me how challenging it was to run the shop during the holidays. Before I knew it, he stopped and pointed at the open street in front of us.

"My friend's house is just up the road on the hill."

Stopping beside him, my heart raced. "Which friend's house are we going to? Is it Hatori's or Taki's?"

"Hmm, so you remembered a couple of my friend's names," he replied. Stepping in front of me, he turned around to smile as he began walking backwards.

"Just the ones you've mentioned."

"Right," he expressed with a happy look, but a distant tone in his voice.

Kai turned back around as I caught up with him so we could continue walking side-by-side.

"It's not either of them, but you have seen him before. He was at the karaoke bar during the mixer; his name is Nobuo, or Nobu for short."

"Oh, I see." Concerned with my introduction, I asked, "Since he doesn't know me, should I call him by his surname?"

"Nah, don't worry about it," Kai reassured. "He's not formal like that.

People he's never met before call him Nobu, too. You'll see why when you have a conversation with him."

"Alright . . .," I answered skeptically.

Once we'd made it up the hill, Kai spotted Nobu's house and pointed it out to me. It was an average, modern Japanese style home, like mine, making it less stressful to approach.

I'm glad this Nobuo guy doesn't have a huge, rich person's house. For some reason, that was the type of house I imagined Kai's friends to have. Then again, Kai lives in a house only slightly bigger than mine, so I'm not sure why I made that assumption.

As we walked up the pathway to the house, the door opened and someone stepped out.

"Kai, man, you're here!" Taki flared as he walked towards us. "Ouu, and you brought Nila with you," he winked and slapped Kai on the back.

Looking at Taki directly in the eye, the corner of Kai's mouth quirked up. "That's Izawa to you, moron."

Taki chuckled under his breath at Kai's remark, then pulled out a pack of cigarettes from his left coat pocket. He took one of the cigarettes out of the package and stuck it in between his lips, patting himself down as he felt around for his lighter.

Watching the guy in front of me made me feel uncomfortable. I couldn't exactly describe this unsettled feeling, but this Taki seemed very different from the Taki who had walked me to Kida's house. He had more of a 'bad boy' vibe compared to the time before.

"Man, you should really give that shit up. You're gonna die young with all the tar and alcohol you consume," Kai warned with a short laugh.

"Yeah, that'll be the day," Taki replied with a smirk, raising an eyebrow in my direction. "The day you two start going out, that is."

"Who says we aren't?" Kai poked sharply.

With Kai's immediate response, Taki's face shifted from joking around, to serious. His lips parted, making the cigarette fall out of his mouth and land in the snow. "What . . .?" he muttered, shocked by Kai's quick wit.

"We're not!" I blurted out, quickly looking at Kai. "Stop spreading rumours, idiot!" *At least I think we're not . . ..*

Kai gave a dry laugh, but at that moment, he never looked more serious. I looked towards Taki to see his reaction and noticed he was already staring in my direction.

Finally finding the lighter in one of his pockets, he bent down to pick up the cigarette he dropped, dusting it off before placing it back in his mouth to light. "So, that's how we're playing it," he said, exhaling smoke while continuing to stare at me.

All his staring had me feeling targeted. *Playing what?*

Kai was apparently finished with the conversation as he walked on past Taki. Before entering the party, he stopped, took a step back, and leaned in towards Taki, whispering something into his ear. I couldn't hear a single word, but it lasted no longer than a few seconds.

"Come on, Nila," Kai insisted as he stepped inside, leaving the door open for me as he disappeared.

As I was about to follow Kai's lead, Taki grabbed my arm. Pulling me in close, he whispered into my ear, sending a cold shiver down my spine. "Apparently, you're very precious to him, Miss Izawa."

I immediately backed away from him as soon as I could and entered the house to catch up to Kai. I didn't dare look back at Taki's face because I was afraid of what expression he wore.

What the hell! Who is this Taki? And what did he mean? Now that I think about it, this is the second time he's said something that I didn't understand. Does he enjoy toying with girls, or is it just with me? I wonder what it was that Kai said to him . . ..

Chapter Eighteen

*B*EING AT THE party was a whole new experience for me. There was a line between my world and Kida's that I had never crossed, not counting the few times she'd tricked me into attending things, like the mixer where I met Kai. Now, I had entered into that world, by my own free will, without realizing I was slowly leaving mine behind. This world was exciting and thrilling, full of things I'd only ever heard about, leaving me interested in the next anticipated step. The party started to make me wonder if Kai lived in the same world as Kida. Deep inside, no matter how hard I tried to avoid it, I feared the answer to my question.

Entering Nobu's house, there were a handful of people standing in the hallway near the entrance, while the majority of people were in the living room. Others also lingered in the kitchen with drinks in their hands. The party was loud; bits and pieces of random conversations were seeping into my ears, along with music playing in the background. Aspects of the party felt very Americanized; from the festive decorations and music, down to the outrageous amount of people packed together.

Kai was a few feet in front of me, greeting people as he went through. Removing my shoes, I remained by the door with my coat on, unsure of what to do or where to go.

"Aren't you gonna go in?" a voice from behind me questioned.

I didn't have to look back to figure out who it was. I continued to stand at the entrance without answering or turning around.

"Taki, leave her alone," Kai said, darting back towards me with his jacket hung over his one arm.

"Hey," Taki raised both hands above his head, playing innocent, "I didn't do anything."

I looked up at Kai and saw a defensive expression on his face. *Is he mad? I thought he and Taki were good friends? All they've done so far is bicker at each other.*

Quickly, Kai reached for my hand to help me up the step of the entryway, then put his arm around my shoulder and pulled me towards him. "Come on, Nila, I'll introduce you to the host."

"Oh-okay," I stuttered, my heart beating faster in my chest. I could feel people staring at us as we weaved through the crowd together. *Everyone's going to get the wrong idea if Kai continues acting this way. I might, too . . ..*

Kai led us directly into the middle of the party. We were no longer side-by-side; instead, he held onto my hand firmly as we pushed our way through the sea of people. Just by looking at Kai's back, and feeling his tight grip on my hand, I could tell something was off.

Hmm. From this angle, Kai's shoulders are highlighted nicely—very broad. Wait, what am I thinking? This is bad! I'm at my first party, meeting his friends for the first time—what is wrong with me?

". . . Niiila, Nila!" Kai repeated, his voice gradually getting louder.

"Oh, sorry! What were you saying?" I asked, diving back into the unfamiliar environment.

"I was trying to introduce you to Nobu . . .."

In front of me stood a tall, foreign-looking guy with blonde hair. His skin was tanned, and his face showed the lightest sign of freckles, as if he had spent time in the sun. Looking down in front of me, I noticed a hand was stuck out to greet me.

"It's nice to officially meet you. I'm Nobuo Nakamura, but please, call me Nobu."

"Oh, um, I'm Nila Izawa," I said while bowing my head, completely ignoring his polite gesture. "Thank you for inviting me! Please accept this box of daifuku!" Holding out the dessert in both hands, I unintentionally forced it upon him.

Nobu chuckled as he used his hand to reach for the bag instead. "Awesome, I love daifuku at New Year's—thanks!"

From the corner of my eye, I could see Kai laughing, which forced me to stand up straight.

"What's so funny?" I asked, turning towards him with a flushed face.

"You, and how formal you're being with this joker," Kai pointed at Nobu with his thumb before continuing to laugh hysterically.

"Well, at least someone at this party has manners," Nobu teased. "You can tell she was raised by a respectable family, unlike some people." He rolled his eyes. "I've already lost two of my mom's favourite vases, and it's not even half past nine—animals I tell 'ya!" Nobu placed his hand over his face, then slowly swiped downward in disbelief.

"Did your parents leave for the night?" I asked curiously.

"Actually, they left with my sisters for the whole week to visit some family in America. Knowing it would be the perfect time to throw a party, I decided not to go with them. I told my parents I'd be having a *few* friends over while they were away," he cautioned wide-eyed.

Oh, from America. That would explain his lighter features.

"A few, huh?" Kai smirked as he looked around the room.

"A few of MY friends turned into a few of EVERYONE'S friends it seems," Nobu said, sarcastically, looking pained.

"I'm sorry for coming," I said, feeling guilty for attending.

"No, no, don't take it like that! You're completely fine being here. Plus, I was interested in getting to know the girl Kai hasn't been able to shut up about."

"Nobu!" Kai hissed.

"Whoops," Nobu said, laughing at Kai's reaction. Just then, Nobu focused his attention on some mischief happening in the corner of the room. "HEY! You three!" he shouted over us. "Sorry you two, I gotta go deal with that. We'll talk later. Nice meeting you!" He turned back and smiled at me, then dashed off.

"He seems nice. Definitely not what I expected," I said, turning to Kai.

"Yeah, he's a super nice guy. A huge partier though."

Looking at Kai, his cheeks glowed a light pinkish colour.

It's probably due to Nobuo's comment. "You know, if you keep doing these kinds of things . . . people will get the wrong idea," I warned, slightly testing him.

"What things?"

"Like coming to my rescue, talking about me to your friends, carelessly touching me . . . kissing me . . .," I listed shyly, ending in a quieter voice.

"And what idea would they be getting exactly?"

"The idea of us being a couple, like dating."

"Oh, I see, I see. Would that be such a bad thing?" he asked, looking at me intently.

WHAT? YOU TELL ME! You do all these things that make me think you like me, but you've never come out and actually said it! Even when we kissed, you said so many sweet things . . . what am I supposed to think? How am I supposed to confirm what was never discussed?

"Yo, Kai! Get in here!" shouted a guy from the kitchen.

Shifting his gaze from me, Kai looked over to the guy and shouted back, "Alright I'm coming!" Turning back to me, Kai spoke softly, "I'll be right back. Want anything to drink while I'm there?"

"Water is fine."

From the corner of his mouth, a swift smirk was drawn. "Somehow, I knew you'd say something like that."

Brushing off his joke, I quickly asked something that came to my mind. "Oh, hey, Kai, before you go, is Hatori coming tonight?"

Turning back sharply, Kai seemed frightened as he turned white. Before replying, his expression softened. "No. He can't make it," he answered over his shoulder, allowing only half of his face to be seen.

"Oh, that's too bad. I wanted to thank him for finding such a beautiful spot near that river. Plus, he's your best friend and all . . . ."

Smiling somewhat sadly, he paused before replying. "He'd probably be too intimidated if you were to thank him like that," Kai exhaled a laugh coldly. "We'll stop by and see him later so you can tell him in person."

"Won't it be too late?"

"Nah. He's not doing anything important."

"Then, if there's time, that would be great."

In a rush, Kai headed for the kitchen to meet up with some friends and left me behind.

"That was pretty rude of him, to leave you alone. Tsk, tsk, he should have brought you along."

Startled by the voice of the person next to me, I nearly jumped out of my skin. To my right stood Taki, shaking his head back and forth as he watched Kai walk off. I turned my face to him.

"If I were him, I would have brought you with me to introduce you to my friends, proudly showing you off. But, to each his own, right?" Taki winked.

"What's with you?" I blurted out angrily.

"Huh?" he said, looking oddly surprised. "What do you mean?"

"You're acting very different from the guy who walked me to my friend's house."

"Is that so?" he pondered to himself childishly, looking up at the ceiling. "I wonder why? Maybe it's the alcohol." He brought his head back down to look at me, then winked. "Let's sit somewhere. You've been standing this entire time, right?"

"I guess . . .."

With nothing better to do, I made my way to one of the couches. Taki sat down first, holding a drink in one hand while patting the cushion beside him with the other.

Hmph . . .. "I'm not a dog, you know. I don't need to be told where to sit."

Choking on laughter, Taki stopped tapping the cushion and started wiping tears from his eyes instead. "Ohhh, Nila. Your sharp tongue and quick wit kill me."

With caution, I sat on the couch under my own command, as far away as I possibly could from him. "So," I began, attempting to start a normal conversation as I finally had the opportunity to take off my coat. "Is Nakamura full Japanese?"

Leaning forward on his knees, he tilted his head. "Why do you ask?"

"Well, for one, he's tanned with blonde hair, and I think I caught a bit of an accent when talking with him. Leaving me to believe he isn't fully Japanese," I debated. "He also mentioned having family in America."

Giving a dry laugh, Taki confirmed. "Yeah, you're right. He's not full Japanese; he's half. His dad is Japanese but his mother is an American beauty. Nobu was actually born in America and came to Japan when he was about ten or so. I think his younger sisters were born here though."

"Wow, that's so cool!" I said excitedly. "I knew he looked foreign. I wonder what America's like."

"Why are you so interested?" Taki asked, raising a brow.

"In who? Nakamura?"

"Sure," he said, taking a sip from his cup.

"I don't know. I just thought it would be nice to take an interest in the person whose party I'm attending?" I answered sarcastically.

Looking over the lip of his cup, he replied, "Alright."

I tried to study Taki's face. *His reactions are much different than Kai's. With Kai, I can read and understand most of his facial expressions, but with Taki, I can't understand what he's thinking or feeling at all. He's so weird—it's vexing! It's as if he has a split personality. Which Taki is the real one?*

All of a sudden, Taki had a malicious grin on his face as he comfortably leaned back against the couch and stared at me.

"What? Is there something on my face?" I asked, wiping one cheek, then the next. *It almost feels like he's studying me.*

"Virgin?"

Startled, my eyes shot open. *What did he just say?*

"You strike me as the type who would be a virgin," he restated confidently.

What the . . . WHAT IS HE SAYING? Why would he ask me something so personal? How embarrassing!

"That's really none of your concern."

Smirking, he pushed further. "But I'm right, aren't I?"

"Shut up."

Quietly laughing in his seat, he continued. "It's a simple question to answer really, but your reaction clearly says it all."

I could feel the rage building up inside me as Taki continued to press every one of my buttons with his words. "You know nothing about me."

"Sure, I do."

"What?" I muttered, dumbfounded by his confident response.

"You're the type who appears to be smart and pure to get guys to fall for her. Then, you pretend you need our help, powerlessly trapping us with your innocence." He looked off to the side and choked out a laugh. "Just like the rest. How else would you have gotten Kai to open up to you so fast?" Returning his attention back to me, his face twisted coldly. "He's been closed off for—"

"Stop," I butted in.

"Hmm?"

"People who judge others like that are despicable. You know my name—not my story. Don't think you can write it before I've finished living it." Immediately, I got my coat and rose from the couch. *Screw you, asshole!*

Fuming, I made my way to the front door, speedily putting my shoes and jacket back on. I kept my head down to avoid eye contact with others; I didn't want anyone to see the tears about to drip from my eyes. The little bit of makeup I applied ever so carefully for this special night, had been all for nothing.

I knew this was a mistake! I have to get out of here. I really want to go home.

"Nila? Where are you going?"

I knew exactly who it was that called my name. Without thinking, I turned around to face the guy who abandoned me, tears pouring from both eyes.

"Nila! What happened?" With great concern, Kai placed the two cups he was holding down on an entry table in the hallway and rushed over to me.

I couldn't find my voice, no matter how hard I tried. I continued to look down and cry as Kai reached over and caressed the upper parts of my arms. Attempting to hide my tears, I shoved my face into the palms of my hands. Within seconds, I was pulled into Kai. His arms were strong and secure and made me feel safe. He held me tight, as if I was something extremely precious that he did not want to lose. My heart raced. I was shocked more than anything as I replayed the whole scene with Taki in my head.

When Kai loosened his grip, I gazed up at his face. The towering body over me glared fiercely at the couch in the living room where Taki sat. Stepping away, Kai darted towards Taki with clenched fists. When Kai reached the couch, he stuck out his arm and grabbed the front of Taki's shirt, standing Taki up to face him. Inches from Taki's face, Kai started yelling.

"What did you do?" Kai demanded, clenching Taki's shirt tighter in his hand.

Taki looked straight into Kai's enraged eyes. "Nothing, bro," he replied satisfyingly. "We were just talking."

"Nothing?" Kai echoed. "Nila wouldn't be crying for 'nothing.' Obviously, you did something! What's with you, man?"

"What's with ME? What's with YOU?" Taki retaliated. "What are you even doing here?"

Kai's eyes flashed with anger. "What?" he shouted, tugging on Taki's shirt more aggressively, almost tearing it.

I couldn't watch Kai fight with his friend any longer. Running to Kai, I latched onto his arm. Kai had a strong grip on Taki's shirt, but I continued to pull on his arm with all my might, trying to get him to calm down.

"Kai, stop!" I pleaded.

A couple of guys rushed over and tried ending it by pulling Kai off of Taki, shoving me off to the sidelines. One guy grabbed onto Kai's arms and shoulders, holding him back, while another one held onto Taki. Since the guys were much stronger than I was, they succeeded.

"Kento! Fujiwara! Why are you guys fighting?" asked the guy holding Kai.

The commotion caused a large crowd of people to form around them. Amongst the crowd was Nobu, forcing his way into the circle.

"What the hell is going on with you two? There's no way both of you are drunk already!" Nobu hollered in confusion.

Because of his assertive tone, the atmosphere in the circle settled. Kai shoved off the guy who was holding him, rolled his shoulders back and forth, and adjusted his shirt.

"I don't know what happened, Nobu, but all of a sudden Kento was all over Fujiwara. We thought we better stop them before punches were thrown," answered the guy holding onto Taki.

Kai unconsciously turned and stared directly at me. Catching my eyes, Kai's fierce face eased into an unsettled one. He walked to Nobu, then bowed to him.

"Sorry, I think it's best if Nila and I leave."

Astonished, Nobu placed his hand on Kai's head. "Kai, lift your head. You guys don't have to go, but if that's what you feel is best, then that's your call. The party will still be here if you decide to come back."

Kai raised his head like he was told, then walked over to me and grabbed my wrist. He led me straight to the entrance but soon released me to put on his boots and jacket, then exited through the front door. During this stressful moment, I didn't say a single word. I was too scared to ask Kai how he was. Silently, I followed him out. I walked quietly behind him as we made our way down the path of Nobu's house and onto the side of the road.

We continued to walk in silence for over ten minutes. All I could do was stare at Kai's back as snow lightly fell from the dark sky. I wanted to break this awkward silence between us, but I was too afraid to speak up. I didn't know what to say to him to make things better; I knew this was all my fault. I caused a scene and made him fight with his friend. I ruined the party for everyone, and most of all, I ruined New Year's for Kai.

He's definitely mad at me and probably regrets bringing me. If I were in his shoes, I know I'd be mad at me. I want to talk to him, but nothing I say will fix what happened. But no matter the outcome, I want to apologize to him before parting ways.

"Kai," I finally spoke up, stopped in my tracks.

"It's not your fault."

"But—" I started, wondering how he knew what I was thinking.

"The thing with Taki, it wasn't your fault."

"But if I wasn't there, then everything would have been fine and—"

He turned around to face me, frustration hardening his face. "Nila, he was just toying with you to get back at me. Truth is, it's actually my fault all this happened."

"How...?"

"It was something that happened between me, Taki, and Momiji," he said, obviously unsettled.

Finding myself emotionally intrigued by Momiji's involvement, I pursued the topic. "What happened?" I could tell Kai didn't want to talk about it, but because Momiji had something to do with it, I couldn't stop myself from asking.

He sighed with irritation. "Long story short, we all went to the same junior high but got split up after; Momiji and Hatori at Naoetsu Gakuen and Taki and I at West Oji Gakuen. Even though we were separated, we all remained good friends and Taki finally told me he liked Momiji. At first, I had no feelings for her whatsoever. But, as things carried on, Momiji reached out to me often and we began talking frequently one-on-one. The two of us ended up spending more and more time together outside of school, and I found out she had feelings for me. Shortly after, I started seeing her in a different way, and in no time, I found myself falling for her, too. This caused conflict between me and Taki, and ever since I started dating her, he's claimed I stole her from him. Then, Hatori came into the mix, and well, you know the rest...."

Listening to Kai, I started thinking about the situation with an open mind. I barely knew anything about this girl and I already disliked her. She was the cause of so many problems, and heartache, that I wished she could feel double the amount of pain Kai had felt over this past year alone. I looked at the situation from Taki's perspective, and then from Kai's.

"But, Momiji and Taki weren't officially 'dating,' since he never made a move," I pointed out. "His feelings were one-sided."

"That's true, but I broke the code," Kai answered with a dull crack of a smile.

"Code?"

"Yeah, guy code. He was the one who liked her first and he confided in me about it, but I snatched her away. I'm really regretting that decisions now though," he chuckled to himself with stress as he tugged on the back of his neck. "Ever since then, my friendship with Taki hasn't been the same. He feels like I betrayed him, which I did, and he's been trying to get me back ever since. Considering you're the first girl I've brought around since that time, you're his prey."

I'm the first? Not knowing how to comfort him, I ended up replying half-heartedly. "I see."

"Yeah. So, if he comes near you or says anything weird, don't believe him. This is between me and him. I'll deal with it when he's in his right mind."

"Okay. I hope things between the two of you blow over soon. A year is a long time," I added.

"I know," he said, gazing up at the dark sky. "I know."

I followed his gaze and noticed stars had appeared in the night sky as snow continued to fall. *The stars look like lights shining through the dark clouds.*

"Beautiful, isn't it?" Kai pointed up. "The sky."

"I was thinking the same thing."

"Hmm," Kai expressed, looking down at me. "Can I take you somewhere?"

He still wants to be with me? Even after everything that's happened? "S-sure!"

"Let's forget about the party. I could tell you were uncomfortable the whole time. I shouldn't have thrown you in there when you didn't know anyone, especially considering I didn't know everyone at the party myself. The next time I try to introduce you to my friends, I'll make sure it's with a small group of them first."

"The . . . next time?"

"Yeah, the next time," Kai smiled gently. "Come on."

Kai took a couple of steps towards me and reached out his hand. This time it wasn't so aggressive. Giving him my hand, he took it into his palm and interlocked our fingers together.

What are we doing? Is this all just some game? What am I to him? These questions, amongst others, were all ones I had a hard time asking out loud, fearing answers I wasn't sure I wanted to hear. Remembering back to the kisses we shared, I became irritated. *I don't understand his feelings for me at all! He does all these things without any explanation. I can't help but wonder if he truly cares for me or just feels sorry for me. But maybe, just maybe . . . Kai has the exact same confused feelings as I do?*

Chapter Nineteen

E TOOK OUR time walking through the streets and caught a couple of buses along the way. I had no idea where he was taking me, but it really didn't matter. I had been expecting to go home after what happened at the party, so it made me extremely happy Kai still wanted to spend time with me. Though our conversations were scarce, I was content with just being near him.

"Where are we going?" I asked, while looking through the bus's window at the forever-changing scenery.

"It's a surprise," he answered sharply. "But we do need to pass by my family's shop first."

I turned back to him. "The flower shop?"

"The one and only. I need to pick something up."

"That's fine."

We had been riding the last bus for more than thirty minutes and I was constantly on edge. There was no way I could relax when Kai held my hand; he hadn't let go since he grabbed it on the street down from Nobu's. We didn't talk much on the remainder of the bus ride as Kai seemed deep in thought. When we reached our stop, Kai took a couple of seconds to react before he stood up.

He seems more and more depressed as the night goes on. I wonder what's wrong . . ..

Observing Kai, I noticed he was aloof and appeared extremely worn out. Getting a closer look at his eyes, they were gloomy and puffy, something I hadn't noticed until now.

Off the bus, we walked for a while longer until we reached an older downtown shopping area. The area was small, quiet, and away from all the commotion of the larger chain businesses, which our town had been gaining more of over the past few years. All the tiny shops were lined up in two strips facing each other, eventually connecting in a circular, courted area. Right in the middle of the court, stood a giant Christmas tree decorated with glorious bright lights and ornaments. The tree looked radiant as it stood tall in the centre of the cozy shopping district, shining proudly for everyone to see and experience.

"Wooow, it's so beautiful! Kai, look at that tree—it's huge!" I shouted in amazement.

Kai chuckled as he watched me. "I'm glad you like it. It was hard work getting it all done up in time for Christmas."

"Huh? Kai, did you put this tree up?" I looked at him, shocked.

"Not alone, that would be crazy," he smiled childishly. "I helped put it up at the beginning of the holiday season with my dad and my brothers, along with a bunch of people who work and live in this community."

"That's incredible! To have such a close-knit community, where everyone pitches in to help each other, is so nice and welcoming."

Kai looked back at the tree. "Yeah, it truly is."

I looked up at Kai and saw the tree's lights reflecting in his eyes. Looking past him, I noticed a sign which read: *Kento Family Flowers*.

Pointing to it, I got excited. "Hey, is that it?"

Following the direction of my finger, Kai looked at the shop. "You are correct, Madam," he replied in a terrible, made-up accent.

We walked up to the front door where Kai used a key to unlock it. He held the door open for me so I could step in before him.

"There's no alarm?"

Shaking his head, he answered surely, "We haven't needed one. Everyone in this community gets along and trusts each other, so it's not necessary. We're our own neighbourhood watch in a sense. I can almost guarantee that none of the surrounding shops have security systems."

"That's kind of refreshing actually."

"It's one of the things I like most about small communities. You know everyone, and everyone knows you," he said proudly.

"Couldn't that also be a bad thing?"

"It could, but that's not how I like to look at it," he grinned.

Stepping inside, I stood in the middle of the entrance and peered into the shop's darkness. Even though it was pitch black, I could smell the strong, perfume-like scents of flowers. Kai shut the door behind him and flicked on the light switch. Within seconds, the shop lit up, and so did all the beautiful flowers; they were even more wonderful than I had imagined. The colours were out of this world; a rainbow had come to life right in front of me. The scent of the flowers alone was enough to leave an imprint in my nose, an aroma I could never dilute, nor wanted to. All around the store flowers were elegantly placed inside water baskets, pots, and even vases. Near the back, the register was positioned on a spacious counter and attached to it was a small, gift-wrapping station.

"It's so cute!"

"It's not cute—it's a very MANLY establishment where MEN work," Kai tried to reassure me, but mostly himself.

Spitting out laughter, I saw Kai's face flicker red. "Does working here embarrass you?" I teased.

"Nooo," he groaned immaturely. "As a matter of fact, I have a lot of faithful FEMALE customers who come in regularly, just to see me."

"Oh, yeah? I bet they're only here to see your good-looking grandpa."

"Ew! My grandpa is not good-looking! He's old and wrinkly," he said with a disgusted face.

"I doubt it. He's probably a catch."

"Grrross! Since when did you have a sick fetish for elderly men? And when did you even see my grandpa?" he accused with playful shock.

I was laughing so hard that my sides cramped. "Are you jealous?"

"Who, me?" he asked in disbelief. "Of my oldest man? Never."

"Pffft— oldest man!"

We had a lot of fun trading jabs at each other. Watching Kai's reactions made me laugh uncontrollably, to the point where tears were shed.

Kai looked at me as if I had lost my mind, but eventually joined in on the madness.

Kai lost the smile on his face as he took a detailed look at the shop and flowers. I couldn't help but watch Kai as he poked through the flowerpots and straightened out a couple of displays. He approached some of the flowers, touching their petals with care. There was a majestic aura emanating from him. It felt warm and sincere, but also sad and depressing at the same time. Making his way around, he carefully inspected the blossoms until he collected enough flowers to make a bouquet. He walked to the back of the store towards the register and took out some plain, white sheets of paper from underneath the wrapping station. He organized the counter's surface before placing the flowers down on top of the wrapping paper. The flowers he'd collected were a mixture of red and white roses, with a single yellow rose placed in the middle.

Making my way to Kai, I stood a few feet back as I watched him delicately wrap the bouquet, using tape and ribbon.

"Is this what we're picking up?"

Taking a break from his intricate work, he looked up at me. "Yeah."

"They're very pretty. Who are they for?" I asked curiously.

Looking back down at the flowers, he smiled. "You'll see when we drop them off."

Hmph, I thought they might've been for me. Wishful thinking, I guess . . ..

"Why only one yellow rose?"

He grinned at me innocently. "It represents a new beginning."

"Oh . . .," I responded quietly, feeling oddly left out in a room with just the two of us. I wanted to ask what he meant by 'a new beginning,' but from the look on his face, I felt like I shouldn't.

As Kai was finishing his wrapping job, his phone rang. He reached into his pocket to get it, then looked down to read the screen and let out a displeased sigh. "Sorry, is it okay if I answer it? It's my little bro."

"Yeah, go ahead."

Kai tapped the screen of his phone with his finger, accepting the call. "What is it, Ryu?" he asked with irritation. "Uhhh . . . I think I left the spare in the top drawer of the stand in the kitchen," he paused. "Sure, I have mine with me," he paused again. "Whatever. I seriously don't understand how you always lose yours," he replied, annoyed. "Okay, bye," he said, then hung up the phone and placed it on the counter beside the bouquet.

"What was that about?"

"Ryu lost his house key, AGAIN. He's going out with his friends, but he'll be home late, so he needs a key to the house. Nila, I swear, we have given that kid about seven keys and he's lost all of them! Where do they go?" he questioned, shaking his head.

I started laughing at Kai's dramatic explanation.

"Why are you laughing? It's true—I swear!"

When I was able to control my laughter, I focused in on Kai's face. "Your family seems fun."

Kai looked surprised by my reply, expressing a soft smile. "They can be."

While we stood there gazing at each other, Kai's phone vibrated on the counter. I took a quick peek down at it and saw the name *Momiji* come across the screen. Reading that name made my heart do a vertical jump in my chest.

Momiji . . .? Like his ex-girlfriend, Momiji? Why would she be messaging him this late on New Year's Eve? Is this bouquet of flowers for her? If it is, I'm going to be pissed.

Kai also looked down at his phone. When he read who the message was from, his eyes narrowed. Without reading the message, he reached for his phone and placed it deep into the pocket of his jeans, then returned to the bouquet.

Are they still in contact with each other?

The mood had instantly changed and the atmosphere between us didn't seem so warm and bubbly anymore. When Kai finished the wrapping job, he tidied up the workstation.

"Ready to go?"

"Yeah," I answered, somewhat unsure.

Holding the flowers in one hand, he headed for the set of switches to turn off the lights.

Walking back through town, we returned to the nearest bus stop to wait for the next bus without exchanging a word. I had no idea where we were going and it didn't seem like Kai was eager to tell me. I wanted to ask about Momiji, but I wasn't sure how to go about doing so, or if I should pretend like I didn't see anything.

Watching the bus pull up, we got on and found a couple of empty seats at the back. Kai took the window seat, leaving me with the aisle. Sitting beside him, I clenched my purse tightly, letting out my frustrations with each fist I made. Kai sat with the bouquet of roses resting over his lap, dragging out the silence.

Five minutes passed, and still no words were spoken. My frustration continued to build until I could no longer contain it. Turning towards Kai, I made up my mind to confront him about the message.

"Kai, back at the—"

"Nila . . .," he interrupted, staring down at the flowers. "Have you ever thought *'Where will I be five years from now?'"*

"Huh?"

Smiling coldly, Kai changed the subject unexpectedly. "Is it okay if I take a quick nap? We still have about an hour until our stop and I'm a bit tired," he turned towards me, waiting for my response.

He looked exhausted from head-to-toe and his hands had a slight shakiness to them. I had planned on interrogating him, but when he looked at me the way he did, I didn't have the heart.

"Okay," I confirmed.

"Thanks."

He told me the name of the stop we needed and within minutes, he passed out. His arms were crossed in front of him and his head hung lifelessly. I couldn't help but admire the way he looked as he slept beside me.

Dammit! Why do you have to be so damn good-looking all the time?

To keep myself occupied, I pulled out my phone to check for any new messages.

That's a surprise; there's not a single message from Mom. Though, she is working.

I scrolled through my inbox and read old conversations between myself and Kida to pass the time. While doing so, I thought of Kenji. *I wonder if he'll stay in tonight or go out with his friends? Maybe he'll spend New Year's with Kida this year . . . Who knows.*

Each time I thought of either one of them, I immediately remembered the unspeakable act that happened between them. It eventually led me to recall Kenji's words once more. *'Nila—I LOVE HER!'* This was the phrase that I could not burn from my memory, no matter how hard I tried.

A sickening pain collapsed the walls of my heart, making it nearly impossible to breathe. Just as I could feel my throat begging for air, something heavy fell on my shoulder. Stunned, I slowly turned my head to find Kai leaning against me, fast asleep.

He must be in a deep sleep. My breathing returned to normal, but my heart began beating faster. *Should I wake him? It's not like him leaning on me is bothering me or anything. My heart may explode, but I enjoy being this close to him.*

Putting my cellphone away, my hand started acting on its own. Before I knew it, I was running my fingers through the top of Kai's almond-brown hair. Admiring his sleeping face, my mind rushed with thoughts of what it would be like to be the one who could always be by his side. *Why do I want you so badly? Why can't I ask you how you truly feel about me? Am I afraid of being rejected? If possible, I want to stay like this . . . even if it's just for a little while longer.*

Time seemed to be speeding up, when truthfully, all I wanted it to do was slow down. With each stop, people were getting on and off the bus until it was finally our turn.

"Kai, Kai, wake up! It's our stop," I exclaimed. I took the flowers from Kai's lap and nudged him.

Flustered, Kai jumped to his feet while wiping the sleep from his tired eyes. "W-what's happening?"

I placed my purse over my shoulder, held the flowers in one arm, and grabbed Kai's hand in order to get off the bus quickly.

"Phew! We made it off in time!" I said, trying to catch my breath.

Kai let out a weak chuckle. "For a second, I didn't even know what was going on. It all happened so fast; I didn't know if I was still dreaming or not."

I also began to laugh a bit. "I didn't want to wake you in a panic to cause anxiety, but before I knew it, our stop had arrived."

"It's okay; no sweat."

Standing up straight, I noticed I was still holding the flowers and onto Kai's hand. "Sorry . . .," I said, releasing his hand. "Here." I passed the bouquet back to him.

"Thanks, but I like it better this way," he replied, reaching back to grab my hand.

He does these things so swiftly, and looks so comfortable while doing them. He's able to take control so easily; I don't know how he does it!

We walked a couple of blocks hand-in-hand, constructing and taking part in short, dull conversations. The night grew progressively colder as snow fell heavier, coating the streets in a fresh layer of white. The second half of our night had been a rollercoaster of emotions. I wasn't sure where we stood. Were we a couple, or two individuals enjoying each other's company over the holidays?

God, we've been walking forever! Where the hell is he taking us? Damn, I should've brought the mittens Kenji gave me for Christmas.

"Kai . . .."

"Hmm?" he looked at me.

"This is probably a silly question, but are we still in town?"

Without warning, Kai stopped walking, forcing me to stop along with him. He looked at me dead on as he bit his upper lip, trying to keep his mouth together. "Pffft!" he burst out in laughter.

Unimpressed by his reaction to my serious question, I hid my face in my shoulder like a child. "I'm being serious!"

Suddenly, his cold hand touched my cheek, guiding my head up. "I know you were. That's why I couldn't help but laugh because you said it so innocently, it was kinda cute. But to answer your question, yes, we are still in town; on the outskirts." Kai grabbed my wrist and pulled me in towards his chest, holding me securely with one arm as the other held the bouquet. "I'm really glad you're with me right now, Nila. I don't think I could do this without you by my side. I just hope you don't hate me after this." Kai loosened his hold on me and took a step back. His hand lingered as it trailed down my arm and back into my palm. "It's getting really cold and we don't have any gloves, so let's keep pushing forward. It's just up ahead."

Still feeling shy from Kai's warm embrace, I nodded and continued to follow his lead.

Eventually, we came across a small shrine with a tiny, wooden hut on the right side of the road, while a large cemetery stretched out distantly on the left. The tiny hut was enclosed with a roof, four unstable walls, and a rickety door that didn't seem to have a lock. As we got closer, a dim light from a candle could be seen flickering through one of the hut's windows. Taped to the window was a sign that read: *Flowers replenished daily.* Walking up to the hut, I cautiously peeked inside.

A cemetery? Why . . . are we here? "They seem to have flowers for sale. Why did we have to go all the way to your family's shop if we could've gotten some right here?"

"The flowers available here are free to those who come. They aren't as good as ours; he wouldn't like them."

"He?"

Kai tugged on my hand. "Follow me."

We crossed the street and approached the entry gate of the cemetery.

"Kai . . . why are we here?" I asked nervously.

With a darkened expression, he answered. "Sorry, I just needed to visit someone, but I didn't have the guts to come alone."

Even with the amount of snow falling, the moon was bright, lighting each step we took through the paved cemetery. After Kai searched multiple rows of stone gravestones, we approached two identical burial sites placed side-by-side. Both were decorated with flowers inside vases and had incense stands placed upon them which, like the gravestones themselves, had been covered in snow. Food items were left as offerings and looked freshly made, making it seem like someone had placed them recently.

From the corner of my eye, I saw Kai take a couple of steps forward to wipe the snow off the gravestones, then kneel right in front of the graves, resting the bouquet over his lap.

"Hey," he spoke to one of the gravestones. "Sorry it took me so long to get here. Every time I tried to come, something held me back. I guess . . . I wasn't strong enough to face you yet." Kai dropped his head. He took the flowers from his lap and laid them at the base of the grave he spoke to. "These are for you." Kai let out an emotionally exhausted chuckle. "They're the ones you always liked and bought for your 'lady friends.' I clearly remember how deliberate you were when selecting them."

Not really understanding what was going on, I walked to Kai's side and knelt down beside him. I placed my hands together and bowed my head in respect for the private resting place I was disturbing.

"Oh right!" he exclaimed as he looked to me, then back at the grave. "This is Nila Izawa—the girl I like. I'm glad I'm able to introduce her to you."

In awe, I raised my head. My hands fell down on my lap as I looked at Kai in shock. *Wait, what? Did he . . . just confess his feelings for me? Right here? RIGHT NOW?*

"It's strange," he carried on. "Life seems like it will last forever, until one day it's gone in the blink of an eye and we realize we didn't do a damn thing that mattered. We live in such a messed-up world where going to school and getting a job is mandatory, but living is not." Kai's face filled with satisfaction, as if in triumph over reaching a milestone. "You know," he began with a broken smile, "I met her at the park where we used to practice playing ball, back in junior high. I also took her to your secret spot, that river you showed me almost two years back—she really liked it."

As soon as Kai mentioned the river, I looked up to read whose grave this was. Tears filled Kai's eyes, then rolled down his cheeks as he choked. I reached for Kai's hand and placed mine on top, watching fearfully as the tears streamed down his face. Not even a second after, I felt tiny drops of warm water drip from my chin and splash onto my cold hand. The cold pavement and wet snow underneath me were seeping through my jeans, turning my legs into icicles. Even though I knew my body was freezing, I was able to withstand it. Without having time to think about my emotions, my head jolted back to face the grave as I cried alongside Kai.

"Hatori . . . I miss you, man."

Chapter Twenty

I'D ALWAYS HATED cemeteries. To me, they were places full of sadness where people came to say goodbye, but not that night. I went there to meet someone special and say hello for the very first time. Even though the circumstances were unbearable, and I couldn't stop crying, I was thankful.

Witnessing Kai breakdown in front of Hatori's grave was the first time I had seen him so vulnerable; I was torn. It opened my eyes and made me realize I wasn't the only one going through something difficult. Being next to Kai, and experiencing some of this pain with him, meant everything. Until now, I only pitied myself and didn't bother to consider the hardships others were facing. At times, everyone's problems seemed less important than my own. Being pressured to achieve ultimate success in school by my mother, no longer having a father figure, dealing with a dishonest best friend and brother—none of it mattered. I knew then how completely wrong and selfish I truly was.

No matter how hard I stared at Hatori's gravesite; my mind didn't want to accept the reality of the situation. Both Kai and I continued kneeling on the snowy pavement, crying until our hearts were content as the cold penetrated through our clothes. I didn't know anything about this person except for his name, but seeing Kai's pain was enough to trigger my own emotions.

"Hatori, I'm very glad to have met you," I spoke up. "I know . . . I know how important you are, and always will be, to Kai." Trying to hold back the tears, I turned to Kai who was already facing me. Tears continued to drip down his face and onto the collar of his jacket, while his eyes looked to me for support. I pushed forward. "He loves you. I hear it in his voice when he talks about you, and I can see it in his eyes because they light up when he thinks of you."

Still locked onto Kai, I saw his face gradually fill with bliss. It seemed like he was being released by something heavy that had, until now, been dragging him down. Without warning, Kai fell onto me, pressing his face deep into my shoulder. Slowly raising his arms, he placed them around me, hugging me from the side.

"Nila . . .."

"Hmm?"

"Thank you."

"For what?"

"For being here. Without you . . . I probably wouldn't have come. I truly mean it. This is my first time coming to Hatori's grave," he said while exhaling warm air onto my neck.

"Your first time? But what about his . . .."

"No. I never went to his funeral. I couldn't even get my pathetic ass out of bed for almost a month after it all happened. I spent my days locked up in my room without speaking a word to anyone—not even my family. They all tried . . . but I just couldn't . . . I'm a terrible per—"

"NO! Don't even say it, Kai!" I yelled, shaking him off my shoulder so I could see his face. "You just didn't know how to cope with the death of your best friend. If it were Kida, I don't know what I would do. I can't even imagine it! No one could possibly know how they will react to something as extreme as this. All anyone can do is say how they wish they could've dealt with it after it's already happened, after it's too late."

"Nila . . .," he looked deep into my eyes with regret. "I don't know if the reason why I couldn't bring myself to attend the funeral was because I couldn't deal with the death of my best friend or . . . if it was because he died on the way to see Momiji, right after he left my house." Kai paused;

his eyes still tightly shut as he shook his head in utter disappointment. "After all this time, I still don't know the answer."

Looking into Kai's eyes was like looking through a gateway into his heart where a dark hole nestled. I could see his warm breath floating in front of him each time he spoke or exhaled forcefully.

Kai took a minute to think before he went on, his face drained and wrecked from crying. "He died in a car accident one year ago today. He was in the car with his older brother, who was dropping him off at Momiji's, just after picking him up from my house. But they never made it. They got into a head-on collision with a drunk driver. The drunk driver survived, but Hatori and his brother . . . they didn't make it."

My heart tightened with each word. I felt my eyes widen as Kai finished describing the horrifying details of the incident. "Kai . . .."

"I'm a horrible person for having these thoughts. The fact that even to this day, I can't make them go away, only proves that I'm screwed up," he said angrily. "Can you imagine the amount of sorrow and pain a parent must go through when losing not just one, but both of their children?" Lifting his head, Kai looked up at the gravestone, shifting to sit on his bottom with both legs bent. He placed his arms over his knees and held onto them tightly, then lowered his head. "Because I couldn't."

Standing, I walked closer to the gravestones and looked down at the engraved names of *Hatori Mamura* and *Haruto Mamura*. After listening to the story about the accident, I took note of the single, wooden sotoba that was placed at both burial sites.

With a moment to think, I opened my thoughts to Kai. "I don't believe that, not even for a second, and I know Hatori doesn't either." I turned back towards Kai. "No matter what happened between you two in the end, the bottom line is, you guys WERE and always WILL BE best friends. And no, you are right about one thing. I can't imagine what a parent in that position would be feeling, let alone how they dealt with it from there onward. But Kai, you also have to know one thing; what happened with Hatori and his brother, no matter what your feelings were at the time or what you wished for based on petty revenge, none of that was your fault."

Kai stood up and came towards me, leaving footprints in the snow behind him. When he was a couple of feet in front of me, he gently placed his hand on my cheek. "Thank you, Nila. I really needed to hear that. I'm really glad I chose to bring you with me. Tonight, out of my own selfishness, I ruined your New Year's because I didn't want to be alone, and for that, I'm terribly sorry."

"Actually," I placed my hand on top of Kai's, "you're wrong. This New Year's has been the best one I've had so far."

"How?"

Knowing exactly what I wanted to say, I still couldn't bring myself to say it out loud. Even with the cold weather, and my face practically numb, I could feel my cheeks burning up. "Be-because, I got to spend the whole night with a guy who means a lot to me. I got to know his true feelings and how deep of a love he had for his best friend. There wasn't anywhere else I would have rather been tonight than right here with you."

Taking a moment, Kai smiled brightly, catching my eye. "You're probably the best person I've ever met, inside and out. Thank you."

His warm lips pressed against mine.

"Kai, not here! That's disrespectful!" I hissed, scared of whatever supernatural beings might be watching.

"I guess you're right. It's about time we get going anyway—it's freezing! We probably have frostbite on our toes without even knowing it. And, I wouldn't doubt it if we both wake up with a ridiculous cold tomorrow," he joked, trying to lighten the mood while wiping away the remainder of our tears.

I let out a small giggle as I reached for the cellphone in my purse to check the time. "Oh my God, Kai!"

Shaken by my sudden outburst, he shouted, "What is it?"

"It's already a quarter past midnight! I have to be home by 1:00 a.m.!" My voice started to crack as I trembled. "There aren't any buses that run at this time, are there? What are we going to do?"

"A quarter past midnight . . .," Kai echoed calmly as he looked back towards Hatori's grave. He bent down and placed one hand on top of the gravestone. "Happy birthday, man."

"Birthday?" I repeated.

"Mhm, his birthday is the first day of the year."

Both of my hands slowly rose up on their own as my raw fingertips brushed my ice-cold lips. I couldn't bring myself to say a word. My whole body went stiff. A ringing sound consumed my ears as my eyes shot open, drying out every tear in my ducts.

"I know what you're thinking, but it's okay," he agreed quickly, grabbing my hand. "Come on we have to go; I promised your mom I'd have you home by 1:00 a.m."

"Are you sure it's—"

"Oh, and Nila . . .," he broke in.

"Hmm?"

"Happy New Year."

The outside air remained cold, but the air between us was warm and fuzzy. I allowed Kai to whisk me away as he led us back towards the road. We called and waited twenty minutes for a taxi to arrive, then sat in the back seat holding hands, until Kai, once again, fell asleep on my shoulder. I, on the other hand, couldn't help but think about the death of Hatori and his brother, along with Kai's confession.

Looking out the window, I tried to stop myself from imagining what Kai and Momiji were like in the past, not wanting to compare their relationship to our untitled bond. From there, my thoughts drifted towards Hatori and Kai and how Hatori began seeing Momiji behind Kai's back. I didn't want to choose sides based purely on hearing the story from one person, but it was hard not to. Plus, I would never be able to hear the story from Hatori's point of view. I turned to the sleeping boy on my shoulder and tightened the grip on his hand.

"You know," I whispered, "you make me doubt myself all the time. Everything you do sets my heart on fire."

The whole ride home was full of anxiety and anticipation. I was fighting time and didn't know how I was going to leave Kai when the time came. A part of me wanted the taxi driver to drop Kai off first so I could make sure he made it home safely, but I knew time was against me. When the taxi finally reached my house, the driver parked the car right in front of the gate and Kai woke up. He brought my hand up to his lips, kissing the top of my hand before letting me go. With a strain on my heart, I examined Kai and felt his aura to be much calmer and settled.

The moment I looked into his eyes, the fear, which had grown inside me, was replaced with peace.

I pulled out my phone to check the time as I stood in front of my house, noticing I had only four minutes to spare before missing my curfew. As I sprinted past the gate, the taxi drove off. I took the keys out of my purse with cold, shaking hands, fumbling a couple of times until I managed to get the correct key into the keyhole. All in one motion, I unlocked the front door, kicked off my boots, and rushed to the small, hallway table for the house phone.

My mother's work number was written in an address book left in the top drawer. I flipped through the pages frantically until I came across it. My hands continued to shake as I punched in the number. Placing the phone up to my ear, it began to ring. Using my cellphone, I checked the remaining time—just shy of two minutes. The hospital secretary transferred me to my mother. The ringing went on for a while until I heard my mother's voice answer on the other end.

"Nurse Kimura speaking."

Kimura, huh? She's already using it. "Uh, hi, Mom," I said, shivering. "It's me . . .."

Now that I think about it, why didn't I have a number that connected me directly to her? I thought she said she had caller ID at work? That was the whole point of me using the house phone to call her!

"Oh Nila, thank goodness you're home safe," she released a sigh of relief through the phone. "Cutting it a bit close, aren't we?"

"Sorry, I lost track of time. I made it home before curfew though," I hesitantly responded.

"Yes, that's true," she paused in defeat. "Is Kenji home?"

"I'm not sure. I just walked in, so I haven't checked the whole house yet."

"I see. Well, message me when you have."

"I will," I replied, my heart slowing its rapid pace.

"Have a good night. I should be home later this morning."

"Alright. Good night, Mom."

As I placed the phone down on the dock, I saw a small piece of torn paper resting at the end of the table. It read:

Nila,

Happy New Year.

-Kenji

Not knowing that such a small piece of plain, ripped paper could mean so much to me, my eyes teared up. Lately, all I ever did was cry; it didn't matter if it was for something happy or sad. Reading only a few simple words from my brother brought a warm smile to my face and tenderness to my heart. My eyes were bloodshot and puffy from the exhausting night, but the amount of pain was worth it.

Making my way to the top of the stairs with Kenji's note in hand, I approached his room. With suspicion, I opened the door quietly to take a quick look. Peeking inside, I saw Kenji sleeping soundly. Seeing Kenji in his own bed, with my own eyes, brought ease to my worrying heart. Turning the knob, I pulled the door towards me and shut it gently. With an idea in mind, I rushed into my room to find some sticky notes from my desk.

Kenji,

Same to you.

-Nila

I peeled off the sticky note from the pad, walked back to Kenji's room, and stuck it to his door. "Good night."

"Kenji hurry! We're gonna get left behind!"

"Niiila, you're too fast! I can't keep up."

"I'm not fast! You're too slow, dummy! We gotta go fast so we don't lose Mommy and Daddy!"

"Nila! Kenji! Come on! We're going to be late if we keep going at this pace," Mom warned over her shoulder. "Honey, go back and get them."

Gripping onto Kenji's hand tightly, we faced our parents' backs as they walked several feet ahead of us. Dad turned around, rushing back to get us after Mom ordered him.

"Here we gooo!" Dad picked Kenji up by the armpits and tossed him onto his shoulders.

"Daddy, me too! Me too!"

"I only have one pair of shoulders, Nila. Your turn will be on the way back from the shrine, okay? For now, is it alright if you hold my hand?"

"Okaaay."

Holding onto his giant hand, we caught up with our mother who waited by the shrine's entrance.

"Daddy, why do people go to a shrine?" Kenji asked, looking down at our father's forehead.

"Because, people typically pray for a good year to come."

"What are we going to pray for?" asked Kenji curiously.

"Mom and I will be praying for good health and fortune for the whole family," Dad replied, looking upwards.

"Wooow! Did you hear that, Nila? Daddy's gonna pray for us to be rich!" Kenji shouted excitedly.

Dad's body shook with laughter. "If only it were that easy."

We walked side-by-side as a family before climbing a huge set of stairs leading up to the shrine. There were groups of people travelling in front and behind us, all heading to the same place.

"What are you guys going to pray for?" Dad asked.

"Money," Kenji answered bluntly.

Laughing at Kenji's reply, Mom asked, "What about you, Nila?"

"Ummm, I don't know yet."

"It's okay not to know. Maybe you will think of something when we reach the top," she advised. Mom grabbed hold of my other hand, then looked up at the sky. "The year is coming to an end. We'll be saying goodbye to it and all of its precious memories. Soon, we'll be saying hello to a brand-new year with lots of new beginnings. It's exciting."

I woke up later than usual the next morning with my shirt drenched in sweat, feeling sore. My nose was stuffed and began to run as soon as I sat up, making it difficult to breathe. I stretched over to the right side of my bed, fingertips extended, reaching for the tissue box that normally sat on the side table near my clock.

Ugh, I feel crappy. It's probably from being outside last night with Kai. He did warn me. Remembering the night with Kai, I reached back to the nightstand for my phone. *Zero new messages, huh? That's depressing.* Lying back onto the pillow, I raised my phone above my face, just staring at it intensively. *I wonder how Kai's doing? I hope he's okay and didn't wake up feeling sick today, too.*

[Line Nila]: Morning, how are you feeling?

After sending a message to Kai through Line, I tossed my phone to the side and got up to change my wet pyjama shirt. Just as I was putting a new one on, my phone lit up on the bed. Barely having any energy, I finished putting on the shirt as I walked to get the phone. Checking my inbox, I was surprised to see who I had received a message from.

[Line Kida]: Hey, can we meet up? I want to talk.

Without giving the message a second glance, I hit the delete button. *Wait! Why did I do that?*

Looking down at my thumb pressed against the screen, I contemplated how I wanted things between Kida and I to be. I was stuck at a crossroads. The questions I had to ask myself were simple: Did I want to try and fix things between us? Or, did I want to give up and take the easy way out, since it might not be worth saving in the long run? Kida had been my best friend for so long, could I walk away from our friendship like it meant nothing? With the countless selfish, irritating situations she had forced me into over the years, was she a person I wanted in my life? How much did I truly value our friendship?

I left the situation at a standstill, once again not having the courage to make a decision about my own predicament. With the way I was behaving, nothing would get resolved. I tossed the issue aside like a coward.

Another day went by and I hadn't received a reply from Kai, nor did I send a message back to Kida. I grew so anxious about Kai's absence in my life that my fight with Kida seemed less important. I'd spent the past couple of days getting over my cold and preparing to go back to school. Kenji was out most of the time and only returned late at night, sometimes, early the next day. He never mentioned the note I left on his door, but I assumed he read it because it wasn't there the following morning.

Chapter Twenty-One

*I*T FINALLY CAME, January 3rd. Today was the day I returned to my final semester of high school. January was probably one of the busiest months out of the whole year for the third-year students. At the end of the month, final exams would commence for the seniors, along with college and university entrance exams. To help prepare, some students decided to attend cram schools after hours or create study groups. Not feeling the need to attend a cram school, but still being nagged to study, I chose to spend my leisure time reviewing my work independently at home.

A lot had happened to me during the break. I tried remembering only the positive stuff as I packed my bag for school. Going back, I knew I would be in class with the same people I was with before the break started. This made me happy for once because Kida wasn't in my class.

In the kitchen, I fixed up a quick bento box for lunch, then headed to the front door to get ready.

"Nila, wanna walk to school together?" At the top of the staircase, Kenji stood tall wearing his school uniform.

Shocked by his request, I blinked a few times before answering. "Uh . . . y-yeah, sure."

He made his way down to the raised entryway and sat down to put on his shoes.

This would be the first time Kenji and I travelled to school together since he became a junior, which was a year and a half ago. We stopped walking to school together as soon as he made new 'friends.' That was around the time things went downhill. This was a request I wasn't going to question, nor pass on, because I wasn't sure if it would ever happen again. *New year, new beginnings, right?*

"Mom's already gone to work; I presume?" I asked generically, attempting to spark a conversation.

"I think so," he answered, grabbing his schoolbag before standing. "She needs to start taking it easy with all these shifts she's picked up. She missed a bunch of them over the break, then recently started accepting so many hours. She's gonna burnout."

Hearing my brother express his concern for our mother really surprised me. I didn't think he paid attention, let alone cared so much about her well-being.

"Now that you mention it, you do have a good point. She's picked up a lot of shifts; I've hardly seen her."

"Hmm," Kenji mused as he looked off into space.

"We should go. Don't want to be late for the first day back," I suggested.

"I guess."

Before walking out the door, Kenji took out a hat from his schoolbag and placed it on his head, adjusting it to comfort.

"Ah, that hat!" It was the one I had given him for Christmas.

"What about it?"

"N-nothing," I choked, turning my thoughts inward. *He likes it!* I couldn't help but smile brightly at the fact that he liked something I got for him.

Side-by-side, we walked, making small talk along the way, neither of us mentioning Kida or Kai. We discussed Christmas, and shared a little bit about how we each spent our New Year's. Gradually, we got closer to my beloved Pink Path. The trees were covered in snow, adding some bright, clean lines to the dark, dormant branches.

"I wish these trees could stay in bloom all year round. The walk to and from school would be so worth it if they were," I vented.

"I agree. They are pretty."

Whoa! Did we actually just agree on something?

Making it to the top of the hill, I could see a person standing by the front gate of our school. Looking closely, I noticed the person was Kida. I stopped in my tracks, frozen stiff, in fear of the confrontation.

"Later."

"Huh? Wait! Where are you going?" I shouted as I watched Kenji walk in front of me, towards the gate.

As Kenji passed Kida, I noticed a small exchange of words between them, but was unable to make out what was said.

How did she know I was coming to school at this time? Did she come early in order to wait for me to eventually pass by? Or, did Kenji tell her we were coming? How sly . . ..

Watching Kenji pass the gate with ease, I attempted to march myself forward as well. I avoided eye contact with Kida, but in the end, it didn't matter.

"Nila, can we talk? Please!"

I didn't want to stop my confident stride because I knew if I stopped to face her, I'd cave. I refused to be the weak person I was before the winter break. Even with the amount of time I'd had to decide, but wasted thinking about Kai, my mind wasn't made up. It had been easy to push the problem with Kida aside. I wasn't forced to live with her like I was with Kenji. What I did know was that I wanted to finally gain some sort of equal power in this friendship.

"There's nothing left to say," I replied coldly, walking past her, right through the gate.

The first thing I did when I got into the building was head straight for the shoe lockers. Along the way, people were wishing a 'Happy New Year' to those they hadn't see during the break. As I passed by some classmates, I decided I should also do the same.

At my locker, I exchanged my boots for my school slippers and prepared myself for homeroom.

Wait . . . I never got my English textbook back from Kai! What the hell was I doing during the entire break? I forgot all about it, and now, I actually NEED it!

Having a small panic attack about not being prepared, I whipped out my phone to send Kai a quick message. Just as I hit send, the opening chimes rang.

Guess I'll have to share a textbook with the person beside me for today.

A few hours into the day, the chimes echoed throughout the school, indicating it was time for lunch. No matter how many times I checked my phone, there was still no reply from Kai.

I ate lunch with my usual group of friends from class, minus Kida. From time-to-time, Kida would come to our classroom to have lunch with us, but today, there was no sign of her. After finishing my lunch, I took a walk downstairs to the shoe lockers, with the idea of going outside to clear my head. Before I could make it there, I saw Kenji and Kida walking together in my direction.

So, that's where she's been. I'm surprised Kenji is still here; I thought he would have ditched school by now. I wonder, did he only stay because of her?

I hid and waited for them to pass the lockers before going to mine. Just as I had finished changing my shoes, and was about to close my locker, the chimes rang to signify lunch was over.

What? I thought I had more time!

Students were scurrying around the hallways on the first floor, making their way back to class, while I stood against my locker, cellphone in hand. *Ugh, still nothing! He hasn't replied to a single one of my messages since New Year's. Is he ignoring me? I thought things were going good between us . . . ..*

I exchanged my shoes once more, slammed the locker door shut, then angrily headed to my next class.

The rest of the day dragged, almost to the point of agony. I had asked the person next to me if they could share their English textbook, and they were kind enough to do so, but I hardly used it. I had a hard time concentrating because my mind kept wandering. I couldn't help but reflect back to all the hardships the holidays had brought me. Images of my father and his new family, and how normal he acted living his new life, randomly passed through my mind. It felt like he was a completely different person from the man I knew and loved. Until now, I had completely blocked from my mind, the fact that I had seen him again, after so long. There was too much going on for me to get held up on a man who purposely left his family to create another. His new situation was also something I wanted to further investigate over the break, but didn't get the chance to. I was still undecided if I wanted to inform Kenji and my mother of my findings; I didn't want to drive my family further apart.

Scenes of Kenji and my mother fighting also crossed my mind, and their voices lingered in my ears. Soon, I was able to block out every word the teacher was saying and replaced it with the avalanche of noise from trouble at home.

Kida's words about losing her virginity to my brother continued to haunt me as well. The memory from the kitchen table knotted my stomach and stabbed deep into my heart. This was an issue I knew I'd have to deal with soon since Kida would constantly be around me at school, unlike my father.

At last, all my other thoughts and worries went silent as soon as Kai popped into my head. He had been the only positive thing that happened to me during the winter break. But despite all of the secrets shared, he had become a major stressing point. I hadn't heard from him in what felt like forever. It was as if he had disappeared.

Everything going on in my life was distracting me from my current task—school. The entire day, I accomplished and learned nothing. During a time like this, throwing it all away seemed better than keeping it all inside and dealing with it alone. Not necessarily better, but definitely easier.

Seniors would continue to be in exam mode for the next couple of weeks while homeroom teachers had been instructed to hand out exam schedules and information regarding standard versus specific college or university testing. We were encouraged to attend each day in the final semester, study hard, work through practices given to us during school hours, and then take more home.

I was dying to close the book on high school and be done with this chapter of my life. I wanted to start something new and have a grand adventure, created specifically for me. I couldn't care less about half of the people in my classroom, and even less for the school's population as a whole. I wanted to get out as quick as possible.

The final set of chimes sang, marking the completion of the first day back. I was usually the last person to leave my classroom, because I wanted to avoid the rush of idiots pushing and shoving their way out, and today was no exception. I tidied my desk and collected my thoughts as I mentally prepared myself for another night of endless studying and college prepping. My classmates hurried out the door, leaving behind the brief sound of meaningless conversations. My teacher didn't waste his time either; soon, the classroom was empty and quiet.

A few minutes passed, and I knew I was purposely moving as slow as possible to avoid encounters with Kida. In the back of my mind, I had been temporarily collecting the things I didn't want to deal with. The room didn't stay quiet for long as a voice called out to me from the doorway.

"Nila . . .."

I didn't have to look in order to match the voice to a face. I kept my back turned to the door as I stood by my desk in silence.

"We might not be on speaking terms right now, but I wanted you to know that you have a guest waiting for you at the front gate. He's been there for quite some time."

Whirling around, I only caught a glimpse of Kida's back as she stepped away from the door. I grabbed my bag and ran out of the classroom as fast as I could. Flying past Kida in the hall, I muttered a quick *'thank you'* over my shoulder.

The school seemed to have gained a couple more sets of staircases because it felt as if I had been running down flights of stairs forever. Finally reaching the bottom, I booked it to my locker to swap my shoes. Not having time to bundle up, I used every last bit of air in my lungs to get myself to the front of the school.

Approaching the school's entrance, I saw Kai leaning against the stone wall of the gate. He was wearing his uniform and his schoolbag hung from one shoulder. I slowed down in disbelief as Kai glanced my way. He shot me a comforting smile, but even though he was smiling, his eyes wavered. I couldn't help but regain speed as I made it closer to him. Not wanting to stop, I ran right into his open arms, bottled up tears blurring my vision.

Huffing and babbling my words in the cold air, I had to ask before I went mentally insane with stress and worry. "W-why didn't you an-an-sw-er my mes-messages?"

"I couldn't; I'm sorry. My phone is broken," he answered calmly, hugging me tightly.

"Broken?" I questioned, looking up at him, teary eyed.

"Mhm, I broke it, smashed it against the wall when I got home on New Year's."

"Why . . .?"

"Don't worry about it; it's all taken care of. It won't happen again."

What won't happen again . . .? Unsure of what to make of his answer, I decided not to mention the number of messages I sent him. Having him stand before me, safe and well, was enough. "Um, Kai . . .."

"Yeah?"

"How did you get here so fast? Our schools finish at the same time."

"I skipped the last period."

"Why?"

"I wanted to catch you before you went home."

Remaining silent in his arms, I took in everything I possibly could from that moment. Then, I remembered my book.

"You still have my English textbook. I realized it when I was heading to class today."

"I know. Sorry, but I didn't bring it with me."

"It's okay. That's all I was messaging you about anyway," I fibbed, digging my face deeper into his chest. My face was in so deep that I could smell his cologne through his thick, uniform jacket.

"Okay."

"Did you get sick, or was it only me?" I asked lightly.

"Oh, I definitely got sick."

Taking note of where we were standing, I backed away from Kai in embarrassment. I peeked over both my shoulders to see if anyone was still around and saw a couple of people lingering about. Some looked at us, while others whispered to their friends, probably initiating a new rumour for tomorrow.

"Let's go," Kai insisted as he grabbed my hand.

"Where are we going?" I asked, following his usual lead.

"Someplace where we can be alone. I need to talk to you."

Hearing those words from Kai worried me, but also had me feeling excited. "Oh, um, Kai . . .."

"Yeah?"

"Please take care of me this year, too," I informed, remembering I hadn't properly greeted him into the New Year.

"Same goes for me."

Chapter Twenty-Two

THE PLACE KAI took us to was exactly where I thought it would be—Hatori's hidden river. With Hatori's memory being so prominent in our lives lately, I had been hoping we would return soon.

Neither of us spoke as we made our way through the trees and onto the hidden path, heading straight to the water. We came across the same bench we previously sat upon and wiped off the snow before sitting. I glanced at Kai who looked past the frozen water. He sat hunched over, resting his elbows on his knees as he fiddled with his fingers.

Is he nervous about something?

"Hey."

I giggled at such a plain opening. "Hi."

"Hey," he repeated.

A smile replaced my laugh as I replied the exact same once more. "Hi."

"If someone had told me that I would meet an important person, the moment I needed it the most, I probably wouldn't have believed them," he said, staring into the distance.

Confused as to where he was going with this conversation, I tilted my head, waiting for him to elaborate.

"When we first met, I honestly had no idea that you would become so important to me. You crossed my mind once and never left."

My heart hammered deep in my chest while my eyes focused solely on Kai. The wind blew lightly, making the top layer of snow dance across the ground as the sun shined upon it, creating a blanket of sparkles.

What is happening right now? What's driving him to say this?

"I could tell you tried distancing yourself from me when we first met, but during that time, my longing for you only grew stronger. I kept getting this tingly sensation inside; my senses kept looking for you, even though I knew you weren't around. Whenever I was alone, I found myself craving the cold tone you used against me; all those cute insults you directed my way, drove me wild." The corner of his lip perked up as he faced me. "Each time I remembered one of your insults, I'd actually burst out laughing." With the sincerest eyes I had ever seen, Kai reached over and placed a hand on my cheek. Gliding his hand up towards my ear, he tucked my hair behind it. "Even the constant look of struggle you wore on your face attracted me."

An embarrassing feeling fluttered inside me. I wanted to break the line of vision we were sharing, but I couldn't look away. I could feel my face burning up; staring into his eyes was intimidating. My heart was past the hammering stage and almost felt like things were smashing around inside my chest. Everything he said, he said with such confidence and certainty. My heartstrings wouldn't stop plucking.

"Where is all this coming from?" For my own sanity, I had to question it. I needed to confirm that what my ears heard and what my heart felt were the same.

The hand on my cheek slowly slid down, until his thumb grazed my bottom lip. The touch of his thumb caused an uproar of enticement inside my entire body.

"I'm so nervous right now. Please, let me finish what I spent hours rehearsing," he said, turning a light shade of pink.

I had no problem eating up the words spilling out of his gorgeous mouth. He silenced every worry I had with just a simple sentence; I was trapped within an enchanted dream.

"From there, all I wanted to do was to help you in any way I could. The challenges you were facing over the short period of time I got to know you, further triggered my curiosity about you. Nila, you are unbelievably strong. No matter what difficulties you have been faced with, you never gave up or stopped caring. You were even able to help me in a way I thought no person could. You saved me, multiple times, and you probably didn't even notice you were doing it." The nervous guy who once sat beside me, had become calm and powerful. Perking up to a bit of a grin, he continued. "Now, forgive me for being extremely cheesy, corny—whatever you want to call it, but to me, you have become the bright light at the end of my dark tunnel, a tunnel which I've been trapped in for so long, aimlessly wandering around in search of something unidentifiable. I haven't felt like this in a while, and for a brief moment, I feared I was incapable of such feelings. Nila," he paused to take a deep breath, "you have no idea how badly I want you. Since I've met you, the sound of my heart won't stop . . . ."

My heart sank; I was overtaken by many emotions. Some overwhelmingly happy, while others were beyond terrifying. My world used to be mostly black and white, with a few grey areas. Since meeting Kai, I could honestly say there were splashes of colour bleeding through in every direction.

IS THIS A CONFESSION?

Untucking the hair from behind my ear, I adverted eye contact with Kai. Brewing within my chest was a heart attack waiting to happen.

Is this seriously happening right now? Kai shares the same feelings I do? There's just no way!

"Nila?" he said, interrupting my thought.

"Cheesy," I said quietly, gazing down at my boots.

"Huh?"

Lifting my head, still unable to face him, I repeated, "You're right; that was too cheesy."

From my peripherals, I could see a smirk rise from his mouth. "The cheesiest."

"Idiot," I said out of nervousness.

"Yeah, I'm an idiot."

Shocked by his agreeable response, I finally faced him. "Kai . . . ."

"Hmm?"

I took a deep breath, knowing I needed to express my feelings in return. "During the last couple of days of winter break, when I couldn't reach you, I learned a few things about myself. I noticed I wasn't laughing as much, I didn't smile as often, and I didn't even feel comfortable in my own skin. Without realizing, I found myself wanting to spend more time with you. I'd wonder where you were, what you were doing, and who you were spending your time with when it wasn't with me." The words were getting caught in my throat. "I . . . I don't want you to be my only source of happiness. If you're the only thing that makes me happy, then how am I supposed to continue in my daily life when you're not around? I don't want that."

Kai stood, breaking our eye contact once more. He took a couple of steps forward, looking to the frozen water yet again.

"Nila."

"Y-yeah?"

"I don't believe that, not even for a second. You're genuinely a warm and joyful person—I'm not the one who robbed you of that. It's not that you don't want this to happen between us, you're just straight-up scared, that's the concurring feeling," he said strongly, still facing the water. "Do you think I planned for this to happen? Do you really think I knew things would get this way between us? I never imagined I'd develop these kinds of feelings so soon." He calmed the intensity of his voice. "Nila, you have too much pride to be able to rely on someone else—I get it, but hey," he looked over his shoulder and winked at me, "that's one of the reasons I tripped and fell so hard."

I wasn't used to hearing all those pleasingly romantic words. Out of embarrassment, I turned my face and pressed it into my shoulder.

Noticing I had hidden my face, Kai made his way to the bench and knelt down in front of me.

"I bet it scares you to put all your faith in one person, trusting them with a part of your heart and letting them carry half the weight you have on your shoulders."

He nailed it, hitting every nail precisely with his words. He wasn't judging me; he knew me. He figured it out, something I didn't even know about myself. That's what terrified me the most. Without realizing, I was already relying on Kai. I had been doing so this entire time.

"Ka—"

"Nila," he overruled, his eyes fixated on me.

"Hmm?"

"Do you know why I brought you here, to this exact place?"

I shook my head in response.

"It's because this place holds a lot of meaning to me." Lost in thought, Kai took a quick glimpse over his shoulder, embracing the nature around us.

"Because of Hatori?"

With an emotionless smile, his lips cracked apart. "Yeah, because of Hatori."

Standing, Kai reached for my hand to help me up from the bench. Rising to my feet, my hand remained in his warm palm as he gestured for the other one. Holding both my hands in his, we stood face-to-face. He took a deep breath, then exhaled smoothly.

"I want this place to continue holding happy memories for me, not sad and depressing ones. I'm sick of feeling sorry for myself and avoiding anything having to do with Hatori. I don't want to fight with someone who physically can't fight back. No matter how hard I try to forget, I can't erase Hatori from my memory, and I now know it's because I don't want to. I want to share all the memories I've had here, with you, as we make new ones together."

My eyes widened and my face and ears instantly grew hot. My heart was at its limit; it was about to explode and jump right out of my chest. *Oh my gosh! I'm literally going to die of a heart attack. He said so many sweet and important things to me that nothing I say back will even come close to matching it.*

Trying to come up with a way to convey my feelings to Kai just as well, my mind kept drawing a blank. Soon, my mouth moved on its own. "When I saw you in the park that one day, I thought you were good-looking." *What the HELL am I saying?*

Surprised by my bluntness, his eyes flung back just before he could laugh. "Oh, yeah?"

"Mhm," I said, my face burning from embarrassment. To avoid the awkwardness of the situation I created, I knew I needed to continue by saying something—anything. "That is, until you opened your mouth."

"Oh, really?" he raised a brow. "You weren't any walk in the park yourself."

"Ah, I see what you did there," I played along.

Our eyes wavered as we both laughed. It felt good to change the pace of the conversation since everything was happening so fast. Not wanting Kai to think I was making light of what he said by joking around, I returned to a steady gaze, trying to find words to help me get my true feelings across. My heart was on the verge of exploding.

"I like you—I really like you," I admitted. "My heart is always pounding when I'm with you."

Kai stood dumbfounded as his eyes blinked irregularly.

"You're right, about everything. I'm not just scared—I'm terrified. I'm terrified of you, of this, of us. I don't know how to do this!"

"And you think I do?" he questioned, with a big grin on his face.

"Well . . . yeah."

Shaking his head, Kai's body pressed up against mine as he squeezed me tightly. "Wrong. This is something new for me too."

"But . . . Momiji," I mumbled into his uniform jacket with worry.

"Nila," he said softly, pulling himself back. "You are nothing like her. I don't want you to make this into a competition. Please, do not compare yourself to her."

"I know I shouldn't, but she was so involved in your life. Especially when Hatori—"

My words were suppressed by a warm and tingly sensation. To shut me up, Kai had kissed me.

Parting his lips from mine, he continued. "Everything, from the beginning to the present, has been at a completely different pace with different emotions. My feelings for you are SO much different than they were for her. This time, things feel purer and more meaningful. It's hard to explain, but you honestly have nothing to worry about. The feelings I experience when I'm with you—nothing can compare to it."

"Okay." *Maybe I'm the real idiot.*

We left the hidden area hand-in-hand. I couldn't put my finger on it, but there was a different air between us. Different in a secure kind of way, as if all my worrying was for nothing. All the doubts and confusion I had towards Kai's feelings for me, were miraculously gone.

Kai took me home, and when we said are goodbyes, he gently kissed me on the lips as if this were to become a regular thing, leaving my whole body numb with excitement.

My mother was still at work when I arrived, and Kenji was nowhere to be found. The rest of my night consisted of thoughts of Kai and his tender lips, with a side of homework. Every time I tried to focus on my studies, I became distracted by images of Kai passing through my mind. My heart spiralled into a furious rush every time I replayed the moment he spoke with such heartfelt emotions, expressing his true feelings towards me. I was left feeling giddy, like the dumb schoolgirl I truly was.

Chapter Twenty-Three

THE NEXT MORNING, I went through my usual routine. I got myself ready, made my lunch, and packed everything up to leave for school. The whole time I was getting ready, my mother was nowhere to be found, and neither was Kenji.

Did either of them even come home last night?

Making my way to the door, I remembered the walk to school with Kenji the previous day.

He played a dirty trick yesterday. I wonder if he'll show up today, too.

Knowing I shouldn't have gotten too excited by Kenji accompanying me, I headed out on my own.

The cherry blossom trees along the road were still bare, adding another disappointment to the start of my day. When the school gate came into sight, I saw Kida standing in front of them once again.

Why is she there? Is she waiting for me or Kenji? This might be my chance to thank her for informing me about Kai yesterday ... Maybe it's the excuse I've been waiting for.

Approaching Kida with caution, I smiled at her faintly. She wore her uniform jacket with a huge, warm scarf wrapped around her neck, as her bag hung by its strap from her shoulder. When Kida's eyes met mine, I received a worrisome smile in response.

"Hey," she started off.

"Hi."

"Um, Nila, I just want to say—"

"Kida," I said firmly, stopping her mid-sentence.

"Yeah . . . ?"

Even though she was my best friend, I sometimes felt like more of a groupie than her equal. The circumstances weren't the greatest, but I felt in control of where this conversation was headed. Not having Kida around was definitely putting a strain on me. She was usually the person I could go to for advice, guidance, and support, even though she wasn't the wisest. I couldn't lie to myself anymore—I missed her.

"Thank you for coming to my classroom yesterday to tell me about Kai."

"Oh, uh, yeah, it was nothing."

It felt good to have the upper hand on her for once. Standing a few feet in front of her, I carried on. "No seriously, thank you. I know we haven't been talking, but what you did was more than I could have hoped for. I hadn't seen or heard from Kai in a couple of days, and I was getting worried about him."

"Yeah, no problem. You know . . . I'm always here for you, no matter what. You're still my best friend," she said, smiling earnestly as tears accumulated in her eyes.

"Don't!" I pleaded. "You're going to make me cry! And I'm really sick of crying."

Watching the tears in Kida's eyes build, I could feel her determination to fix things between us and couldn't help but shed a few of my own. She walked towards me with arms out, ready to hug. I allowed her to come close and wrap her arms around me because I knew it was what I had been secretly waiting for. We stood at the school gate, crying hideously. I knew things weren't magically perfect between us, but it was definitely a step in the right direction.

Kida and I walked into school side-by-side, trying to hold back any future tears from falling. She asked me if we could meet up at a new sweets shop down the road from school. We needed to catch up on each other's lives and finally get a proper chance to discuss her relationship with Kenji. I accepted her offer in order to solve, and hopefully fix, our broken friendship. I hadn't otherwise given her the chance to share her side of the story.

At lunch, Kida and I ate together in the stairwell leading up to the roof. We finally sat down and caught up with each other as we briefly talked about what had happened during our holidays. I ended up sharing more than I wanted; I told her everything. Having taken over the conversation, I told her stuff about my family, about Kai, and about Hatori. I continued to ramble on and on about the previous day, and what went on after she informed me that Kai had been waiting for me.

"I still don't know exactly what we are to each other. Like, he said all those sweet and meaningful things, and we confirmed we liked each other, but he never stated if we were 'dating,'" I muddled my words with uncertainty.

"Nila, Nila, you are so naive. You guys ARE dating."

A warmth crept across my face as I turned away. "I don't know . . . ."

"Well, I do!" she said, jumping to her feet and moving right in front of me. "He confessed his love for you!"

"L-love!" I shouted, choking on a rice ball from my lunch. "He didn't mention the word LOVE at all."

"It was implied. No guy says all that JUST to remain friends. Plus, he even kissed you! And if I remember correctly, you guys have kissed more than once."

"Jeez, when you say it like that, it seems like a common thing we do," I confessed with embarrassment.

"I didn't mean it in that way. I'm just saying, if you guys had kissed once and didn't keep in contact, then it was probably a one-time thing. But, since you guys have hung out more than once and have kissed more than once, then to me, it seems like you're dating. You've both confided in each other with many personal things; it only seems natural now, don't you think?" she said with a warm smile as she returned to my side.

"I guess . . . it has begun to feel like a normal thing with Kai. I feel like I can honestly tell him anything. There isn't much he doesn't already know."

A depressed smile slowly appeared on Kida's face. "I'm sorry."

"Hmm?"

"Don't get me wrong, it's great you had Kai to confide in during the break—I'm all for you guys getting together! I guess I just feel a little left behind," she explained, a sadness lingering in her voice. "I know it's my fault for having these feelings, because I'm the one who screwed everything up, but . . .," she paused, as tears glistened in her eyes, "I wanted you to confide in me with all this stuff, y'know?"

Smiling, I answered, "Yeah, I know. Just like I've always done in the past, I wanted you to be the first person I told, but this time . . . you weren't there."

"Nila, I tried . . .."

I put my bento down on the step beside me and turned to face her straight on. "You did, just not hard enough," I admitted, tears building. "Do you know how devastated I was? How devastated I STILL am? You dropped this huge bomb on me, and I know I didn't really give you the chance to explain, but Kida come on—he's my brother! The one who's been there every single time you've come over, the one who's watched movies with us late at night, the one who's slept in the room right beside us when you stayed over—MY LITTLE BROTHER!"

Just as I finished lashing out, the school chimes played. Lunch was over, but our conversation was far from it.

"We'll pick this back up at the sweets shop after school," I demanded.

"Yeah . . .."

We walked to our classrooms in dead silence, smiling faintly as we parted ways before entering. I made it to my seat near the window, hung my bag on the hook attached to my desk, and pulled out the stuff I'd need for the next lecture. Once the teacher arrived, and class started, my mind drifted. I can't say I gave the teacher my undivided attention, but, at least, I was physically present. I kept checking the clock on the wall; twenty minutes went by and each minute made me more anxious as I sat in my seat.

School will end in a few hours. Today I'll finally get to hear what Kida has to say.

Suddenly, there was a knock on the door at the front of the classroom and my teacher paused his lesson to answer it. Sliding the door open, my teacher blocked the guest's face with the book in his hand so we couldn't see who it was. A guy, who sat at the front of the class, closest to the door, leaned over his desk to see who the mysterious knocker was.

"It's the principal's secretary," he whispered to the class.

"That's weird," another one of my classmates added. "She doesn't come down personally unless it's something important."

The whole class began whispering ideas of what or who it might be regarding, creating rumours within mere seconds.

Our teacher shut the door, then turned around to face the class. Instead of heading towards the front, he walked through the sea of desks until he reached mine at the back near one of the windows. He placed a hand on my desk and slowly leaned in.

"Miss Izawa, you're wanted in the principal's office. Please bring all of your belongings with you."

Principal's office? ME? What did I do?

Scattering like a maniac to collect my things, I carelessly shoved everything into my bag and rose from my desk before my classmates could begin gossiping. Weaving through a few desks, I felt the sharp eyes of everyone in class on me as I made my way to the back door. As I walked out, the class got rowdy with questions and random ideas leading to false accusations I knew would soon spread throughout the school.

I marched my way through the empty halls and down a few flights of stairs to the main level where the principal's office was. When I reached the office, the secretary wasn't back yet. Not knowing what else to do or where to go, I took a seat on one of the chairs lined up against the wall in the reception area.

It's weird she didn't get back before me. I wonder what this is all about?

Moments later, the secretary walked in. She smiled at me kindly as she made her way to a door which read: *Principal Goda*. She knocked on it twice before poking her head inside, mumbling something to someone behind the door.

"Miss Izawa," she turned back towards me. "Principal Goda will see you now."

As I got up from the chair, a familiar face walked through the doorway.

"Kenji?"

"Nila?"

"Great, you've both arrived. Principal Goda will see the two of you in his office now. Right this way."

Uselessly leading the short distance, the secretary held the door open for us. Kenji and I both stared at each other with confusion as we stepped inside. The secretary closed the door behind us, leaving us in a small room with a man I had only seen a few times during school assemblies.

"Hello, Izawa's," Principal Goda said with composure, as he walked around to the front of his desk.

"Hello, Sir," Kenji and I greeted in sync, bowing to show respect.

"I guess you're both wondering why you were called here today."

Too nervous to answer, I nodded my head while Kenji stood silent.

"Yes, well, the school received a call from the hospital where your mother works. We were informed she collapsed during her shift."

My eyes jolted at Principal Goda's words.

"IS SHE OKAY?" Kenji blurted anxiously, stepping forward.

"From what they've told us; she is stable. They wouldn't give us much information, but they said to send you both over immediately," Principal Goda said calmly.

Glancing at Kenji's face, a shadow was cast, displaying a look of horror. Without a second to spare, Kenji flung the principal's door open, and dashed out of the room.

"Mr. Izawa!" Principal Goda shouted, taking a few steps after him. "Wait just one moment!" The principal's words couldn't reach Kenji; he would stop for nothing and no one. Turning back towards me, Principal Goda touched my shoulder. "We have called a taxi to take you directly to the hospital. Do not worry about the fare; the school will pay for it. The driver is waiting out front."

With those final words from Principal Goda, I bowed, then rushed after Kenji, but he was no longer in sight. I ran to the lockers in hopes of finding him, but there was also no sign of him. Making my way outside after switching shoes, I headed to the front gate where the taxi was said to be waiting. When I opened the door to hop in, Kenji wasn't inside.

Kenji, where did you go?

The driver asked for confirmation on the destination before taking off. During the ride, I tried calling Kenji's cellphone, but was unsuccessful at getting through. I sent a quick message to Kida to let her know I had to cancel our plans because I was on my way to the hospital. Not even a minute later, I received a reply from her.

[Line Kida]: OH MY GOD! Is everything okay? Why are you going to the hospital?

[Line Nila]: My mother collapsed at work, so Kenji and I are heading there now.

[Line Kida]: HOLY SHIT! Is she alright?

[Line Nila]: I don't know.

[Line Kida]: Are you okay?

[Line Nila]: I'm not sure. Inside, I'm freaking out, but somehow, I'm still remaining calm . . .? I don't know what to expect when I get there.

[Line Kida]: Let me know if everything is okay once you find out!

[Line Nila]: Okay.

Our town was small, meaning the hospital was also small, with fewer resources than the ones in larger, neighbouring towns and cities. My mother was the head nurse on her floor. She was one of the few nurses who had made a name for herself at such a young age here in town.

When I was younger, I would visit the hospital with Kenji often. We would be our mother's 'little helpers' by performing easy tasks like delivering towels and blankets to each room, or food trays for the patients during lunch. Now that I think about it, I'm not sure how she got away with having kids around.

"Miss, we've arrived."

As I had reminisced about the past, I had also withdrawn from the world around me. The car had stopped, and the taxi driver was staring bluntly at me through the rear-view mirror, waiting for me to get out.

"Sorry!" I apologized, removing my seatbelt and shuffling out.

I jumped out of the taxi and shut the door behind me. As soon as I was out, the driver sped off, leaving me to face the hospital by myself.

This is it. Kenji, seriously, where the hell did you go?

Cautiously, I approached the front doors of the hospital, anticipating all the terrible possibilities I could imagine inside my head. When the sliding doors opened, I saw a huge desk with a sign hanging above it reading: *Front Desk—Check In*. The front entrance was completely different from when I was a kid. It had been redone nicely, with modern furniture and a fresh colour scheme, giving it a welcoming atmosphere. Even though it seemed welcoming, it still smelled like a hospital.

Walking up to the front desk, I noticed an unfamiliar face sitting behind it.

"Um, pardon me. Could you please tell me which room Shino Iza—um, I mean Shino Kimura is in?" I asked.

"Hello, dear, you're here to see Nurse Kimura? May I ask your relation to her?"

"Yes, I'm her daughter."

"May I ask your name?"

"Nila Izawa."

"Perfect," the lady at the desk accepted without any further persuasion. "She's in a private room on the second floor. Number 208."

"A private room? Why?" I questioned, my heartbeat picking up in pace.

"I'm not sure on the details of her report, but if you head up to the unit, the doctor can fill you in on anything you want to know."

"Thank you very much."

I made my way to the elevator and pushed the up-arrow button, waiting patiently for it to arrive. As I waited, I saw a huge blur go by from the corner of my eye.

"WHICH ROOM IS SHINO IZAWA IN?" a voice shouted abruptly.

"Sir, please step back and calm down," the lady at the front desk said, trying to defuse a possible hostile situation.

I looked to see what the commotion was about and found myself shocked to see my brother hovering over a frightened lady at the front desk.

"Ken-KENJI!" I shouted at the top of my lungs.

Hearing my voice call out his name, Kenji looked over. "NILA!" he exclaimed, rushing towards me. "How's Mom?" he asked desperately, his chest heaving.

"I don't know; I just got here. Where did you go? The school arranged a taxi to take us."

"I ran a portion of the way, then hopped on the bus. Sorry," he answered with uneven breathing.

"It's alright; I'm just glad you're here."

As I said that, the elevator doors opened before us. We got in and I pushed the button to the second floor.

"What room is she in?"

"208, a private room."

"Private room? What the hell—what for?" he asked, raising his voice angrily.

"I don't know."

Agitated, I watched Kenji tap his foot repeatedly as we rode the elevator up. The elevator finally stopped, dinging to inform us of our arrival to the second floor. We dashed out, running down the halls frantically as we looked for room 208. When we found it, an older male in a long, white coat was exiting the room, making sure to shut the door behind him.

"Hey, doctor!" Kenji shouted from down the hall. "What's wrong with our mom?"

"You must be Kenji and Nila—Shino's children," the doctor addressed with a smile. "I am Dr. Ashima."

As we came to a halt in front of the doctor, Kenji answered for the both of us. "We are. What's wrong with her?"

The doctor took a deep breath before releasing a long sigh. "She collapsed from overexertion during her shift this morning."

"Overexertion?" Kenji processed.

"Who directed her to be in a private room?" I asked.

"Well, she is an employee of the hospital, and since we had available rooms, we took advantage of it—at no charge of course. The cancer has taken a severe toll on her body, so we wanted to make sure she was comfortable, while monitoring her closely for the next couple of days."

"Cancer?" I echoed, my heart at a standstill. *What . . . ?*

Kenji, with his eyes narrowed, raised his voice once again. "What do you mean 'cancer'?"

"Yes, cancer. Did your mother not inform you of her condition?" Dr. Ashima asked, looking puzzled as he lowered his chin.

Kenji and I looked at each other, both signalling to one another that we knew nothing before turning back to Dr. Ashima.

"No . . .," I answered. My heart sunk as I listened to the doctor's words.

"Oh dear, this is troublesome," Dr. Ashima said, shaking his head. "Well, I do not know how to put this lightly, but your mother has stage two breast cancer. She has been fighting it for almost six months now."

Looking at Kenji again, I saw him with his head down and clenched fists. "You're lying."

"Son, I wish I were. I am an Oncologist, and although I have been trying to treat your mother for quite some time, she never makes time for her regular appointments, even though she knows better. I have also been telling her to cut back on her hours at work, but she ignores everything I suggest. I heard from some of the other nurses on her team that she has been picking up shifts for other employees, even for those not on her floor. Maybe, with you being her children, she will finally listen. She is strong enough now for you both to go in and see her. Just try not to put too much stress on her," Dr. Ashima concluded, peeking into the window on the door of our mother's room before walking away.

Even though the doctor gave us permission, neither Kenji nor I could move. Kenji, with his head still hung, appeared frozen in time. I looked past him, just staring at the door to our mother's room, not being able to bat an eye.

What . . . just happened? This is some kind of joke, right? My mother can't have cancer—that's impossible! "Kenji, he's wrong. This doctor doesn't know what he's talking about. Mom can't have cancer. Like, come on—she still has all her hair! Hair loss is one of the signs, right?"

Kenji didn't make a single gesture or take a noticeable breath. He was completely absent from the conversation I was trying to engage him in. I took a couple of steps forward and placed my hand on his shoulder. With the sensation of my hand barely sinking in, Kenji shook it off, almost as if I were a disease.

"Hey," I said, trying to figure out the expression on his face.

Before I could say anything else, Kenji got closer to the sliding door and opened it. He didn't take a single step inside. Instead, he stood in the middle of the doorway, just staring intensively into the room. I followed shortly, like a shadow behind him as I took a look. In the room, I saw my mother sitting upright in a hospital bed as she gazed out the window.

Without much thought, I called out to her. "Mom . . .?"

Turning her head quickly, she placed her focus on us as we stood at the door.

"Ni-Nila! Kenji! What are you two doing here?" she asked, shaken by our presence. "They didn't have to call you—I'm fine. I just passed out from working too hard, is all. I'll probably be home tonight."

My mother was trying to play it off, as if she wasn't a sick patient in the hospital. She smiled a lifeless smile, one without colour or warmth; it was the smile of a sick person, very white and pale. Seeing my mother like that was unbearable, to the point where just looking at her made my heart ache. The last time I saw her, she looked nowhere near as bad. Even though the doctor told us the shocking news of our mother having cancer, it didn't seem to register until I actually saw her with my own eyes. The sound of her speaking my name was enough to tug on my heart and rip it out of my chest.

"Who are you kidding?"

Forgetting Kenji was standing next to me, I looked to him. There wasn't a single sign of sadness on his face. Instead, the only emotion I could read was anger.

"Who do you think you're kidding?" he repeated firmly, refusing to set foot in the room.

"Kenji, what do you mean?" my mother replied, stunned by Kenji's harsh approach.

"Look at you, sitting there, telling us you'll be home tonight. You're only kidding yourself—YOU'RE DYING!"

"Kenji!" I shouted, tugging on his arm.

"No, Nila!" Kenji fought back. "I'm not walking on eggshells around her, and you shouldn't either! SHE'S DYING—she has cancer and she's dying! One day we'll wake up, and she won't be there because she'll be dead."

Without much thought, I slapped Kenji across the face as hard as I possibly could.

"Nila!" my mother shouted as she pulled the sheets off her, attempting to get out of bed.

After the slap, Kenji couldn't look me in the eye. Before my mother could even get one foot on the floor, Kenji spun around and booked it down the hall.

"Kenji!" I yelled, turning to run after him but stopped in order to remain insight of my mother.

"Nila, go after him!" my mother pleaded. "Make sure he's okay; we can talk after!"

Following my mother's orders, I ran down the hall in a hurry after Kenji. Catching up to him, he took the exit to the stairway, instead of using the elevator, and made his way down to the first floor. I followed his every move; each turn he made, until he bolted outside. When I reached the hospital's entrance, I ran out and saw him standing near a huge support pillar, a short distance from the building. He had placed both hands on the pillar, bent to stretch his arms and back, then hung his head in between his biceps as he spat and coughed excessively. I stood by the doors watching Kenji, like my mother requested, as he took some time to himself. The moment didn't last long before he pulled out a pack of cigarettes from his coat pocket, placing one in his mouth as he searched for a lighter.

"WHAT THE HELL ARE YOU DOING?" I yelled, running to him before he had the chance to light it. Ripping it from his mouth, I tossed the cigarette on the ground and stomped on it with my boot in disgust.

"Fuck off, Nila."

"No! You fuck off! Are you for real right now? We just found out our mother has cancer, and you're going to purposely do something that can cause it? If so, then you're actually a bigger idiot than I thought."

Kenji fell silent, still not being able to look at me.

"Dr. Ashima told us not to put stress on Mom, and look at what you're doing. You're doing EXACTLY that! What has gotten into you lately?" I said, toning down my voice.

After a long pause, Kenji spoke. "How can you be so fine with all this?"

"Fine? How am I fine? I'm freaking out, just as much as you are," I argued back.

"NO, you're not! Look at how fucking calm you are! Like shit, Nila."

That moment, it hit me. Why was I so calm? Inside, I knew my heart was aching, but on the outside, I hadn't even shed a tear. I usually cried about every little thing, so what was wrong with me now? I wished I could have avoided such an unsettling confrontation altogether.

"Uh . . . um, I don't really . . . know."

"Can you go? I want to be alone for a bit," he asked as he lightly kicked around chunks of ice which had most likely fallen from the lip of the roof.

"Yeah, I'll go. Just please, don't leave the hospital. Take all the time you need—just don't leave," I begged.

"I won't."

I left Kenji and went back inside. I did a couple of laps around the main floor of the hospital, preparing myself to face my mother again. Pacing, I tried to make sense of everything.

What am I supposed to do? Really, what can I do? Please . . . someone . . . tell me what I need to do to fix this.

I started getting cramps from the on and off sprinting I was doing, so I took a seat on the closest chair available. I ended up resting in a waiting area designated for surgery. The hospital was fairly quiet, which explained why there were only two other people seated near me.

Randomly, in a state of panic, I remembered Kida and how I told her I would let her know what was happening once I knew. I took out my phone and saw my inbox flooded with messages from both Kida and Kai.

I haven't even told Kai anything. I don't want to worry him, but . . . I really want to see him right now.

I chose to knockout the one message from Kai, versus the million I had received from Kida. His message was short and unpredictable, compared to his usual opener.

[Line Kai]: Hey, I fixed my phone! Let's walk home together. Is it okay if I pick you up from school?

School . . ..

[Line Nila]: Hi, sorry, but I'm not at school.

That was pretty bland of me.

After replying to Kai's message, I read through Kida's to see what they all said.

[Line Kida]: Nila, is everything okay? How's your mom?

[Line Kida]: Girl! What's going on?

[Line Kida]: NILA! IT'S BEEN MORE THAN AN HOUR!

[Line Kida]: Kenji isn't answering his phone either! NILA, WHAT'S GOING ON?

Just as I was about to reply to Kida's messages, the new message icon appeared across the top of my screen. Erasing the message I was typing to Kida, I went back to my inbox to read the new one.

[Line Kai]: Oh, did you stay home today? Are you sick?

No. Kai, I wish it were that simple . . . I wish you were here.

[Line Nila]: No, I'm not sick.

After sending the message to Kai, I stood up and made my way to the elevator. While I waited for it to arrive, Kai messaged backed.

[Line Kai]: Is everything okay . . .?

I read the message just as the elevator doors opened. Stepping into the elevator, two female nurses walked out, chatting away about their plans for the night. I pushed the button for my mother's floor and watched the elevator doors close before me. Staring at my phone, I re-read Kai's message. Crouching down in the elevator, I typed:

[Line Nila]: No.

Pushing send took all the courage I had left. I had suppressed my feelings for the past couple of years; I had not relied on a single person, except myself. I had built that tiny amount of courage all on my own, and then, just like that, I gave it all away with a tap of a button.

Am I weak? Have I really become THAT needy?

Everything was now so different, so strange compared to the way it was before. Things were no longer the same, not at school, not at home, not with my friends, and definitely not with me. Nothing was reliable, and all the things that brought me comfort, simply vanished in mere seconds.

Each breath I took got tighter and shorter. My throat was constricting itself, leaving me with little to almost no airway to breathe through. The walls of my air passage felt like they were thinning out, while the inside of my chest was burning aflame. The elevator felt like it was closing in around me; the tiny, rectangular space was getting even smaller the more time I spent inside. The short ride up to the second floor seemed to go on forever.

As my body continued acting out, my phone started vibrating vigorously. I was getting an incoming call.

"Hello?" I managed to answer quietly.

"Nila, what's wrong?"

Hearing Kai's voice snapped something inside me. My vision fogged from tears, and immediately I began to cry. Not being able to cry before, now I couldn't stop. I tried to focus on controlling my emotions before replying, but I couldn't do it.

"Everything."

"Everything? Nila, what happened? What's wrong?"

"I ... My mom ... I'm at ...."

"Your mom? What's wrong with her? Where are you?" I heard panic rise in his voice.

"Hospital," I answered, trying to swallow the saliva sticking to the back of my throat. "I'm at the hospital. I need you ... I really need you."

Chapter Twenty-Four

*A*FTER THE PHONE call with Kai, the elevator dinged and opened its doors to the second floor. Remaining crouched down inside, the doors slowly shut and the elevator stayed at a standstill. I slowly stood up and pushed the number to a different floor. I decided to wander the other floors of the hospital for a while longer to try and calm down. I didn't want my mother to see me this way.

Presented with the chance once more, I was eventually successful in exiting the elevator on to the second floor. I walked the floor at a much slower pace, the destination of my mother's room fast approaching. With clenched fists, I made it to the corner before having to turn down her hallway. To my surprise, Kida and Kenji were sitting outside of the room on the chairs positioned along the wall. I locked eyes with Kida immediately.

"NILA!" she exclaimed as she rose from her chair and rushed the short distance towards me.

My mouth was immobile. I wanted to acknowledge Kida's presence with at least a few words, but my lips remained sealed.

"Nila!" she shouted again before embracing me with a hug. "How are you doing? Kenji just finished filling me in."

How am I doing? "Honestly, I don't understand the way my body is reacting right now. None of this feels real."

Kida continued to hug me tighter, trying to console me as if my mother were already dead. I knew those weren't her intentions, and she was just trying to show her support by being there for me, but that's what it felt like at the time.

"While you were gone, Dr. Ashima came back and told me Mom's gonna stay in the hospital for a few nights," Kenji informed, as he stood up and walked towards us.

Kenji seemed much calmer and more composed than before. I wasn't sure if it was Kida's doing, or if it was merely due to the time he had to himself, but whatever it was, it had my stomach in a knot.

"I'm going to stay here tonight with Mom," he said.

Moving away from Kida, I looked at him. "Actually, would it be alright if I stayed with Mom tonight?"

Thrown by my suggestion, Kenji looked at me warily. "I'll stay with her tomorrow then. I'm gonna head home to get a couple of things for Mom, want me to bring you anything?"

Looking down at my clothes, I realized I was still in my school uniform. "Maybe a change of clothes."

Giving me a look of understanding, Kenji went back to get his bag from the chair, then walked on past us. As I watched him turn the corner and out of sight, I started to feel nervous.

"Nila, I don't want to interrupt any more of your family's time, so I'm just gonna give you what I brought before heading out myself." Walking to the chairs, Kida scavenged through her bag, pulling out some class notes and a pile of worksheets.

Slowly walking towards her, I held out my hands.

"I was told you didn't get a chance to get the worksheets before you left. Also, I made copies of my notes, since we're learning the same things. You probably don't care about these right now, but with finals, and college entrance exams coming up . . .."

I felt a soothing smile make its way onto my face as I looked down at the papers in my hands. "Thanks."

Kida smiled back faintly as she gathered her things. "Message me if you need anything, or if something changes, alright?"

"I will."

With both of them gone, I was left alone in a huge building that reeked of illness. The more I concentrated on the smell, the more I felt sick to my stomach. I made my way closer to the door of my mother's room and slid it open with a shaky hand. Inside, my mother was resting on the bed, reading a magazine. Taking note of my presence, she closed the magazine and placed it on the side table next to the bed. Stepping foot inside, I shut the door behind me, then made my way to a chair positioned in the corner of the room. I dragged the chair closer to the bed before taking a seat.

"Nila," she whispered sadly. "Thank you for finding your brother."

Studying her pale face, I couldn't help but get straight to the point. "Why didn't you tell us?"

The corner of her mouth quirked up a bit. "I didn't want to worry you."

"Worry us? What do you think THIS is?"

Before answering, she took a quick evaluation of my face. "This is very unlike you, you know."

"Unlike me? How?"

"That's a very stern and confident tone emerging from you, one that I haven't seen too often. I'm going to have to admit though, lately, I've begun to notice it coming out a lot more."

I could feel my emotions bubbling inside, brewing angrily by my mother's aloof attitude to my question. "Why didn't you tell us you were sick? We could have helped you!"

"No," she asserted.

"No . . .? Why not? This isn't just a mere cold, Mom—this is cancer!"

"Nila, I know what I have."

"I . . . I don't really think you do," I said sincerely, swallowing my tears.

"What difference would it have made if I told you two? All it would have done was cause you stress and anxiety every time you left the house. You're in your final year of school, working hard and concentrating for your college entrance exams, while Kenji is always out, doing God knows what around town. If I were to have said anything, you would be stressing out in school all day, and Kenji would probably be getting into worse things than smoking."

Surprised by my mother's keen knowledge, I couldn't help but ask. "You know he smokes?"

"It wasn't hard to figure out. He smokes in his room, so whenever I go in, I can smell it right away."

"Oh . . .." *My room's right next door, I'm surprised I couldn't smell it myself.*

"Mhm."

"What treatment or medication has the doctor prescribed?" I asked, not knowing much about cancer, or how to deal with it.

"He's prescribed them all, but I'm not on anything."

"Huh?" *What does that mean?* "How could you NOT be taking anything?"

Again, with a strict expression, she repeated. "I mean, I am not taking any medication OR going through any treatment."

"What? WHY?" I shouted desperately, jumping to my feet.

"The only things which could possibly help are chemotherapy and radiation, but I refuse to do either."

"WHY?"

"Nila, lower your voice," she hissed. "If I were to begin chemotherapy and radiation treatments, I would start losing my hair, along with having other side effects, causing others to become aware of my illness. I don't want to worry you or Kenji, and I sure as HELL don't want the neighbours to see me without hair. Imagine all the rumours and gossip that would spread throughout the neighbourhood—I can't have that."

"You're unbelievable! You work in healthcare but you care more about your appearance in the eyes of others, others who don't even matter, instead of your own well-being and your family. That's outrageous!"

"Nila . . .," she said, shocked by my outburst.

I knew I was losing my temper, and I shouldn't have been yelling at my mother, especially in this situation, but I couldn't help it. The doctor told us not to stress her out so her body wouldn't become weaker, but after receiving such a dumb answer, I no longer had control.

"Do you understand how much of a shock it was for Kenji and I to be told that our mother has cancer? DO YOU?" Tears gushed from my eyes as I lashed out with the heavy emotions locked inside me. "Like Kenji said, what if we wake up tomorrow and you're gone? JUST GONE! Cancer can take you away from us at any moment! You've gone for half a year without any means of treatment; the odds are not in your favour. You can't be gambling with your life, Mom!"

I could see the terror building in my mother's eyes as she listened to each concern I vocalized. I knew I couldn't continue to look at her without sobbing uncontrollably, so I buried my face into the palms of my hands and I sat back in the chair, whimpering quietly so people outside the room wouldn't hear. Seconds later, cold hands grabbed hold of my arms, pulling me upwards onto the bed. Within seconds, I was beside my mother, being tightly held in her arms as she comforted me. Leaving a couple of her own tears in my hair, she kept me close to her body, enough for me to hear her heart beating. Her heart sounded regular, just like mine, leaving me with the slightest bit of hope that this would all blow over and my mother would be fine. She petted my head, running her fingers through my hair as we stayed in each other's arms, silently rocking side-to-side.

After our heartfelt moment, I wanted to go to the washroom to regroup and better compose myself. There was a small bathroom in my mother's room, but I needed a moment away to breathe. Excusing myself, I left the room. To my surprise, I saw Kai in his uniform, waiting outside on a chair facing the door. As soon as I closed the door, our eyes met and he rose from his seat, immediately rushing towards me.

"Nila!"

"Kai," I said softly, calmed by his presence. Remembering I had asked him to come all the way to the hospital without any explanation, I knew my actions were a bit rude. "Sorry for making you worry. How long have you been waiting out here?"

"Don't worry about that, if my girlfriend is in trouble, then of course I'd come running. I've only been here for roughly five minutes anyway. I peeked through the window on the door and saw you and your mom talking, so I didn't want to interrupt."

My eyes widened while my heart did a three-sixty loop before stopping dead in my chest. *Girlfriend! That's what he said right? I'm not imagining it? He really . . . did say it.*

Embarrassed by the sudden confirmation I received, I found it hard to look at him. "Oh, um, okay. That's good," was all I could fumble out of my mouth.

"How's your mother? When I asked the lady at the front desk for the room number, she wouldn't give me any information."

Suddenly, the fact that Kai had called me his girlfriend seemed so trivial and unimportant. Finding it easier to face him, I stared into his eyes and caught a glimpse of concern. "My mom has cancer," I said, breaking eye contact so he wouldn't notice my tear stained face. I was sure my eyes were already bloodshot from before, so I was also pretty confident he'd figured out I had been crying.

I didn't have to see Kai's face to know what expression I'd find. All I had to do was understand the immediate touch that followed my destructive news. As soon as the words left my mouth, his arm was around my head, pressing my face deep into his chest while his other arm rested at his side. With his body's quick response, I couldn't help but grab onto his uniform jacket and cry silently into it. This unvoiced comfort was exactly what I needed, and somehow, he knew.

Changing my mind about the washroom, I poked my head back into the room and informed my mother I was going for a walk around the hospital instead. I took advantage of the time I got to spend with Kai by walking a few laps within the disease-infested building. We walked around the halls slowly as I informed him of my short day at school, and how Kenji and I were brought into the principal's office where we were first told about my mother's hospitalization. Then, I explained everything the doctor told us once we arrived. The whole time I talked, Kai didn't say much. He attentively listened as I vented and complained about everything going through my mind.

We spent about half an hour together, enjoying each other's company in such a dreadful place. Coming across the elevator for the hundredth time, I knew I should've been heading back to my mother's side, but a huge part of me wanted to leave the hospital with Kai.

"I should get back."

"Yeah, you've been gone pretty long," he replied as we came to a stop. "I'll walk you back to the room."

"It's okay; you don't have to."

Looking at me, he admitted earnestly, "But I want to."

A smile crept its way onto my face. "Alright."

We turned around and made our way back towards my mother's room. Each step taken felt more uneasy than the last. I was scared to go back and spend the night with her, all alone in a room that had probably witnessed numerous deaths.

As we approached the door, Kai pulled my arm back before we passed by its window.

"Hmm?" I mumbled.

"I don't want her to see me," he said, right before putting his hand on my cheek. Pulling me in close, Kai placed a gentle kiss on my lips.

"K-Kai!" I raised my voice, slightly louder than a whisper.

He put a finger over his lips as he walked back down the hall to leave. Startled and embarrassed, I watched him turn the corner and vanish out of sight.

I had to get rid of my idiotic, romantic, teenage smile before re-entering the room where my mother waited. I didn't want her to see me all flushed and ask a series of questions. I stood with my eyes shut and my back to the wall beside the door, inhaling and exhaling deep breaths in order to regain my composure.

While doing so, someone tapped me on the shoulder. Jumping, I turned to my left and saw my brother standing beside me with a bag in his hand.

"Kenji!" I exclaimed, seconds away from a heart attack.

"That guy was here."

"Guy?"

"The one who was at our house before. I just passed him as I got off the elevator."

He passed by Kai . . .. "Oh, yeah, um, he was here to give me—"

Before I could finish my excuse, Kenji stopped me. "You don't need to explain anything to me. Anyway, here are your clothes. I'm gonna go in and say goodnight to Mom before heading back home."

"Oh, okay," I replied hazily, as I took the bag from him.

Kenji walked into the room as I stayed dumbfounded in the hallway.

Good night to Mom? He's definitely calmed down quite a bit from earlier. Lately, he's been showing a lot more of his emotions. This is a side to him I haven't seen in a while. It's kind of nice.

Before following Kenji, I sent Kai a quick message to thank him for coming all this way for such a short period of time. After hitting send, I walked into the room to join my family.

Kenji was standing beside the bed with his backpack resting on the edge of the bed's metal frame. He pulled out a couple of books and half a dozen magazines, before handing them all to her. She looked extremely pleased as she received them. From the doorway, I saw a huge smile appear on our mother's face as Kenji stood by her.

"Thank you, Kenji."

"I thought you'd be bored, so . . .," he attempted to explain.

"It's perfect. They will come in handy, I'm sure," she replied, unable to mask the smile on her face.

"Then I'm gonna head home," he said, zipping up his bag and throwing it over his shoulder.

"Oh, Kenji," I said, remembering something last minute.

"Yeah?"

"I'm not going to school tomorrow. If you could please let my homeroom teacher know, and collect my homework at the end of the day . . .."

"Sure."

"Nila, you have to go to school tomorrow," my mother argued.

"It's fine; I'm caught up in everything. We're basically just studying for exams, which I can do here."

My mother wasn't too pleased that I wanted to skip school, but eventually accepted my decision. "Just make sure you go the day after. I don't want you to fall behind."

"Okay."

A couple of hours went by and visiting hours were over. The hospital became much quieter than it had been during the day at its peak, except for my mother's room. For the rest of the night, my mother and I chatted about almost everything and anything. We talked about school and my plans for college and I reassured her that my plan to attend the local college hadn't changed. We discussed which program I wanted to explore, and I told her I was still deciding between an Elementary School Teacher or an Executive Assistant for a well-established business corporation. I knew my mother really wanted me to get into business because she had mentioned it to me several times before, but I was still undecided.

Touching upon the future, and life in general, made me wonder how much longer my mother would be in mine. We stayed on the topic of education for quite a while before switching to Kenji. We discussed the gifts we received from him at Christmas, his recent improvement in school attendance, and even his willingness to help regarding my mother's current illness. I didn't mention anything about him and Kida. I figured it wasn't something my mother should concern herself with at this time, plus I hadn't properly discussed it with Kida, so I didn't know all the details myself.

"What about this Kento fellow?"

"Hmm?" I squeaked in panic at her sudden mention of Kai.

"You know what I mean. You haven't mentioned him lately. Has he become your boyfriend?"

"Would you be mad if he was?" I said, not knowing how she would take the news of her daughter dating.

"Nila," she said, a bit cross.

Only finding out about it today, I wasn't sure if I should tell her or lie about it. In the end, I decided to confess the new relationship between me and Kai. "Um . . . yes?"

"I see. When did this happen?"

"I'm . . . I'm not really sure. Recently . . .?"

With eyes far from amused, she continued asking questions. "What is it you like about this boy?"

What do I like about, Kai? Wow, um, I'm not too sure how to answer. There's so much I like about him, it's impossible to narrow it down. Plus, it would all sound so stupid confessing it to her.

"Well, there's a lot I like about him. But I guess the first thing that comes to my mind is his persistence to entangle himself within my life."

Interested by my response, she squinted her eyes. "What do you mean?"

"Weeell, at first, I really disliked him. I wanted nothing more to do with him than to retrieve my textbook, but, as time went on, he was somehow involved in everything I did without me even realizing it." I giggled under my breath. "To this day, I haven't seen my textbook. It's almost as if he doesn't want to give it back."

I guess my response was enough for my mother because she seemed much more relaxed on the subject of Kai, which made me happy. I could tell she was still uncertain about him, but her negative comments towards him appeared to have lessened. She didn't seem to like the idea of him before, so I wondered what it was that changed her mind.

A nurse came in to do a check on my mother before she fell asleep, making sure everything was okay and set for the night. The nurse brought in a small futon for me to sleep on, which I set up at the end of the room against the far wall. Before my mother went to sleep, I said goodnight to her and changed into the pyjamas Kenji brought for me.

On the rolled-out futon, I checked my phone for Line messages and saw one from Kida and one from Kai. I opened Kai's first, reading his reply to my previous message.

[Line Kai]: Of course. You don't have to thank me for something like that. It made me happy knowing you could count on me. Anytime you need me, I'll be there.

Reading his message put an immediate smile on my face and in my heart. In such a short time, things had changed drastically between us. Even though I was scared about how fast things were progressing, I was unexpectedly excited to experience it all for the first time. It felt like I was finally growing up and could now be compared to every other girl in high school who'd been in a romantic relationship.

I closed Kai's message to open Kida's.

[Line Kida]: Hey, I know things are chaotic right now, and you're gonna be spending most of your time taking care of your mom, but do you have some time to meet up tomorrow? I really want us to finish our talk.

I agreed with what Kida was asking.

[Line Nila]: Yes, we really need to finish that conversation. Tomorrow after school, let's meet up.

I had a hard time falling asleep in an unfamiliar place. The pile of papers Kida had brought sat on the chair, untouched. My mind raced in circles with thoughts about today and everything going on until I mentally exhausted myself. I placed my phone under the pillow and was finally able to doze off.

The next day, I woke up with a sore back. The thin futon was nowhere near as comfortable as my bed at home. As kids, Kenji and I grew up on futons, but they were never as crappy as this one. I sat up and looked at the bed my mother was in. I saw her sitting up and reading one of the books Kenji brought for her.

"Morning," I greeted, stretching out the sleep within me.

Peeking over the top of the book, she greeted back. "Good morning, Nila."

"How did you sleep, Mom?"

"I've had better nights."

"Yeah, me too."

A moment later, there was a knock on the door.

"Nurse Kimura, are you awake?"

"Yes, come in," my mother answered, laying the book flat on her lap.

A nurse I didn't recognize, slid the door open and poked her head through. "You have an early visitor. I wasn't sure if you were awake, so I didn't let them in alone."

I checked the time on my phone; it read 9:12 a.m.

"A visitor?" my mother questioned with a twisted expression.

"Yes, should I let them in?" the nurse asked.

With a questioning look, my mother accepted. "That's fine, thank you, Nurse Ikeda."

From the futon, I watched the nurse's head retract from the doorway as the door slid wide open. A horrified look overcame my mother's face as she stared intensely at the door.

"Shino," a deep voice called out.

I didn't have to see the face attached to the voice to figure out who the visitor was. The horrified look my mother wore, copied over to me.

"Youji . . .," my mother whispered.

Chapter Twenty-Five

MY SUSPICION WAS correct, but how I wished it wasn't. He took a step into the room, holding an arrangement of flowers in a vase as he continued to face her. Within seconds, my presence in the room caught his attention.

"Ni-Nila," he said, startled.

I could feel my stomach drop at the sound of my own name. "Dad . . .."

"What . . . are you doing here?" he asked, his eyes wider than ever.

Before I could answer, my mother spoke for me in a furious tone. "The real question is, what are YOU doing here, Youji?"

Fumbling his words, he attempted a reply. "I, uh, heard you were hospitalized, so I—"

"Leave," my mother said forcefully, overruling him.

"Shino . . .."

My mother turned away from him, putting her head down. "You have no business here. I am no longer your concern. Now, leave."

He took a few more steps into the room, reaching out a hand towards her. "Shino, please."

I stood up from the futon. "STOP!"

He flinched as he looked at me. The man who had been missing from my life for the past two years, was now only feet away and looking straight at me. Pulling his hand back, he stopped moving forward and stood up straight. "Nila, I thought you'd be in school at this time."

The more he spoke and said my name, the more my stomach turned and my chest tightened. The tone he used towards me was unfamiliar. He spoke to me as if I were a stranger, direct and proper. I could sense uneasiness in his voice, and each time he looked my way, he was covered in a cloud of gloom. There was so much I wanted to say, but I was too stunned to say anything. I had a million and one questions to ask him, but could not think of a single one. All I could do was answer his simple question.

"I took the day off."

"I see. To be with your mother no less. Well then," he smiled at me distantly, "I can see she's in good hands."

He bowed to me, then faced my mother and did the same. He placed the flowers on the small stand beside my mother's bed and turned around to walk out the door, shutting it behind him. In that moment, my body took control over me and I was running to the door, sliding it open before flying out of the room. Everything happened in a blur; I heard my mother's voice call out to me in the background, but I continued anyway. When I got into the hall, I took a couple of steps away from the door and watched my father walk away from me once again.

Please look back . . . please look back . . ..

Inside my heart, I desperately wanted him to turn around. I wanted him to face me properly, but he never did. Deep down, I wanted to summon the nerve to call out to him, and I wanted him to turn around after hearing my voice. I wanted to know why he left us, without so much as a word to explain where he was going or when he'd be back. I wanted to know why he didn't love us—why he didn't love me. I wanted to know so many things, but my pride held me back.

Why . . . why did you come?

With my head hung, I went back into the room to face my mother. I could feel that his sudden appearance had stirred her emotions and set her heart racing. The atmosphere in the room felt heavy, but she didn't mention him after he left, nor did she ask me why I chased after him. We acted as if nothing had happened, as if he had never appeared before us or even existed.

Hours went by and I realized that I hadn't seen Dr. Ashima since yesterday. I was ready to talk to him, but thought it would be best to do so with Kenji present. Now that I was able to wrap my head around the fact that my mother had cancer, I had put together a series of important questions to ask him. I had many opportunities to reflect upon my own feelings and work through complicated emotions. I wasn't sure why I was handling things so well today; something inside me felt very off.

Keeping my mother occupied became extremely hard. I quickly figured out we had little to nothing in common, unless we spoke of school or reflected upon memories from the past.

Stepping out of the bathroom in my mother's room, I received a message from Kida saying she, instead of Kenji, would be dropping by the hospital after school to give me my homework. She also asked if it was okay for us to leave right after in order to continue our talk. Her message did all of two things: comfort me and give me anxiety. I was excited she would be passing by, but her reason for coming made my stomach turn.

Once school was over, it didn't take Kida long to arrive. I met her on the first floor where she handed me a couple of worksheets to add to my uncompleted pile.

"Thanks," I said, juggling the items in my hands.

"Anytime," she replied with a caring smile. "How's your mom?"

"I'm not too sure. She seemed fine throughout the night, but that doesn't mean much when you take into account what's going on inside her. I plan on talking to the doctor with Kenji before I go to school tomorrow. I'll probably end up missing homeroom again."

"I'll let your homeroom teacher know," she informed helpfully. "I'm sure the talk with the doctor will go fine. Just keep me posted."

"Thanks."

Shortly after Kida arrived, I received a message through Line from Kenji.

[Line Kenji]: I'll be there soon. If you have stuff to do, it's okay to leave before I get there. I'm gonna be staying the night anyway.

He probably knows Kida and I are having our talk today.

[Line Nila]: I do, thanks. And okay, I'll tell Mom. Also, before I go to school tomorrow, I'm going to pass by the hospital so we can talk to Dr. Ashima together. Don't tell Mom.

Kenji replied with a simple '*okay*,' giving me the confirmation needed to inform our mother of the plan for tonight. I asked Kida to wait for me on the main floor as I went upstairs to speak with my mother.

We took a bus halfway, then walked the rest of the way to the new sweets shop Kida mentioned yesterday. During our travels, we initiated small talk. She proceeded to ask more questions in regard to my mother and how crazy it was that we didn't know she had cancer. I didn't have many answers for her because I knew very little myself. I had no issues talking about my mother, since I wasn't really ready to dive into the topic of her and my brother.

When we arrived at the colourful shop, a girl in a maid's outfit greeted us before taking us to our table. She seated us at a window-side table and we both ordered milkshakes, which came to the table in no time. From the way Kida was fiddling with the straw in her glass, I could tell she was uncomfortable.

"I didn't know the uniforms here would be so cute. Maybe I should apply," Kida joked.

I didn't have much to say on the topic of uniforms, so I answered by smiling politely.

"Um, well, I'm not really sure where to start," she admitted, quickly changing the subject and avoiding eye contact. She swallowed hastily. "Remember last summer, when I went to that bonfire party with Risa Kobayashi from class 3-4?"

Thinking back to the previous summer, I tried to remember the specific party Kida was referring to. She went to so many parties, it was hard to keep track of them all. "The beach one you asked me to come to because boys from other schools were going to be there?"

"Yeah, that one! It was a huge party, right on the beach. Of course, you turned down my offer though," she laughed dryly.

"I remember," I said, trying to speed up the conversation.

"Well, that night, Kenji and his friends showed up. I spotted him within the crowd of unfamiliar boys and went to talk to him. Now, keep in mind, there was alcohol at the party, so everyone was drinking, everyone except Kenji. He didn't have a single cup in his hand the entire night."

So, he wasn't drinking . . ..

"Risa bailed on me to go flirt with some guy, and usually, I'd be doing the same, but instead I hung out with Kenji. Of course, I've known him since we were little," Kida rambled, "but it wasn't until that night that I had an actual conversation with him as a friend. I remember being a bit tipsy, so I don't even know if half of what I was saying made any sense to him. What I did remember was the stupid little crush I had on your brother, for all those years, didn't feel so stupid anymore. There might've been a party going on in the background, but when Kenji and I were talking alone, it felt like we were the only ones there," she paused to look up at me.

Surprised by her confession, I couldn't help but question it. "You had a crush on my brother . . .?"

I could see my reflection in her eyes as she looked at me. Her eyes screamed of worry and guilt, while her fingers trembled as she continued playing with her straw, aggressively twirling it in circles around the edges of the cup. "Mhm . . .."

She never mentioned my brother in THAT way before. She has dated SOOO many guys. How do I know she isn't lying?

I tried to deny knowing which part of her story was coming up next, but realistically I knew. No matter how hard I tried to prepare myself, I knew what was coming.

"We decided to leave the party early and go to a cheap love hotel. I don't know what came over me. Maybe it was the alcohol, but . . . I wanted to be with him no matter what."

EW! WHAT? That escalated insanely fast! "Stop!" I cut in. "I don't get you."

"What, don't you . . .."

In a stern, clear tone, I voiced my observation over her reply. "You say you 'like' my brother, and have for a long time, but I know you've flirted and dated many guys afterwards. So how? How can you say you like him when you've never shown signs of it?"

Kida's face caved in from the harsh tone and direct hit of my question.

"Nila," she said gently, almost purring, "if I were to have told you I liked him back then, how would you have reacted?"

Her body language shifted. She no longer looked like a scared little kitten. Instead, I could tell she was seriously asking me for my opinion in order to prove a point. Everything would have played out differently if she told me she liked my brother, before telling me she slept with him.

"You're right. I probably wouldn't have taken it well. But Kida, I can guarantee I would've reacted much differently than I am now. How are we supposed to move forward from here?"

"What do you mean . . . ?"

"We can't just have conversations like we did before. We can't talk about boys, or future romances anymore, because I don't want to hear about Kenji in that sense. It's too awkward for me. From here on out, no matter what we do, things will be different."

Coming to the same realization, she finally understood. "I guess you're right."

The conversation went dry from there. The waitress came back to the table and handed us menus. Since this was our first visit, the waitress was happy to share her favourite items on the menu with us as she described how each one of them looked and tasted. We took a couple of minutes to decide before placing our orders.

As the waitress walked away, I glanced at Kida who was gazing out the window beside our table. I knew she was thinking about something important because whenever she looked off into space like that, it meant she was deep in thought. I looked away from her to take a sip of my shake.

She soon broke the silence. "You know, I really do like him. I could possibly love him for all I know."

Finishing the sip of my milkshake, I almost choked as it went down. "I never heard you mention the word 'love' before when talking about a guy."

"Yeah, because I didn't keep them around long enough to figure it out," she said, still looking out the window. "With Kenji, I want to keep him close. I get scared every time I fight with him, because I know at any minute, it could be over if he really wanted. At the beginning, we talked a lot, sending messages back and forth and meeting up secretly. It was almost as if we were really dating, but I knew in my heart we weren't. We never brought up the topic of being in a 'relationship' until a couple of months ago. I guess I wanted more. I asked him what we were to each other and that's when the fights began."

Somehow intrigued with her story, I felt myself getting sucked in. "What were the fights about?"

Turning back from the window, she looked at me dead on. "You."

"Me?"

"Yeah, and our friendship. Kenji didn't want to ruin it, so he slowly started backing off after he realized the possibility of our friendship ending. I realized it too, but I played dumb. I tried to convince myself everything would be alright if we talked to you about it together. Since you guys weren't very close, and hardly spoke to each other, he denied my request to try and make it work. He said you'd never understand and he didn't want to be the reason we stopped being friends. I knew he was absolutely right. There was a moment though, where I was ready to throw it all away to be with him. Don't worry though; I realized how ridiculous that idea was. I didn't want to become the clingy girl guys were afraid to get involved with, so I did the same as him and pulled away."

As Kida laid everything on the table, spilling her heart out to me, I couldn't help but think back to what Kai had said to me once before:

"We call them 'best friends,' but the moment they do something we don't like, we demote them from their position. Don't let things drag on longer than they should. Before you know it, it'll be too late and you'll be full of regret."

Only now understanding what Kai meant, was I able to relate it to my own situation. He was right; if I didn't put in the effort to fix things, then nothing would change. I didn't want to be full of regret like Kai said; there was no way I could let it eat away at me, every day, for the rest of my life. I knew what I should do, but I couldn't bring my heart to agree with my head. My heart still ached from being betrayed; it was at war with my brain and I knew it wasn't going to be as understanding or easily swayed by emotion.

The more I paid attention to Kida's expression, the more I wanted to cry. No matter what I did, it wouldn't change the fact that she and my brother had feelings for each other. I knew how he truly felt about her, from the haunting words he left me with, and how she felt about him. So, the real issue wasn't with them, but with me. I was the only obstacle standing in the way of their happiness. If Kida felt anything similar to how I felt with Kai, then I couldn't bring myself to lecture her further. I recognized that it was impossible to choose who you fall in love with. So, if she truly loved Kenji, the only thing left to do was acknowledge and accept it. The sooner I came to terms with the situation, and what I expected to come out of it, the sooner we could all move on.

"What happens if you guys break up? It will be awkward either way."

Her head perked up. "Break up?"

"I guess . . . he has been attending school more often. I wonder if you have anything to do with that?"

"So, you're saying . . . ."

"Yeah."

Her eyes lit up until she beamed. She exhaled deeply and her upright position slouched until she was moulded to the chair. Kida put her hands over her mouth and promptly burst into tears. Then, she flew over the table to hug me, knocking over the remainder of our shakes. Her body quivered as she wailed in my ear. I put my arms around her shoulders and did the same. From the corner of my eye, I saw a bunch of people staring at us. Even though we were causing a scene, I didn't care because this moment was way overdue. I needed Kida to be by my side as my best friend during this difficult time, and of course, Kenji did, too. I might not have fully agreed with the relationship between my brother and my best friend, but I didn't have the right to stop it if they were both happy.

When the waitress came back with our orders, she had an immediate reaction of shock then concern, asking us if we were both okay. Quickly ending our hug, we reassured her everything was fine. Before placing the desserts on the table, she wiped up the spilled milkshakes with a clean cloth.

We sat back down to eat our desserts properly as I expressed my feelings and concerns to Kida about her relationship with my brother. I told her I had some conditions. I didn't want to hear about their romantic relationship or see anything that would disgust me and make me want to throw up. She laughed, but understood my underlying message. I also told her I would prefer it if Kenji would go to her house whenever they wanted to spend time alone together, and when she came over to ours, it was to spend time with me. This way, I didn't have to wonder what they were doing while I was under the same roof. I felt a bit demanding, but those were the rules that felt reasonable. She seemed to agree because all she could do was laugh and smile in her chair.

"If I marry Kenji, we'll be sisters!"

Listening to her ludicrous thought, I choked on a piece of cake.

"Too soon?" she teased, smiling from ear to ear.

"Just a bit," I replied, as I grabbed a napkin to wipe my mouth.

Once we finished our treats, we left the shop and walked towards our school. On the way, we chatted and joked about this and that, just like we used to. When we hit the school, we made it down the colourless Pink Path like we normally would if we were walking out of school together. The end of the blossomless path led to a fork in the road, which would force us to split up and go our separate ways.

"I can't wait until spring when these trees will gain their beautiful colour back. Right now, they're pretty ugly, just like every other tree during this time of year."

"They're not ugly—they're just naked!"

She laughed at my protectiveness. "Sorry, sorry," she said, waving her hands back and forth in defeat. "I am glad the snow's already melting though. It felt like it just got here, and now it's already going away."

"I agree. We didn't get much snow this year compared to previous years. Usually, we would start getting signs of snow weeks before December."

"Yeah, exactly. I can't complain though; I hate winter. I'm just glad we had snow on Christmas, that's the only time I really want it around," she shared.

"Same here."

Looking up at the bare branches of the cherry blossoms as we walked down the path, I couldn't help but feel warm and protected. Kida dashed past me, skipping merrily through the path like the idiot she was. Even though she looked foolish skipping through the patchy areas of snow, I couldn't fight the need to join her. Together, we skipped down the path like two insane teenagers until we reached the fork where we had to part.

Spending that time with Kida was extremely precious to me, something I didn't think would ever happen again. We were talking and acting normal with each other, just like before. Even though my heart was heavy from my decision, I was happy to continue to hold Kida dear. Kai was right; fixing things with Kida was well worth it. The only thing I can say I regret is that it took me so long to do it.

When I arrived at my house, I saw Kai sitting on my doorstep all bundled up in a jacket, still wearing his uniform. Wondering what brought him, and how long he had been sitting there, I bolted through the gate to meet him.

"Kai! What are you doing here?"

Looking up at me with his emerald green eyes, he smiled brightly. "Waiting for you, of course."

"But, why? How did you know I'd be here at this time?"

"To be honest, I thought you would've been here a while ago," he said, sticking his tongue out as if to mock my tardiness.

Still not understanding what he meant, I stuck my tongue out to match him. "You could have messaged me! How long have you actually been waiting? And you still haven't told me what you're doing here."

He let out a sigh of disappointment. "You're no fun. You're trying way too hard to expose my mysterious, spontaneous side," he teased as he stood up from the step, shaking the snow off the back of his pants. "I went to the hospital to see if you were there, but instead, I found your brother. I ended up chatting with him for a bit, then asked him when you'd be home. He told me you should be arriving at home shortly, so I decided to head over straight from the hospital. Turns out, he was wrong. You definitely didn't come home straight from the hospital like I did," he joked, taking a step forward as he tousled my hair.

"Oh," I answered rather simply, taming the mess he created on my head. "Wait, you spoke to my brother! About what?"

"Nothing really. I can't say we actually had a full-on conversation. We just answered a few questions each other had," he briefly explained, still beating around the bush.

"What kind of questions?" I pursued, still rather suspicious.

"You don't need to worry too much about that. The main reason for me coming is I wanted to make sure you were doing okay."

Accepting his concern on my behalf, I instantly remembered my father's brief appearance at the hospital. "Actually, do you have a minute? There's some stuff I want to tell you."

"Yeah, of course. Should I be worried?"

"I don't think so," I answered truthfully. "Let's go inside."

With a look of uncertainty, Kai followed me into the house.

Kai left his stuff by the door, then bowed. "Pardon my intrusion."

"No one's home. You don't need to be so formal."

"I know, but still . . .."

Directing him to the kitchen to wait for me, I hung up my coat in the entrance closet. From the corner of my eye, I saw a blinking red light. The answering machine on the hallway table flashed, indicating an unheard message.

Not wanting to keep Kai waiting long, I walked over and hit the play button, hoping all the messages were short. The computerized voice notified me of two unheard messages. I played the first message which was from a lady my mother worked with at the senior home attached to the hospital, asking her to call her back regarding a shift. The message was left before word had spread of my mother being hospitalized, so I chose to delete it. The machine continued onto the second message.

'Next unheard message, sent today at 10:24 a.m.':

"Hello, this message is for Nila and Kenji . . ."

The second I heard the caller's voice; I knew exactly who it was.

"This is your father. I'm sorry to be calling like this out of the blue . . ."

As soon as I heard the machine talking, I slammed my hands down on the small table. Hearing the noise, Kai came rushing out of the kitchen.

"I was wondering if the two of you would consider meeting me for a cup of tea—or coffee, or whatever you prefer. I would really like to see both of you. I have a lot I'd like to discuss with you two, and I'm sure you have questions of your own. I'll be waiting at the café in front of the train station at 5:00 p.m. tomorrow. The one I used to take you both to as kids sometimes after school. I'm really hoping you will come, but if you choose not to, I'll also understand."

And just like that, the message ended. From start to finish, I held my breath, in fear of exhaling too loudly and missing a single word of the message. My hands shook and my knees wobbled. It got to the point where I didn't know if I was still standing or if I had already hit the floor. Apparently, I was on the floor because when I looked up, Kai was hovering over me with a horrified expression on his face.

It was strange, I could see his lips moving, but I couldn't hear anything he was saying. My chest was acting up again, the same feeling I'd had when I was upstairs in my room with my mother and Kenji. Each time I took a breath, I choked on the air filling my lungs. Before I could curl up in a ball on the floor, Kai picked me up into his arms and brought me to the couch in the living room. I tugged at his shirt aggressively, gasping for air, but by the look on his face, he had no idea what was going on. He didn't know what to do; he wasn't trained like my mother was, so I could understand his panic. Everything felt like it was moving in slow motion around me. It was as if my voice had been stolen; I couldn't communicate with words. The world around me was closing in and moving slowly, but the pain inside my body was spreading quickly.

I'm not dying, right, Mom? This is the same thing that happened before, right? Mom, what did you do before? What was it that you did to help me? Tell me so I can tell Kai. You used a bag, wasn't it? Mom? Mom? Please, answer me . . ..

Something clicked, leading me to the realization that my mother wasn't coming to my aid and I was on my own. I quickly figured out my body was reacting this way because I wasn't breathing normally, meaning I had to calm myself down. In a fuzzy blur, I watched Kai shuffle from standing to a kneeling position and back to standing all in a matter of seconds as he maintained eye contact with me the entire time. Tears formed in his eyes, clouding his vision in frightened anticipation. I had to focus so I could show Kai everything was okay, that he didn't need to worry.

Within a couple of minutes, my vision became much clearer and Kai's voice drifted into my ears. My breathing regulated to a controllable pace, and the constricting chains around my chest started to loosen. Kai knelt back down beside me and I latched onto him, pulling myself up into his arms as we sat up on the couch together. In return, Kai held me tightly, keeping me as close as possible without physically crushing me.

"Nila! NILA!"

"Kai," I let out with a gust of trapped air.

"What's happening?" he asked in desperation, his eyes shifting back and forth, skittish.

"Kai, it's okay now," I tried to settle him, hugging him securely.

"Okay? NILA, THIS IS NOT OKAY!"

"Kai, please calm down. Shh, I'm okay," I said calmly, hoping he would hear my voice over his.

Pulling away from me, he held onto both sides of my face with his big hands, forcing me to stare directly into his ravishing green eyes. "Nila," he lowered his voice. "What just happened? Are you sure you're alright? I was calling out to you, but you never responded—you were looking right at me but weren't responding!"

"Yes, I'm alright," I said, trying to make him feel more comfortable. "I can't really explain why, but I'm alright. It's happened before and my mom used a paper bag to help me control my breathing. I think she told me I was hyperventilating. It's when—"

Still riled up, Kai cut me off sharply. "I know what it is. How long has this been going on? Do you need a bag right now?"

Trying to think back to my first episode, I attempted to explain its severity during certain peaks. "Right before Christmas, it happened; when Kida first told me about her and Kenji. It comes in waves and in different strengths; sometimes, it's worse than others. Around the time my dad left, that's when I first noticed I was starting to feel different. It was like I was suffocating whenever I thought of something out of my control."

He removed his hands from my face and placed them around my

body, then brought me close to his chest once more. "You weren't responding, that was the scariest part. Man," he said, on a stressful exhale, "I've never been so scared in my life. Nila, you don't even understand what was running through my mind."

Kai repeated himself over and over, and I let him until he was able to calm down.

"Each time I called out to you, you'd vacantly stare at me. I had no idea what was going on or how to help you. I completely froze; I didn't even call an ambulance! What if I lost you?" he asked, somewhat rhetorically.

His whole body quivered, shaking down to each finger that touched me. Before I could say anything, the words dissolved in my throat and turned into tears. I couldn't imagine being in his shoes. If it had been him who'd had the attack, and was left unresponsive, I probably would have reacted the same way.

"All I knew was I wanted to stop you from crying. I listened to the emotions from your facial expressions, and before I knew it, I could hear your voice going through my ears. The only way I thought I could help you was to get you to hear my voice," I explained.

"I don't understand. How come you were unable to speak?"

"I don't know. All I know is that my chest became tight, stopping the words from coming out and preventing air from reaching my lungs."

Kai held onto me for a while longer, making sure I was fine and everything else was okay before letting me go. He wondered if hearing my father's voice on the machine was enough to trigger something traumatic for me. I told him about my father's appearance at the hospital earlier this morning and he asked if I had experienced a similar episode there as well, which I informed him I didn't. I wasn't sure why I had an attack just by listening to a voicemail from my father, rather than when I saw him in person. There was no explanation I could think of.

Unsure of the idea, after what had just taken place, Kai asked if I was going to go through with meeting my father at the café. He also asked if I was planning on telling Kenji about my father's visit, or about the voicemail. In the end, I decided against both.

We continued to talk about things in each other's lives and I reported that Kida and I finally patched things up. I also told him I agreed to let

Kida continue seeing my brother, with the exception of a few rules. From the smile on his face, I could tell he was very pleased I managed to fix things with my best friend.

Sitting side-by-side on the couch with Kai, having such a deep conversation, was by far the closest I had ever felt to him. The whole time we talked, he held onto my hand as if he didn't want me to go somewhere out of reach. His hand was warm and his presence felt secure, making me feel safe all around.

Hours flew by, and I knew it was almost time for Kai to go. Sitting on the couch, I dreaded the thought of him leaving and remaining by myself in a house I had grown to hate so much. This house was full of so much heartache and terrible memories that it became uncomfortable to be in.

"Nila."

"Yeah?"

"I don't think I can leave you alone tonight."

"What . . . do you mean?"

Kai shut his eyes. "Just the thought of you being alone . . . what if something happens? What if no one's around and you have another attack? It makes me nervous, just thinking about it."

"I'll be fine. Don't worry so much." I tried to sound convincing.

Opening his eyes, with a determined expression, he shook his head. "Would it . . . be alright if I stayed here with you tonight?" Unable to look at me directly, he turned red. "When I needed you, you were there for me. Now, let me be here for you."

Shocked by his sudden request, I lowered my head, nervously nodding yes.

Chapter Twenty-Six

TAKING OUT AN extra futon, a pillow, and a couple of blankets, I prepared a spot on the floor near my bed for Kai. As I set things up, Kai was on the phone with his father to explain that he would be staying at a friend's house for the night to finish up some last-minute homework.

"Yeah, uh-huh, okay," he repeated a few times. "Thanks, Dad, it'll be fine. I'll wash my uniform at Taki's or just borrow one from him. I'll be home tomorrow, good night." He hung up the phone, then came to help me finish preparing the futon.

"So, your parents think you're staying at Taki's?"

"Yeah. My dad didn't have a problem with it. He just wanted to know if I had my uniform for school tomorrow."

"Oh, I see," I said, nervously. "By the way, how are things between you and Taki?"

"The same," Kai gave a weak smile, as if not wanting to get into it further.

Switching topics, I remembered I had to meet Kenji tomorrow morning. "I have to go to the hospital really early tomorrow to talk to the doctor before I go to school. Sorry . . .."

"That's fine, don't worry about it," he said understandingly. "I'm a morning person anyway."

"Thanks."

Kai responded with a supportive smile as he unbuttoned his shirt, revealing a white undershirt.

Oh my gosh, I thought he was about to strip! "W-would you like to wash your uniform?"

"If you don't mind," he grinned with his teeth clenched together.

"Not at all. Just hand it over and I can wash it for you."

"Uh, what about my pants? I mean, I have boxers underneath, but . . .."

"Oh, um," I mumbled, my face catching fire.

"I usually sleep in them, but I don't know if you're gonna be okay with me walking around half-naked . . .."

"You-you'll need a change of clothes to sleep in, of course!" I shouted in panic. "Kenji probably has extra clothes you can borrow. You're roughly the same size."

"If he doesn't mind."

"He won't find out. It's no trouble," I replied anxiously, trying to escape the awkwardness I felt in the room. "I'll be right back."

I went into Kenji's room in search of a pair of pyjamas or a tracksuit that Kai could use for the night. I found an old T-shirt, along with a pair of track pants which looked like they would probably fit him.

When I returned, Kai was moving around, looking at pictures and objects around my room. Observing him from the doorway unnoticed, I watched carefully as he picked up one of the stuffed animals sitting on my shelf. A light smirk appeared at the corner of his mouth as he squeezed it in his hand.

"Here," I said, tossing the clothes to Kai as I stepped in. "Kenji's a bit shorter than you, but I believe they'll do for one night."

Startled by my sudden appearance, he quickly placed the stuffed animal down, trying to hide the fact that he was snooping. He caught the clothes against his chest, then held them up to take a better look. "Great, thanks. Can I use your bathroom? I'll change in there so you can have your room."

"Yeah, it's just across the hall."

"Thanks."

He walked past me, brushing against my shoulder. I grabbed the handle of the door to my room, shutting it slowly as I watched Kai close the bathroom door behind him. With my door shut, I turned my back to it, taking a few steps backwards until it caught me. Sliding my back down the door, I realized what I had agreed to. I sat on the floor in a daze, shocked at who I was becoming. The reality of Kai and I being home alone together, all night long, started to sink in. I knew I wasn't going to get any sleep with him literally inches away from my bed.

Kai . . . he's staying over—sleeping over, in MY room! WHAT THE HELL AM I DOING? How could I have agreed to this? At the time, it didn't seem bad, but . . . I can't have my boyfriend spending the night, especially behind Mom's back. She'll kill me if she ever finds out!

My stomach was fluttering out of control, as if butterflies had been trapped inside. Just the thought of being alone with him in this situation drove inappropriate thoughts through my mind. My heart pounded at full throttle, shaking my whole body, down to the tips of my fingers. While I was at war with myself, I heard the doorknob to the bathroom unlock.

Crap! He's done changing already? I haven't even started!

Quickly jumping to my feet, I ran to my dresser and flung the drawers open in desperate search for one of my cuter pyjamas. Not even seconds later, there was a knock at my door.

"Is it alright if I come in?" Kai asked from behind the door.

"Uh! Just need a few more minutes!"

"No problem, take your time."

I frantically continued my search. Finally coming across a nice pair with bows, I ripped my clothes off and raced to put on the pyjamas. Tossing my dirty clothes into the hamper, I ran to the mirror beside my dresser for a quick hair and face check; heart racing.

Everything looks normal. Okay, he can probably come in now. "I'm done," I called out.

"Pardon my intrusion." Kai opened the door and took a step in. As he did, our eyes met. "Wow . . .."

"What?" I asked, extremely self-conscious.

A light shade of pink crossed his face before he tried to cover it with his hand. "Nothing, it's just you look really . . . cute." He turned around quickly to close the door behind him.

Even though he was wearing Kenji's clothes, they looked much different on him. He was actually much taller than I expected and had a larger build compared to Kenji. The clothes had an all-around tighter and smaller fit. I knew I must have been blushing a ridiculous amount as well because my face felt extremely hot.

"Th-thank you," I said shyly.

"You're welcome."

Kai was holding his uniform, and I walked closer to retrieve it from him. "I'll go wash this for you."

"Oh, yeah, thanks," he said, passing his clothes over to me.

Walking downstairs to do the laundry, I could smell Kai's scent seeping out from his uniform. Sneakily bringing Kai's school shirt up to my nose to get a better whiff, the pleasant smell of the one I liked burned straight into my nose. Feeling perverted, my insides started boiling.

Ugh, what am I doing? If Kai saw me right now, he would probably be so grossed out. How embarrassing!

After placing Kai's clothes into the washing machine, I went back up to my bedroom. Entering the room, I saw Kai patiently sitting at my desk.

"You look very stiff," I teased.

Looking back at me with laxed eyes, he replied, "I wasn't sure what to do while you were gone. It's the first time I've been in your room."

Grabbing the pillow that I had laid out for Kai, I swung it, smacking him in the face. "Now you're making me nervous." An uncomfortable silence crept upon us again. Trying to lessen the awkwardness of the situation, I took the first step in breaking the silence as I sat on my bed. "It will take about half an hour before we can hang your clothes."

"That's fine," he said, tapping his fingers against the desk. Within seconds, Kai got up from the chair and made his way to a floating shelf near my dresser. "This is a picture of you and your brother, right?" he asked, pointing to a small frame.

"Oh, um, yeah. We were at the beach on a family vacation."

"How old were you? You look so cute."

GAH! How embarrassing! Leaping from my bed, I ran to grab the picture from the shelf, wanting to remove it from sight. "I was five," I said, reaching for the photo.

Inches from touching it, Kai took the frame and held it as high as he could above me. "What are you doing?"

"Give it back! It's humiliating," I said, jumping up and down, trying to climb his arm and retrieve it.

Laughing, Kai tried to playfully fight me off. "Humiliating, how?"

"It just is!" I continued to struggle, also joining in on the laughter. "Look at that haircut and swimsuit! I had no style or fashion sense back then."

"Oh, and you do now?" he teased.

"Shut up, idiot!"

Continuing to horse around, we talked about the places we've been on vacation with our families. Kai stated he'd been to a few different countries, such as Russia, England, and Canada, where I, on the other hand, have never left Japan. It was nice to hear about some of the childish adventures he's had with his brothers when they were younger. Hearing him talk about his family always brought a smile to my face because he also wore a smile each time he spoke of them.

The jingle from the washing machine played throughout the quiet house just as we were wrapping up our conversation. Although I stated that I could do it alone, Kai insisted on coming downstairs with me to help hang his clothes. After we were done, we returned to my room for the night.

"So, um, we should probably get ready for bed. We have to wake up early tomorrow."

"You're right," he agreed, making his way to the futon.

Turning off the lights, we tucked ourselves in, lying face up to the ceiling. I immediately learned that we didn't have to be touching for my heart to race at an uncontrollable pace. Being near Kai made me feel vulnerable; I never knew a single person could occupy so many of my thoughts. Lately, all I wanted to do was be around him as much as possible; I could feel myself changing, whether I liked it or not.

"Kai."

"Hmm?"

"This is weird, right?"

"What is?"

"You and me, sleeping in the same room," I confessed, still looking up at the ceiling.

"Is it?"

Confused by his response, I leaned over the side of the bed to see him on the floor. The room was dim, moonlight from the window was shining through, allowing me to see his face clearly. "You don't think so?"

Glancing up at me, he chuckled. "Yeah, it is."

"Huh? Then why'd you . . . ."

"I just wanted to see what expression you'd make," he smirked mischievously.

"Idiot."

"Guess I am," he said, as he sat up on the futon.

On his knees, inching closer to my bed, he stayed kneeling as he reached my bedside. He put his gentle hand on my chin, tilting it up ever so slightly before he leaned in towards my lips and brushed them softly with a kiss. When it came time to breathe, he pulled away and looked into my eyes, then leaned in once more. Bringing his lips back to mine, he kissed me again, this time much more passionately. His gentle pecks, had become fierce, breathtaking kisses. My lips soon separated; his tongue was in my mouth, applying more pressure with every movement.

Oh my God! What is his tongue doing?

Each kiss was more intense than the last. He moved his body closer to mine until he was pushed up against my bed frame. It must not have been close enough because he grabbed my arm and pulled me down onto the futon. We rustled around a bit, changing our positions until I was on the bottom with him hovering over me. His arms were extended out beside my head, holding his body up like a tower as he looked down at me. His face was much different than before; I had never seen him with such an intimate expression.

NO! Stop it, Kai!

I repeated the word 'no' over and over in my head, but it never left my mouth. I knew where this could potentially lead, and if I didn't say something soon, I might end up doing something I could regret. Of course, I liked Kai, and I knew that eventually, possibly, maybe, I'd consider having sex with him one day, but today wasn't the day and this wasn't the right time. I didn't want to be forced into something like this. I always thought of sex as something that happened naturally between two people who loved each other, something they both agreed on without having to say a word. But right now, that's not how I was feeling.

Kai began lowering his body onto mine as he ran his hand up under my shirt, slowly approaching my breasts. Squinting my eyes, I held my breath as a single tear trickled down my cheek.

"Nila?"

All forms of contact between us had come to a halt. Kai's hands were no longer touching my bare body. I opened my eyes to find him hovering over me again, staring at me point blank.

"Nila?" he repeated, a concerned look swept his face as his narrowed eyes softened.

I placed my hands over my face to hide my tears. "I'm sorry."

Not hearing a reply, I spread my fingers to look through the spaces. Kai was no longer above me; instead, he was sitting in an upright position beside me.

"Kai?" I whispered, lifting myself up.

He had one knee bent with one arm resting on top of it, supporting his head. "I'm so sorry, Nila. I'm so unbelievably sorry."

"Kai?"

The guilt which filled his eyes spread onto his face as he expressed his concern. "I can't believe I just did that. I forced myself on you. What the fuck am I doing?" Dropping his knee, he turned to me. "You were crying; I made you cry!"

"It's okay," I forgave, leaning over to give him a comforting hug.

"No, it's not!" Shaking me off, he looked at me with angered eyes as he grabbed my wrist. "I tried to take advantage of you, Nila! You looked terrified, as if I was some sort of monster."

Looking into his eyes, I could see they were unsettled and filled with regret. I knew I needed to express how I truly felt in order to reassure him. "Kai, I'm not terrified of you. Yes, I admit, I was scared of things progressing. I was afraid it might have led to sex, but that doesn't mean

I don't want to do it with you. I just feel like everything we do is a new experience for me, but common for you. We just started dating and we're still learning about each other; I feel like it's too soon to go that far. Plus, with my mother being in the hospital, my mind is elsewhere and my emotions are screwed up. Kai, I like you—I really do! But your pace is so much faster than mine. At times, it's like you're on a whole other level I can never advance to. Don't be sorry; I just want us to work together until we can walk at the same pace, running hand-in-hand if we need to."

The heavy look on his face lightened as a faint smile eased through. "Okay, I can live with that answer." Reaching for my hand, he brought it up to his mouth and placed a gentle kiss upon it. "Let's try this 'sleeping' thing one more time."

Smiling at him gently, I stood up and got back into my bed. Laying my head on the pillow, I turned to face the wall. "Hey . . . ."

"Hmm?"

"Have you, uh . . . have you . . . done IT before?" I asked before turning to face him, not knowing if I should've asked such a question, or if I even wanted to know the answer.

Stopping the rearrangement of his futon, he didn't look at me. Nothing was said at first; there was a long pause before Kai responded. "I have."

My heart dropped. An immediate tightness grabbed onto it and began squeezing it tighter with each beat. "With Momiji?" I kept firing questions without running them past my brain first.

Lying down, facing away from me, he answered again. "Yeah . . . and others."

"Others . . . ?"

Continuing to face the opposite direction, a wave of silence filled my room once more. "Nila," Kai said, disappointment continuing to linger in his voice, "I was in a bad place after Momiji cheated on me; I slept around to forget about her. Then, when Hatori passed, and Momiji tried to get back in contact with me, I gave up on relationships and started messing around frequently. Even while I was doing it, I never felt fulfilled or satisfied. I hated the person I had become, but after getting in so deep, I didn't know how to get out. It lasted for half a year until I smartened up. I confided in my brother, Sosuke, who knocked some sense into me, literally."

Not knowing what to say, I froze in silence. I was scared of the person Kai described to me. That wasn't the kind, loving Kai I had come to like and treasure dearly. Having no words, I broke from my frozen state and turned away from him. Taking in his truth and breaking it down, was I willing to accept this person? What part was it that got me so upset? Deep down, I guessed he wasn't a virgin. The strength he had during that moment, already told me everything I needed to know.

"Nila," Kai spoke firmly, "I can't change the past."

"I know that!" I shouted unknowingly. "It's just . . .."

Before I could continue, my bed rocked back and forth. Strong arms wrapped around me, trapping my own arms against my chest. Kai leaned his head on my shoulder, adding just a little more physical weight to my emotional baggage.

"No matter how much I hate my past, I can't go back and change anything. You have opened my eyes to how great it is to be with someone special, that not all relationships are the same. The feeling I get when I'm with you is so pure; I want to cherish it for as long as I possibly can. I like you a lot, Nila, so the thought of worrying you sickens me. I don't want to ruin anything we've already built, I just wanna keep making it stronger. So, please, don't be hung up on stuff I can't erase."

Understanding the pain I was causing him by bringing up his past, I held my tongue to any further inquiries regarding Momiji or his other sexual partners.

Kai lifted his head off my shoulder and released his hold on me, making his way back down to the futon. "Good night, Nila."

Feeling terrible about pressuring Kai to talk about someone he no longer was, I wasn't able to find a comfortable position, and sleep eluded me.

Half an hour passed and a good night's sleep was still far from my reach. Wondering if Kai was also having a hard time falling asleep, I rolled over to the side of my bed and decided to take a peek. To my surprise, there was a pair of eyes staring right back at me. Not knowing we would both be facing the direction of the other, we were taken by surprise.

"You're still awake?"

"Yeah, you too, I guess?" he answered, lying on his side with one arm exposed over the blanket.

"Mhm."

"Can't sleep?"

"Not really," I admitted. "My mind keeps thinking about absolutely everything and anything. It won't shut off."

Laughing under his breath, he rolled onto his back and looked up at the ceiling. "Me too."

The single arm once exposed out in the open, now rested behind his head as support.

For whatever reason, I want to be closer to him right now. Would it be weird if I asked him to lie in bed with me? What am I even saying, of course it would!

Hesitant to ask my inner thoughts; words began to tumble out on their own. "Ah, um, if it's al-alright with you, could you lie with me in my bed . . .? Just until I fall asleep?"

Surprised by what I was asking, he looked at me with widened eyes. "Are you sure?"

"Mhm."

"Y-yeah, I can do that."

"JUST until I fall asleep though!" I reassured.

"Okay."

Kai pulled the covers back and stood up, cautiously making his way to my bed once again. I scooted closer to the wall, making room for him. Once we were both settled in, I faced away from him out of embarrassment. My heart was beating a thousand times per second. Clouded thoughts, mixed with constant fear and anxiety, ran through me. I was starting to rethink my decision, but now it was definitely too late to back out. His body was so close to mine, and his breath was blowing against the hair on the nape of my neck. My body began to tense up.

OH MY GOD, OH MY GOD, OH MY GOD! What am I doing? This isn't like me! Never in a million years would I have suggested something like this before! Why did I think this was a good idea? When I'm with him, I never seem to know what I'm doing. Even though I'm nervous as hell, and every part of my body is FREAKING OUT, having him close is also oddly comfort-ing. I'm really glad he asked to stay over.

While I was zoning out, a soft laugh came from behind me.

"What?" I asked, turning halfway to talk to him.

"Nothing."

"Liar! What is it?" I said, completely flipping over to face him.

With a playful smirk, he grabbed my face with one hand and squeezed my cheeks together, squishing my lips to mimic a fish. "You're worrying way too much. Nothing is gonna happen. I promised, remember? Even though you're insanely toying with my manly urges," he teased, ruffling my hair. "I won't do anything. So, go to sleep."

"Okay," I said quietly.

He pulled my face closer, placing a kiss on my forehead. "Good night."

As if we weren't close enough, he pulled me into his arms and held me like that for the remainder of the time I spent awake.

"Nila, what should we order? Tea perhaps?"

"Yeah! Oh, Daddy, can I get a cookie? Please, please, please!"

With the usual warm smile, he nodded his head. "Of course. What about you, little man?"

"No tea, Daddy—juice!"

With the same smile, he answered, "You got it, Ken."

At our regular café, with the regular waitress, he placed our regular order. Like usual, the waitress mentally jotted everything down before scur-rying off.

"Daddy, how come we always come here?"

"Well, Nila, Tuesday is Daddy's only early day off work. That means I can come and pick you and Ken up from school. And, since this café is close to your school, Daddy thinks it's nice to stop in, just the three of us. Don't you agree?"

"Yeah!"

"Me too, me too!" Kenji added, not wanting to feel left out of the conversation.

With a satisfied chuckle, he placed his hand on top of Kenji's head, messing up the hair our mother spent time styling earlier that morning. "I'm glad you both like coming here, because Daddy likes this place very much."

"Yeah, they have good cookies!"

"And the bestest juice!" added Kenji.

"The 'bestest,'" our father repeated with a smile.

Chapter Twenty-Seven

THE NEXT MORNING, Kai woke me up with a soft kiss on my forehead. When I opened my eyes, he was already fully dressed in his uniform.

I hope I didn't snore last night! Flipping over onto my stomach, I shoved my face into the pillow to hide my embarrassing morning self from Kai. *Hmm, the pillow smells just like him.*

Kai told me he wanted to leave before me for all of two reasons: one, he knew I had to leave early to meet up with Kenji, and two, he didn't want my neighbours to see us leaving together in case word got back to my mother that he had spent the night. He was thoughtful and always planned ahead when it involved me, that was one trait I really liked about him. No matter how pushy Kai could be at times, he was always considerate.

Not paying attention to the time, I was almost late in meeting up with Kenji at the hospital. Still unsure about whether or not I should meet with my father one-on-one, my heart was left in turmoil as I gave myself a headache just thinking about it.

Preparing for a school day had become a robotic routine since junior high. Each day I dressed in my uniform, packed my bag, and boxed up my bento, and today was no different. I hardly had a chance to look at the homework from the last couple of days, which was unlike me. Most of the readings were already completed because I had worked ahead, but the worksheets Kida brought me were barely touched.

I caught the next bus and rode it to the hospital, passing my school in the process. The early bird students were entering through the main gate, chatting happily with each other as they did every morning. For a quick moment, I was envious of the boring lives some of the students at my school led. What amazed me most was that in such a short period of time, I went from living a quiet, isolated life, interacting with the few people around me, to living a loud, threatening one.

Deep in thought, no longer paying attention to the world outside the moving window, I had come to a stop in front of the hospital. I sent Kenji a quick message through Line to let him know I had arrived and would be up to our mother's room shortly.

Just like yesterday, I went to the front desk to sign in. The lady at the desk wrote my name, the date, and the time I arrived on a clipboard hanging on the wall beside her, giving me the okay to go up.

During the elevator ride, my heart began to beat faster. Stepping off on the second floor, the realization that I would soon be discussing the depths of my mother's cancer with Dr. Ashima, smacked me in the face. No matter how hard I tried, all I could think about was the probability that Dr. Ashima would be informing Kenji and I on how much time our mother had left.

Walking down the hallway towards my mother's room, I saw Kenji sitting outside on one of the chairs.

"Kenji," I said in a loud whisper, walking faster to meet him. "Why are you sitting out here?"

Looking in my direction, he rose to his feet. "Mom's still sleeping; I didn't want you to come in and wake her."

"Oh, okay. Are you ready to speak with Dr. Ashima?"

"Yeah," he said in a monotone.

"Everything alright? How did last night go?"

"I told Mom . . . ."

Before he could continue, Dr. Ashima popped out from around the corner of the connecting hallway.

"Ah, good, you are both here. If you have time, I would like to have a word regarding your mother's condition."

Although longing to know what Kenji was about to say, I was forced to put the thought on hold in order to speak with Dr. Ashima. "We were about to come and find you for the same reason," I stated.

"Excellent. Let us take this into my office. This way."

Dr. Ashima led the way to his office as Kenji and I silently followed. His office was on the opposite side of the second floor, alongside some other offices and a small cafeteria where a couple of nurses were on break drinking coffee and watching TV.

When we entered his office, Dr. Ashima directed us to sit down in two chairs facing a large wooden desk with a luxurious leather chair behind it. As we took our seats, he shut the door and made his way behind the desk. Even though the office was spacious, having the door closed made things feel smaller and more confined. Coming here today, I told myself I was prepared to speak with Dr. Ashima, but now, it felt like I was trapped in a shrinking room, unsure of what to say or how to escape.

As the doctor collected some paperwork, most likely in regard to our mother, I peeked at Kenji from the corner of my eye and saw a blank expression masking his face.

"Alright," Dr. Ashima commenced. "Today, I want to speak with the two of you as your mother's friend, but she has also authorized me to inform you about the basics of her illness. She feels that if the information comes from me, in the form of a mediator, there will be less conflict."

As her friend . . . ?

"I will also discuss things medically, as I am obligated to do so, but I want to speak freely with you. As I previously informed you, your mother has cancer and has been dealing with it for quite a while now, without any form of treatment. After running a few tests, we were able to confirm that the cancer has spread to both her breasts. At this time, we are still uncertain how far, or how quickly, it may spread, but her platelets are dangerously low. Breast-Conserving Surgery or a Mastectomy are on the table for discussion amongst the doctors, but as of yet, nothing has been determined as the best possible route, since your mother is also hesitant to proceed."

There it was, the words I feared the most. The thoughts which had run through my head in the elevator moments ago, were slowly becoming a reality, soon to affect my entire world. Looking at Kenji, he wore the exact same blank expression as before.

Why isn't he reacting? He lashed out the last couple of times when it came to Mom . . . What's going through his damn head?

"Now, I do not want to scare you, that is not my intention, but I do not intend to sugar-coat things like your mother wants me to do. As your mother's friend, I am begging you, help me convince her to proceed and finish treatment." Dr. Ashima shifted his eyes back and forth between us, waiting to receive some sign of reassurance before looking down and sighing heavily. "I know the situation with your father is not ideal . . .."

"It's not anything," Kenji added strictly, interrupting Dr. Ashima.

I looked at Kenji and saw his face finally shift, showing some emotion. He looked heated at the mere mention of our father. I began to wonder. If I were to tell him about our father's recent activities, would he lose it?

"Yes, well," Dr. Ashima pressed forward. "Are there any other family members you can consult with about this matter? I will do my best to help you, but dealing with a parent who has cancer is hard on a family with both parents in the picture; I cannot imagine the two of you dealing with this on your own. We also need to take into account the fact that you are both underage, for legal matters."

Waiting to see if Kenji would be the first one to respond again, I remained silent for a few seconds before answering for the both of us. "No, we have no close family who live nearby. Our mother is an only child, and our grandparents on her side have already passed. We haven't spoken to the relatives on our father's side since our parent's separation."

Watching the uneasiness increase in Dr. Ashima's face, made me worry more than before. It was at times like these that having a big, close-knit family was desirable. Being the older sibling always came with added pressure, as if I were expected to figure everything out.

Dr. Ashima seems willing to help us, but how can we convince Mom to go ahead with treatment? We're just kids!

Trying to avoid the unruly family dynamic, Dr. Ashima composed himself before moving to the next topic. "I would like to discuss the options of chemotherapy and radiation. Now I warn you, these methods of treatment have a high probability in altering your mother's body drastically. Noticeable to the human eye, she could lose her hair and appetite, which may cause weight fluctuations. There may also be discoloration of her skin. Even with all the side effects, I do highly recommend these methods considering the stage of your mother's breast cancer. These are the treatments with the best-recorded results. She will also be prescribed other medications to take daily. Most of these medications are already covered by insurance and by the hospital, in part because your mother is an employee here—I will make sure of it. However, that does not necessarily account for anything that may change with future developments. Now, I know this is a lot to think about, and I am giving you both a lot of information to try and process, but there will be remaining medical expenses I cannot help with. I am not sure how you want to deal with the method of payment for the remainder of treatment, considering I do not know your family's monetary situation, but the financial department can better assist you in that area. Normally, this responsibility is not left with minors such as yourselves, but Shino is a valued employee here, and a dear friend—we need to act fast."

Dr. Ashima ended his explanation, giving us time to let everything sink in.

This isn't the first time he's called Mom by her first name.

Thinking back, I remembered how highly my mother spoke of Dr. Ashima, and how much she admired him as her superior and as a professional. His name never left a bad taste in her mouth. Apparently, he'd been working at the hospital long before my mother even started.

Focusing on what we should do next, I looked to Kenji for some sort of guidance, and for the first time within this meeting, he glanced back with the same kind of expression.

"Kenji?" I said, almost in a whisper.

Turning back towards Dr. Ashima, as if he understood what I was thinking, he responded. "We will convince her to go through with the treatment. I have a bit of money saved up from my part-time job, so I should be able to cover the first round of expenses, then we can go from there. Our mother is a private person, so I have no idea where we stand financially."

Part-time job? When did he get one? Mom's never allowed us to have jobs because of school, so when did he . . . .

"Perfect. Miss Izawa, are you on board with these treatment options? I would like a confirmation from both of you before speaking with your mother and directing my team."

"Y-yes," I answered, a bit shaken by the fact this whole discussion could possibly lead to my mother's death shortly down the road.

"Alright. I will have a proper discussion with your mother. There is paperwork that needs to be filled out, but we can worry about that part later. We will—"

"What if she denies treatment?" Kenji asked, cutting the doctor off from his constructive speech.

"Let us not wander down that path just yet," Dr. Ashima advised.

Kenji sat upright in his chair. "No, tell it to me straight," Kenji's eyes were aflame. "She'll die, right?"

"Mr. Izawa . . . ."

"Tell me, Goddammit!"

Stunned by Kenji's outburst, I didn't know what I could do to control him. "Kenji!"

"Mr. Izawa, you are correct. Unfortunately, this is not an illness that will treat itself. My goal here today is to make sure we are all on the same page before your mother's condition worsens. I am hoping you and your sister will help me persuade her to agree to receive treatment. While she is still able, she can go through the paperwork and sign off on it herself. The staff and myself were hoping . . . ."

"I get it," Kenji said powerfully. "We'll try. But in the end, it's her choice to live—not ours. Don't put that kind of pressure on us." With those final words, Kenji rose from the chair and walked out the door.

Though it was harsh and sickening to hear, I knew what Kenji said was true. The fact that Dr. Ashima left it up to us to convince our mother to go through with the treatment, was ridiculous. I already previously brought up treatment with our mother, and she turned it down. How were we supposed to get her to accept treatment after she's been refusing it for so long? After all, we were just a pair of hopeless, teenage kids.

I bowed and thanked Dr. Ashima for his time, then rushed after Kenji. By the time I reached him, he was already back in our mother's room. When I entered, he was standing by her bed discussing chemotherapy and radiation.

"You're gonna start receiving chemo. It's already been decided," Kenji informed harshly.

"Excuse me? I most certainly will not! That imprudent Ashima—what did he say to you?" she fought back.

"Don't be stupid!" Kenji retaliated.

"Watch what you say to me, young man, I am your mother!"

"And that's the way I want you to stay," he said, intensively looking at her. "What are you afraid of?"

"Kenji . . .."

"No, you're not even trying; it's like you've given up. This is not a simple cold, Mom. Do you want to leave us that badly?"

Again, Kenji was right. That was the exact attitude my mother was having towards this situation, and he was finally able to put it into words. She wasn't getting treatment for the cancer; she wasn't slowing down or monitoring her condition at all. In fact, she had worked harder, picking up shifts, as if she was purposely trying to shorten her life. Instead of facing it, trying everything in her power to get better, she'd spent most of her time at work and away from home—away from us.

"Of course, I don't want to leave you! Why on earth would you say such a thing?"

"Because, you've been working a lot more recently and we barely get to see you, even though you know you're sick," I chimed in from behind.

"Nila . . .," she spoke softly.

"Mom, please. Dad's not around . . . we can't lose you, too," I choked, trying to hold back the tears.

My mother's composure broke. Kenji stood in silence with his head lowered as she cried before him. With Kenji's back towards me, I couldn't see his face, but I knew it must have been in rough shape, just like mine. My mother was wiping the tears from her eyes, but they fell quicker than she could remove them. With her teary eyes shut, she nodded in agreement. I ran to give her a hug, while Kenji turned around, making his way out.

Before stepping through the door, he held onto the frame with one hand and spoke over his shoulder. "I'll go tell Dr. Ashima everything's been decided."

I embraced my mother quietly, giving her as much time and comfort as she needed. She had her arms wrapped around my waist, hugging me tight. I didn't dare look down at my mother's face for fear I'd be unable to control my own tears from falling.

"Nila, weren't you supposed to be in school?"

"I was going to go in for the second half, but I don't think I will."

Pulling away, she looked at me with deep concern, flaring her nostrils. "You shouldn't be missing school so close to exams. I've told you this already," she scolded.

"Mom, I know, but this isn't something I want to miss. Plus, I wouldn't be able to concentrate knowing you were here like this."

"I'm sorry. Things will return to normal soon."

"Your definition of 'normal' is slightly distorted."

"You might be right," she answered distantly, sitting up straight as she wiped the remaining tears.

It wasn't long before Kenji returned with Dr. Ashima and a nurse carrying a large file folder. The nurse opened the folder and went over the chemotherapy and radiation treatments, as Dr. Ashima explained all options to us in detail. There was a prearranged schedule Dr. Ashima thought was best suited for our mother to begin with. At first, our mother would go through a couple sessions of radiation, followed by chemotherapy. Later on, the dosage amounts would be altered accordingly, depending on how well her body responded.

In the file, the nurse wrote down pieces of information my mother gave her regarding eating habits, daily routines, family history, and many other things which made absolutely no sense to me. Each time Dr. Ashima or the nurse spoke of a drug my mother would be taking, I felt like a child listening in on an adult conversation.

My mother had a series of appointments pre-booked at the hospital with Dr. Ashima and his team before she could receive any medication. With all this talk about cancer and medication, anxiety built inside me, crawling up my throat and painfully straining the tiny air passage. The noise in the room intensified. Each time Dr. Ashima spoke in medical terms with my mother, I wanted to cover my ears. Trying to avoid drawing attention to myself, I started taking quiet, deep breaths in my seat, hoping to end the small panic attack before anyone noticed.

Concluding the conversation, Dr. Ashima announced that my mother would be on a leave of absence from work and could only return once she achieved remission. For some reason, in the back of my mind, the word *when* kept turning into *if.*

School was done by the time Dr. Ashima and his nurse finished discussing the treatment plan with us. I left Kenji in charge of our mother as he prepared her things to go home. As per Dr. Ashima's orders, she was allowed to go home freely after each appointment until the chemotherapy sessions started.

I lied to Kenji by telling him I had a couple of things to pick up for our mother before heading home. He waved me off, assuring me my absence wasn't a problem and that he could handle taking our mother back on his own. With his go-ahead, I took my first steps into the direction of a familiar emptiness.

While Kenji dealt with our mother, I headed downtown to the café in order to meet with our father. The whole time Dr. Ashima spoke to us, the more I sat and thought wholesomely about our broken family. I compiled a list of questions I wanted answers to, and the only way I was going to get them was through my father.

Lately, the town's main source of transportation was where I spent most of my time. Travelling from one place to another, the bus became one of the places I did most of my thinking and decision making. Looking at my phone, Kai had sent a couple of messages throughout the day, asking if everything was alright and if there were any updates on my mother. With a quiet moment to myself, I sent a message back letting him know what my family and the doctor had decided. In the same message, I also informed Kai I was on my way to meet up with my father, like the voicemail requested. Immediately, I received a reply. Kai asked if I was ready to do this alone or if I wanted him to accompany me. Thanking him for his offer, I kindly declined.

I don't know how this will turn out, but Kai, I'm so glad to have met you. You came into my life EXACTLY when I needed you.

Getting off the bus and making my way to the train station, my heartbeat increased. The station had new renovations almost every year as our small town slowly expanded. A new section was always being added or redone in order to maintain the building and keep it looking modern for tourists. This was one of a few reasons I avoided taking the train. Another was that it was mainly used to connect people to major cities or larger stations with bullet trains, something I rarely needed to do. Other than that, the train only ran between two places in town: the station and the local college. So, if you wanted to get out of here, this was your best ticket.

In front of the train station stood a statue of a man named Etsuko Miyata. The station had been renamed after Mr. Miyata, for his devotion to the town's homeless children. One day, on our way to the café, my father told us the story of a great man who took in and watched over abandoned children in all neighbouring towns. Without expecting payment or recognition, Mr. Miyata did everything he could for the children out of the kindness of his heart. Every time we passed Miyata Station, my father put on a serious expression and bowed to the statue, silently thanking the man for his selfless work. Now, every time I walked by it, regardless of who I was with, I felt obligated to do the same.

Without a snowfall in a while, the weather outside had improved to a tolerable temperature. Instead of a thick layer of snow, the ground was drowning in slush, turning what was once dirt into mud. The trees were still bare, but somehow felt livelier than they did before Christmas. Looking up, the sky was grey with bright blue pockets peeking through.

The closer I got to the café, the more fear spread through me. My heartbeat continued to accelerate until it reached the pace of an unsteady drum.

Arriving, approximately ten minutes before the scheduled time, I marched to the door and reached for its handle. With my hand hovering over, I couldn't grab it for the life of me. My brain commanded my hand to 'just grab it,' but my heavy heart pulled back, pleading 'don't touch it.' With conflicting emotions, I went with the judgment of my heart. I dropped my hand to my side and took a step back. Behind me, a small line of people wanting to enter the café formed. Their whispers of *'What is she doing?'* startled me. Not wanting to disturb anyone, I stepped off to the side, facing the café's huge, top to bottom, glass windows.

What am I doing here? I can't do this. There is no way I can meet this man after two years like nothing's happened. Why did I even convince myself to come? I'm not ready to face him . . . and I don't even know if I want to.

"Nila."

With my name called, I froze into a complete sheet of ice. Having absolutely no confidence in my ability to turn around, or to give myself time to process who the voice belonged to, I used the window as a mirror to reflect the person standing behind me. To my pleasant surprise, it wasn't the man I feared it would be.

"Kai!" I shouted in relief, turning around to hug him.

He hugged me before taking a step back to catch himself. "I know you said you could do this alone, but something inside me told me to come. I hope you're not mad?"

Unable to verbally admit I was glad he disobeyed my request, I shook my head with assurance. "How did you know I'd be at this specific café?" I asked, pushing away from his chest to look up.

"Yesterday on the couch, you mentioned a café near the train station, and since there aren't many around here, I pieced it together."

"Thank you." My eyes were smeared with tears.

"Nila, are you sure you're okay?" he asked, wiping my tears with his scarf.

Without looking at him, I admitted what was buried in my heart. "I don't think I can do this. I don't know if I actually want to see him."

Grabbing onto my shoulders, he pulled me in towards him again. Using the window as a mirror once more, I saw Kai's head turn from side-to-side as he looked all around us.

"Here, this way." He grabbed my hand and led me back across the street into a small ice cream parlour beside Miyata Station. We sat at a window-side table for two.

"What are we doing? It's way too cold for ice cream. We're legitimately the only ones in here."

"Clearly," he answered sarcastically, using his hand as a guide to unveil the empty shop. "We're here to wait."

"Wait for what?"

With an accepting smile, he answered, "Your dad."

The only employee in the entire parlour came out from the back of the shop and quickly took notice of our appearance. As the employee was about to make his way over to take our order, Kai stopped him.

"It's okay, man. We just need to borrow this space for a bit. Sadly, ice cream's not in the cards."

The employee shrugged his shoulders and went straight to the back again.

"So, we're just going to wait here?" I asked.

"Yep. This way, you decide when you're ready to go."

A smile crept upon my face as I turned to look out the window, watching random people enter and exit the café.

Minutes later, the man I was terrified to face, appeared in front of the building. He took a quick look around before heading in, most definitely keeping an eye out for me. Twenty minutes went by as I continued to sit in the ice cream parlour with Kai, not saying a word. It was hard to believe that across the street from where I was, my father waited for me. No matter how hard I willed it, my legs wouldn't budge from the seat.

"Nila . . . it's been quite a while."

Still facing the window, I thought out loud, "Do you think he'll wait there for an hour?"

"Not sure. Do you intend on making him wait that long?" Kai reversed the question.

"Not sure."

Until the hospital incident, I thought my biggest fear would've been seeing my father again. When I went to Kai's house and saw that my father had been living carefree next door to the Kento residence all this time, none of it felt real. The fact that he lived so close with his new family, never coming back to see us, was eating me up inside.

Sitting in the empty parlour, I finally realized my fear wasn't in facing my father; it was what came after that haunted me. What would I get out of this 'talk'? A sense of worth? Acceptance? Recognition that I'm still important to him? Before, it was easy to push him away because he simply wasn't around. Now, he's made multiple appearances, and I wasn't sure what to make of it or what he was planning. Just as I was getting used to not having a father present in my life, he popped up out of the blue.

Tired of being at war with myself, my legs started to move on their own, standing up nice and tall, with a bit of shakiness to them.

Kai remained seated as he looked up at me from the table. "I'll be here when you're done."

With an unsure smile, I signalled my understanding and made my way towards the exit. Standing outside the parlour, I paused. The option of turning back was there, an easy way out was just an arm's length away, but my legs pressed forward. They continued taking me across the street until I was faced with the café's door for a second time.

Chapter Twenty-Eight

ITH MY HAND on the handle, walking inside was the next step, but it was hard for me to move. I held my breath, as if I were about to dive underwater, and finally opened the door. Inside, I scanned my surroundings. Within a second, I made eye contact with the man once known as my father. Watching me enter, he waved his arm back and forth obnoxiously. For a moment, I remained frozen at the entrance. He was sitting at a table for four near the back, away from any windows, with a cup of coffee placed in front of him. There was a small bowl of sugar in the middle of the table, along with a second cup off to the side that looked to have already been used. Approaching the table, he stood, then adjusted his dress shirt and straightened his tie, making me feel slightly underdressed.

"Peaches," he said, eyes full of excitement as he gestured me to have a seat.

The hair on the back of my neck stood up after hearing the nickname he used, while panic coursed through my entire body. My hands became moist and clammy. I could feel the heat of flames engulfing me as the fire intensified, burning straight through my cheeks and engraving itself onto my face.

"Sorry . . . old habits," he said, smiling nervously. "Please, sit."

I took off my jacket and placed it over the back of my chair. As I did this, my father sat down.

"Kenji couldn't make it?"

"No."

"I see," he said with a crooked smile. "I'm terribly sorry to be troubling you like this. I'm sure my message came as a surprise."

"Just a bit," I added snobbishly. I could feel myself harbouring an unpleasant attitude and using it towards him unintentionally.

Half smiling, he brushed off my rudeness. "Tea, and a cookie, perhaps?"

"Hmm?"

"Your usual order. It's my treat. I'll order it for you."

"No, thank you. I'm fine."

"You sure? Because it's no trouble—"

"STOP!" I shouted out of frustration, slamming my hands on the table in response to the unsettling environment my father tried to create. "Stop trying to make this seem like old times, because it's not."

I watched my father's face shift from being shocked, to a half-assed smile like before. His calm demeanour was starting to get on my nerves.

"Sorry, I guess you're right." Taking a sip, he changed the topic. "How's your mother doing?"

How's my mother doing? Why does he even care? "Fine . . .?"

"I see."

With frustration only building, I couldn't help but ask the question bouncing around in the back of my mind. "Why am I here?"

Placing his cup on the table, he pushed it closer to the centre to prop his elbows down, leaving both arms crossed in front of him. "Nila, you have to understand something. Your mother and I loved each other very much, but it wasn't enough to keep us together."

Hearing my father admit he no longer harboured feelings towards my mother, made my heart ache.

"I know why you came, and I intend on answering any questions you have, but I also came here for a specific reason. Your mother has given you her side of the story, and I want to give you mine. I will not make excuses for anything over these last few years. Decent human beings can still do terrible things; I know I'm at fault and what I did was absolutely wrong. All I ask, is for you to please keep an open mind when I give you the answers you seek."

His face looked sincere; his dark brown eyes begged for my understanding. I nodded in agreement, but truthfully knew I couldn't keep any promises.

"Where should we start?" he asked, straightening out his back in the chair.

Start? I never really thought about what my first question would be. All this time, acting out scenarios in my head about how this conversation would go, and what I'd ask him when the time came, were pointless. I had no idea where to begin.

Noticing my struggle, my father took the initiative. "You're graduating this year, right? How's school going? I'm sure you're still at the top of your class," he smiled.

I can't do this. I can't do this normal, small talk. A conversation like this would usually be done during dinner with your family . . . a family who shows up to dinner. Not like this, not with him. "I can't . . .," I commenced, lowering my head. "I can't talk like nothing's happened."

"Nila . . .."

"There was no doubt in my mind you would keep your promise to come back, but you never did. Hours, days, weeks, and even months went by as Kenji and I waited for you—all for nothing. You make it seem like you've only been gone for a few weeks, when in reality, you've been gone with the new family you abandoned us for, for more than two years. TWO YEARS!"

Looking up, I could see my father's serious face, as his mouth stiffened and his neck and back stretched tall. The eyes from patrons around us quickly focused their attention on our table.

I rose, reaching for my things. "This was a mistake."

As I was about to walk away, the sound of customers clearing their throats became overpowering, a polite warning to settle down. One of the waitresses even made eye contact with me as if to ask if everything was alright.

"Nila," my father's voice projected assertively, "sit down."

I recognized this tone. It was the tone my father used when he was upset. This tone often came out when he was speaking with Kenji or my mother, but not usually with me. I sat back down, tossing my things onto one of the empty chairs, regretting my decision to have come at all.

With the same stern tone, he continued. "Nila, what do you want me to say? That I'm sorry? Will that fix everything? Because if it will, I'll say it a hundred—no, a thousand times. But, for some reason, I don't think a mere 'sorry' will correct my wrongdoings."

My hands were clamming up again. I quaked in fear, listening to the forceful voice my father rarely used on me, even as a child. Staring into his intimidating eyes, I could tell he was starting to notice I was uncomfortable and scared.

"Sorry," he apologized, placing his hand above his eyes and slowly sliding it down, ending the motion at his chin. "I didn't mean to be so harsh with you, that is not why I arranged this."

"You lied. You lied to me."

"Lied to you . . .? What do you mean?"

Trying to hold back the tears that choked me, I attempted to clear my throat so the words wouldn't come out in a slur. "You . . . promised," I said slowly, eyes full of water. "You p-promised you'd be back, but . . .." That was it. Those were the only words I could get out before a single tear rolled down my cheek in defeat; I never knew my chest could hurt so bad. "You never came home!"

I've once heard that when you see someone crying, it makes it harder to refrain from crying yourself. It must have been the case with my father because when I looked at him, he was crying as well. This was the first time I had ever seen my father cry.

He reached out for my hand, and I didn't hesitate to give it to him. Holding my hand with such a strong grip, I could feel an extreme warmth caused by the cup of coffee he held. His hand, much bigger than mine, was familiar, a rough texture I had almost forgotten. For as long as I can remember, my father never had smooth hands like my mother. My mother used a lot of lotions, while my father had permanent scars and calluses all over his. Though it was long ago, it was easy to picture his giant, sandpaper-like hands, tickling my sides during our tickle wars.

It hurt to see my father shed tears. It made me realize, being an adult didn't mean you knew everything, and it didn't mean you always made the right choices. Oddly, it made him human. As I grow older, I understand that all humans make mistakes, but from a child's perspective, parents weren't supposed to make mistakes. Unfortunately, his mistakes didn't affect him alone. It shattered our entire family into pieces.

Composing himself, he wiped away the tears from his eyes and released my hand. "I received the divorce papers from your mother the other day. I thought you should know where your mother and I stand as of now."

"I see," I said lightly, inhaling cautiously before continuing. "So, she finally did it."

"Did what?"

"I took a peek at the paperwork she left lying around in the kitchen, but didn't realize she had filled it out so quickly. She has been talking about divorce for a while . . .."

"Nila . . .." Speaking my name in confusion, his expression turned grim. "Your mother wasn't the one who filed for the divorce, I was."

Not wanting to misunderstand what my father was telling me, I politely corrected him. "No, I saw the documents on the kitchen table. She went as far as changing her last name and everything."

"Nila . . . I sent her those papers because I plan on remarrying soon."

What . . .? Devastated by my father's words, I leaned back in the chair as my hand left the table and fell directly into my lap. My jaw dropped. "Re . . . marry? ALREADY? To that woman who had your 'lovechild'!" I accused loudly. "Are you insane?"

My chest tightened with each word I spat out. I wished I could have avoided such confrontation; the words leaving my mouth were disgusting, making me want to vomit. My heart raged with anger and hatred for this 'mistress' of his. The one who gave birth to my 'half-brother' and future 'half-sibling', about whom I almost forgot. I wasn't sure who I hated more; this mysterious woman who ruined my parent's marriage, or my father for being so easily swayed by a whore.

"How . . . do you know about the child?" he asked, caught off guard.

Lowering my eyes, I stared blankly at my father's cup, watching the steam vaporize in the air. "I met him—Yano . . . on my way to my boy-friend's house."

My father didn't respond right away. Still choosing not to face him directly, I waited until his reply was ready.

"You've . . . met him? My son, your brother, Yano," he said in amazement. "He never mentioned any—"

"He didn't know who I was."

"Who is . . . your boyfriend?" he asked, somewhat frantically.

"Kai Kento, your neighbour," I announced with devilish satisfaction.

"Kento . . . Boy . . . friend. Boyfriend! But you're . . .," he stopped himself, knowing what he was about to say was inappropriate. "How long have you known where I live?"

"Does it matter?"

A look of deeper concern washed over his face as his eyes widened. "Does Kenji know?"

"I never told him, so he doesn't know about Yano, or your future child with THAT woman."

"So, you know we're expecting again," he muttered under his breath, placing his hand on his forehead and ringing it up through the tips of his hair. "How stupid. To think I could break this news to you in person, was foolish." My father seemed troubled by the way he rubbed his temples in circles. "Can you please not call her 'that woman'? Her name is Chizuko."

He can give her whatever name he wants, but I will call her whatever I want. This woman ruined everything; I will never accept her OR her bastard children. "How can you have two children with a woman you aren't even married to? How despicable."

"Nila," he said strictly. "No matter how much you dislike me right now, I am still your father. Please watch what you say and how you say it."

Rolling my eyes, he continued to talk as if I was interested in hearing about his new woman. Pretending to listen, I remembered Kai said he would wait in the ice cream parlour until I was done; approximately thirty minutes ago.

"Your mother," he went on, changing the flow of the conversation, "is sick. The reason I showed my face at the hospital was because Dr.

Ashima's nurse called to inform me she had cancer and had been hospitalized. She still has me listed as her emergency contact."

I felt myself choking on air each time I took a breath. Everything about this meeting was a mistake, and I made the biggest one of all by thinking I could get closure by hearing him out. There was nothing he could say that could fix what was broken, because he was the problem, not the solution.

Using a much calmer tone, he continued. "Your mother and I only just filed for divorce, so legally I'm still the first point of contact for emergencies until everything changes over. I decided to visit her that morning because I figured you both would be in school, but I should've known you would be by your mother's side. I went to the hospital to tell her exactly what I'm telling you now." He paused, taking a forced breath. "I want to end this war between your mother and I. I want to be able to see my children, like any father would."

Angered by my father's greed, I bit my lip because nothing but more disrespectful words wanted to come out. I needed to calm down before I said something I would regret. I wasn't sure what my father had thought he would gain from seeing me, but right then, nothing worked in his favour. He'd spoken as if my mother had been the one keeping us from seeing him, putting the blame solely on her, but that wasn't the case in the slightest.

"Why didn't you come back? Why didn't you come back to visit us? We didn't move; we stayed in the same house, a house you once lived happily in!"

My father looked down at his cup which no longer steamed, silently keeping to himself.

Frustrated by my father's lack of communication, I pressed on questioning him. "You promised you'd answer my questions, or was that a lie, too?"

Finally having the courage to look up, he stared straight into my eyes. "I was terrified to face you and your brother. Fear kept me away. The fear of you both hating me and saying it to my face, would be unbearable. I knew you were probably cursing me behind my back, and I deserved every bit of it because I ran like a coward. I made an unacceptable mistake, one I cannot take back. I do not regret any of my children; I never have, and I never will. I'll also never regret the amount of love I've had in my lifetime. Just like Etsuko Miyata, I could not abandon such a young child and mother who needed my support. If I did, then what kind of man would I be?"

"BUT YOU ABANDONED US! You are THAT kind of man because you did it to us!"

Frightened by my aggressive and cut-throat tone, his wide assertive eyes turned soft and depressed. If everyone in the café wasn't staring at us before, they sure as hell were now.

"Nila, you're absolutely right," he said in a quiet voice, taking control of the sound level. "I guess, at the time, I figured you were both old enough to handle yourselves and would be okay if I wasn't around all the time."

"You weren't around at all," I corrected.

"I KNOW . . . I know. The more I stayed away, the more ashamed I was to call myself your father and go back. Then, after hearing from your mother how you both felt about me, I thought it was best to stay away permanently."

"From Mom? What does she have to do with you abandoning us?"

Tilting his head, he replied, "She told me you both wanted nothing to do with me, and if I never showed my face again, you'd be better off."

Confused by my father's words, I attempted to correct him again. "We never said that! At least I didn't. Yes, there were countless times when we said we hated you, but I don't remember us ever saying we no longer wished to see you. Every day, we waited endlessly for you to return home."

"Ah," he said sadly. "So, it was like that then . . . ."

Hesitating once more, he got up from the seat across from me and sat in the one beside me. Leaning over, he hugged me as tight as he possibly could, while I was at a loss for words. It all happened so fast; I was left completely defenceless. My arms remained motionless at my sides as I desperately tried to hold back tears.

To me, there were two main categories of emotions which produced tears: happy and sad. For me, I was able to add an extra category, much smaller and more complex. These were tears I'd kept locked away for the past couple of years, solely triggered by my father. They were the tears I'd cried two years before, the ones that fell for a month straight after he left. After a whole month of having bloodshot eyes and barely going to school, I had decided it was best to lock away those feelings and replace them with hatred. I never wanted to feel those heavy emotions or cry that much again. As soon as my father embraced me, the lock on my heart broke, allowing all those emotions to escape.

"I'm so sorry, Peaches," he whispered calmly into my ear. "I'm so unbelievably sorry."

My obnoxious crying and deep breathing returned, overpowering his. I had no control over my breathing and ended up choking many times on air and tears. Tears flowed out of me like a river, streaming down my face and soaking my father's shirt. His shirt smelled of the cologne he always wore, giving me a familiar sense of comfort. This was it. This is what I had wanted for so long, my father's heartfelt embrace. I was soaring on the wings of happiness as my once bottled emotions raced wildly within me, finally breaking free.

My father never returned to his original seat. Instead, he brought his cold cup of coffee to his new spot. We continued talking about the past before switching over to things currently going on in my life, lightly touching upon Kenji and how he was carrying on. Our conversation drew to an end as my father pulled back his sleeve to check his watch.

Rising, my father faced me and bowed. "Nila," he commenced, remaining in a bent position, "I know there are no words or actions I can say or do to make up for all the time lost, and I won't excuse my poor behaviour either. I know I'm a good-for-nothing man, and even more so a good-for-nothing father, but I want to try and repair what was lost. I want to fix it as best I can, and treasure it for the rest of my life, like I should have been doing all along. You have both gone without a father for too long; I don't want you to go through the rest of your lives without me. Nila," my father raised his head, "even if we take baby steps, please— PLEASE, let's try to make this work. I want to be a part of your lives and I want you both to be a part of mine."

Standing up straight, my father stared at me as he waited for a reply.

Not being able to find the words, I nodded. I wasn't sure about a single thing; in fact, instead of getting all the answers, I accumulated more questions. Even if I agreed to try, would anything get resolved? Could things be remotely close to how they once were? Unfortunately, these were questions I knew no one could answer.

I gathered my things, buttoning up the last button on my coat before returning to face my father. He stood with newfound confidence, hugging me one final time before needing to part. It was during this hug that I realized, my father didn't just want to be forgiven—he NEEDED to be. In front of me stood a selfish individual, who put their own happiness before their family. Was I really able to forgive such a person? He knew my forgiveness was something he couldn't buy; it needed to be earned. Things were changing, but at what cost?

We both took a step back from each other as he brought his hand up to my cheek to wipe the remainder of my tears, smiling peacefully.

"My graduation ceremony is on March 23rd. Come, if you like."

I had never seen my father's face light up with so much joy like it did at that moment. Seeing his happy face, filled me with a strange, overpowering warmth.

Walking back to the parlour across the street, I saw Kai through the window. Still sitting at the exact same table, I noticed a couple of empty ice cream bowls in front of him. Swinging the door open, I poked my head inside.

"Wasn't it 'too cold' for ice cream?" I asked with a smirk.

"That was an hour ago. After an hour, it became the perfect time," he winked as he rubbed his stomach. "Sooo many flavours."

Chapter Twenty-Nine

KAI AND I walked to the bus terminal, slowly, to give me enough time to tell him everything about the meeting with my father. He had many questions, more than I was able to answer or had even remembered to ask at the time. When the terminal came into sight, Kai asked a final question.

"So, what's gonna happen now?"

"I have no idea. Kenji knows nothing, and I'm too afraid to tell him I went behind his back to meet our father. Our relationship has been decent lately, I don't want to screw it up."

"Nila, he has to know—you have to tell him. It'll be worse if he finds out you met up with your old man from someone other than you. That's what'll ruin your relationship."

I let out a burdened sigh. "I know you're right, but it's easier said than done."

"I'm always right. You need to learn this skill of mine quickly or else you'll find yourself in trouble," he snarked.

"Oh, dear God! My brain is going to explode from your idiotic remarks."

"You love them."

Waiting for our buses to arrive, I couldn't help but laugh at Kai's stupid comments. Standing with my eyes closed and my mouth open from laughing, Kai snuck in a kiss. Immediately, my eyes popped open. Kissing was something I was slowly becoming more accustomed to. He always sprung it upon me when I least expected it.

Parted by two different buses, we got on and rode them in opposite directions. Remembering I had lied to Kenji, telling him I had to pick something up for our mother before heading home, I was forced to make an unnecessary stop at the grocery store.

"I'm home," I announced, entering the house.

"Welcome home," Kenji's voice greeted.

Being at home for mere seconds, knowing my family was inside, felt emptier than it did earlier in the morning with Kai.

Joining Kenji on the couch as he watched TV, he explained that our mother was already tucked away in her bed upstairs. He continued to fill me in on the information Dr. Ashima went over with him in my absence. Listening to my brother talk about our mother so informatively and passionately, made me feel inferior. It took me well over an hour, after Kenji finished talking about our mother, to build up the courage in order to talk to him about our father. When I was finally ready to confront him about it, he started a fresh conversation of his own.

"Nila."

"Yeah?" I turned to him.

"Thanks," he said, looking forward at the TV.

"For what?"

"Kida," he paused, breathing calmly. "Thanks for being okay with everything."

Stalled by his words, I started to wonder if bringing up our father would change this deep, meaningful moment. "I can't say I'm okay with *everything*, but you both seem to care for each other, so I don't want to stand in the way of your happiness. I wish the best for you guys, truly. I don't want this to end ugly, because you both play a major part in my life, and like it or not, you will constantly encounter each other whether you're together or apart."

Hearing the words flow from my mouth, I became really proud of how I worded my thoughts. I finally felt like a big sister giving advice to her little brother. This was a precious feeling that had been missing from my life. With all the tension and lack of communication, in a weird way I felt triumphant conveying my feelings to Kenji, a person around whom I consistently walked on eggshells.

"Don't worry; I'll cherish her."

Such sincere words coming from my brother, pulled at my heart. This soft and kind natured Kenji hadn't been seen in such a long time, I almost forgot what he was like. It made me happy knowing he took the relationship with Kida seriously, just as I knew she did. Not only was Kida one of my supporters through everything, now she could be Kenji's as well.

Not wanting to destroy the atmosphere we had going, I knew I had to bring up our father one way or another before we called it a night. Holding onto the couch cushions for support, I squeezed tightly, digging my nails into them. The harder I squeezed, the more a tingling sensation of pins and needles spread through my fingertips.

"Kenji," I said, unable to look at him. "There's something I really need to tell you."

"What is it?"

Antsy from the anticipation of his potential reaction, I lifted my feet onto the couch and turned my back towards him. Wrapping my arms around my knees, I huddled against them for a sense of protection. When we were kids, this is how we communicated things to each other when we knew we did something the other wasn't going to like, or if we were going to cry but didn't want the other to see.

Within seconds, I felt Kenji's wide back pressed up against mine. It had been years since we sat back-to-back like this; Kenji's back felt both odd and familiar. He was much taller than me; feeling his body tower over mine was intimidating. For a while, I kept quiet, not sure of how to go about starting this conversation when I knew he would only be hurt from it in the end.

With my mind about to explode, I chose the cheap way out and blurted, "I saw Dad! Once unintentionally at the hospital, and then once on my own. That's where I went today after I left the hospital . . . ."

I waited for him to lash out angrily, or to at least click his tongue in disapproval, but not a single sound was made. He didn't speak, nor did his body shift. It wasn't until I felt him inhale deeply that he finally spoke.

"Why?" he asked, almost whispering. "He came to the hospital—why?"

Looking at the ceiling, I answered, "The hospital contacted him. They told him Mom was in the hospital . . . so he came to visit."

I could feel Kenji's shoulders stiffen. "Visit . . .? He's been gone for two whole fucking years and now— NOW he comes for a 'visit'? That's bullshit! He came because she's dying, and he feels like a piece of shit for leaving!"

"Kenji!" I shouted, twisting my shoulders to turn around.

"Don't! Don't look at me."

At his request, I remained still and kept my back to his. "We can't shout, Mom will hear us."

I watched Kenji's shadow on the floor. He brought his arms up and rested his elbows on his knees before covering his face with his hands. "What did he say?"

"At first, he didn't say much. He was more surprised to see me in the room than anything. He had flowers in his hands," I described.

Again, Kenji fell silent. I could tell he was fuelled with rage, not understanding what to make of the situation, just like me. Even after meeting with our father, and agreeing to try and make things work, I still harboured negative feelings towards him, so I could only imagine Kenji trying to work through the same.

"And you voluntarily met with him?"

"Mhm. He left a voicemail on the house phone, asking for us to meet him at the old café."

"Why didn't you tell me?"

Silence filled the room. I reached for my own legs again, grabbing hold of them and pulling them in, even closer to my chest. "I . . . I didn't know how to."

"Ni—"

"I was afraid you'd go off somewhere!" I unintentionally shouted with a shaky voice. "Off somewhere where no one could find you. I was scared to death of you blocking me out again. We've just started getting back to normal; I didn't want to screw it up. If I did end up telling you, I don't think we would be here on this couch, back-to-back, like we are now."

"Nila, you can't fix something THIS broken. What, do you think you can slap a bandage on and everything will magically go back to the way it was before?"

Taking what he said to heart, I internalized the meaning behind his words. *Is that what I'm trying to do? Fix something that can't be fixed? What would be the point of trying to make peace with Dad if it'll end up going nowhere? No, I don't believe it's broken—it just needs some repair. In time, I can fix this.*

"Kenji, you're wrong. It's not broken . . . WE'RE not broken! THIS family is NOT broken! Everyone simply stopped trying, that's all," I finished, my speech lacking the enthusiasm and strength it started with. "If there are results, then it's not time wasted. If Dad's willing to try—"

"Dad? Are you serious?" he exclaimed in disgust. As he whipped around to express his anger, I slipped off his back and was forced to face him. "You don't even know this man! He's not the same 'Dad' from two years ago, Nila. He's a completely different person. We know nothing about him OR his new fuckin' family!"

"Family?" I asked curiously. "How do you know about his new family?"

Realizing he blurted out something he wasn't planning to, Kenji turned around, waiting for my back to reunite with his. I did as he requested and connected our backs again. A long silence followed as I anxiously waited for his answer.

"I saw them," he said, breaking the suspenseful silence.

"Who?"

"His pathetic new family—his mistress, along with a kid. I saw them one day at the supermarket, so I followed them home on my bike and it led me to his new house."

He saw the new woman? I haven't even seen what she looks like.

"The kid is our half-brother. His name is, Yano," I said, bypassing everything else, but wondering how much he really knew.

"Half-brother . . .? You've met him?"

"I met him unknowingly during the winter break when I went to Kai's. Dad . . . is Kai's next-door neighbour."

"Really?"

"Mhm."

"Wow . . .," Kenji said, distraught.

With a deep breath, I asked one final question. "Did you recognize her?"

"No," he answered coldly. "I've never seen her before."

Chapter Thirty

WEEKS WENT BY, and my mother began losing her hair in large quantities as she started chemotherapy. Kenji and I found bundles of it in the sink and in the shower. It was devastating to see my mother with patches of hair missing because the more hair she lost, the more her character changed. Each day, her face grew paler and swelled up, while her weight fluctuated due to stomach bloating. My mother, once a proud, strong woman, was now pitiful and weak. She barely stepped outside as she lived in constant fear of the neighbours seeing her. She became a miserable, empty shell who stayed cooped up indoors. The only time my mother left the house was to go to the hospital for her treatments and other appointments, but even for that, she begged us not to take her. She would start shouting nonsense, saying she would rather die than go through any of it. She cried a lot; spending multiple hours locked up in her room, or in the bathroom throwing up. Occasionally, we even heard loud, terrifying noises from her throwing objects aggressively within the house.

When Kenji could no longer take her self-pity, he ended up doing something drastic. One day, he went off to the shed in the backyard and managed to find our father's old electric shaver. Our mother had placed a bunch of our father's things into boxes and stored them in there when he never came back. After storming back inside, Kenji ran up to the bathroom. Within moments, an electric buzzing was heard throughout the house. Running to see what crazy thing he was doing, I got there in time to witness pieces of hair fall into the bathroom sink as Kenji shaved his entire head.

Watching my mother struggle and wage war with herself, and with us, was too painful to bear. I found myself taking on a motherly role as I prepared meals for the family, making a separate meal for my mother each night based on her new diet. Somehow, Kenji put on a brave face and remained calm every time he stood in front of her, even with all the verbal abuse she spat at him.

Sometimes, late at night, I would see Kenji sneak out to the shed and have a cigarette. At a time like this, no matter how much I disliked it, I couldn't blame him. He was too important to lose right now, so if I wanted him to continue sticking around, I had to look past his disgusting smoking habit.

Dr. Ashima phoned the house, offering the option of private home care for our mother if we were finding things to be too difficult to deal with on our own. Of course, there was an additional cost not covered by insurance, but Dr. Ashima could arrange an employee discount if we decided to go that route. With the first payment mark coming up, we decided to break up the payments in smaller, manageable installments. To Kanji's surprise, when he went to the hospital to give them the first deposit, he was informed that all costs had already been paid for and would continue being covered under the name: *Youji Izawa*. When Kenji came home and told me, I could see a temper building inside him. I was able to convince him our father was probably doing it so we could focus on school and our mother's wellbeing, but he still wasn't able to calm down. Kenji never once mentioned our father after that. With everything happening so quickly, I'm sure he had no clue how to deal with our father's interference.

Kida, of course, was up to date on what was happening with my mother and what Kenji and I were going through, so she backed off a bit. There were times, after my mother went to sleep for the night, Kenji would sneak out to meet Kida, or she would pass by for a bit. Despite everything going on with my mother, Kida and Kenji seemed to be happy.

They had a strong connection, a supportive relationship which was exactly what my brother needed right now.

Kai also kept his distance for a while, sending more messages than visiting, which was understandable because the college entrance exams were still taking place. Even though the entrance exams were wrapping up, finals were also around the corner. Kai's messages may have been through Line, but his support was still clear.

Going to school became a challenge. Kenji and I rotated which days we would attend school, while the other stayed home to take care of our mother. Once a week, a nurse from the hospital would come to the house, which my mother loathed. On the days the nurse came, we both attended school, giving us an extra day to be regular teenagers. Kenji suggested I should attend more days compared to him because this was my final semester before college, and the marks from this semester were extremely important—but I couldn't do it. I couldn't let him be the main caregiver, especially when I knew I was doing better than him in school. Our mother was probably capable of staying home on her own for a few hours, but both Kenji and I worried more about her mental state, considering most of our vases and plates were already shattered into millions of pieces.

The school accommodated our needs, as long as our grades didn't drop. Thankfully, with my nearly perfect attendance record from the previous semesters, and prior years, I had enough days to graduate. Plus, I was confident my grades were high enough to maintain a passing score, even if they were to slip a little bit. Even though I knew it was time to buckle down and get serious about college, I had no motivation and began second guessing the idea of even applying. If I were to go off to college, no matter how close it was to home, my schedule would change and probably conflict with Kenji's, leaving our mother alone more often. She was already in a rough state, and it would only go downhill from here if her body didn't respond positively to treatment. Keeping my doubts aside and to myself, I decided it would be easier to just take the damn tests, then choose the right path later on. This way, I knew my mother would also remain satisfied.

Through Line, Kai scheduled for us to get together this weekend to study for exams. In this sense, it was nice because it didn't matter if we went to different schools, the material on our exams would roughly be the same.

We decided to get together at his house, due to my mother's unpredictable state. Though I had been to Kai's house before, this would be the first time I would actually be going inside. The thought of being in Kai's house made me nervous as hell because it meant there was a high probability that I'd be meeting his parents. Not just as a friend, but as his girlfriend.

One morning, I prepared breakfast for Kenji and myself, plus a separate dish for my mother when I heard her rustling around upstairs; a clear sign that she was getting up. I placed all the medications my mother needed to take with her breakfast beside her plate at the table. It wasn't long until she came down the stairs, wearing a winter hat, along with a poorly wrapped bathrobe that she had been wearing all week. If she had been wearing a traditional kimono or yukata, she would have looked disgraceful.

She came into the kitchen, slumping down into one of the chairs at the table. "This again? Didn't you make this yesterday?"

"Mom," Kenji said with warning eyes, gripping his chopsticks firmly.

"I'm sorry. It's hard to make dishes from the list of foods you can eat, Mom . . .."

"You're right," she said, looking at me with regretful eyes. "I'm sorry."

"It's alright," I answered, trying to brush off her unkind remark.

Kenji finished his plate promptly, cleaning up after himself before leaving the house. Today it was my turn to watch our mother while Kenji went to school. I took my time eating because I knew the day ahead would be long and tiring, so if there was any time to rest, I took advantage of it.

"This is ridiculous. You should be heading to school as well."

"Mom, we've talked about this."

"I know," her voice drifted as she focused her attention to the window overlooking the backyard. "It's just, I feel like a child who needs constant supervision whenever one of you stays behind. I'm slowly starting to lose face as an adult, especially as a mother."

We sat at the table for another twenty minutes, her food and medication hardly touched. Watching my mother suffer in silence, I thought back to the day my father and I met up with each other. Through these past weeks, the thought of telling my mother about it kept crossing my mind. Not knowing how the information might affect her, I held back.

If I told her, would she freak out or be reasonable and understanding? If she never found out, everything would remain the same, right?

No matter how hard I tried to convince myself, I knew it was wrong to keep such an important thing from her. She said she didn't want to be treated as a child, well then, here goes. "Mom . . .."

"Hmm?" she muttered, her gaze leaving the window and returning to me.

"There's . . . something I need to tell you."

"What is it?" she asked, sitting up with concern.

"Well, um . . .."

"Stop mumbling, Nila, and say it," she said with a lack of patience.

"I met with Dad," I confessed, frightened in my own skin.

Her eyes protruded almost out of their sockets. She changed from shocked to upset, then quickly to devastation. The final look she gave me was close to that of betrayal, as if I had deceived her, which knowing my mother, was probably accurate.

"YOU DID WHAT?"

"He invited Kenji and I to meet him at the café he used to take us to when we were little. I didn't mention it to Kenji until after the fact, so he didn't come."

Her look of betrayal had turned ferocious. "Nila . . . how could you?"

Automatically feeling guilty, I dropped my head in order to cut the intense eye contact between us.

"Why did you agree to meet him?"

With fear leaving me, my blood boiled. I lifted my head from its ashamed state and stood up, towering over her. "Why did I agree to meet with HIM? Why? Did you ever stop to think I've wanted to know where he was all this time? Why he up and left us and started a new family?" I said emotionally, my vision getting foggy.

Her eyes got even wider. "A new family? How did you . . .," she said faintly, a blank expression drawn on her face.

"Because, I've met him."

"Met who . . .?"

"Yano," I said confidently, trying to swallow the shock of power stuck in my throat. "Dad also said you told him to stay away because WE wanted nothing more to do with him. You know that's a lie! Why would you say that? It was YOU who wanted nothing more to do with him! You know we never wanted him to leave us. That was not your decision to make!"

The look my mother gave me made it seem like she knew exactly who and what I was talking about. Taken aback by my sudden outburst, she turned away from me and back towards the window. Gazing out at the landscape of the yard, she commented, knowing full well she would not get a response.

"Why . . . why couldn't you have left things the way they were, Youji?"

The talk with my mother didn't go much further. We sat in silence like two strangers until she got up and left the kitchen, leaving a full plate of food and untouched medication. I knew I had disappointed her, but I would have rather told the truth and have her be upset with me, than continue to lie.

Chapter Thirty-One

SUNDAY COULDN'T HAVE come soon enough; if it were a day later, I probably would have gone insane. I needed to get out of the house and away from my mother, so I was glad Kai and I had scheduled to meet up at his place to study for exams.

Since the conversation about my father, my mother had grown hostile and distant towards me, exchanging many words with Kenji, but very little with me. Choosing to separate myself, I spent those next few days reading many books and articles about how to deal with loved ones who have cancer, to learn if my mother's behaviour was considered 'normal.' I had asked Kenji if she said anything about me when they spent time alone together, but all he would reply with was: *"Give her time, she'll come around."* With him being so optimistic, I wasn't sure if he was saying that on my behalf or hers.

Making my way to Kai's was nerve-wracking. I was headed there with the intention of studying, but I would also be meeting Kai's parents for the very first time as he confirmed they'd be home. Terrified of what their first impression of me would be, I knew, as Kai's girlfriend, I had to put my best foot forward.

Getting closer to the Kento residence, I sent Kai a message to let him know I was almost there. He waited for me outside the gate wearing an unzipped jacket and unlaced boots.

"Nila!" Kai shouted, waving.

About to wave back, I froze, realizing the house I would need to first pass was my father's. I cursed my fashion decision by choosing a jacket without a hood. Using what I had, I puffed up my thick scarf, making sure it covered everything except my nose and eyes. From the short distance, I watched as Kai's expression changed from excited to something just above a meek smile. He gazed up at my father's house, then back at me.

"It's okay," he reassured, holding out his hand in comfort.

Walking as fast as I could past the forbidden house, I reached for Kai's hand. "Thanks."

A gentle smile from Kai was all it took for me to understand that he knew how grateful I was for his support. Approaching the front door of Kai's house, he held it open for me to enter ahead of him.

The smell inside the Kento's house was much different from mine, along with the pictures hanging on the walls. The creamy-orange colour of paint was bright and welcoming, making it peaceful to enter. Kai's house was filled with chatter, both from people and the television, which produced a comforting atmosphere. The door slammed behind us, echoing loudly. The volume of the TV decreased, chatter silenced, and I could hear the sounds of people shuffling around.

"Here we go," Kai sighed under his breath.

Peeking at him through my scarf, I knew what he meant. The nervousness in the pit of my stomach grew, making it nearly impossible to undo my coat. I fiddled with the last button, attempting to take off my coat before his family reached the door. Halfway through undoing the last button, I decided it would have been smarter to start with my boots. Now, without finishing one task, I awkwardly began another.

"Yo, Kai, is this your girlfriend?"

With my coat nearly undone, and one boot on, I looked up to see where the voice came from. On the bottom step of the staircase to the main floor stood a boy, who looked to be the age of a junior high student, with his arms crossed as he leaned against the wall.

"Oh, Ryu," Kai said, taking off his jacket and hanging it on one of the hooks near the door. "Yeah, this is, Nila Izawa."

"Hmm," Ryu pondered disinterestedly. "She looks like she's struggling."

Embarrassed by my mess of an appearance, I quickly undid the remainder of my coat and took off my other boot before someone else came and saw how pathetic I looked.

"Ryu, that's rude!" Kai shouted as he went to Ryu and slapped the back of his head. "You caught her off guard."

"Ow! Asshole!"

"RYUSEI KENTO!" a woman's voice shouted from around the corner. "How dare you use that language in this house! Show some respect—we have a guest."

The woman was much older. She wore a modern, knee-length skirt with a white blouse tucked in at the waist, and an apron on top. Her eyes were the same shade of emerald green as Kai's.

"Ah, but Mom, he . . .," Ryu attempted to explain.

"Enough!" The woman walked closer to the entrance where I stood. "I'm terribly sorry for my son's attitude so early during your visit. I hope my *other* son remembers the manners he was brought up with when he's with you." Kai's mother looked at him, giving him a stern look of expected obedience.

To avoid his mother's the intense stare, Kai quickly came back beside me. "Mom, this is my girlfriend, Nila Izawa."

As soon as my name left Kai's lips, I instantly bowed in panic. "Excuse the intrusion! Thank you for having me in your lovely home!"

"Oh my," Mrs. Kento giggled. "She is very polite. That's how you can tell she was raised in a good home." A hand gently patted the top of my head. "Lift your head, dear. You may stay as long as you like."

As soon as her hand left my head, I stood up straight and was faced with a welcoming smile. "Thank you, Ma'am."

"Honey, who's at the door?" an older male asked before turning the corner and appearing at the entrance from the hallway himself. "Oh, a young lady."

"Dear, this is Kai's girlfriend."

I panic bowed again. "Hello, Sir, my name is Nila Izawa. Thank you for having me."

"Izawa? Isn't that the name of our—"

"Allllright, well, I'm going to take Nila up to my room so we can study for exams," Kai took over, as he held my shoulders and directed me towards the stairs.

"That's fine," Mrs. Kento replied. "Would you like me to bring up some tea?"

"Yeah, sure, whatever is fine!" Kai frantically shouted midway up the stairs. "Thanks!"

When we reached the top, Kai let out a massive sigh before looking at me.

"Sorry, they don't know, and I didn't want you to . . .."

"Thanks," I smiled.

"Yeah," he smiled back. "My room's this way."

Kai held my hand and led me in the direction of his room. Along the way, we passed a couple of closed doors and an opened one revealing the bathroom. Once we arrived at his room, he escorted me in before closing the door, leaving it open a small crack. Kai's room was fairly spacious. He had his bed against the wall, like mine, a medium-sized dresser with a TV on it, some sports equipment in one corner, and an average chabudai table with zabuton cushions in the middle of it all.

"If I shut the door all the way, she'll freak," he said under his breath, signs of embarrassment seeping through.

"It can't be helped. My mother wouldn't even let a guy come into my room, no matter who they were." Remembering that Kai already spent the night at my place, in my room no less, caused my cheeks to flush.

"Just how many guys have you tried to bring up to your room?" he teased.

"Ha . . . ha," I said, rolling my eyes. "We should start studying."

"Boooring," Kai moaned like a child.

Taking my first step further into his room, I looked back at him to match his childishness by sticking out my tongue. I walked to the table, bent down, and sat in seiza as I took books out of my bag.

"OH, YEAH!"

"What?" I shouted in panic, flinching from his sudden outburst.

Without answering, Kai walked to his bed and knelt down to look underneath.

What is he doing?

After a few seconds of blindly searching through the mess under his bed, he pulled something out. "Found it!"

I couldn't believe what I was seeing. "No way . . .." In Kai's hand was my English textbook. "Wow, I had completely forgotten about it."

"Me too."

"How terrible! You probably weren't ever going to give it back."

"No, I was. I just needed it for a bit longer than promised," he said mischievously.

"Why?"

"Well, at first, I was gonna give it back right away like promised, but then, I found myself becoming more and more attracted to you each time I saw you, giving me the desire to keep it longer. The longer I had it meant the more frequent our encounters would be, and I couldn't pass up those precious opportunities. This book became my connection to you, and for that, I truly enjoyed keeping it captive." Holding out the book in his hand, he passed it to me. As I reached for it, Kai swiftly avoided my hand, causing the textbook to drop onto the table as he stretched out to grab hold of my arm, pulling me in close. "I love that book, but I love you more."

Kai's words set off an explosion in my heart, igniting into an enormous chest burning fire. *Did Kai . . . just say . . . he LOVED me?* The beating of my heart was nonstop; things inside of me were out of control. My face was buried so deep into his chest that I couldn't see what type of face he was making. I knew I should reply with something quickly. I didn't want him to think my feelings weren't mutual, because they were.

Just as I was about to express my feelings in return, there was a knock at the partially opened door.

"Kai, I've brought the tea."

Kai and I quickly separated, taking an upright, sitting position on our knees at the table before Mrs. Kento entered.

"Come in," Kai eventually answered.

The door swung open and Mrs. Kento came waltzing in with a tray carrying two cups and a small, red teapot. She bent to the table's level before placing the tray on top.

"Here we are," she said with a delighted smile as she poured tea into both cups. When she was done, she placed a cup in front of me, then one in front of Kai before resting the pot back on the tray. Looking up, she stared in my direction. "You know, it's wonderful to have another woman in this house full of men. Granted, I do have a wonderful daughter-in-law, plus a beautiful granddaughter, although sadly, they don't come to visit as often as I would like."

"That's because they live far," Kai answered, sipping his tea.

"Doesn't matter! It gets terribly lonely in a house filled with men," she teasingly snapped at Kai's reply. "A grandmother never gets tired of seeing her grandchildren. You wouldn't understand."

Kai shook his head in response to his mother's exaggerated explanation while I couldn't help but laugh at their quarrel.

With a final smile directed at me, Mrs. Kento stood and walked towards the door. "I'll leave you two to study. I expect perfect scores from the both of you."

"Don't jinx us!" Kai said.

"Oh, please," she said, shutting the door until it rested lightly against the frame.

"You have your mother's eyes," I said, as soon as Mrs. Kento was out of the room.

"Yeah. My mom's half Japanese, she gets the colour from my other grandpa who's Russian. That's also where we get our light-coloured hair."

"Wow," stunned by Kai's family heritage, I couldn't help but become extremely interested in finding out more. "That's amazing."

Slightly pink, he smiled. "Thanks."

"She's really nice by the way," I expressed fondly.

"She can be. She's really just an ordinary mom though."

"Maybe," I said quietly. "I'd say she's much more." Opening my workbook to a fresh page, I switched our focus to studying. "How are you in math?"

With the back of the mechanical pencil in his mouth, Kai sighed helplessly. "Not terrible, but not great."

Smiling at the sight of his frustration, I put my pencil down in the crease of my workbook. "What's your favourite subject?"

"Who has a favourite subject?" he joked, glancing up from his page.

"I do."

"Gym then," he said with another sigh.

"Oh, come on, gym isn't even a real subject," I pestered.

"Is so! If I have to take it in school, AND get graded for it, then it's definitely a subject."

"Okay, I'll give you that," I said, giggling. "Seriously though, do you have a favourite 'in class' subject?" I asked more specifically.

"Science."

"Really?" I said with surprise.

"Yeah," he replied, seemingly embarrassed about his answer.

"Why science?"

"Well, mostly the environmental categories, like plant life, because I'm good at that stuff. But sadly, it's only touched upon briefly," he explained.

Wanting to learn more about Kai's interests, I pursued answers to further questions. "So, you like science because you're good at it? Do you think it has to do with your family owning a flower shop?"

"Probably. I learn a lot from working there, so, naturally, I've become good at it. Eventually, I noticed some of the topics and questions regarding plants were easy to answer, considering I do similar things at the shop. My teacher noticed it too because soon the responsibility of maintaining the school's garden fell upon me—so annoying."

Listening to Kai talk about school made me feel happy and relaxed. School and studying were something of second nature to me. When I heard others talking about their favourite subjects or hobbies, it oddly piqued my interest. No matter how hard my mother pushed me, deep down, I guess I didn't mind it as much as I thought.

"What colleges are you thinking about?"

Looking up at me with wavering eyes, Kai took another sip of his tea. "None."

"None? What do you mean? The deadlines to apply have already passed, you know?" I informed, worriedly.

"I know. I don't plan on going to college," Kai said sternly, placing the cup back down.

"Why not?"

"Because, it's not in the cards."

"Cards? I don't . . . get what you mean?"

With a thin smile, he answered, "I'm taking over the shop. Well, my grandfather and father will be running it for a while longer, but after graduation, I'll be working there full-time. Like I mentioned before, my grandpa plans on retiring soon, since him and my grandma want to move back to the countryside. My dad has already stated that he finds managing the shop to be too much work for one person to handle alone; so, that's where I step in."

"The shop? You mentioned something like this before, but what about your older brother?"

He leaned back from the table, resting his shoulders against the bed frame as he looked up to the ceiling. "He doesn't want it. He works at a law firm and wants to continue to grow himself in the company. His future goal has always been to become a successful lawyer for a huge corporation, not an owner of a dinky flower shop."

Lowering his head, I was able to make eye contact with him. "And your parents are okay with your plan?"

"They suggested it."

"So, that's your dream then? To be the owner of a small flower shop?"

Quarrelling with my eyes, Kai seemed somewhat upset by my confronted statement. "If it was, would you drop the subject?"

"Probably not," I answered truthfully, trying to pull more out of him.

Smirking by my quick remark, Kai brought one knee up and placed his elbow on top, resting his head against his palm. "Dunno why I bothered to ask, I already knew the answer."

With silence filling the room, I decided to pick up my pencil again and continue studying. Knowing Kai had no desire to further the conversation, I chose to give him what he wanted by 'dropping it.'

"What about you?"

Lifting my head from my studies, I found myself staring at Kai who was once again looking up at the ceiling in thought. "Me?"

Kai sat upright and brought himself back to the table. "What do you want to do after high school? What's your dream job?"

Taken aback, I restated his question. "My dream job?"

"Yeah."

"I'm stuck between two different career paths."

Kai's eyes lit up. "Really? Which ones?"

"An Elementary School Teacher or an Executive Assistant for a profitable business close by." Continuing to look at Kai for a reaction, I expected him to tease me about my choices, but instead, he seemed pleased.

"I can see you as a teacher," he said, smiling with sincere support.

"Yeah?"

"Yep," he winked, leaving one eye closed as he continued. "A very strict teacher."

"Hey!" I shouted, as I threw my pencil at him. "How rude! I can be nice and easy-going."

"You?" he said as he hugged his sides, falling over from laughter. "Yeah, right! You need total control over everything."

Not impressed by his reaction, I turned my head away from him and crossed my arms. "I never have control when it comes to you."

"It's me who doesn't have control."

Afraid to lock eyes with Kai, I remained with my face turned away. *What does he mean HE doesn't have control? He's always in control! Every time I'm with him, he has control!*

From the corner of my eye, I could see a dark figure crawling towards me. Startled by his presence, my body acted on its own and I threw myself back until I was forced up against his dresser.

"Um, Kai, you're too close," I said, shutting my eyes.

"In this relationship, I'm not the one with the control. It's hard enough to scavenge the willpower just to resist you while my whole family is in the same house, let alone when I have you all to myself."

Placing a hand on my cheek, I could feel Kai's intense stare. Choosing to open my eyes, I saw his were like arrows, piercing straight through my chest and aiming only for my heart.

"You don't even understand how my disgusting mind works. Every second I'm with you, I can feel my self-control deteriorating. Your eyes hold the things my heart thirsts for, Nila. It's weird to say, but it's like I want to attack you by making every inch of you mine."

With every word, Kai got closer, until the only thing separating us was the musky air of our heavy breathing. Our lips were so close that by barely moving, they could touch.

"Kai," I whispered, the hot air bouncing off his lips.

"Nila," he spoke my name softly, allowing me to experience the same hot air. "I'll say it again; I love you."

The same heart throbbing feeling from before returned. While my heart felt like it was about to jump out of my chest from complete excitement, it also ached from anxiety. There weren't any disruptions this time around, so I had no way of avoiding this frightening moment. I knew what my true feelings were, so there wasn't anything to be afraid of, but no matter how many times I had rehearsed it in my head, I was still scared. "I . . . Kai, I . . . I love you, too."

There was no time to react because as soon those powerful words left my mouth, Kai's lips were already on mine. Our kisses came one after the other, each more intense and longer than the last. I could feel myself getting lost in him, lost in the passionate kisses he guided me through. Never had I experienced something filled with so much passion, an emotion I once thought I lacked completely. He was opening so many new doors for me, ones which left me more exposed and vulnerable to the world than I felt comfortable with. He was a poison ready to consume me until I became an infected shell, leaving me with thoughts of just him.

Reality kicked in. I realized that technically we weren't alone. We were in Kai's room, which was connected to a house, a house in which his family was walking around just one floor below us.

"Stop! Stop! We have to stop!" I whispered, pulling away.

"Huh?" he said, full of lust, his eyes revealing his craving for more. "Why?"

"Because, your family is home! Have you forgotten where we are?"

"Right . . .," Kai replied with disappointment as he held himself back. "For a moment, I kinda forgot they were here."

"'Kind of forgot'! Are you mental?" I continued to shout in a lower tone as I pushed him further away.

We returned to our upright, proper positions at the table as I desperately tried to focus and get back into studying. Kai also went back to studying without any complaints.

About ten minutes passed and I was really surprised that Kai kept quiet the entire time. Glancing over at him every now and then, I could tell he wasn't enjoying himself. He was either stuck on something or he was just flat out bored.

Taking it upon myself to break the silence, I decided to retouch upon the subject of the future. "I just want you to know, I understand your reasoning for taking over the family business, and I admire you for it. Sorry if my reaction didn't show it, I just think you shouldn't limit yourself." Listening to the words that came out of my mouth, I felt hypocritical. "Yet again, I'm pretty much doing the same thing . . . so, what do I know?"

With a gentle smile of understanding, he asked, "What schools have you applied to?"

"Only two. Napa College of Business and Education, here in town, and KT University, just outside of town. My homeroom teacher was upset about my career survey, saying I didn't push myself to apply to more challenging schools, given my consistent academic track. But, this way, I can be close to home to look after my mother while still attending college."

"Limiting," he teased dryly.

"Yeah."

"But I'd probably do the same," he said, with the gentle smile he used against me all the time. "I have no desire to leave this town."

An hour flew by and I had already finished all the practice questions, plus bonus assignments from school, and was now helping Kai finish his. In opposition to my prejudgment about his academics, Kai exceeded my expectations. He was well-rounded in each subject; his only problem was lack of focus.

"Kai, can I ask you something?"

"What is it?"

"Why did you initiate this study date if you don't plan on attending college?"

"Well, I still wanna do well on finals; might as well finish on a high note, and I knew you could use some time away from home, so why not study together? It also didn't hurt that I would get the chance to spend time with you," he said mischievously as his teeth clenched together, smiling widely.

"Thank you. I appreciate it."

"Yeah."

Mrs. Kento popped in a few more times, bringing us each a piece of cake, plus a refill on our pot of tea. Each time she made an appearance, she sat at the table and attempted to join in on our conversation, while Kai tried his hardest to shoo her away.

It was getting late, so I closed up my books before packing them into my bag, making sure to include my long-lost English textbook.

"Hey," Kai initiated.

"Hmm?"

"When's your birthday?"

"September 8th, why?"

"Just wondering. I knew you wouldn't be the type to come out and openly tell me, so I thought I'd better ask before I missed it."

Giggling at his accuracy, I nodded my head. "You're probably right. When's yours?"

"March 30th, a week after graduation I believe."

Dropping my bag from shock, I looked at him. "That's soon . . . like two months!"

"Two months isn't THAT soon," he laughed at my reaction. "Don't worry; I don't expect anything fancy for my eighteenth birthday—just a car, no big deal."

"HA! Yeah, right! You're looking in the wrong direction if you think you're getting it from me."

"You're getting me a car!" he shouted in an exaggerated tone of excitement. "Wow, I have such a nice girlfriend. Who knew?"

"Hilarious. My boyfriend thinks he's a comedian."

With the word 'boyfriend' leaving my lips so casually, I prayed Kai would overlook it.

"Boyfriend, eh?" he repeated, raising a brow.

Crap . . . .

"I think that's the first time you've called me your boyfriend. I like the way it sounds," he expressed with a smile nearly touching his ears.

Caught by my carelessness with words, I couldn't help but feel a tad bit giddy that such a simple thing made him so happy.

As we headed downstairs, Kai insisted that he'd walk me home. No matter how many times I assured him I would be fine on my own, he stood his ground. I placed my bag on the floor near my boots and took my coat from its borrowed hook.

"Kai, you better be walking this lovely lady home," Mrs. Kento's voice echoed through the hallway before she reached the entrance.

"Already on it," Kai said, reassuring his mother.

"Good," Mrs. Kento nodded, a proud look of parenting worn on her face.

Mr. Kento approached the front entrance shortly after. "Leaving already?"

"Yes," I answered, quickly bowing my head. "Thank you for having me."

"Anytime dear," Mrs. Kento answered with a smile. "It was a pleasure meeting you. Please continue to look after my son."

"I will!" I said abruptly, as Kai chuckled.

Kai opened the door and I stepped out first. As he shut the door behind us, Kai let out a sigh of relief.

"Finnnnally free! Sorry about them."

"Don't be, they're lovely."

Kai hopped down the steps before me. "You're just saying that because you wanna get in good with your in-laws."

Startled by his upfront declaration, I paused in immediate shock, not being able to go down a single step. "My . . . who?"

With a wink leaving me utterly confused and embarrassed, Kai continued to make his way down the walkway ahead of me. Managing to pull myself together, I placed one foot in front of the other as I tried to catch up to him.

This idiot spits out nonsense like it's his second language!

Before even making it halfway to Kai, an uncomfortable pair of eyes were fixated on me. Standing in the neighbouring yard was my father. He wore a business suit and carried a briefcase, the type of outfit he usually put on during the week for the desk job I assumed he still had.

"Nila . . .." My name left my father's lips in a loud whisper.

With the sound of my name, Kai quickly appeared by my side in defence. He remained close, to the point where I could see his chest inhaling and exhaling through his jacket, while his arm was firmly placed out in front of me.

Seeing my father standing beside a familiar vehicle, on an unfamiliar property, struck me in an unpleasant way. With a feeling of satisfaction from the way we parted at the café, I wasn't prepared to see him so soon. I couldn't find a single ounce of courage to even smile, let alone say hello, leaving me with awkward eye contact. In return, my father smiled at me softly.

"Mr. Kento," my father called out, acknowledging Kai's presence as he bowed in our direction before turning around to walk to his front door. About to take his first step onto the stairs leading to his porch, he turned halfway, cocking his head and shoulders back towards Kai. "Take good care of my little girl."

My father's voice sounded pained as he uttered those words. The way he said them made it seem like he was giving his unspoken approval.

"I intend to."

I looked up at Kai; his facial expression was something more than earnest as he stood tall and confident by my side. Glancing back at my father, another smile appeared at the corner of his mouth as he continued to press forward into the house.

The sound of a door shutting echoed through the quiet street as I continued to stare blankly at the strange house in front of me.

Suddenly, Kai grabbed my hand. His giant hand was like a warm glove engulfing mine. "Come on, Nila."

Before allowing Kai to whisk me away, I remembered something I had discussed with my father at the café. "I invited him . . .."

"Invited him?" Kai stopped. "Invited him to what?"

"My graduation."

"Are you sure you're okay with that?"

"I don't know. At the time, it seemed like a good thing to do."

"Can I come?"

"To my graduation?"

"Yeah."

"Sure. But Kai, isn't yours on the same day?"

"Well, if it's at a different time, then . . .."

"Are we even allowed? I thought we could only invite family?"

"Then, we're just gonna have to be sneaky."

Smiling foolishly, I squeezed his hand. "Okay."

Part Two

Chapter Thirty-Two

$\mathcal{A}$ MONTH LATER, AFTER finishing all my exams, two letters addressed to me were left on the small table in the hallway beside the answering machine. They were acceptance letters from both colleges I had applied to. In the end, I decided to accept the offer from Napa College of Business and Education, for the Elementary School Teacher program.

February rolled in and out, taking the sweet scent of Valentine's Day along with it. With the months flying by, winter melted away and White Day soon appeared, leaving the guys in my school dumbfounded with hopes of last-minute romance. My beloved cherry blossom branches regained life and were slowly starting to bloom. The whole town brightened again with signs of new beginnings.

All my exams went well, as expected, and Kai also did marvellously on his. Kenji did surprisingly well, which brought tears and a ton of joy to my mother when he showed her his results. It was heartwarming to see my mother holding Kenji's test results in her hands with approval. I knew how long she waited for the day to come when Kenji would take school seriously, like he did when he was younger.

With graduation in less than a week, my mother seemed more

agitated than usual. She tried her hardest to be in good spirits, but was still overcome with misery. Her hair had completely fallen out at this point. Even with small signs of certain areas attempting to grow back, nothing stuck, and it eventually fell out as soon as she touched it. She continued taking her medication and going through with chemotherapy treatments, but physically, nothing changed. Her mood frequently varied from extremely positive, to downright negative and harsh. Sometimes, it was unbearable to watch or be around her.

During recent hospital visits, Dr. Ashima advised us that our mother's condition wasn't getting any better. He assured us that his team was trying their hardest to maintain a positive level, with the goal of eventually eliminating all signs of the breast cancer. We were told that our mother would have to adjust her medication and chemotherapy treatments, as well as come in more frequently for checkups, which I knew was never a good sign. As a family, we always hoped for the best.

The last week of school, seniors had a couple of days off from classwork to prepare for the graduation ceremony. Those involved, had to attend mandatory practices in order to rehearse school cheers, songs, speeches, and understand the order of how the ceremony would run. The juniors were also given important tasks by aiding the seniors when asked or needed.

Luckily, I wasn't selected to do any readings or speeches, which brought some light to my cloudy days. Kai and I compared our graduation schedules and found out that our ceremonies were held at different times, allowing us to secretly try and attend each other's.

Not wanting to further upset my mother, I never mentioned the fact my father might decide to attend. I asked Kai to remind my father about the day and time of my graduation ceremony, as I purposely tried to avoid the chance of meeting any more members of his other family.

[Line Kai]: Can you believe it? We'll be graduates soon! Setting off into the real world to become adults.

[Line Nila]: Yeah . . ..

[Line Kai]: What's wrong?

[Line Nila]: I don't know. It all seems so surreal. We won't be in high school anymore; just tossed aimlessly into the real world. Before, I couldn't wait for it to be over, but now, as the end draws near, it's kind of scary . . .

[Line Kai]: I see your point. Guess it's a bit intimidating from that aspect.

[Line Nila]: Yeah.

The late-night conversation with Kai died after a few more messages. The fact that Kai didn't have to worry about attending another day of school in his entire life, made me kind of envious. I was excited to start a new chapter of my life, but also terrified. What if I could succeed at high school but not at college?

Kida was the same as Kai, happy to leave high school behind and experience a new part of life head on. Surprisingly, Kida got accepted into college on her first try. She managed to get into the same college as me, but for a Social Work program. When making her choice, she insisted on staying close to Kenji and me. Kenji showed signs of happiness and was congratulatory towards her acceptance into a program of her choice, but I could tell he was worried about separating and attending different schools.

Chapter Thirty-Three

"BEEP, BEEP! HONK, honk!" Kenji repeated countless times, while playing with his toy cars on the kitchen table.

"Dear, tell your son to stop playing on the table as I'm trying to prepare it for dinner."

"Ken my boy, your mother is going to explode with anger if you don't listen," our father said, pretending to act assertive.

"Like a bomb?" Kenji asked in shock, dropping the car in his hand.

"BOOM! Just like a bomb!" he joked.

Her eyebrows flared. "Youji . . .."

"Mommy, no! I'm sorry! I'll stop!"

"That's my boy."

Both our parents laughed at Kenji's fearfulness as the table continued to be set by our mother.

"Peaches, why are you so quiet?" Dad asked from across the table.

"At school today, my teacher asked us what we want to be when we grow up . . .."

"And, what did you say?"

"A ninja, but she said I couldn't."

An energy of excitement flew out of our father as he held his sides. "A ninja? Why a ninja?"

"She only wants to be a ninja 'cause I wanna be one. She's a copycat!" Kenji argued, crossing his arms.

"Nuh-uh!"

"Yeaaah-huh!"

"I could be a better ninja than Kenji any day!"

"NO!"

"Alright, alright," our father said, stepping in to break up the quarrel. *"You can both be ninjas."*

"NO WAY!" we both snapped.

"Of course, you can, and I'll tell you why."

Sparking our interests, we turned to face him.

"You see, we come from a long line of undercover ninjas. Even your grandfather became one during the war."

"WOW!" Kenji's eyes sparkled. "Grandpa?"

"You betcha."

"Are you a ninja?" I asked, going over as I tugged on his sleeve.

"Not anymore."

"Awe, why not?" I sulked.

"I'm retired. You can't have a family and be a ninja at the same time."

"Why?" Kenji questioned, jumping up and down in his chair.

"Too much risk. Samurai are ninjas worst enemies, and samurai like to eat children. When Nila was born, your mom said, 'NO MORE!' So, I retired."

Taking a seat back in his chair, Kenji glared at me from across the table.

"What?" I stuck out my tongue.

"You ruin everything."

"Nuh-uh!"

"Yeaaah-huh!"

Our father zipped around the table, grabbing Kenji and I each in one arm. "You're both my little ninjas."

Dropping to his knees, our father started a three-way tickle fight on the floor, right in the middle of the kitchen.

"Dear," our mother sighed, "you're just as bad as the children."

It was the day of graduation, and my most well-kept high school uniform was neatly prepared for its last day of use. Kenji left the house in advance to meet up with Kida, informing me he would see us at the ceremony, thus leaving me alone to deal with our mother. Along with Kenji, Kai also said he would meet up with me at my school because he was running late and had to make a quick stop somewhere beforehand. My ceremony was scheduled before Kai's, so right after mine, we would need to rush over to his.

The night before, it took both Kenji and I hours to convince our mother to attend my graduation. She was obsessed with not wanting to be exposed to people she knew, allowing them to figure out, based on her appearance, that she was sick. Kenji eventually calmed her down, forcing her to listen to the outrageous excuses coming from her own mouth, almost stopping her from attending her only daughter's high school graduation. With the present day at hand, I was glad to see her dressed and ready to go when I went to her room to check on her.

My mother and I took a taxi to my high school, where the ceremony was taking place. As we pulled up to the gate, I sent both Kenji and Kai a message to let them know we'd arrived. The ceremony was set up inside the school's gymnasium because it was where all assemblies and events were held.

Kenji, being the first to arrive, had already saved a seat for both my mother and Kai. I dropped my mother off with Kenji, then made my way to my classroom to prepare. At this point, there was no sign of my father. In the classroom, each student was given a corsage to pin to their uniform jacket, along with a ribbon that was made to dangle below the flower as part of the graduating attire.

Kai messaged me right before the ceremony was about to begin, announcing he had just got to the school and was sorry for being late.

The ceremony opened with the graduating students filing in and taking their designated seats in the front rows facing the stage. Multiple sets of bows and introductions were made, shortly followed by the students singing Japan's national anthem, Kimigayo, as they faced the Japanese flag.

Throughout the ceremony, school songs were sung, and numerous, boring speeches were given, followed by more respectful, robotic bowing. After the final graduating student had received their diploma tube, the student body president spoke for a while on topics related to the future, and how much each of us had grown throughout our time at Ogawa Gakuen. He mentioned memorable moments, such as: school festivals, sports days, and other events hosted at the school, in order to trigger everyone's emotions. Each of us were seated in rows with our classmates, and each person around me was either tearing up or already crying. For some reason, I couldn't get past the little tickle wedged in my throat, making it hard to swallow. Kida was seated two rows in front of me with her class. She, on the other hand, couldn't wipe the tears fast enough.

As the school's director and principal approached the podium, all students rose once again. While our principal commenced his speech, I browsed behind me and made eye contact with Kai who winked back at me. I shifted my gaze to Kenji, who looked oddly happy to be here, as he sat facing the front, smiling brightly. When I glanced at my mother, she was crying, blowing her nose with tissues, but trying to draw the least amount of attention to herself as possible. Continuing to look around, I couldn't find him.

Maybe it's better this way . . ..

The ceremony came to an end with final words from the principal, as he wished us all good luck and prosperity in our future endeavours. All at once, an ocean of students stood and bowed before leaving the rows to meet up with their families and underclassmen friends. Many people were hugging and taking photos in every direction I turned. The crowd forced everyone to shuffle outside, whisking me away in a wave of people as I made my way past the back rows and out the gymnasium doors.

The warm spring air blew over me once I stepped outside. The wind dragged cherry blossom petals through the air, placing them on shoulders and heads of students, faculty, and parents all around. The cherry blossoms were blooming all over town, covering everything in a pink blanket. Their touch against my skin was relaxing, but also left me with doubt and worry about the future as I knew they bloomed for a short period of time.

How many more times will we, as a family, be able to see the cherry blossoms in full bloom?

Outside, my mother and Kai stood next to each other. Kai was standing with a mixed bouquet of flowers. The closer I got to him, the broader his smile became.

"Congratulations, 'Miss High School Graduate,'" Kai said, handing me the bouquet.

With my face warm from embarrassment, a smile managed to squeeze its way through. "Thank you. Was this the reason you were late?"

"Maybe," a sly smirk rose at the corner of his mouth. "I needed some time to prepare one for you, and one for Kida."

"For Kida?"

"Mhm. Your brother came into the shop a few days ago and asked me."

Looking around for Kenji, I couldn't see him anywhere. "Where is he?"

Kai grabbed my shoulders, turning me towards one of the cherry blossom trees growing within the school's grounds. Underneath the tree stood Kenji and Kida, with her bouquet in hand. Kida hung off my brother's neck like a foolish girl in love.

"So, is it true? They have become an 'item'?"

Standing next to me was my mother, catching me completely off guard.

Does she know? Is that what Kenji meant when he said 'I told, Mom'? Scared to reveal any unknown information regarding Kenji and Kida's relationship, I played dumb. "I'm not . . . sure."

"I see. Are you okay with this? She is your best friend after all, and he is your brother. Things could go sour."

"I will be."

"Well then, can we head home?"

"Um, I'm going to attend Kai's graduation ceremony, which is in about an hour, so Kenji will be the one taking you home. Is that okay?"

"Do I have a choice?" she asked, taking the diploma tube from me before turning away.

Not wanting to further upset my mother by answering a question not needing a reply, I gladly gave her my diploma and rushed to fetch Kenji. As I approached the happy couple, Kida attacked me with a hug, drenching me in tears of joy and sadness.

Soon, we all said our goodbyes and parted ways; Kenji went with our mother, Kida stayed behind with friends, and Kai and I rushed to leave.

With my bouquet in one arm, Kai reached down for my hand, lacing our fingers together.

"It's like we're walking home from the same school together."

"Yeah," I giggled.

Making our way to the gated entrance, an outline of an older gentleman appeared against the stone wall. As we got closer, I realized the gentleman was my father. Kai tightened his grip on my hand as we approached with caution.

"Hello, Nila, Mr. Kento," my father said directly with a smile, one arm kept behind his back. "Congratulations on graduating."

"You came . . .," I said with surprise, shocked by my father's appearance before me.

"Of course. I told you I wanted to. I sat at the back, far from your mother," he said, rubbing the back of his neck as a sign of discomfort. "I'm not ready to face her again. Last time didn't go so well . . .."

"Yeah," I replied, unable to find any words to keep the conversation going.

Still smiling, he removed the hand from his back, revealing one peach coloured rose. "For you, Pea— Nila."

As I reached for the flower, Kai pulled my arm back.

"A simple rose cannot buy the respect and love of your daughter. Please remember that, Mr. Izawa."

Allowing me to accept the gift, Kai loosened his grip as I hesitantly received the flower from my father. After holding the rose for no longer than a second, Kai tugged on my hand, wanting to lead us away to avoid any other gesture or conversation with my father.

"You're right," my father said quietly as we passed him. "You're absolutely right."

I looked up at Kai with great concern as we walked down the hill. The usual calm and collected guy I knew, was fuming with immense frustration as his face shot red. Speed walking down the path of my school, Kai didn't say a single word.

"Kai?"

"I'm really sorry, Nila," he stopped in his tracks. "I know it wasn't my place, but he . . . I just couldn't, because he . . .," Kai attempted to explain, but the emotions flowing through him easily took control.

"It's okay. I know why you did what you did. Thank you, but I can't have you coming to my rescue every time I encounter him. Eventually, I'll need to handle things on my own."

"I know, I know," he admitted in defeat, still holding onto my hand securely. "I wish I could save you from every encounter you have with him, even though I know it's not possible." The strength of his hold loosened, as my hand slipped out of his. Kai looked down at me. "You should go back before he leaves."

Thinking carefully about what to do, I reached for Kai's hand and squeezed it. "I'll be back in a minute."

Walking back up the hill, my father continued to grace the school entrance with his presence. Getting closer to him, I noticed that he was taking a call. As soon as he saw me coming, he quickly ended the conversation.

"Nila . . .," his voice cracked.

When I reached a comfortable distance, I lowered my head. "Thank you for paying for Mom's hospital bills. Kenji and I were shocked when we received notice that the remainder, not covered by insurance, was paid for and a future payment plan had been arranged by you. Also, thank you for coming today. I really appreciate it. Take care . . . Dad."

After spitting out everything I had wanted to say for a while, I raised my head and turned around, trying to prevent eye contact. Even though my body moved away, I secretly waited for a reply.

"Of course, Peaches."

Overwhelmed with everything involving my father, his words became daggers jabbing into my heart. If I were to have looked straight into his eyes, tears would have fallen from mine within a matter of seconds. The way he answered was far too familiar; it was bitter-sweet to hear.

Sprinting back down the hill at full speed with flowers in hand, I could see Kai patiently waiting for me at the bottom. Even with his figure closing in, my body refused to decrease in speed. Kai stretched his arms out wide to catch me, and like a child, I allowed myself to be caught. His big arms embraced me, wrapping me up and hugging me securely like a blanket as he rested his head on top of mine.

"Everything okay?"

I brushed my face up and down in his chest. "It was enough to know he came."

Kai let out a burdened sigh which I easily felt against my face. "I understand." Holding onto me for a few more seconds, he squeezed and almost suffocated me. "We have to get going or else we won't make it."

With my shoulders and ribcage about to shatter, I pulled away playfully. "You're right!"

Kai reached for my hand again and I grabbed his without hesitation. We started to run as fast as we could, as if we were being chased. He led me towards a taxi waiting on the street, one he'd previously arranged. Taking a bus, with such a time limit, was dangerously unpredictable at a time like this.

Nothing but good and happy feelings ran through my body as we raced time in order to make it to Kai's school. We hit stand-still traffic halfway there, so Kai decided to pay the taxi driver what we owed and book it the rest of the way on foot.

Running hand-in-hand with Kai felt foolish, but it was the kind of foolishness I wanted in on. Rushing wildly down streets probably made us look like a dumb high school couple, which we were, to those who were watching. This was the kind of high school experience I had missed out on during my three years as a student. I wasn't sure if these warm, crazy feelings were triggered by Kai or by my father having kept his promise by attending my graduation, but I wanted to hold onto these feelings for as long as possible.

Kai's school had a similar style and shape as mine; big, white, and rectangular with an outrageous number of windows. We made it in time, quickly meeting up with Kai's family after he snuck me inside. The ceremony was held in a large gymnasium, just like mine. Nervous about being caught in a different school's uniform, Kai instructed me to stay with his family as he went to his classroom to prepare. I took the second seat in from the aisle in between Mrs. Kento, who kindly welcomed me, and Ryu, who awkwardly stared at me for at least two whole minutes.

When Ryu finally spoke, nothing more than light insults directed at me came out, shortly followed by a smack across the back of his head from Mrs. Kento, who reached around from behind.

When the graduating students came out all properly dressed in their straightened-out uniforms, they took a seat in the designated rows. Looking around at the many faces who wore the same uniform as Kai, it took me only a few moments to spot him—the best looking of them all. There was something about seeing him act so serious that got me riled up. He looked so mature and confident, almost like he was glowing, making it hard to take your eyes off him.

The ceremony was roughly the same length as mine, and with the thought of already having sat through one full graduation, I was surprised at how attentive I was during the second. Watching Kai go up on the stage to get his diploma tube was heartwarming. Our high school lives were ending, and the future was right in front of us, waiting for us to reach out and grab it.

After the ceremony, students scattered like ants across the gymnasium. With the diploma tube in one hand, and nothing in the other, Kai came running at me with full force, pulling me close into his chest and slightly lifting me off the floor effortlessly with one arm.

"We did it! It's finally over!"

Knowing the eyes of his teachers, friends, and family were on us, I tried to push him away out of respect due to our public display of affection, something Kai cared little about. No matter how hard I pushed, he held me with double the strength.

"Kai, people are watching! I'm not even supposed to be here, remember?" I whispered loudly.

He brought his lips to my ear, "No matter how embarrassed you get, I will always show the world how much you mean to me."

Baffled by his straightforward statement, my heart couldn't help but melt. I could feel the heat rising to my face, blushing promptly.

With the clearing of his throat, Mr. Kento had appeared beside us, with Mrs. Kento and Ryu trailing behind. "Congratulations, son. You have made both your mother and I proud. We never doubted you, nor your ability to complete high school. You have truly made us the happiest and proudest parents."

Our bodies separated as Kai looked directly at his father, listening attentively. The look Mr. Kento returned to Kai was one of honour and acceptance as a growing adult. Mrs. Kento was finding it hard to keep it together as she had cried during most of the ceremony. As soon as Kai's father finished, his mother pounced on him, hugging him with obvious love and tears of joy.

I couldn't help but smile and watch as the interactions between Kai and his parents deepened with affection. In my peripheral vision, I realized someone was waiting for us. Taki leaned on the door frame closest to us and tapped his diploma tube against the gymnasium wall. As soon as he caught my attention, his eyes locked with mine. A terrifying shadow lingered over me with memories from our last encounter at the New Year's party.

What does he want?

Kai must have noticed Taki's presence as well, because shortly after, he began wrapping things up with his parents in a hurry. "Mom, Dad, is it okay if I meet you guys back at home? I just want to spend a little more time with Nila before she has to go."

"Yes, of course, son, we understand," Kai's father answered. "Just make sure you don't drop her off too late and make her parents worry. I'm sure they would like to spend time with her as well. Also, your mother wanted to cook your favourite meal tonight, so try not to come home too late."

"I won't, thanks," Kai said with a brief smile.

As his parents and Ryu walked off, Kai locked eyes with Taki.

"What does he want?"

My hands trembled. "I'm not sure. He's been there for a while."

"Stay here," Kai said sternly, placing a gentle hand on my back. "I'll go find out what this asshole wants."

"Kai," I said, tugging on his sleeve as he walked away. "Please don't . . . ."

"Don't worry. I won't do anything to get me in trouble on the last day," he said, talking over his shoulder.

His words had assured me, so I let go of his sleeve. Kai's back was straight, displaying confidence, and a bit of anger, as he walked. Each step he took closer to Taki, made me more nervous than the last.

A couple of minutes went by, and from where I stood, everything seemed calm. With Kai's body blocking Taki's face, I couldn't see Taki until he stepped to the side of Kai. When he did, Kai also took a step in the same direction as if to block Taki from seeing me. Taki placed one hand on Kai's shoulder, which Kai immediately shook off. Just then, Kai looked back at me. He seemed irritated as he rolled his eyes, but signalled for me to come over. Hesitant to get in the middle of their friendship, I took baby steps towards them.

"Taki has something to say to you."

Standing beside Kai, I looked back and forth between them both. The Taki standing before me seemed rational and easy to approach. Almost instantly, Taki bowed before me.

"I'm extremely sorry, Izawa. I'm sorry for my inexcusable behaviour at the New Year's party. I was completely out of line. I was upset with Kai and used you to get under his skin. I've come to terms with my jerk-like behaviour and wanted to apologize for ruining your night and making you feel uncomfortable."

Looking at him, I could see the same Taki who walked me to Kida's house, not the jerk from the party. "It's okay . . . I forgive you."

As soon as the reply left my mouth, Kai grabbed my hand and pulled me back. "We're done here."

"But Kai . . .," Taki started, lifting his head to stand. As Kai was about to turn away, Taki reached for his shoulder to stop him. "Come on, man; I'm trying to apologize here."

Grabbing the hand Taki placed on him, Kai threw it off. "Just because she forgave you so easily, doesn't mean I will."

Kai continued to walk away from Taki, taking me along with him. Watching Taki's dreadful expression as we walked off, I remembered the meaningful words Kai once said to me.

"Kai, wait!" I shouted, pulling my arm back to stop us.

"What is it?" he asked, agitated.

"You're going to regret this decision. High school is over now, and you won't be able to see more than half of these people every day like you used to. Don't you think it would be better to deal with this now before it's too late?"

Kai's body language shifted. He went from clenched fists, to loosened and relaxed. With a heavy sigh, he looked up at the ceiling, then back at me with a smirk. "I hate that you're using my 'not-so-wise' advice against me."

Feeling quite proud of myself, I beamed with achievement.

"Yo, Taki!" Kai shouted, looking over me as he projected his voice.

Taki, already walking in the opposite direction, quickly turned around.

"Don't be a stranger; you know where to find me," Kai finished, reaching out for my hand as he turned back around to continue walking out of the gymnasium.

Grabbing hold of Kai's hand, I was eager to look back at Taki's reaction. When I did, Taki's face lit up with a smile emerging from one corner of his mouth to the other. This type of parting was easier to accept because I knew Kai could walk away from this with his head held high.

On the way home, during the bus ride, Kai held my hand openly for everyone to see. This time I wasn't bothered by our public display of affection. It felt like we achieved something great together, and this small reward was more than precious. With the final day of high school coming to an end, I was glad to put my high school life in the past and welcome a brand new one.

"Hey," Kai said softly, holding out his other hand in a closed fist.

"Hmm?"

"Hold out your hand."

"Why ...?" I asked hesitantly, bringing my hand out slowly.

Scared to find out what he was about to give me, I shut one eye, leaving the other open to peek, as if he were handing me something gross and slimy.

"Take a look."

Opening both eyes, Kai had given me all the buttons to his school uniform jacket.

"Your buttons?"

"Yeah. I thought about just giving you the second one, but I wouldn't dare give any of them to anyone else. That's why I want you to have all of them," he smiled.

With a tight chest, all I could do was smile happily. The fact that Kai exceeded the expectations of a traditional gesture did not surprise me.

So far, our relationship had been fresh and exciting; each passing day became a step closer towards a future I wanted to hold onto. The time I spent with Kai had changed me. In such a short time, he showed me that it was okay to open up to others and experience different things with them. I had been exposed to new things and many firsts when it came to relationships, it was all so exhilarating. If only I had met him sooner, high school could have been more pleasant.

The bus slowly emptied, dropping people off at each stop. Kai continued holding my hand, playing with my fingers as he rubbed over them gently. Our chatter slowed as Kai focused his attention to the passing scenery outside the window.

"Oh!" Kai suddenly straightened up and looked at me.

"What is it?"

"I forgot to tell you; I won't be able to see you for the next couple of days."

"Huh, why's that?" I questioned; a sense of worry lingered as I thought about the short time I had off before college started.

"My parents and Ryu are taking another trip to see my grandparents. So, before they go, my dad wants to show me some business-related material about the shop so I can learn how to run it on my own. Starting tomorrow, I'll pretty much be working full-time. So, until I get the hang of things, I won't be able to see you much. My dad said it's only gonna take a few days, so it shouldn't be too long."

"Oh, I see, sounds exciting." I attempted to smile. "You already ran the shop on your own before, didn't you?"

"Yeah, I did. I've opened and closed it too, so I got those procedures down with no problem. I think my dad wants to start training me to become a partial owner."

Kai looked bright and vibrant as he talked about the shop. This made me realize how my expression before was rude. This was Kai's future, and for him to be working hard towards it so quickly, at such a young age, was truly amazing.

Feeding off his energy, I responded with more excitement. "Congratulations. It's amazing that your goal is in reach."

"Thanks," he smiled. "While my parents are gone, I'll be pretty busy, but I'll try to find time to spend with you."

"It's okay if you can't. I'll also be busy preparing for college and . . .."

"Nila, I want to see you; therefore, I'll make time for you."

His expression was collected and solemn. His eyes darkened with a mysterious notion that lured you in the moment he looked at you. Each time he spoke in such a way, my body became weak.

"Okay . . .."

Chapter Thirty-Four

*A*LMOST A WEEK went by before I saw Kai again, though messages between us were exchanged daily. He had informed me of how hectic the flower shop had become, while I kept him up to date with my college preparations, plus other things I did to keep myself busy. Kida came over a few times to plan for college with me, complaining every chance she could about the short break we got in between. High school finished during the third week of March, and the first week of April was the start of college.

Since graduation, my mother's spirits seemed to have lifted. She acquired a greater sense of hunger and participated frequently during dinner, almost finishing everything on her plate. When it came time to take her medication, she took them without much fuss, but still complained about it. Kenji also seemed to have noticed our mother's change because he walked around the house with a new positive attitude. Things were starting to look up.

Kai's birthday was two days away, and I had completely forgotten about a present. We agreed to meet up for his birthday on the actual day, since the shop was closed on Sundays. In order to come up with some possible gift ideas, I called Kida. She gave me the great idea of buying Kai a nice watch for his new business career look, so, off to the store I went.

After shopping around for a few hours, I managed to select one

I thought would suit him. As I was leaving the shopping district, a toy shop caught my eye. In the window were multiple toys, but the one which grabbed my attention was a small toy car. Laughing at the memory of our birthday conversation during our first and only study date, I couldn't help but chuckle.

This is perfect.

The days flew by and Kai's birthday quickly came. The thought of giving him my gift gave me butterflies, I could only hope he liked it as much as I did. Even though excitement ran through me, I was anxious about going to his house while his family was away. Unfortunately, Kai's parents had to extend their trip a few extra days because Kai's grandmother fell ill again. Before making my way over, I stopped at a bakery to pick up a cake for Kai.

Arriving onto Kai's street with a few bags in hand, Kai waited outside like usual, only this time he stayed at the edge of one of his neighbours' properties. It was past noon when I arrived and the sun was shining brightly, enveloping everything in its warmth. The light spring air blew through the trees, enriching them with energy along my way.

Kai, who stood in the distance, was wearing a black printed, short-sleeved shirt with jeans as he stared down at his cellphone. From afar, he sparkled gracefully like a rich object just out of reach, extremely pleasing to the naked eye. Just like before, passing my father's house was required before reaching the Kento residence.

When I was within sight, Kai looked up from his phone, placed it into his pocket and smiled to welcome me. Kai, once again, held out his hand, waiting for me to reach out and grab it so he could escort me past my father's house, but I was less terrified than before. I didn't even feel the need to look back as we walked past it.

Inside Kai's house, I remembered to remove both shoes before taking off my sweater to avoid the same embarrassing fate as before.

"Kai!"

Surprised by my sudden outburst, he jumped back. "What is it?"

Fidgeting with the straps of the bags between my fingers, I had a hard time concealing my uneasiness. "Happy birthday!"

Smiling, he took a couple of steps towards me and grabbed my chin, tilting it upwards. "You're so damn cute; it weakens me."

With playful words, he kissed my lips tenderly. My face burned like fire as I stood completely still, allowing him to soak me in and take control. We had already kissed multiple times, but each kiss set me aflame all over again.

"Thank you," he said after our lips parted. "But you don't have to be so timid and shy. It would be nice if you could relax when you're around me. Where's that feisty girl I know and love?" Removing his shoes, Kai walked down the hallway, not waiting for my reply.

"Hey," I called out to him before he left my sight. As Kai turned around, I stuck out the hand holding both bags. "Here."

"What's all this?" he asked while reaching for the bags.

"Your cake and birthday present."

"My cake . . . and present?"

"Mhm."

Kai's eyes filled with joy like a child's. "Wow! You didn't have to get me anything. It was enough just getting to spend time with you."

"Sorry, it's nothing fancy, but I hope you like it nonetheless."

He smiled brightly. "Can I open it?"

"If you want," I said, the embarrassment continuing to have influence. "It's yours after all . . .."

Not a second later, Kai gently placed the bag with the cake down on the floor, then unwrapped his gift excitedly. "Awesome, a watch!"

"Yeah, it's to go with your new business lifestyle, you know, like your first gift as an adult. Kida gave me the idea. If you don't like it, I can return it for something else . . .."

With my blabbering, there was no time to realize I was already trapped within a hug.

"I love it. Thank you."

Taking a step back, Kai began fixing the watch upon his wrist.

"You're putting it on now?"

"Why not?"

"Well, um, I don't know. You technically can . . . I guess."

"I'll wear it every day—for two reasons."

"Two reasons?"

"Yep. One, because you gave it to me, and two, because it represents my future success."

"It's just an ordinary watch . . . Success is not guaranteed."

"Sure it is," he winked. "I believe in it." As he fixated on the watch around his wrist, he noticed something else. "Oh, what's this?" Pulling the toy car out from the bag, Kai's face twisted as he looked at me with confusion.

"I couldn't afford a real car, obviously, so this will have to do."

Looking down at the car in his hand, then back up at me, Kai burst out laughing. "You remembered!"

"Of course."

"This is even better than the watch!" he shouted with exaggeration, still laughing.

"Well then, I guess I'll return the watch."

"No! It's my favourite watch!" he exclaimed, possessively gripping onto it.

"Your favourite? How? You only just got it?" I said sarcastically, one eyebrow raised.

"Yeah . . . and? I've already built a strong rapport with it; therefore, it's my favourite."

"Idiot." I was able to spit out before busting a gut.

Kai picked up the cake and took it into the kitchen to open it. He placed it on the counter before removing it from the plastic bag. Promptly following him, I needed to explain my purchase before he had the chance to see it.

"It's just a little something. With your parents being away, I thought you might not get the chance to have one, so . . .."

Looking at me, Kai's smile continued to widen. "So far, this is the best birthday I've ever had. It looks great, Nila. It even has my name on it," he beamed.

"I got them to write on it before packaging it up. I hope you like it."

"I love it. I love the fact that you're here, I love the watch and the car, I love the cake, and most of all . . .I love you. I couldn't have possibly wished for anything better."

My heart pounded explosively. I couldn't look directly at Kai's face, in fear of setting off the bomb in my heart. My knees weakened, like an idiotic girl in a shoujo manga. "Well," I coughed uncomfortably, clearing the knot in my throat, "what did you want to do for your birthday? Did you want to go out or . . . ."

"Can we just stay in for the day?"

As I focused my attention back to him, he looked at me with timid eyes.

"Yeah . . . sure." *What's with that expression?* "Did you have anything specific in mind? Oh, did you eat already? If not, I can prepare something quickly. I'm not a fantastic cook or anything, but I can . . . . "

As I blabbed on, a quiet chuckle from Kai soon turned into a deep laugh.

"What?" I flared.

His face quickly melted into a grin. "Nila, you kill me."

Is he making fun of me?

"I already ate, but thanks. If you stay until dinnertime, then maybe we'll have the chance to eat together," he winked.

Angered by his cunning charm, I crossed my arms. "I'm not your maid, you know! If you're hungry later, then you're going to have to make something yourself. I'm only offering my services as of this instant."

Uncontrollable laughter emerged from Kai as he placed one hand on his forehead, doing a full-face swipe downward over his eyes and nose, ending at his chin. "Jeez woman, make up your mind. First, you'll cook for me; then you won't. Some girlfriend you are. Depriving her boyfriend of a fresh, homecooked meal, on his birthday no less," he said dramatically.

"That's right! I'm a terrible girlfriend! Find some other girl to prepare meals for you." Still with crossed arms, I rolled my eyes and turned away.

"Not possible," Kai said, pulling me into his chest. "The only meals I'll eat are from the girl I love, only yours . . . and maybe my mom's."

Kai's chest smelled of the same cologne from the New Year's party, it was pleasant. His arms were as sturdy as ever, strong enough to hold me securely, but gentle enough that I was comfortable. Within his arms, I felt protected from everything. My hands were pinned near my chest, though I had the ability to reach out and touch him at any moment. With the temptation of wanting to touch him intensifying, I took my hand and pressed it firmly against his upper body. Although my hand wasn't directly over his heart, its beat was strong and picked up speed, each beat faster than the last.

What am I doing? I'm nervous beyond belief that my anxiety could crush me, but I can't pull away.

Kai placed his hand over the one I had resting on his chest. The heat from his hand seeped through, melting me into a state of bliss. He brought his other hand to my face, caressing me softly as he tucked a piece of hair behind my ear. Bending, Kai caught me with a kiss. This kiss felt different than usual; it was much longer and deeper. My lips parted, making room for Kai's tongue to enter. It was different from the last time Kai kissed me this way. It was strange, but not unpleasant.

The hand holding mine glided its way down towards my waist where Kai lifted me up onto my tippy-toes, bringing me in as close as he could to his body. His hand triggered a sharp signal up my spine to my neck. Kai's heat soaked through my clothes and onto my skin, as his warm breath bounced off my face.

"Let's watch a movie."

"Huh . . .?"

Kai removed his hand from my waist and released me from his grasp, then walked out of the kitchen.

"We can watch the movie in my room and eat the cake at the same time. I'll prepare tea to go along with it. You're okay with tea, right?" he shouted from the hallway.

What . . . just happened? "Uh, yeah. Tea's fine," I shouted back, dumbfounded.

"Cool. I'm gonna set up the DVD player, then you can wait in my room as I bring up the rest of the stuff."

Poking my head out from the kitchen, I yelled, "Want me to at least cut the cake?"

"Sure."

As I was about to pull back into the kitchen, I remembered something important. "What about singing Happy Birthday?"

"Nah, it's fine. I'm too old for that. Plus, I don't need to make a wish. I already have everything I need."

"Okay . . .."

Facing the kitchen counter, I searched for a knife inside the drawers. *Did I just imagine all of that? His embrace? The kiss? Did I . . . do something wrong?*

Opening a few drawers to locate the utensils, I got lost in thought. Taking my finger, I traced my bottom lip. "That did happen, right?" I whispered to myself.

The moment Kai and I shared was thrilling. My body felt like it was slipping away from me with each kiss, like I had become a different person—it was scary.

"Here they are." After finding the knives, I pulled one out, then shut the drawer before walking back to the cake. *Oh, we need plates.*

I began opening and closing cupboards.

"They're in here."

Kai appeared from behind me and reached over my head to pull out two small plates from the top shelf. His sturdy chest was pressed against my back as he leaned closer to grab stuff. That slight touch got me going all over again.

Removing the knife safely from my hand, he walked over to the cake. "Never mind, I got it. I don't want you cutting your fingers off or anything," he smirked.

"I'm not stupid. I can cut a simple cake."

"I know, I just like teasing you."

"Idiot," I folded my arms.

"Yeah, yeah. Go wait in my room; the movie's all set up."

"What are we even watching?"

"Oh right," he looked up at me with a goofy expression. "Guess I never told you. Thought we could watch Hachikō Monogatari."

"Hatchi? But, it's so sad!"

"So, you've watched it?"

"Of course, it's a classic! I cry every time. They even made a statue to commemorate the dog in Tokyo."

Smiling, he turned to me. "I love that movie. It's definitely one of my all-time favourites. The relationship between them is unbelievable. It's amazing how an animal can rely on a human and get so emotionally attached. After watching the movie for the first time as a kid, I asked my parents for a dog, but they refused. I pushed for one each year and wished for one on each of my birthdays, but still nothing. I came to the realization that if I wanted a dog, I'd have to move out and get one myself. So, that's exactly what I plan to do. That's why I don't need to make wishes on cakes anymore, because the cake can't miraculously make what I want appear. Besides a dog, I have everything I need. I didn't need to make a wish on a birthday cake to get you; I did that on my own. Wishing is great when you're a kid because it gives you something to hope for and believe in, but when you become an adult, you gotta work for what you want. That's how I think anyway."

Amazing. Everything he said makes sense. I can't help but agree with every word.

"Here," Kai said, handing me a slice of cake.

With mesmerized eyes, I accepted the cake without words. This guy, who I had constantly insulted, was capable of speaking so much truth that the life of an adult became less appealing and the life of a child became quite desirable. Throughout high school, I wanted nothing more than to escape the rumours and people with whom I walked the halls. I spent so much time worrying about my grades and being accepted, when in actual fact, I should have focused on preparing myself for adulthood.

"Hey, you okay?"

"Hmm? Oh, yeah, I'm fine," I said, snapping back into the present moment.

Looking at me with unsure eyes, he headed out of the kitchen. From where I stood, through the archway, I could see Kai reach the staircase with his cake in hand. "Come on."

Making our way up the stairs and into Kai's bedroom, we placed our plates on the table.

"Crap, I forgot the tea. I'll be right back. Start the movie without me," Kai scrambled for words before dashing out.

"You sure?" I shouted after him. "I can wait until you get . . . back . . .."

My sentence faded as he left from my sight. "After all, this is YOUR favourite movie . . .."

I walked to the DVD player and pressed play, then went to one of the zabuton cushions and sat in seiza. As the movie started, I could hear Kai rustling around downstairs in the kitchen. With the anticipation of his imminent return, my hands became sweaty and clammy, while my pulse picked up in speed.

Calm down, Nila, it's just a movie. We're just hanging out and watching a movie. You can do this.

Nervousness slowly consumed me. Even though the movie was playing right in front of my eyes, my mind wouldn't focus. I looked down at my forgotten piece of birthday cake. With a shaky hand, I grabbed the fork and took a bite.

Oh, it's so good! I'm glad I picked chocolate. I hope Kai likes it, too.

Moments later, I heard Kai running back up the stairs.

"Got the tea!" he blurted as he entered the room like a gust of wind, holding a tray.

"Careful not to spill it!" I said, slightly jumping up, preparing to catch it.

"Stop pestering me, woman," he stuck out his tongue.

Copying him, I also stuck out mine.

As Kai placed the tray down on the table, he laughed. "You're just like a kid."

"Shut up! I'm not a child . . . idiot," I said. Saying this, of course, only made him laugh harder.

Kai put a cup in front of me, pouring tea into it before his own. "Careful, it's hot."

"Stop pestering me, MAN!" I mimicked, as I reached for the cup.

Shaking his head in defeat, a smirk appeared on his face. "Don't freak out when you burn that ridiculously loud mouth of yours."

Ignoring his snarky comment, I sipped the tea. "AH!"

"Told you, 'Miss Know-It-All,'" he mocked.

"Dammit. You made it extra hot on purpose . . .."

"Yes, of course, that must be it. I prayed to the Tea God and begged him to make your first sip hot enough to burn you. You caught me," he expressed dramatically, bringing his hands together to pray.

"I knew it . . .."

With both of us laughing, I looked at the TV and realized we had missed the beginning of the movie, and probably wouldn't be catching the rest of it if we kept up our foolishness. Things slowly settled, giving us time to finish our cups of tea and slices of cake, while we gave our best attempt at focusing on the sad movie.

With only a few drops of tea remaining in my cup, I tilted my head back and tried to finish the last little bit.

"Shoot!"

"What's wrong?" Kai looked over to see what had happened, noticing the spilled tea on my blouse. "Oh, shit!" Quickly standing, he ran to his dresser and pulled out a plain, white shirt, tossing it at me. "Here."

"Your shirt . . .?" I said, catching it.

"Yeah, change into it while I put yours in the wash."

Feeling shy and uncomfortable about wearing his clothes, I kindly decided to refuse his offer. "I'm fine, thanks. I'll wash it when I get home. I can just pat it dry with some napkins for now."

"Stupid! It'll stain by then!" he said angrily. "I'll step out of the room, so hurry and change. Let me know when I can come back in, alright?"

"Uh . . . sure."

Kai left the room promptly, leaving me alone as the television echoed in the background. Peering down at my clothes, I noticed a tea stain visible on both my blouse and skirt.

Crap, I thought the tea only dribbled a little on my top, not my skirt, too. At least it didn't get on my white stockings . . ..

Taking Kai's shirt, I lifted it in front of my face to get a better look at it.

Wow, his shirt is huge! He's tall after all, so it only makes sense that his shirts need to be long, but still . . ..

I took off my stained clothes and rushed at top speed to put on the shirt Kai lent me. Before slipping it over my head, I caught a look at myself in my underwear in the stand-alone mirror next to the dresser.

It feels weird to be practically naked in my boyfriend's room. This is humiliating.

As I panicked, a knock was heard at the bedroom door.

"How's it goin' in there? Almost ready?"

"Not yet!" I answered in a shaky, high-pitched voice.

"Take your time."

"Thanks . . .."

Finally throwing it on, I looked down and measured how far the shirt was above my knees. *Oh, it goes down as far as my uniform skirt did.* "This could pass as a temporary dress," I whispered in amazement as I adjusted my stockings back up to my knees.

Standing up straight, a familiar scent caught my nose. The smell was coming from his shirt. I pulled the shirt's collar up to my nose to get a better whiff. The shirt was embedded with his usual smell, and a bit of laundry detergent, as if he were holding me in his arms. I wrapped my hands around my shoulders, hugging myself. His scent was more than captivating. Placing my hands all over his shirt, somehow felt perverted, so I quickly stopped.

Taking my dirty clothes, I walked to the door and opened it. Poking my head out, I found Kai leaning against the wall beside the door. "All done," I said, holding out the clothes.

Turning to look at me, Kai remained silent.

"What?"

"Why'd you take your skirt off?" he asked, his eyes widened as he received my clothes.

"Oh, um, there were a couple of tea stains on it as well, so I thought it would be best to have everything washed together. Is that okay?"

"Yeah . . .," Kai's voice wavered.

Looking up, I glanced at Kai's face before he turned away. "Hmm?"

"I'll, ah . . . go put these in the wash now, so, uh . . . hopefully they'll dry fast!" he said quickly, then descended the stairs.

"Okay . . .," I replied, my voice hesitant. *What was that? His face was red.*

Kai returned ten minutes later, still unwilling to look me in the eye. Standing inside the entrance of his room, he stopped in front of me.

"Hey . . . did I do something to upset you? If I did, please tell—"

Before I could finish, he shot me down. "No." He looked down at his feet. "You didn't do anything wrong. I just, uh," he paused, rubbing the back of his neck, then tugging on it aggressively with his hand. "Man . . .," he exhaled stressfully, "you're killing me."

I stood absolutely still with no idea what I had done to strain him. "Sorry . . . I don't understand."

Completely ignoring my response, Kai went to his dresser and began aimlessly opening the drawers, desperately searching for something.

"Kai . . .?"

"Dammit! Where did all my shorts go?" he shouted frantically, tossing clothes back and forth inside the drawer.

"Why are you looking for shorts?"

"For you to wear!"

"For me? Why? Your shirt is so long; it's like a dress on me," I giggled.

Kai whipped around and grabbed my arm, shoving me towards the bare wall beside the mirror and pinning me up against it.

"Ow, what the . . .," I said, shutting my eyes before colliding with the wall.

Before I could get angry with how rough he was, I opened my eyes. He had both arms pressed against the wall as if blocking me in, while his body towered over me, creating a shadow. There was no way of escaping the sturdiness of his hold. His body, form fitting against mine, left me with little to no room to move, let alone breathe. Quickly searching for his eyes, I realized they were nowhere to be found, which triggered some sort of uneasiness. Within seconds, my one shoulder felt heavier than the other. Kai's almond-brown hair brushed against my cheek as his head rested on my shoulder; a slight moisture accumulated against my neck from each one of his exhaled breaths. Kai's body was so close, it was as if he was using mine as support to hold up his own.

"K—"

"You don't get it," he overpowered.

I couldn't do anything. "What's wrong?"

"Looking like that. With a guy's shirt—my shirt. IT'S DRIVING ME CRAZY!"

Flinching from the shouting done close to my ear, I froze with an unknown fear.

"I'm sorry . . .," he whispered in my ear. "With you, I can't keep control."

Kai's breath lingered at the edge of my ear as his lips slowly worked their way to my earlobe, nibbling it gently. He then placed multiple kisses on my neck.

"Mm— Kai . . .."

The atmosphere changed; the jokes and laughter from before quickly came to an end. Kai lifted his head and now wore an expression so intense; it frightened every inch of me. Squinting my eyes, Kai eased his hand under my jaw as he lined it with his thumb, right before moving it up to my lips, brushing them softly. Even though I was scared, I opened my eyes to see if he still wore the same expression. Never taking the time to notice how long Kai's eyelashes were, I caught him looking down at me. Different from before, his eyes devoured me in a devilish gaze, electrifying every vein running through my body.

Kai brought his lips closer to mine. "I want you to say that you'll love me endlessly."

My heart tightened, then stopped beating completely. Moving in, Kai pressed his lips to mine. My vision clouded with emotion from each passionate kiss. The way Kai continued to kiss me was comparable to nothing I had experienced before. I wasn't even sure if I was doing it right. Kai's tongue slipped into my mouth numerous times; a warm and thrilling sensation poured into me each time our lips connected. His hand assertively held onto my face to direct my lips to where he wanted them, while our bodies remained close together. He kept me from crumpling to the floor.

The long passionate kisses came to a halt as Kai grabbed my waist and lifted me into his arms, which forced my legs to wrap around him as he carried me towards the bed. Kai placed one knee on top of the mattress and slowly lowered me down. With Kai applying so much pressure to the mattress, I easily sunk into it. The sheets on his bed were warm and soft and smelled just like him.

Lying on my back, I could see an assertive Kai, with disheveled hair, gazing down at me. He looked so manly the way he hovered over me; I couldn't help but grow even more attracted to him. His arms were stretched out at both sides of my head; you could see the veins running through them. The short sleeves of his shirt seemed much tighter, almost like it was made to fit his exact figure, lining his triceps in a way that made my mind race in a dangerous thrill.

This side of Kai was one I had briefly interacted with before. He acted this way during the night he slept at my house. Last time Kai terrified me, he was forceful and unfamiliar. This time, my body was crying out for him as I anxiously awaited his every move, his every touch. Kai's emerald eyes were intoxicating, just looking into them sent me on a selfish trip—I wanted to be trapped by him. He was a strong force I wanted to be captured by.

Kai rose from his towering position and balanced all his weight onto his knees, which were placed on each side of my waist. He reached for the back of his shirt with his hands, pulling it up and sliding it off over his head. Above me was now a half-naked Kai, a body of impossible perfection. Only in magazines or in movies had I seen male bodies as glorious as his.

Oh my God! His shirt is off! I'm freaking out! Is this really happening?

Kai tossed his shirt onto the floor, then slowly lowered his body back on top of mine.

"K-Kai, wait . . .."

He continued with his passionate kisses; kisses full of lust and desire. Each time our lips met, I melted from the joyous sensation. Kai's hand played with the end of my borrowed shirt, slipping under it and stroking my hip, gradually making his way up my bare body towards my breasts.

"K . . . ai . . .," I said, an unidentifiable noise escaped from my throat.

He didn't hesitate. With his hand finding its way to my bra, Kai began fondling my right breast. No one had ever touched my breasts. My emotions threatened to run away from me. I couldn't help but panic silently as I allowed him to continue. Finding it hard to admit, I started to crave this new sensation more and more.

I kept my eyes tightly shut as Kai took control. Next, he lifted my shirt. With the shirt trapped because of my arms, he guided my body to an upright position and brought the shirt up to my shoulders, then slipped it over my head in one swift movement. Not caring where it landed, Kai tossed the clean shirt onto the floor. With only my bra and my not-so-cute underwear on, a powerful feeling inside of me took over and instructed me to latch onto Kai's neck, slowly pulling him down closer to my lips. I couldn't get enough of him. My body continued to act on its own, while my head and heart waged war deep within.

A warning light went off in my subconscious as I focused on the insecurities I had with my own body. I was concerned how my breasts might look to him, so I quickly released his neck and covered my chest with both arms.

"What are you doing?" he asked, glaring at me with fixed eyes.

Too shy to look at him, I whispered, "They're not very big, so . . .."

Kai lifted my chin, so our faces lined up with each other. "Don't hide your body from me. I love all of it," he said, as he grabbed the arms that guarded my chest and gently pulled them over my head, pinning them down. "I want to see your amazing body and touch every last inch of it. Nila, I know I'm being selfish, but I want your body to belong to me and only me."

With a heated face and a heart tainted by love, I nodded, giving him permission.

That answer was the confirmation Kai needed, because he came back down closer to me, pushing us deeper into the mattress without breaking our embrace. He kissed my lips once more, this time slowly working his way down to the nape of my neck. Each kiss he left on my body was instantly absorbed into my skin, like water on a sponge, filling my body with an indescribable heat I wasn't sure I could handle. His sweet kisses made their way past my neck and onto my chest, going down closer to my breasts. Fondling my breasts over the bra, he placed many kisses just above the bra line. Kai was touching places I had never imagined a guy would touch. His hands were so gentle, but also extremely powerful. With each kiss getting closer and closer to my actual breasts, I fell into bliss from the touch of his lips and the graze of his tongue.

With great strength, Kai arched my back up smoothly, leaving him enough room to unhook my bra with one hand. He struggled for a short moment, but eventually got it, the whole time keeping my lips occupied with his. As he slid the straps off my shoulders, his kisses left my mouth and progressed down my jawline to my collarbone, finishing off at my shoulders with absolute care.

Everything was moving so fast. Kai had total control over my body like a drug, getting me to a high intoxicating enough to make my chest heave. My skin was on fire, engulfed by flames trying to burn through, while butterflies danced in the pit of my stomach. My heart pounded at full throttle, quaking down to its very core. I could feel him everywhere. He invaded my heart with a love so terrifying, so captivating; I was losing the reflex to resist.

I'm scared! I'm scared to have sex! What if I'm not good at it? Kai already has so much experience. What if She's better than me? My mind was running wild; I could feel my eyes filling with tears from the stupid paranoia playing out in my head. "Wait!"

"Nila . . . ?"

My eyes were completely shut and the weight over my body decreased as I heard my name come from the person I cherished so deeply. Opening them, I could see Kai's half-naked body fully extended above me. The passionate kisses, full of sweet emotion, had stopped and an unsettled expression was worn by the person I was about to fully open myself up to.

"Nila . . . why are you crying?"

I raised the tips of my fingers to my face, padding the tears trickling down my cheeks and onto my hair. Not understanding why tears were falling, I answered truthfully. "I . . . I don't know."

Alarmed by my reaction, Kai quickly sat up. He placed both feet on the floor and hunched over, resting his arms on his knees.

He's mad! Why the hell am I crying? Why can't I do this? People have sex every single day with people they don't even know, so why can't I share this moment with the one person I love the most?

"Kai, I'm sorry," I said. I sat up and covered my chest with my arms.

Kai turned to me. "Why are you sorry? I'm the one who should be sorry! I keep forcing you to do things you don't want to do."

Disappointed with myself, I corrected him. "No, you don't understand . . . ."

"What is it I don't understand?"

"I want to do this with you—I really do! I'm just scared to do it. I heard it really hurts the first time . . . and you already have so much experience and, and—it's going to hurt, right?"

A gentle smile returned to his face. "I was afraid of being too pushy with you again. I don't want you to force yourself to do this with me if you're not ready or don't want to. I love you so much and I know this is something I want to experience with you. I just wasn't sure if you . . . felt the same."

Wait, Kai was questioning my feelings for him?

Trying to find a way to make it up to him, I crawled up behind Kai and hugged him. With my naked breasts pushed up against his smooth, muscular back, I placed a single kiss on his shoulder before resting my head on him. "I love you, too."

As my face was pressed to his back, I could hear and feel his heartbeat increase as we continued to sit close. Not even a second after, Kai turned around and faced me.

"You're so damn beautiful, how did I get so lucky?"

With the kindest of words flowing into my ears, he threw himself on top of me, pushing me back onto the bed. Pulling back the sheets, he guided our bodies underneath. Lifting the covers with his broad back, he began undoing his jeans, awkwardly sliding them off, along with his socks. He released one arm from the sheets and tossed his clothes onto our small, disorganized pile. Kai slowly slipped my stockings off and threw them onto the floor.

With both of us down to our last garments, we couldn't help but have a good look at each other's bodies. My face was filled with embarrassment as I felt Kai's eyes examining my body up and down, judging every inch of me. When I glanced up at Kai, his face was also red, making me feel slightly less anxious.

Carefully, Kai discarded our final pieces of clothing, then moved right back on top of me. Nothing separated our bodies now. As he lingered over me, he smiled softly and slipped one of his hands into mine. He brought our intertwined hands up past my head, then leaned on his forearms.

"Your body is absolutely gorgeous, Nila."

My body temperature increased to its max. Every word, every kiss, left me breathless. He had become the happiness I felt deep in my heart, the kind of happiness I truly yearned for. I followed his every movement impulsively, teeth clenched together as my vision faded into a white bliss from such intensity. Kai gripped my hands tighter, almost crushing my fingers. The instant our fingers seized, was the moment we shared one breath. That was the moment I felt most alive. As I laid in Kai's bed, having dropped all my defences, I drifted into ecstasy.

The movie continued to play in the background, like white noise, neither of us paying any attention. That was my first time.

Chapter Thirty-Five

AFTER HAVING EXPERIENCED sex for the first time, I felt different, somewhat changed. Within less than a year, I got my first boyfriend and lost my virginity, something I didn't expect to lose so early. The entire time it was happening, Kai kept asking me if I was okay, and that night, after going home, Kai sent me many messages through Line, making sure I was still okay. The whole thing happened so quickly; it was embarrassing to look back on. I could vividly remember the way Kai looked at me with his beautiful eyes. It was a look I would surely remember for the rest of my life.

The short week before college started, Kai and I spent as much time together as possible before things got busy. I was nervous to start fresh at a brand-new school with brand-new faces, but Kai encouraged me each step of the way.

Before I knew it, I was already a month and a half into my college program. My classes were much more challenging compared to those of high school, and I wasn't the only one who thought so. Kida had a difficult time adjusting to the change, and to the amount of assignments given by the professors in her program. Even with the heavy workload, I was really enjoying my time as a college student. It was a nice change not having to wear a uniform every day.

While I was enjoying college life, Kai worked hard at the flower shop each day. By then, he was fully able to run the store on his own, which gave his grandfather the peace of mind to finally retire in the country-side. Kai took his job at the flower shop seriously, even more so than before. No longer based on expectations or obligations, Kai grew to enjoy the responsibility of managing the shop.

On a weekly basis, I would go and visit Kai at the shop to watch him in action. The way he managed the store, while interacting with custom-ers, put a silly smile on my face. Observing him in his new surroundings was enough to make me acknowledge the beneficial decision he made for his future.

With college being further away from home than my high school, Kenji was left to take care of our mother for the majority of the mornings. My days started a bit earlier than Kenji's, so he was in charge of breakfast, plus lunch preparations, while I was left with dinner and medication dispensing. The night before, I would measure out all of our mother's medications and leave them on the kitchen counter for the next morn-ing. With both of us away from the house during lunch, it was up to our mother to fend for herself, unless it was one of the days that the nurse was around.

As time went on, we noticed most of the lunches prepared for our mother were being thrown out in the garbage outside around back. When we discussed it with her, she ignored our questions and called our persistent hovering annoying. This confused us, as she had been eating and doing so well not long ago.

Over the course of a month, my mother's hospital visits became more frequent as her health deteriorated, with the three of us making trips almost every other day. The doctor's discovered tumours had spread from her breasts to her lungs, with signs of new masses lining the outside of her liver. It felt like each time my mother went into the hospital, more bad news came about. Going to the hospital had become its own dis-ease entirely. Depression and frustration hung over me like a dark haze I couldn't shake.

There were a few times when Dr. Ashima had looked at me with cau-tion, but I turned a blind eye. I couldn't accept what was taking place right in front of me. Kenji wore his emotions on his sleeve whenever my mother wasn't looking. I could see that he was burning himself out as he used up all of his strength and positivity to comfort her with his fake smile. Anytime I tried to have a conversation about our mother's condition, he would click his tongue in disapproval and storm off.

One night I came home later than usual, my mother was already in bed, and I caught Kenji folding a bunch of paper cranes at the kitchen table. Pieces of rainbow origami paper consumed every inch of the kitchen, like small bodies of water uniting. Cranes were stacked on top of each other on all surfaces; from toppled over piles on the table, to bundles resting on the counters and falling onto the floor.

The origami art of folding and stringing a thousand paper cranes together represents good health and longevity. It was once believed that one who could fold a thousand paper cranes, would have their wish granted. It had become a symbol of hope and healing during difficult times. I personally never folded cranes for a greater purpose other than when the teachers would tell us to do so in school, usually for festivals. For someone to fold a thousand of them with a special person in mind, to me, it reflected the feeling of losing hope.

That night, I watched my brother from the kitchen entrance with tears clouding my vision. Kenji looked up from his work and saw me sobbing. When he invited me to the table with his eyes, I took a seat. Night slowly grew into morning as we completed one thousand paper cranes together; hands full of papercuts and hearts emotionally drained. Not wanting our mother to see, we stuffed the cranes into large bags and placed them in the closet on the main floor. Thankfully they all fit, but I had no idea what Kenji planned to do with them.

Chapter Thirty-Six

ANOTHER MONTH WENT by and summer began to appear in June. My first set of exam preparations were already underway. Some days, I would even forget to eat because there was no time to balance everything going on in my life, let alone study hard for perfect scores. There were mornings in which I would wake up feeling nauseated from the lack of food intake, sometimes throwing up nothing but water. Without a doubt, my body hated me. Most mornings, I would oversleep and miss breakfast, because I'd rather sleep than eat, so I would mooch food off of Kida if I managed to catch her in the building before our first class. Other than that, most mornings were going according to schedule, up until the day of my first written exam.

"Here you go, drink this," the nurse got up from her chair and handed me a cup of water.

"Thank you," I said before taking a sip.

"So, Miss Izawa," the nurse started, making it back to her seat, "the school records say this is your first visit to the infirmary. Have you been feeling alright lately? I know exam time can put a lot of stress on students."

"Well, I guess I haven't been eating regularly. There's some stuff going on at home . . . and with exams . . . I guess it's been getting the better of me," I answered honestly.

"I see, well, I'm not a psychiatrist, so I'm not going to get into personal matters, unless you wish to discuss them. I just want to make sure you are taking care of yourself during these stressful times so that throwing up all over your exam paper doesn't happen again."

"Yes, Ma'am."

"How have your sleeping patterns been lately? Are you going to bed at a consistent time?"

"Not really . . .."

"Alright," she said as she typed information into the computer at her desk. "From what I gather, it seems you're demonstrating signs of anemia. I suggest you find more time in your schedule to let your body have the proper rest it needs, and things should start going back to normal in no time."

Standing up, I set the cup on the nurse's desk and bowed. "Thank you."

Reaching down for my bag, I grabbed the strap and pulled it over my shoulder as I made my way to the door.

"Oh, Miss Izawa, before you go," the nurse looked over from the computer monitor. "Make sure you check in with your professor and tell them I have submitted approval for you to have the opportunity to rewrite your exam. It will be up to the professor to decide when."

At the doorway, I bowed my head in her direction once more. "Thank you very much for taking care of me."

Making my way down the hall towards my class, uneasiness bubbled in my stomach again. Before heading back to class to speak with the professor, I stopped at the closest washroom and threw up in the toilet. With my upset stomach subsiding, I was able to pull myself together to go speak with the professor.

When I reached the classroom, there were still a few students writing their exams, so I patiently waited outside the door until they were done. As soon as the last student left, I went in to inform the professor of what had happened and he kindly agreed to let me rewrite my exam on the weekend.

A few days later, I went to Kida's house for our first sleepover since becoming college students. With my usual items in hand, Kida and I walked up the stairs to her room.

"Hey, you okay?" Kida questioned as she shut the door, setting my bag on the floor beside her bed.

"Yeah, I'm fine. I've just been a bit queasy lately."

"Do you feel sick? Did you catch something at school?"

"I don't know, maybe?" I said, not sure where I could have caught this bug.

"Hmm, well, if you need anything, let me know. We've got some medicine downstairs."

"Thanks."

The night carried on, but the same unsteadiness in my stomach continued. Depending on how I was sitting or lying down sometimes made a difference in my level of discomfort, but for the most part, it still ached.

"How did your first exam go? You said you had one this week, right?" Kida asked as she sat on her bed.

"Yeah, I did, but um . . . it didn't go too well," I said, taking a seat beside her.

With a look of confusion, Kida tilted her head like a puppy. "What do you mean? What happened?"

"I got sick during the exam and threw up all over the paper. I don't really remember exactly what happened, but the next thing I knew I was in the infirmary. I think someone must've escorted me there."

"SERIOUSLY?" Kida jumped at me, grabbing my shoulder. "Nila, that's not good—like at all! What's gonna happen with your score?"

Jolting back due to the sudden closeness of her face, I reassured her. "I'm going to rewrite the exam on Sunday."

"Like, this weekend?"

"Yeah."

"Man, that sucks. Guess you won't be able to see Kai this weekend, huh?" she dropped her arms, pulling away slowly.

"It's okay; there will be other weekends."

"I guess," she sighed, falling back onto the bed and looking up at the ceiling.

Following her lead, I also laid back.

"How are you guys doing anyway?"

Catching me off guard, I turned red as I remembered Kai's birthday. With school and life being so hectic, Kida and I hadn't really had the time to hang out or catch up until now. Not wanting to tell her about my first time through Line, I kept pushing the news off until I had the chance to tell her in person.

I played dumb from nervousness. "What do you mean . . .?"

"Come on, you know," she turned her head to look at me. "Everything okay in paradise? Any progress?"

Should I tell her now? UGH! Why is it so embarrassing to talk about sex? Hesitant to get into this conversation and fall into Kida's trap, I remained calm and collected. "Things are . . . fine."

She rose halfway, turning her upper body to face me as she propped her arm on the bed, then placed her hand under her head to hold it up. "Just 'fine'?"

Turning my embarrassed face in the other direction, I stayed quiet. I knew exactly what she was getting at, and even though she was my best friend, it felt awkward to say such a private thing out loud.

"Nila, come on!" she teased, tugging at my shirt in hopes I'd turn back towards her.

As I rolled my head back to face her, our eyes connected. Within seconds, a sly grin crept upon her face. I quickly covered my face with my hands to hide.

She flung up like a catapult. "SHUT UP! NO, YOU DIDN'T!"

Shocked by her cleverness, I immediately jumped and covered her loud mouth. "SHH! Your parents!"

"Right, right! Sorry!" Her voice sounded muffled under my hand. "But . . . OH MY GOSH! I can't believe you guys did it! My little Nila is no longer a virgin!"

"UGH!" I grunted in frustration. Removing my hand from her mouth, I reached for one of the pillows on her bed to cover my embarrassed face. "Shut up," I moaned desperately into the pillow.

"I can't believe it. Nila, all grown up. This is a day for celebration!" She jumped off the bed and ran for the door. "I think we have some sweets downstairs, the kind you like! Since you're not a big drinker."

I removed the pillow from my face and placed it on my lap. "Please don't, I beg you," I said, sitting up with a displeased look.

"I'll be right back," she sang as she left the room.

Slumping back on the bed, I took the pillow and buried my face into it once more wanting to scream. "UGH! I'm such an idiot . . .."

Sounding like a stampede of animals, rummaging through the kitchen, Kida finally made it back to her room with a bag of candy in hand as she slammed the door with incredible strength.

"KIDA!" Mr. Nazuka called from downstairs. "DON'T YOU DARE BREAK THAT DOOR OR ELSE IT'S COMING OUT OF YOUR POCKET!"

"Sorry Dad!" Kida faced the door while replying. Right after, she whipped around and ran to her bed, taking a huge leap onto it. "Here, Nila," she said excitedly, tossing the bag at me.

Moving my face away from the bag's line of impact, it ended up smacking me in the chest, knocking the wind out of me. "Ow . . . thanks."

I opened the brand-new bag of Melon Tart Chew, my favourite candies, and shoved a few into my mouth.

"Sooo," Kida perused, "tell me! Tell me! I wanna know the juicy details."

Choking on the candy, I replied in frustration. "You're so embarrassing!"

"Embarrassing, how? I'm your best friend! The problem isn't that it's embarrassing, the real problem is you're too secretive. When were you planning on telling me if I hadn't asked?" Her mouth opened in awe. "Were you even planning on telling me?"

"Enough questions!" I expressed in defeat. "I'll tell you. Just keep your voice down."

"Got it!" she said in an elevated voice, pretending to zip her lips with an imaginary zipper and locking it with a key.

Rolling my eyes, I explained the start of Kai's birthday. When it came to the part about his gift, I told her that her watch idea was a success and how thankful I had been for it.

"It happened on his birthday? That was months ago! You're only telling me now?" she asked, partially offended.

"I know, I know!" I replied in a loud whisper. "Things got sort of busy . . . Sorry."

As I continued to talk about Kai's birthday, my stomach started acting up again, to the point where I had to stop speaking and rush to the bathroom before all the candy I just ate ended up on Kida's bed.

Kida followed me to the bathroom down the hall in a panic. "What's wrong?"

After throwing up into the toilet, I backed away from it and placed one hand over my mouth and the other on my stomach, rubbing it slowly. "It's my stomach; it's acting up again."

"Is it from all the candy?"

"Possibly," I pondered. "I haven't been able to keep much down, so maybe the candy isn't agreeing with me."

"But you eat this candy all the time? That can't be it."

Looking up at Kida from the bathroom floor, I watched as her face went from concerned to almost petrified as her eyes broadened.

"What?"

"Um," she paused in a shaky voice. You could almost see the wheels in her head turning as she stood deep in thought. "Just a crazy thought . . . like seriously crazy, but um . . . have you . . . gotten your period recently?"

Trying to remember back to the last time I had my period, I came to the conclusion it hadn't appeared in quite some time. "Now that you mention it, I don't really remember the last time I had it. It's been a while."

"Uhhh . . . huh," she said suspiciously. "Here's another crazy question—again crazy, but . . . did you and Kai . . . use a condom?"

"A WHAT!"

"Shut up, I'm serious! Did you, or didn't you?"

Thinking back to Kai's birthday, I relived the moment of my first time, a moment I would never forget. Going through each movement and every embrace, the image of a condom never came. My eyes widened in a shock like no other as my mind instantly drew blank.

The same expression crossed Kida's face. "Okay—um—wow!" her voice grew louder and full of panic. "Okay, everything's fine!" Kida quickly shut the door to the bathroom, then instantly began pacing back and forth.

"Ki-Kida . . .."

"Don't freak out. Don't panic."

"YOU'RE MAKING ME FREAK OUT! STOP MOVING!"

"Shh-shh!" She rushed to my side and placed a hand over my mouth, struggling to silence me. With the eyes of a crazy woman staring into my soul, she jumped up. "I'VE GOT IT! Nila, stay here and lock the door behind me, okay?"

Still in shock, I reached for her hand. "Where are you going?"

"Don't worry, I have a plan, well, an idea," she said, her voice trembling at different pitches. "I'm gonna go to the corner store; I'll be right back. I'm gonna tell my parents I need to go to the store to get some more candy. So, if they ask, that's what I'm getting, okay? OKAY!"

"Okay . . .."

With my uncertain confirmation, Kida rushed out of the bathroom and closed the door behind her. The stampede of animals returned as she rushed down the stairs, shouting something quickly to her parents before the sound of the front door opening and closing was heard. Just as Kida instructed, I locked the door behind her, then curled up into a ball in the corner beside the toilet.

There is no way . . . There's just no way.

Fifteen or so minutes passed before Kida returned. Her parents had remained downstairs the entire time watching TV, so I was off the hook for any explanations. Kida knocked on the bathroom door, informing me she had returned. When I opened it, Kida was discreetly holding a scrunched up, brown paper bag at her side.

"Here," she whispered, handing me the bag.

"What is it?"

"Two pregnancy tests," she whispered again, letting herself in partway.

"TWO WHAT?"

"Shh! You'll need to use both tests to make sure the first one's accurate."

My heart grew heavy. "Kida . . .."

"I'll be right outside the door."

Kida forced the paper bag into my hands, then backed up and shut the door slowly, again, leaving me alone in the compacted room.

Even though I knew what Kida was getting at, and I knew exactly what was inside the bag, my body stood frozen in fear behind the closed door. My brain was smart enough to understand the current situation, but time felt like it had stopped.

Unable to control my breathing, the exhaled air leaving my body got caught in my throat, making it impossible to swallow the built-up saliva lingering in my mouth. My chest grew tight, as if someone were stepping on it with all their might. With the air so thin, I began to hyperventilate. I fell to my knees and dropped the bag on the floor.

What is this? This life . . . What's happening?

A faint knock was heard at the door.

"Nila, you okay in there?"

The sound of Kida's voice snapped me back into a calmer state, enough for the intense, raspy breathing coming from my mouth to lessen.

I'm not alone. Kida's here.

"Nila?"

"Y-yeah . . . I'm okay."

"Let me know when you're finished."

"Yeah . . .."

I read the instructions on the box carefully before opening it. Inside was another paper, tightly folded up, along with a long, thin plastic stick. Unfolding the paper, I could see another set of instructions with pictures. The pictures were stupid diagrams, explaining the method and stance to use when urinating on the end of the stick.

For a girl to be able to aim was already a task all on its own. The hardest part was to accumulate enough liquid out of thin air in order to actually go on command. After a few minutes of forcing myself to pee, my body conveniently decided it needed to go.

When both tests were completed, I couldn't even look at them. Taking a minute to clean myself up, I unlocked the door for Kida to enter. As soon as the lock unhitched, Kida burst in, again locking it behind her. Looking down at her hands, they were shaking.

"Sooo, what do they say?"

"I couldn't bring myself to look at them."

"Do you want me to do it?"

Nodding my head, I turned around to face the opposite wall. It took no longer than a few seconds before a devastating response was heard from Kida.

"Nila . . . what are you gonna do?"

Looking back at Kida wasn't an option. I knew exactly what she meant when she asked that question. In just seconds, my legs weakened and I fell to the floor. All the strength and support of my legs turned into mush, while my arms and hands trembled with an unending quake. The irritably fragile heart of mine lapped different cycles of pressure, tightening, releasing, and stopping completely.

'*What does this mean?*' were the only words continuing to play in my head.

Kida placed a gentle hand on my shoulder. "Nila, I'm not sure if you're going into shock, but I want you to know no matter what happens, and no matter what your decision is, I'm gonna be here for you every step of the way."

Kida's words rang kindness through my ears, but they couldn't register. I tried hard to focus, but I wasn't sure what I should be focusing on.

"Will you keep it?"

I turned around to face Kida who was kneeling on the floor beside me. "Keep what?"

" . . . The baby?"

"The . . . baby . . . ."

Kida grabbed my face and brought it closer to hers. "Nila, you're having a baby—Kai's baby! Do YOU understand?"

A baby with Kai . . . WAIT! KAI! A panicked and devastated expression crept onto my face. "KAI! WHAT DO I TELL HIM? What will he think of this? OF ME?"

Kida cupped a hand over my mouth. "SHH! Nila, shh. It's okay, breathe—breathe in," she took a deep breath in, "and out," then exhaled.

She repeated this demonstration a few times until I caught on and followed her lead.

"That's it, just like that. Now, listen here," she said with a stern voice, still cupping my mouth as I continued to breathe deeply through my nose. "Tomorrow is Saturday. We're gonna put on our clothes and head off to school like usual, but instead of going to school, we're gonna take a bus and go straight to the hospital to confirm things with a doctor. Just in case the tests were faulty, okay?"

Unable to form words, I nodded, agreeing with her plan. Watching Kida's mature actions and put together attitude, was comforting. Usually her plans were inappropriate and extremely unorganized. But this time, for my benefit, it sounded carefully thought out which gave me the assurance and guidance I needed.

Kida stood, releasing her hold on my face as she went back to the pregnancy tests resting on top of the small counter. She placed both tests, and all other evidence, back into the brown paper bag, rolling it up tightly.

"I'll get rid of these; meanwhile, you head back to my room and wait for me there."

"Alright," I said without confidence, nodding my head with vacant eyes.

Kida walked out with determination, while I remained knelt down on the floor inside, the door slowly creaking as it swayed back on its hinges. Staying in the bathroom might have caused a scene if the Nazukas walked in, so I managed to pick myself up and move to Kida's room like instructed.

As soon I got inside and shut the door, I instantly collapsed. My body shut down; crying didn't feel possible. All the tears inside of me had dried up, like water in a desert. The future I had set in stone for myself, was now crumbling and so unclear.

Some time later, I couldn't even tell how long, Kida returned empty-handed.

"I took care of the tests."

"Okay," I mumbled from the bed where I had eventually crawled to, tears recovered enough to fall and soak into the pillow I was lying on.

Kida sat beside me and ran her fingers through my hair. "Nila . . .."

"Hmm . . .," I spoke through silent tears, gazing at my quivering hands.

"Tomorrow, if we find out you're actually pregnant, will you choose to keep the baby?"

Unable to formulate such a thought, let alone the answer, I closed my eyes. "I don't know."

"What about Kai? You're gonna tell him, right?"

I fell silent. "I don't know."

Kida stopped playing with my hair and moved her hand down my back, rubbing it slowly. "I think you should, well, I mean, eventually you're gonna have to. Kai's a really great guy, Nila. He'll be there for you every step of the way, just like me and Kenji will."

With my brother's name mentioned, my heart elevated. "YOU CAN'T TELL KENJI!" I shot up. "Definitely not! You can't tell anyone!"

"Okay, okay! I promise—I won't tell him. But Nila, eventually, you're gonna have to tell him, too."

Lying back down into the same position after hearing her promise, I buried my face deep into the damp pillow. "Yeah . . . eventually."

Kida laid beside me and continued to rub my back until I fell asleep, which wasn't for a few hours. By that time, the pillow was drenched with tears, along with one I hugged against my chest. We didn't say much because all I could do was cry. Like an intoxicated person, I expressed feelings about not being able to finish school and other future aspirations in babbling nonsense as Kida stayed beside me, listening quietly. Towards the end, my eyes were extremely sore and puffy from crying. I tried to hold back tears out of pain, but my body had every intention of continuing until I passed out.

Before drifting off into a deep sleep, I couldn't help but think of the two plastic sticks currently holding so much power over my life. Even though the two pregnancy tests came out positive, every bit of hope inside of me prayed for a miracle, that tomorrow the doctor would deny me of being pregnant this young.

Chapter Thirty-Seven

THE NEXT DAY, Kida and I got up early and packed our bags like usual. With her father having already left for work, we wore fake smiles and waved goodbye to her mother before taking off.

The bus ride was dreadful. Without saying a word, Kida sat beside me, linking arms with me the whole way to show her support. There were times my heart rate rose, and times in which it settled. When I tried concentrating on breathing, my breaths became irregular, causing me to choke on air.

When we arrived at the hospital, Kida was the one who approached the front desk and asked for directions to the pregnancy centre so that rumours wouldn't spread around, eventually tracing back to my mother. After confirming which wing it was in, she waved me over casually and we went on our way.

At the pregnancy centre, there was a small waiting room with one older woman sitting and reading a fashion magazine. Looking over at the receptionist's desk, I was glad to see an unfamiliar face sitting at it. The receptionist was a young lady who wore a certified nurse's badge on the left side of her uniform. Kida was first to approach the desk.

"Hello."

The receptionist looked up from her computer screen. "Hello, how may I help you?"

"My friend needs to confirm if she's pregnant. Is there a doctor in?" Kida stepped aside, leaving me in direct sight of the young receptionist.

"Yes, Dr. Toma is in. She's the Obstetrician here today," she responded kindly. "There is one person before you. You will be called in when it's your turn. May I have your name?"

Kida looked over and signalled at me with her eyes to respond.

"Um, it's Nila Izawa," I said quietly.

The receptionist smiled. "Thank you. I'll need you to fill out some paperwork before you see the doctor," she said, handing me a preorganized clipboard. "You may have a seat as you fill it out."

Kida and I bowed, then walked over to the two closest chairs to take our seats.

"It's gonna be okay," Kida said under her breath, trying to put on a confident smile.

"Mhm."

After filling out all the questions on the clipboard to the best of my ability, I turned in my new patient information sheet.

Fifteen minutes went by and the door to Dr. Toma's office opened. A young-looking couple, possibly newlyweds, walked out of the room with bright, beaming smiles on their faces, shortly followed by an elderly woman in a long, white lab coat. The elderly woman wore a badge, similar to that of the receptionist, on the left-hand side of her chest which read: *Dr. Sakura Toma.* Dr. Toma had a friendly face as she said goodbye to the couple, making me feel a bit more at ease. Also, seeing Dr. Toma was a female, gave me great comfort.

Dr. Toma read from a list and called in the older woman who sat in the waiting room across from us. Closing the magazine, the woman placed it on the small table in the middle of the room, then walked to Dr. Toma as they entered the office together.

With fear and anxiety building as my turn grew near, I reached for Kida's hand and squeezed it as tight as I could. Squeezing back just as hard, Kida looked at me.

"Nila, it's going to be okay. Whatever happens, just remember, I'm here for you."

Squinting my eyes shut, I nodded.

A while later, the door to Dr. Toma's office reopened and the older woman walked out alongside Dr. Toma. Again, the woman seemed pleased as she bowed to thank Dr. Toma before heading off. Dr. Toma read from the clipboard in her hands, then brought her gaze up to meet mine.

"Nila Izawa."

Kida and I both jumped to our feet and made our way to the door where Dr. Toma commenced walking into her office ahead of us. Once we were both inside, Dr. Toma had already made it to her desk.

"If the last one in could please shut the door," Dr. Toma asked.

"Sure thing," Kida said, shutting the door behind her.

"Now, which one of you is Miss Izawa?"

My heart jumped once my name was said. "Th-that would be me."

"Perfect. If you could come sit here on the bed, dear," Dr. Toma said, directing me over to the examination bed. "Your friend can sit on the chair," she pointed to a stand-alone chair against the wall opposite from the bed.

Kida quietly took her seat, while I sat on the bed.

"So, you are here to confirm a pregnancy, I see."

"Y-yes, Ma'am."

"Have you taken any form of pregnancy test?"

"Yes, I've taken two over-the-counter tests, both came out positive. I guess I'm here to triple check . . .," I answered, my voice shaking with each word.

"Understandable. I have been doing this for many years, and I know those tests are not always one hundred percent accurate," Dr. Toma said as she wrote some stuff down on her clipboard. "When was your last period, dear?"

"I'm not . . . exactly sure. Two or three months ago, maybe? I don't normally keep track . . .."

"Alright," she continued to write. "Have you been taking any form of birth control?"

"No."

"Okay. Any signs of uneasiness, like throwing up, mostly in the mornings, or feeling dizzy and tired out of the blue?"

Recalling the times my stomach felt unsteady for the past while, plus the time I threw up during my morning exam, I folded my hands together to stop them from shaking. "Yes. I've experienced all of that."

"When was the last time you were sexually active?"

With my head lowered, I answered, "About two and a half months ago."

I looked at Kida who was already smiling back. No matter how many times I looked at her, she wore the same smile of reassurance. Having her here was probably the only way I could have gone through with this, there was no way I could have done this alone.

"Okay, Miss Izawa," Dr. Toma said as she stood and placed the clipboard on top of her desk before walking to a cupboard. "I will need you to put this on," she said, handing me a hospital gown. "You can change behind the curtain if you feel uncomfortable." She pointed to the corner beside the bed where a small curtain hung from a wraparound bar.

I reached for the gown in Dr. Toma's hand. "Th-thank you."

Heading to the curtain, I was glad to see it reached the floor, because as soon as I pulled it around me, I crouched down to my knees, hugging the hospital gown as tight as I could. Behind the curtain, I was breathing stiffly, trying to hold back tears, cautious of my surroundings. Here I was, at the hospital with my best friend, confirming if I was in fact pregnant. Not being able to keep it in any longer, I started crying silent tears into the gown, refusing to let out a single sound and cause a scene.

Eventually putting my emotions in check, I quickly took off my clothes and put the hospital gown over me, then stepped out from the curtain.

"Excellent," Dr. Toma announced. "If you could kindly take this jar and make your way to the washroom," Dr. Toma continued, handing me a small clear jar. "I need you to provide me with a urine sample. Once you are done, make your way back to the bed and we can continue the examination. If you need water, there is a small fountain near the washroom in the hall."

Slowly, I took the jar from Dr. Toma and made my way out. Kida followed me to the washroom and waited outside in case I needed anything. Finally, after being able to provide a sample, we both went back into Dr. Toma's office.

After handing the sample to Dr. Toma, I sat on the examination bed as instructed. Dr. Toma took the sample to a small lab table she had stationed near her desk. On this table, there were a few unfamiliar machines and incubation holders where she proceeded to run a few tests with my sample. Leaving the sample in one of the incubators, she came back towards the bed.

"Alright dear, as we wait for that, I am going to proceed with a Pelvic Exam. Do you prefer to have the curtain covering you or are you alright with it open?"

"Um, open is fine. What's a pelvic exam?" I inquired.

"A pelvic exam is a physical examination where I will mainly inspect the vagina, cervix, ovaries, uterus, and a few other parts for any signs of illness. For this exam, I will need you to lie down on the bed. Your friend may stay in the room or you can ask her to leave, that is completely up to you," Dr. Toma explained.

"Um, I prefer it if she stayed," I said, in fear of Kida leaving me alone.

Dr. Toma smiled. "As you wish."

Stretching myself out on the bed, I could feel my body shaking from head to toe.

"I am going to need you to relax, dear. The more relaxed you are, the less discomfort you will feel."

"I'll try . . .," I said, unable to convince even myself.

Dr. Toma began the physical examination. Never having something so weird done to my body, I regretted my decision to have Kida in the room. Once Dr. Toma was finished, I was able to finally relax.

"The pelvic examination is complete. Everything seems fine, I have no concerns," Dr. Toma stated as she headed back to her lab table. Lifting the sample to take a better look, she turned around to face me. "Congratulations, Miss Izawa, you most certainly are pregnant," she said, lifting the urine sample up in my direction.

Kida immediately jumped out of her seat. "YOU'RE KIDDING!"

"Now, there is a final test we could do at this stage, but I do not believe it is necessary because I am fairly confident you are indeed pregnant. It would be a blood test which we would need to send over to the lab here in the hospital, but we would only receive the results in a few days. Ultimately, the choice is yours, Miss Izawa."

Not being able to move, let alone blink, I stared directly at Kida who no longer wore her comforting smile as she stared back. Robotically, I answered. "That's . . . alright."

A shiver ran up my spine and to my head as my whole body broke out in a cold sweat. On its own, my mouth answered questions Dr. Toma continued asking. Even though I looked directly at her lips, I had no idea what she was saying. The same went for Kida. She grabbed onto my hand and began saying things my deaf ears couldn't pick up, as tears rolled down her face in fear and mild excitement.

The world around me was still moving rapidly, but it was unbelievably silent. The saliva at the back of my throat completely dried out, so, every time I went to swallow, it felt like my throat was being attacked by cats with sharp claws. Nothing about my body felt right; it was an unknown mystery to me. What was this life I was living?

With everything spinning and spiralling out of control, things instantly stopped as soon as Dr. Toma asked me, "Do you plan on having this baby, Miss Izawa?"

Trying my hardest to focus solely on her, I had no answer to her question. "The . . . baby . . .."

Dr. Toma continued. "There are options. You can consider adoption, or there is the choice of aborting the baby if you do not wish to have it. Though, if you choose the route of abortion, I suggest you do so quickly before the baby furthers in development. There are some pamphlets I will send home with you today to better explain all the options."

I couldn't think straight. I had no idea how I should have been reacting. With my ears ringing on the word 'abortion,' I looked at Dr. Toma with gunshot eyes. "Okay . . .."

"Go home, look over the pamphlets, weigh the outcomes, and give yourself some time to think about it. I do not know the current living situation you are facing, or about the father, so I advise you to look at all possibilities before coming to a decision."

For the remainder of our time in the office, Kida asked Dr. Toma a bunch of questions while I sat in silence. Nothing around me felt real, not even the skin on my body. It felt like I was watching someone else's life unfold through their eyes, like I was along for the ride merely to observe.

A baby. What does it even mean . . . to have a baby?

The bus ride to school was mentally exhausting. Kida was now a jittery chatterbox. She went on and on about the baby as if it were already born, as if it were alive, describing all the things she's going to buy them if it turns out to be a girl. As she blabbed on, I concentrated on the scenery outside the window, counting the passing trees and clouds, anything to get my mind off of the fact I was pregnant. It wasn't until we passed by a mother and her child walking along the road holding hands, that I realized an even bigger problem. What was my mother going to say?

That night, I couldn't sleep. With the escaping hope of being able to close my eyes and fall sound asleep, I turned on my side and stared at the blank wall beside my bed, contemplating. If I were to abort the baby, all my problems would go away. If I were to give the baby up for adoption, a loving family would happily raise them, probably better than I ever could. If I were to keep the baby, my whole life would change. Thinking back to the cruel things I said to my father about having children out of wedlock, now haunted me.

The next day I went into school to rewrite my exam. Unable to focus or study the night before, I left half the questions blank, failing the entire exam.

Chapter Thirty-Eight

*J*UNE FLEW BY in the blink of an eye and the first week of July rolled in. By this point, I was starting to show. No matter how many baggy shirts or sweaters I was able to get away with before, my body was at its 'skinny' limit. My stomach had grown faster than I could keep up with in loose clothing. Kida had said since I was fairly tiny to begin with, so was my baby belly—but not in my eyes. I still hadn't mentioned my pregnancy to anyone except Kida, but I knew I couldn't put it off any longer because those around me had started to comment on my fashion choices. It was time to tell Kai. We hadn't had much time together in recent weeks, which made it easier to avoid the topic. I was terrified of the possibility that Kai would hate me and want nothing more to do with me or the baby, but as the father, he deserved to know. I didn't want to believe he could be the type of hateful person my mind was making him out to be. In the end, it was up to the both of us to make a final decision. I knew time was ticking, and the longer I waited, the more complicated things would get, medically and emotionally.

School became a challenge, especially morning classes due to the non-stop morning sickness. When I had gone to see Dr. Toma, I thought the nausea was at its all-time worst; but, after barely surviving the sudden change in my body, I would have given anything to go back. My morning sickness wasn't just exclusive to mornings; it happened sporadically throughout the day and during the night.

My mother touched upon my sudden weight gain and I told her I was stress eating due to my tough college classes. She was the last person I wanted to find out, and I didn't want to put any more stress on her in case her condition worsened.

Another tumour was found inside my mother, growing in a different area besides her breasts, and even though the doctor said it was small, the cancer was still spreading and nothing was helping to stop it. We were past the option of surgery because my mother had waited so long to make a decision, but I believe, she avoided it on purpose. Each time we had stepped foot into Dr. Ashima's office, my mother fell silent, her fighting spirit crushed. Her face was as slim as an anorexic model and her wrists were thin as twigs. She was constantly feeling weak and frail, any hope left in her had vanished. The expression of a person who was giving up was written all over her face.

When Dr. Ashima spoke about the cancer, he tip-toed around us as if we were fragile, porcelain figurines. It got to the point where Kenji was the only one with the strength to get mad anymore. Eventually, the two of us had come to accept it—our mother was dying. Nothing the doctors and nurses did had worked, and there was nothing more they could do. Cancer is a killer; from day one I knew that. The amount of effort I put in trying to fool myself into thinking everything was going to be okay, was a waste. You can only fool your heart for so long before you're forced to listen to your brain speak the harsh truth.

Whenever we spoke with Dr. Ashima, even just the word 'cancer' got my blood boiling. There was a possibility my mother would soon disappear, disappear to a place where we could no longer reach her.

With the news getting worse, my mother's mood never changed. She continued to lock herself in her room more than ever, and refused to eat anything unless physically forced. The denial stage remained longer than expected, according to the nurse who had given me the list of my mother's newest medications. Anti-depressants had now been added.

During this period, I thought the relationship between my mother and I would strengthen, but reality proved to be different. I knew my mother less than I did before. Even though talking and sharing feelings were not my strong suits, I would have liked my mother to communicate some sort of emotion to either Kenji or I so we could try and help her in whatever way possible.

One night, I was sitting at the desk in my room, attempting to catch up on homework, when Kenji passed by my bedroom. Even though the door was opened, he didn't step inside. Instead, he remained in the hallway out of sight.

"She's going to make it, you know."

I spun my chair around until I was facing the door. His statement played in my mind while an unsure answer lingered in my mouth. What did I actually believe? What was it that I wanted to believe?

"Yeah . . .," I replied, half-heartedly.

After that, the sound of Kenji's bedroom door opened and shut. Not knowing if I answered correctly, homework became less important.

Without realizing it, I had begun to avoid Kai. It wasn't until he'd bluntly asked, that I noticed.

[Line Kai]: Hey, how are things? I have a free day coming up, want to meet up?

[Line Kai]: Feels like we haven't talked or seen each other in a while . . . Are things okay? How's your mom?

[Line Kai]: I'm starting to get worried. Is everything alright at home?

[Line Kai]: Nila, why are you ignoring my messages?

A couple of days went by and I received multiple new messages from Kai, all of them left unread at the top of the inbox on my phone. It wasn't until he showed up at my doorstep, that I was forced to face him.

"Kai!" I exclaimed nervously, as I cracked the door open ever so slightly to see him.

"What's going on? Did I do something?"

Taking a quick peek behind me down the hall, I could see Kenji sitting on the couch in the living room. Turning back to face Kai, I answered, "No, you've done nothing wrong."

With a look of utter confusion and despair, Kai's eyebrows elevated as he stepped closer, placing one hand on the door to prevent me from closing it. "What's wrong then? What is it you can't tell me?"

Anxious from his closeness, I felt suffocated. "Um . . .," I took a step back.

Noticing my body language, Kai also took a slight step back. "Nila?"

Kai's face was full of panic and distress; he looked hurt by my unexplained actions. I knew he had every right to be upset with me because I had left him in the dark for so long, there was no way he wouldn't be confused. If I was in his shoes, I would be, too. Knowing I was causing him so much discomfort, why couldn't I tell him something so crucial? There were many pathetic excuses holding me back, but it wasn't a lack of trust or ability to confide in him; it was fear of what would come next. If I were to tell him, where would it leave us? What would happen to the *us* right now? What I needed to do was take responsibility.

"Can we . . . go for a walk?" I asked, hanging my head.

"Of course."

With the park in mind, we walked silently hand-in-hand until we reached the place where we first met. We headed to the same swing set as before, both taking a seat as we swayed back and forth, almost bumping into each other during times of opposite rhythm. The park was silent, empty of any children or adults. Kai was the first to break the silence.

"Are you breaking up with me?"

"WHAT?"

"Well, I don't know! You've been avoiding me lately. Not answering my messages or calls. What am I supposed to think? When I actually think about it, you've been acting weird for the past month."

I shook my head. "I'm sorry . . . it's nothing like that."

"Good," he exhaled heavily. "I'm glad. I was so worried; you have no idea. Well, actually, I had no idea," he chuckled at his own joke as he pushed both feet off the ground with great strength, increasing speed.

"It's the very opposite . . .," I whispered.

"Huh?" Kai said, slowing back to his original pace. "I didn't catch that. What did you say?"

Hopping off the swing, I stood with my back towards him. "I . . . I'm . . . I don't know what to do!"

For the slightest moment, the shrill song of cicadas was the only thing heard throughout the entire park. The summer air was still, keeping the trees and plant life quiet. The chirping of the cicadas gradually became louder, until finally the sound of feet stomping on the dirt behind me could be heard.

"Is it your mom? Is everything okay?" he asked, as the squeaking noise from his swing coming to a stop loudly screeched.

"STOP!" I shouted as I turned around, marching towards him. "Please, stop! We can't talk about her right now," I grabbed the chains of his swing. "If I don't tell you now . . . now's my only chance, so I have to . . . tell you now—it HAS to be now!"

Tears trickled down my face as Kai placed his hands over mine, securing my grip on the chains, leaving me no room to escape. "Tell me. I want you to tell me."

With tears overflowing, all things rational no longer applied. "You'll leave! I know you will! I mean, we haven't been dating very long. You didn't ask for any of this, you—"

Kai stood up, and before I knew it, I was tightly wrapped in his arms. My face was pressed deeply into his chest as the tears fell, absorbing into his shirt. His heartbeat continued at a normal pace, soothing my ears with its steady sound as he inhaled deeply.

"Nila, nothing you say can get rid of me. I've already decided I'm here to stay, whether you like it or not, I'm not going anywhere. You have to be in my life, because no one else makes sense. So please, tell me what's wrong."

"I'm pregnant."

Kai's body tensed up. The strong arms holding me slowly weakened and eventually slipped off. Regardless, my face was still pressed into his chest. I didn't dare look up at the man who stood before me. The sound of Kai's breathing became choppy and unpredictable, as though he had forgotten how to breathe. The hesitated silence was nerve-racking, driving my heart rate to an impossible pace.

"...What?"

In a muffled voice, I spoke into his chest. "I know you heard me...."

Kai's body caved, shifting downward to the ground, taking me along with it until our knees reached the dirt. Still pressed against him, afraid to glance up at his face, I took parts of Kai's shirt and scrunched them up in my palms. The tears continued with no end in sight.

Kai's hands rested in the dirt at his sides. "How? We've only... we've only done it once...."

I backed my head off his chest, focusing my eyes down at my palms. "It only takes one time."

Kai was silent for a moment, then spoke to himself out loud. "I can't believe I didn't use one... I can't believe I didn't use a condom." Kai paused. "Why... didn't I use one?" he shouted. "How could I be so dumb?"

The sound of cicadas reappeared, echoing loudly through my ears as the sun beamed down on us. My skin was warm but full of goosebumps. In my head, the image of Kai's face haunted me. The fear of seeing disappointment and regret stopped me from looking up at him. I had just ruined the life of the only guy I've ever loved.

"So, we're... having a baby?"

"Yeah."

"There's... a baby... inside you?"

"Yeah."

"Did you... take a pregnancy test?"

"Multiple."

"Wow, this is, uh, a lot to take in."

"Mhm," I sniffled, trying to hold back more tears.

"Who, uh... who else knows?"

"Just Kida."

Taking a painfully long moment of silence, Kai finally responded. "So, this is really happening... isn't it? We're having a baby," he repeated, raising his hands past my line of vision. "WE'RE HAVING A BABY!"

My ears rang with an explosion of abrupt exhilaration. When I finally looked up at him, Kai had his hands on his head, pushing back the pieces of hair from his hairline. His face was bright, lit with an expression of pure bliss as his mouth bounced between a smile and being left wide open from shock. Kai didn't blink once as he dragged his hands down the sides of his face until they reached his mouth.

"Wow, okay."

Hanging my head once more, I folded my hands and rested them on my lap. It was no longer just my eyes, my heart was crying, too. "I'm sorry. I'm so sorry, Kai."

"Sorry?" He reached out to grab my chin, lifting my face up until our eyes met. This was the first time in a while where we truly looked at each other. His ardent gaze stayed fixed on my eyes, not blinking even once. "Nila, I don't EVER want you to apologize—not for this. A baby is a blessing. OUR baby is a blessing. I can't even imagine anything more important, more wonderful than this moment right now. To have a baby with the one I love, the one girl I want to spend the rest of my life with, is a dream." Kai reached out his other hand and placed it on my stomach. "Right here, inside of you, is our baby. I couldn't be happier."

Tears were still flowing, more than ever before. I was so relieved to hear how Kai felt, it made me wish I had told him sooner to release my self-induced stress. Leaping forward, I jumped into his arms, causing us to tumble and plummet into the dirt. Our clothes were filthy, but we didn't care. I clung to his shirt to once again scrunch it into a ball in the palms of my hands, as I cried out the excruciating pain I had held within. The realization of actually having a baby finally hit me after Kai said it out loud, causing my mind to wander into further suppressing issues.

"W-what about the sh-shop?" I asked between sobbing breaths, laying on top of him. "And s-school? I won't be able to continue my program. What about our parents?" With each discouraging thought, a darkness overwhelmed me. "This baby will ruin everything!"

I could feel my chest pounding aggressively against Kai's each time I spoke as my body quivered. These negative thoughts consumed me, making it impossible to breathe, all early signs of an attack.

I pushed away from him. "I mean, I'll be eighteen in a month's time, with my whole life ahead of me—just like you! What if I were to have an abortion? Then things would go back to normal!"

I knew I needed to calm down before an attack started, but the heavy emotions wouldn't stop. Kai's eyes were locked on me the entire time I lashed out, not once stopping to interrupt me. He waited until all my concerns were out in the open before replying. After all the yelling, the warmth of two strong arms came up and slowly embraced me.

"Nila, stop."

As my name left his lips, I looked into his eyes. This wasn't the first time he's broken my trance. His eyes gave me the ability to focus, helping me to calm down and practice breathing slowly before continuing. When my breathing was back to a steady pace, I started. "Kai . . . everything was going great . . . everything was stable. How are we going to handle this? I don't know how to be a mother! What if I'm terrible at it?"

Kai fell silent, making me worry even more. Normally he would reply with a quick, suitable response, but his silence was killing me. Kai pulled back and rose to his feet, then reached out his hand to help me up. After dusting himself off first, he gently patted me down, attempting to clean the dirt from my clothes. With his big hand holding onto mine, his gaze shifted from my face and down towards my stomach as he smiled tenderly.

"First of all, you are not having an abortion. Please, never mention that word again. Just the thought of giving up this baby, without even trying to make things work, is unfair. I mean, I just found out we're having a baby. We haven't properly thought about what our lives would be like if we were to keep this baby. How can we possibly give up on him or her so easily?"

Kai's words touched me. His ability to think rationally during this difficult time was astonishing, something I truly admired. The concerns he came up with so quickly, were selfless. It never once crossed my mind to think about the future of this baby inside me, while Kai thought about it effortlessly. He was talking about the baby as if it were already a living person, like Kida had.

"Kai . . . ."

"Secondly, no matter what our parents say, this baby is coming, and no one will stop it—I won't let them." He placed his hand on my stomach. "No doubt my family is gonna be shocked, and probably disappointed, but I'm more worried about your mom finding out considering her condition. Telling her is going to take every bit of strength and courage we have. I don't want to make things worse for her, but she needs to know before the baby gets any bigger."

Kai's confidence gave me the ability to settle and sort my emotions. The unpleasant sobbing passed, leaving me to concentrate specifically on something Kai said. "Everything *we* have?"

He looked at me with a strong smile. "Together, we're gonna tell your mom. From now on, we're doing this together. I'm never going to leave your side. Nila, you're the precious mother of my unborn child. I haven't met our baby, but I already know I love you both very much."

My hands immediately covered my mouth to mask the amount of happiness trying to escape. Even through this exhausting time, hearing Kai's supportive declaration made me the happiest and luckiest person. The fear and loneliness I once felt had all seemed to vanish with his assuring words. Not knowing what the future had in store for us, the road didn't matter, as long as I had him.

Placing my hand on top of his, which continued resting upon my stomach, I squeezed it firmly. "Thank you so much."

Kai's smile faded. "The only thing I'm actually concerned about is your schooling. I know you mentioned it was something you were worried about, and that you have anxiety about being able to remain in the program, but how have things been going?"

The mention of school weighed me back down. On a scale, every happy feeling I felt was so light compared to the heavy burden of my declining education. I had never told Kai school was becoming difficult, but there was nothing to hide anymore, we had already come so far.

Focusing on the remaining dirt on my long skirt, I took a deep breath. "It's not good . . . I'm failing almost all of my classes."

Kai's eyes grew wide. "Why didn't you tell me?"

"I couldn't, I . . . didn't want to burden you. Things were going so good for you at the shop, and—"

"Nila," he interrupted, placing a warm hand on each cheek, pulling my face closer to his. "I want you to be able to tell me when things are getting hard. I don't want you to carry all this by yourself, I need you to tell me these things. We're a team; stop struggling alone . . . please."

With his compelling eyes staring into mine, I decided to confess something else I had been hiding from him. "I threw up in class."

"You threw up?" his voice escalated as his hold on my face weakened.

"During one of my exams, before I knew I was pregnant."

He raised his brow in suspicion. "When did this happen exactly?"

Dropping my head, Kai's hands fell from my face. With a faint voice, I was scared to answer. "A little over a month ago . . .."

"WHAT? A MONTH!"

Cringing from the anger in Kai's voice; I flinched, my arms pulled into my chest, my shoulders tensed, and my neck shrunk.

In a stern tone, he continued firing questions. "How . . . far along are you?"

"You should know . . .."

"Nila!"

". . . Around three months."

"THREE MONTHS!" He grabbed my shoulders firmly, lifting me to my tippy-toes. "You've been pregnant for THREE MONTHS and haven't told me?"

"I'm sorry!" I burst out in tears, praying for forgiveness. "I found out just recently. I didn't know I was pregnant; I didn't put two and two together. I wanted to tell you as soon as I found out, but I wasn't sure how you . . .." I cut my excuses. "I'm so sorry."

Releasing the firm hold he had on me, he dropped his arms. "I've missed three months of my child's growth. I can't believe it." Kai rubbed his face up and down, stretching his skin in every direction. "GOD! How could I not have noticed the signs?"

Feeling worthless, I tried to explain. "We had sex on your birthday. It's been about three months since . . .."

"My . . . birthday . . .," he said, using his fingers to count.

Sadness lingered in Kai's voice, triggering me to open up and face him properly. My tense shoulders stretched out as I brought my eyes to face his again. I reached out my hand and placed it over his beating heart. "I'm sorry. I'm so unbelievably sorry."

Looking disappointed in himself, Kai took a deep breath. "I'm sorry for my actions, I didn't mean to be so rough with you. I know it isn't your fault."

The sound of Kai's heart was quick but strong. Each second my hand rested above it, it decreased in speed and back into a steadier rhythm. With my hand on Kai's chest, I thought about the baby in greater detail.

"Will you come to the first ultrasound with me?"

Immediately, the lifeless eyes I was staring into filled with colour. "The first— yeah!" Kai answered unexpectedly.

"Okay."

Kai's eyes were no longer solely filled with colour; instantly, they watered. "I can't express what I'm feeling right now. There are literally no words that can convey even an inch of the feelings inside me." Kai leaned forward to slip his hand through my hair and graze my neck with his fingertips until he stopped behind my ear. "Nila, I love you."

Kai's earnest gaze set my heart on the right course and my happiness fell out in an ocean of more tears. From all the crying, my eyes were getting puffy and sore, a common occurrence lately. As we continued to stand alone in the park, all covered in dirt, I opened myself and welcomed his kiss. "I love you, too."

When our lips parted, I was faced with great determination from Kai as he refused to advert his eyes from mine.

"Nila, I know we haven't been together long, and people may judge us solely on that, but I can promise you this; I will work hard so I can take care of you and our baby, and no one can tell me differently. I'm gonna create a life into which our child will be proud to be born, even if it kills me. This baby deserves to have everything it desires, and I plan to deliver it all. Same goes for you. Whatever you need and whenever you need it, I'll be there. This is our family now, and I'll do anything in this world to protect it."

Like Kai said: *'There are literally no words that can convey even an inch of the feelings inside me'*—that is exactly how I felt. I was over the moon with joy and excitement; it was written all over my face and in my heart. All I could do was keep doing what I did best, and that was cry.

A warm smile returned to Kai's face. "Come on, let's go."

Placing my faith in him, I asked, "Where?"

"My house. The shop should be closing soon, so I want to tell my parents."

"Right now?"

"It's already three months too late."

He spoke the truth. We were late on sharing the news with our loved ones. It takes about nine months to have a baby, and I was already a third of the way there.

The sun was setting; everything around us glowed in a shade of vibrant orange. Taking Kai's hand, I was prepared to walk an unstable path, only hoping for it to be full of love and support from those closest to us when we reached the end.

"I'm ready."

Chapter Thirty-Nine

KAI WORE A troubled smile the whole way to his house, trying his best to put on a brave face in front of me. On the bus, he held my hand, occasionally rubbing my stomach with his other while no one was watching. The way Kai was acting made me feel loved, like everything was going to be okay, even though I had many doubts. Kai was an amazing person, but I didn't realize how truly amazing he was until today.

He asked me if I had felt any kicking and I informed him I hadn't. I knew very little about babies and pregnancy milestones. We discussed when we should go for the first ultrasound appointment and decided to also make a list of questions to ask the doctor. Watching Kai's enthusiasm about making appointments, and willingness to be so involved in the pregnancy, gave me the strength to keep myself together. If he had taken the news negatively, the thought of abortion would have been something to further consider.

As Kai's neighbourhood grew near, my nerves skyrocketed. When I looked at Kai, his smile lessened to something more serious as his leg bounced rapidly in one spot. It was easy to sense he was nervous, too. When our stop came, Kai was the first to stand, reaching out his hand to escort me off.

Kai hovered over me every step of the way, right until I hopped off the bus. I couldn't help but laugh as I trailed behind him.

"You know, I'm not huge yet."

Confused, Kai looked over his shoulder with an earnest expression. "Huh?"

"You're treating me as if I'm too big to stand on my own two feet," I giggled.

"Sorry, that wasn't my intention," he said, walking ahead. "I'm just scared of you falling or bumping into something. Each day the baby's growing, and until he or she is out into this world safely, I'm going to continue worrying."

Touched by Kai's protectiveness for our unborn child, I pulled his arm back and stood up on my tippy-toes, planting a kiss on his cheek. "I'm glad I get to see this side of you. Thank you."

For the first time in a long time, Kai blushed all the way to his ears. "This side's gonna appear a lot more. And if we lived together, you'd see it every day."

Standing close to the road's edge, my heart stopped. "Lived . . . together?"

Kai turned towards me with a serious face. "I was thinking about it on the bus. Let's move in together."

Taken aback by his sudden request, a few important matters came to mind. "Where . . . where will we get the money? I've never had a job. I'm still in school. How will we afford—"

"I've saved up enough money to get us started in an apartment. It's not a lot, but it's a start. I'll pick up more hours at the shop; I'll get a second job if I have to. I'll do anything in order to start our life together. Nila," he pulled me closer, placing an arm around me, "I'm going to treasure you in a million different ways. I want this to work, but for it to happen, we have to work hard. We have to learn how to become adults a lot sooner than planned, whether we like it or not. This is our life, and we have to take control of it."

The famous waterworks started up again. Everything seemed to trigger my tear ducts a hundred times worse than before. Kai's words made my heart throb; just being close to him set me on fire. "I love you, Kai," I said wholeheartedly, tears bouncing off my swollen face.

Kai squeezed me tighter, then placed his lips firmly against my forehead. "I love you, too." Pulling away to look at my face, he used his thumb to wipe the falling tears. "You sure do cry a lot," he chuckled. "But you look your best when you're smiling."

Embarrassed by his kindness, I couldn't help but smile at him with warm, rosy cheeks. From here on out, I knew my world was going to get bigger and a lot more complicated.

Eventually making it to the Kento residence, Kai reached for my hand as we approached the front door, taking deep breaths with each step. Faced with uncertainty, Kai reached for the handle. Signalling with a nod of his head for me to enter first, I let go of Kai's hand, following his non-verbal instruction. Taking the first step inside, I immediately shuddered with dread of unknowing.

"Nila!" a welcoming voice shouted from atop the staircase. "What a pleasure to see you, dear." Looking at the stairs, Mrs. Kento stood halfway up with an inviting smile as she slowly descended to greet us. "I'm sorry, I didn't prepare a large enough dinner. I wasn't expecting you tonight. If worse comes to worse, you can have Kai's portion, since he failed to inform his loving mother, we would be having company," Mrs. Kento expressed with mock surprise, giving Kai a stern look.

At this moment, Kai stepped into the house behind me.

"Oh, um," I hesitated, remembering to quickly bow mid-sentence before taking my shoes off. "Thank you, but I'm fine."

"Well, if you change your mind, Kai's portion is on the counter," she explained as she reached the bottom.

"Okay."

"How's your mother doing by the way? Any change?"

"Um, she's . . .."

"Mom, we don't have time for that right now," Kai stated.

I looked back and forth between Kai and his mother. Mrs. Kento's face was pricked with rage. "What do you mean there's no time? Rude child! This is your girlfriend's—"

"Mom," Kai interrupted with an assertive tone, "where's Dad?"

Thrown by Kai's manner, Mrs. Kento fumbled over her words. "Um, your father, yes, he's in the living room. Is everything alright . . .?"

"We'll go see him then. Mom, I need you to follow us into the living room. There's something Nila and I need to tell you."

I followed Kai's lead straight to the living room without hesitation. Mrs. Kento followed from behind with much concern as she hurried with care, not understanding what could possibly be so important.

"Hello, Nila, how nice of you to stop by," Mr. Kento left his seat to greet me. As he watched us all file into the room, he slowly sat back down. "What's going on?" he asked with raised brows, peering over his glasses.

Kai looked back at his mother. "Mom, please have a seat next to Dad."

Without asking questions, Mrs. Kento did as she was told. On the opposite couch from where Kai's parents sat, Kai had taken a seat, leaving me room to join him. With everyone sitting in silence, and with Kai's parents confused beyond belief, the only sound heard was the television Mr. Kento had been watching. Reaching for the remote on the table, Kai turned the TV off.

"Son, what's wrong?" Mr. Kento asked.

"Is it about Nila's mother?" Mrs. Kento also questioned, her face stressed with a frown.

"No. This has nothing to do with Nila's mother," Kai reassured.

Letting out a small sigh, Mrs. Kento placed a hand over her heart. "Thank goodness. With you being so serious, I thought something might have happened."

"Something has happened," Kai immediately fired back. "Just not with Nila's mother."

"What is it, son?" Mr. Kento sat at the edge of his seat, shifting his gaze between the two of us.

I placed my hand on Kai's shaky knee. Acknowledging my support, he placed his hand on top of mine, squeezing it tightly for reassurance. My heart was ready to explode at any minute. The look Kai's parents were giving us from across the room was enough to pierce through me. I had never been so scared. What if they were to forbid us from seeing each other and having the baby? What if they came to hate me?

Underneath my hand, Kai's leg instantly stopped moving. "Nila's pregnant."

With our confession out, I shut my eyes and held Kai's hand for dear life. The room fell silent; the sound of a pin would shatter glass if one were dropped.

"Come again?" We heard the disciplined voice of Mr. Kento first before anything else. "Son, what did you . . . say?"

Partially opening my eyes, I peeked at Kai's face. Kai wore the same strict expression he had started the confession with. "Nila's pregnant," Kai repeated. "She's about three months along."

"What do you—" Mr. Kento began to ask, but was interrupted by Mrs. Kento.

"How— HOW DID THIS HAPPEN?"

Both Kai and I remained quiet as we dropped our heads.

From the top of my narrow, downward vision, I could see Mrs. Kento's legs extending and shooting up. "HOW COULD YOU HAVE LET THIS HAPPEN?"

"Mom . . .," Kai expressed, his voice begging for forgiveness as he looked up at her.

"Dear, sit down," Mr. Kento's calm voice cancelled the anger from Mrs. Kento's. "This is not a time where we can afford to lose our heads."

Raising my head to face his parents, I listened wholeheartedly to what Mr. Kento continued to say.

"Nila," he directed his attention at me. "I'm sorry to ask such an insensitive question, but does this child belong to my son?"

"DAD!"

Pulling Kai's arm back, I answered his father's question without hesitation. "Yes, he is the only one I've ever been with."

"I see. Well, then, do you plan on having this baby?"

Just as I was about to answer, Kai jumped in. "Of course, we do!"

"Hold your tongue," Mr. Kento snapped.

Witnessing such an unpleasant and scary side of Kai's father, my hands commenced to tremble, shortly followed by my whole body building up a cold sweat. "Yes. I plan on having this baby and raising it to the best of my ability, with Kai by my side," I looked at Kai with a fragile smile.

With a gentle smile back, Kai looked into my eyes and enveloped me with strength. Right after, Kai rose, bowing towards his parents. "I beg you; please, give us your blessing. That's all I ask for . . . just your blessing."

Kai's voice quivered as he stood in front of his parents. Just as he did, I stood beside him and grabbed hold of his hand, then bowed.

"The two of you are so young, and you hardly know each other," Kai's mother expressed; her voice raspy from holding back tears. "You have no money. How will you support this baby?"

Kai straightened up, as did I. His shoulders were wide and demonstrated confidence in response to his mother's justified concern. "I know this situation isn't ideal, but if I have to work a million jobs in order to support Nila and the baby—I will. I already have enough money saved just from our shop alone for the first rent payment. I will continue to save money to protect my new family, no matter what."

Kai's passion for our unclear future brought out an overflowing number of tears. I was so unsure about my own future that thinking about a future forever connected to Kai's, was overwhelming. There was a pure little life inside of me which I became responsible for overnight. Barely having my own life together, I was suddenly accountable for shaping the life of an innocent child, one who knew nothing about the scary world he or she would be born into. Mrs. Kento was right; we were so young, so inexperienced—could we really do this?

Not wanting Kai's parents to see me crying, I wiped my tears quickly with the thin sleeve of my shirt. Mrs. Kento had tears of her own pouring from her eyes, but I wasn't sure where she stood with all of this. Shifting my eyes back and forth between Kai's parents, Mr. Kento fixated harshly on Kai, as if judging his credibility.

"Son, have you found something worthy of protecting? Even if it means sacrificing your own life?"

"Yes," Kai said automatically, not a single ounce of hesitation lingered in his reply.

"Then, don't let it go," Mr. Kento said strictly.

"Dear?" Kai's mother questioned, standing dumbfoundedly as her hands fell to her sides.

"You know, you sound just like me when your mother was pregnant with your older brother, Sosuke," he said with a lighter tone. "I was in your position, standing exactly where you are now, across from your mother's parents as I made similar promises to them. Of course, at the time, we

352

were a little older than what you are now, but the promises were the same. I swore to protect my family with absolutely everything I had; I was going to fight until I couldn't fight anymore."

"Dad?" Kai's voice sounded eager.

"You have my blessing, but only if you uphold everything you just proclaimed. Once a child is born, there is no turning back. You will have to grow into adults much quicker than most people your age." A smile cracked from his lips. "But I believe in both of you, individually and as a pair. It's going to be extremely challenging, at times, you will want to give up, but there is no doubt in my mind that the two of you will pull through. There is no greater gift than a child."

Mr. Kento's supportive words brought a smile to my face. Before I even looked at Kai, he had already lunged at his father. Just like a young boy, Kai flew into the arms of his father and hugged him dearly. I wasn't sure if my eyes were deceiving me, but I could've sworn that both Kai and his father shed a few tears. Watching them together made my heart feel eternally warm. I brought my hands to my face to shield my emotions from everyone. As I did, a pair of arms wrapped around me.

"You're right, dear. They are just like us." Mrs. Kento took a step back as she stared into the eyes of my weeping face. "I can't believe it, our second grandchild!"

With a new perspective from Mr. Kento, I felt more confident in our ability to become parents. I was especially glad to have Kai's mother backing us. She was someone I looked up to, a strong and powerful female role model, much like my own mother.

When the touching moment between Kai and his father ended, Kai turned towards his mother. Mrs. Kento gave me one final squeeze before being embraced in her son's arms. The same feelings from before took over as I watched Kai holding his mother dearly. It brought me immense joy knowing that Kai had a great relationship with his parents.

"Nila."

Turning to my right, Mr. Kento moved closer to me. Somewhat intimidated, I felt the need to stand up straight. "Mr. Kento . . .," I said in a shaky voice.

"I do have one question." He took a weight-bearing breath, "What will you do about school? I understand you're in a teaching program here in town. Will you continue to attend?"

Being put on the spot, I thought carefully about what was asked.

"We haven't really talked about what we plan to do with her education," Kai answered for me, slowly letting go of his mother.

"Son, with all due respect, this is not something you have a say in. Unless she absolutely cannot be on her feet, or her health is at risk, this is Nila's decision."

"But Dad—"

"Kai, your father's right," I said. "School is something I need to decide on. With me already three months along, it's only going to get harder as the days go on." Returning my focus back to Mr. Kento, I already knew my answer. "Like you said, Mr. Kento, there will come a point, closer to my due date, where I can no longer keep busy on my own two feet," I took a confident breath before pressing on. "But I want to continue attending my program until the end of the semester. This way I can complete some of the classes and receive credits for them, allowing me to return to the program at a later date if I choose to do so."

With a smile, Kai's father reached out his hand and patted me on the head. "I think that is a wise and grown-up decision."

Looking at Kai, he wore a smile of acceptance, leaving me satisfied with my response.

Kai's father removed his hand from my head. "If there ever comes a time in which you feel uneasy, and school becomes a burden, please do not push yourself to continue. Unfortunately, in this situation, academics can wait; a child coming into this world cannot."

"That's right, Nila," Mrs. Kento added, standing beside me. "You are a part of the Kento family now. You, Kai, and this baby are of the utmost importance to us. Please take care of yourselves and each other."

Kai instantly ran to me, grabbing my hips and lifting me up high into his chest. "I'm going to protect this girl with my entire life," he announced confidently. "And the precious little life we created, too." Kai looked up at me. "I truly love this girl. Nothing will change that."

Beyond embarrassed, I shied away from Kai's confession in front of his parents to bury my face into my palms. My heart was pounding out of control. If it were to beat any faster, it would've flown right out of my chest. With everything that just happened, I got choked up. In a soft, quiet whisper, I replied, "I love you, too."

I could sense Kai's parents staring at us from the corner of my eye, making it uncomfortable to express such heartfelt emotions right in front of them. I was never spectacular at expressing my feelings whenever Kai and I were alone, but in front of others, especially his parents, it seemed wildly inappropriate.

Coming over to Kai's house to tell his parents about the pregnancy turned into a joyful celebration. Kai and I sat at the kitchen table with his parents to further converse about the near future. Mr. and Mrs. Kento asked us if we had already spoken to my mother about the news, and we informed them we hadn't. When Ryu returned home, Kai decided he would inform his younger brother about the news after seeing me home.

Kai escorted me back to my house, constantly asking me if I was feeling all right. The next two nights, Kai did the same. We spent most of our time at his house, living in fear of how we should approach my mother with the topic. Trying to avoid any confrontation with my mother before we were ready, threw off the entire care schedule Kenji and I created for her.

On average, Kida would send me five messages per day, asking me how things were and if I was feeling okay or needed help. With everyone so concerned about my wellbeing, I wondered if my mother would react the same.

Not used to having so many people care about me, I sat in a dark space between two closed doors of trust and betrayal. Afraid of the outcome, I was traumatized by opening the wrong door to the wrong person. Soon, I became obsessed with the future; I couldn't stop thinking about how things would turn out. Everything I had done, leading up to that point, didn't matter anymore. I desperately wanted to meet my future self to simply ask how my life would turn out. What does the end of this hardship look like?

I also came to realize, the more prepared you were, the more things fell apart. Being the type of person who liked having my life planned and organized, left little to no room for interruptions or mistakes in my ideal world. Having everything outlined gave me peace and tranquillity, making it easier to work through and conquer each day. I had made sure no surprises would put a bump in my road and screw up what I worked hard to accomplish. Although, life enjoyed tossing in frequent jokes, creating obstacles and delaying my route. Slowly, I've come to accept that nothing ever turns out right, and nothing is as it seems.

Throughout my short time with Kai, I'd learned many things. One of them being the world is full of things I don't know. I've also learned that if you go with the flow, not worrying about stupid speed bumps, an unexpected path may appear.

Chapter Forty

*K*ENJI CAME BARGING *into the kitchen.* "Mom, where's Dad?"

"He's still at work."

Glancing up at the clock, Kenji seemed puzzled. "Shouldn't he have been done about an hour ago?"

Our mother followed his gaze. "Actually, you're right. Maybe he's running late? What did you need from him?"

"He said we could toss the ball around for a bit after he was done work. I gotta practice for baseball tryouts next week . . . ."

"Have you finished your homework?"

"I'll do it later."

Rolling her eyes, she replied with a suggestion. "Try calling his cellphone."

Stepping into the hallway, Kenji took the phone off the dock. There was a silence that ran through the house as Kenji dialed the numbers.

Shortly returning to the kitchen, Kenji wore a look of disappointment. "It went straight to voicemail. I think his phone's off."

"That's strange . . .," *our mother pondered.* "He charged it last night, so the battery shouldn't be dead. I wonder what he's doing?"

"He came home late yesterday, too," *I said from the table.*

"Man!" *Kenji kicked the base of the kitchen wall lightly with his foot.* "I wish he'd hurry up. It'll be dark soon."

The next day, I was in high spirits and decided to get up extra early to make a bento for Kai and take it to him at work for lunch. It was the first time in my entire life that I made the decision to cut class without being sick or getting permission. My body felt good, no signs of dizziness or having the urge to throw up. I started preparing common bento favourites like tamagoyaki and chicken katsu. Not having attended the same high school as Kai, I wondered what his everyday high school self was like. What did he eat for lunch? Did he bring his own lunch, or did he buy it from the cafeteria? Where would he eat his lunch, and with whom? So many unanswered questions, holding little to no importance now.

Before discarding the leftovers, I made two separate, smaller bento boxes for Kenji and my mother and placed them in the fridge. With time to spare, I also prepared breakfast. When everything was done, I covered the breakfast to maintain its warmth, temporarily staging it to the side of the counter. Going over to the table, I set it for two. When everything was ready, I placed the wrapped breakfast on the table for Kenji and my mother to easily see. As I stared at the middle of the plain table, a pleasant vision of having flowers in a vase came to mind.

I'll pick some up from Kai's shop before coming back.

"Morning."

"JEEZ!" I jumped. "I didn't hear you get up, Kenji. You startled me."

Heading back to the counter, I placed Kai's bento in a cloth and tied it, as Kenji stepped into the kitchen.

"What are you up to?"

Making sure my stomach faced away from my brother, I glued myself to the edge of the counter. "Bentos; this one's for Kai."

"Where's mine?" he asked, looking around to find it.

I pointed to the fridge. "It's in there, but your breakfast is on the table."

"Thanks," he said, patting my head as he passed me.

Stunned by his little gesture, my eyes followed him as he left my peripherals from one side and reappeared from behind me at the other. "...Yeah."

"Did you put tamagoyaki in it?"

Not paying attention to what was asked, I turned to him. "Huh?"

"Tamagoyaki . . .? Did you put any in the bento?"

"Oh, yeah, I did."

A grin appeared at the corner of his mouth as he sat at the table. "Awesome."

Looking at him with a puzzled expression, my heart tightened from his tiny, hidden smile. Even though the interaction with my brother was brief, it added to the greatness of my morning. Kenji had come a long way since we'd found out about our mother's cancer. He had become more involved in things at home and at school, but overall, even though our mother was sick, he generally seemed happier. Kenji had, once again, become a joy to be around.

"I'm going to be leaving shortly for the flower shop, to bring Kai his lunch. While I'm there, I was thinking about getting some flowers to decorate the table for Mom," I explained.

Kenji looked at the plain table before him. "She'll like that," he said with the same upbeat grin.

"I should be home before lunch. Will you stick around until I get back?"

"I'm just gonna step out and drop something off at Kida's; then I'll be right back. Mom will probably still be asleep before I return."

"Alright. Think she'll eat breakfast?"

"Probably not. She hasn't for the past few days."

"Oh, I see . . . ."

"Sorry, I know you took time to prepare all this," Kenji said compassionately.

"It's okay." Wanting to stay clear of depressing topics, I quickly changed the subject. "So, you're going to see Kida? I'm surprised she's up this early," I teased.

Kenji laughed lightly. "She's getting ready for her morning class."

An unsettled feeling came over me as soon as Kenji mentioned the word 'class.' "Right . . . ."

Kenji's smile faded. "Speaking of, don't you usually have class this early, too?" he raised a brow.

"Um, well, normally, yes. But my class got cancelled today," I lied terribly.

"I see . . .," Kenji answered with suspicion.

"Annnyway, don't take too long at Kida's. I get anxious when Mom's left alone, and the nurse isn't coming today."

"She's not handicapped, Nila. She has to be able to do some things on her own."

"I know, but . . .."

"I'll be quick, stop worrying."

"Okay."

I went to check on my mother before heading out. With her sleeping soundly in bed, and things looking normal, I got my stuff and left before Kenji was done with breakfast. Walking along the street, it was impossible not to notice all the beautiful flowers blooming in the surrounding neighbours' gardens. Looking over my shoulder, ours was a pathetic display I was sure Kai would have found laughable. In the past, my mother had taken pride in maintaining the greenery at our house, but she had no passion or motivation left for anything.

It would be nice to have a tiny house, with a lovely garden that grew many flowers of all different colours. A small house with a small family . . .. Stopping the thought of my own selfish desires, I wondered if this is what people considered a dream, something that I could slowly work towards?

Eventually, I came to my frequent bus stop where a cluster of people stood in a jagged line. The stop was full of businessmen and all types of students, some even wore my old high school uniform. Great, big trees hung over the bus stop, creating a lovely shaded area to stand under during excruciatingly hot days. When the bus pulled up, a few people got off before everyone waiting outside filed in. As soon as I got on, I was instantly shoved up against some stranger. The bus was packed; most people chose to remain standing, in fear of sitting and getting trapped, possibly missing their stop.

With the nice weather, things were getting hot, especially in the bus. Being so close to people, I was able to feel their sweat on my skin and smell their body odour, making me want to puke. Attempting to continue the positive day, I tried my best to think of things that wouldn't make me feel like vomiting. Sadly, that didn't work too well because, in the end, I threw up all over a businessman's shoes. After apologizing profoundly, I immediately got off at the next stop before dying of embarrassment. The gentleman was kind enough not to ask for money to clean or replace his shoes after telling him I was pregnant. Still trying to keep my pregnancy a secret, I didn't like using the 'I'm pregnant' card, but it was my last resort since I had no money to pay for such expensive-looking shoes.

Finally approaching the famous Kento Family Flowers, there were endless amounts of gorgeous flower displays set up all around the front. Anyone who walked by, regardless of being directly in front of the shop or across the street, could easily see the vibrant colours that illuminated from the flowers.

With my purse over my shoulder, and the bag with the bento box in hand, I crossed the street with a cheerful attitude. As I did, I noticed Kai through the glass, wearing an apron as he cleaned the large shop windows from inside with a rag. He seemed focused on cleaning, because no matter how close I got to the window, he didn't notice me standing in front of him on the other side. Trying to be funny, I smacked my hand on the glass to scare him. With success, Kai dropped the rag and jumped back with enlarged eyes. After realizing it was me, he picked up the rag and threw it at the window as he laughed nervously. My hand remained on the window the entire time as I laughed at how scared he got. Just as I was about to remove it, Kai closed his eyes and brought his face closer to the window, placing a kiss on the glass that separated my palm from his lips.

I felt my face warm up as I looked at my hand. Butterflies whisked through me as Kai reopened his eyes. Without even touching me, I could feel his warmth. This guy meant a lot to me, and I discovered that I was no longer afraid to admit it. Every little thing he did, only made me love him more.

After pulling my hand away, I ran for the entrance. Kai got to the door first, opening it with a smile as the shop's bell chimed. My face tingled with joy as we came face-to-face.

"Hi."

Without warning, he grabbed me by the legs and lifted me high into his arms. "Good morning."

Embarrassed by the scene he created, my heart pounded aggressively. "Morning."

"Your face is extremely red right now," he said, laughing under his breath.

"And whose fault is that? Idiot!"

His laugh lightened into a refreshing smile. "An idiot in love."

Avoiding his embarrassing notion, I shoved the bento in his face. "Here!"

Placing me down gently, he held up the bag. "What's this?"

Casting my gaze at my sandals, I answered shyly before looking up. "Lunch."

With a smile glued to his face, Kai went through the bag. "Wow, it's a bento!" he exclaimed, pulling it out. "Awesome! Did you make it?"

"I wasn't sure what kind of foods you liked or disliked, so I made some common favourites from my house. Hope that's okay."

Kai wrapped his one arm around my head and pulled me closer towards him, covering my eyes with his chest. His apron had a strong floral aroma, one which would probably seep through clothing if worn for too long. The wonderful smell of flowers was cleansing my nose from the terrible stench of sweat and body odour from the bus.

"Thank you so much. I can't wait to eat it," he said, holding me tightly.

"Mhm."

Kai ran inside to put his lunch away, zooming past Mr. Kento at the register, then came back to water the flowers outside with a hose. He said this way, he could use 'watering the flowers' as an excuse to look busy in front of his father as he talked to me for a while longer. Feeling useless as I watched him work, I noticed a watering can sitting on the ground beside one of the flower beds, so I took it and filled it with water. With us talking and laughing as we watered the flowers together, more customers stopped to admire and smell them. Kai kindly greeted each person who passed the shop, even if they didn't enter. Watching him deal with people so casually and confidently, made me genuinely proud to stand beside him. The regular customers greeted him, making note of my unfamiliar face. Each time Kai introduced me, they playfully teased him about having a girlfriend. The atmosphere around the shop was safe and attracting.

As soon as we were done with the water, we put our tools away and went back to the entrance of the shop to say goodbye. As per my request during our conversation, Kai quickly arranged a lovely bouquet for me to take home for my mother.

"KENTO!"

With Kai's name being called out unexpectedly, we both turned our heads.

"Kenji . . .?" I said, faintly.

Hurling towards us in a fit of rage, with teeth bared and clenched fists, Kenji reached out and grabbed Kai's collar.

"Hey, man!" Kai shouted with confusion, grabbing hold of Kenji's hand, struggling to loosen his grip. "What the hell are you doing?"

"YOU SON OF A BITCH! HOW DARE YOU LIE TO MY FACE!"

Kai's eyes narrowed. "What do you mean?"

Trying to defuse the situation, I grabbed Kenji's arm. "Kenji! What are you doing? Let go of him!"

Kenji ignored me as his face went fuming red. "Don't pretend you don't remember! At the hospital, you made me a promise—I FUCKING TRUSTED YOU!"

Kai's eyes didn't waver, he continued to look straight at Kenji. "I didn't break the promise I made you."

"Promise? What promise?" I asked, still tugging on Kenji's stiff arm.

Kenji loosened his grip on Kai's collar, releasing him as he tossed him back, causing Kai to land on top of the flowers we just finished watering.

"KAI!" I shouted as I ran to him, throwing the bouquet to the side as I knelt down beside him.

"YOU FUCKING ASSHOLE!" Kenji shouted, overtop me, breathing heavily and speaking loud enough for everyone to hear. "How DARE you get my sister pregnant! I TOLD YOU TO TAKE CARE OF HER!"

Shocked from Kenji's announcement, I looked up at my brother and froze. *He knows . . .?*

Beside me, Kai carefully moved the flowerpots and trays out of his way, trying not to further damage them before standing. Once on his feet, he dusted himself off from top to bottom, then confronted Kenji.

"As I said before, I didn't break the promise I made."

"LIAR!" Kenji took a step forward, throwing a punch.

"KENJI STOP!" I begged, covering my eyes to avoid seeing the physical connection of his hand on Kai's face. Even though I couldn't see it, I heard it.

"Feel better?"

Removing my hands, I looked up and saw blood drip from the corner of Kai's mouth and smeared on Kenji's knuckles.

"Kenji, do you feel better now?" Kai asked again, totally unfazed.

The Kenji in front of me looked like a completely different person from the brother I knew and grew up with. He was like a monster. Never in my life had I seen or heard about my brother initiating a fight. I knew there was only one person who could have told him I was pregnant.

Repeating himself for a third time, Kai projected his voice. "Do YOU feel better now? After hitting me, did it make YOU feel any better?"

Kenji looked at Kai with unforgiving eyes, hate and anger floated within them as he remained silent.

As I got up slowly, Kai took quick notice and turned around to help me. When I went to stand beside Kai, he placed his arm in front of me, forcing me to take a step back as he guarded me from the unpredictable Kenji.

"Yes, what you're saying is true," Kai stated protectively. "Nila is pregnant, and it is my fault. But I do not regret a single thing. If anything, this baby has only made me realize how much I truly love and cherish your sister. Whether you like it or not, Nila and I plan on having this baby. So, you can either choose to be a part of our unborn child's life, or remain silent. I will continue to take care of Nila, just like I promised you, nothing has changed. The choice is yours, Kenji."

Chapter Forty-One

KENJI'S FACE FILLED with anger like no other before he ran off. Kai chased Kenji down the street but eventually lost him in a crowd. When Kai returned to the store, it was easy to see how riled up he was as he paced back and forth, rubbing his temples in circles. Unfortunately, Kai was unsuccessful at calming himself down because he punched the shop's cement wall with all his might, giving me the scare of my life. His hand dripped with blood, matching Kenji's.

To try and defuse the situation, I helped Kai tidy up the mess out front, but felt my presence was only causing him greater turmoil. Once everything was cleaned, I apologized to Kai and Mr. Kento, and thought it would be best to take my leave to keep the shop's respectable appearance. Kai and I decided to discuss things after he finished work, giving us both time to think and cool off. A part of me wondered if Kai didn't like getting angry when I was present, as if he was uncomfortable showing me that part of himself, like at the New Year's party. Even though his confrontation with Kenji was dealt with on a much higher and respectable ground, he seemed disappointed in himself above all, shaking his head as he mumbled stuff under his breath. Not wanting to leave Kai in such a state, I didn't know what else to do.

Later that night, Kai came over and we went for an evening walk around my neighbourhood. His face looked swollen compared to when I saw him earlier, but he denied any pain. He informed me that after he saw me off, he made his way back into the shop where his father approached and told him he had witnessed the scene between him and my brother through the windows. Mr. Kento, though understanding, ended up dismissing Kai for break, telling him to go to the backroom and compose himself before dealing with any customers. Hearing about the amount of trouble my family had caused, I apologized profoundly for Kenji's behaviour, but Kai said not to worry since it was out of our control. I knew he was right, but I felt incredibly unsatisfied and responsible.

That night, Kenji never came home.

The day after the shop incident, I spent an hour on the phone arguing with Kida about her opening her big mouth when she had no right, after promising me she wouldn't. The whole time I was yelling, Kida listened quietly in the background, accepting everything being lashed out at her. After I was finished, I asked Kida if Kenji was with her. She told me she snuck him into her house last night after her parents fell asleep, but he left early in the morning before anyone woke up and hadn't heard from him since.

The distance I spent so much time closing between my brother and me, had re-opened and grown to immeasurable length—another thing to weigh me down.

Four days passed, and Kenji hadn't stopped by the house even once, leaving me to look after our mother all alone. Things were becoming harder each day we let stuff slide. I knew it was time for Kai and I to tell my mother about the pregnancy, before Kenji did so in a destructive way.

During the time I wasted waiting for Kenji, I made peace with leaving my mother home alone and was able to attend two full days of classes at school. Thankfully, one of those two days, the nurse came over, which lessened my worry. If I wanted to pass finals, it was time to buckle down and focus, using every bit of energy I had left. Between school and waiting for Kenji to return, Kai and I decided we were going to be straightforward and tell my mother everything.

Discussing only a few things together, Kai kept unusually quiet when it came to how we should approach such a delicate conversation with my mother. As he kept to himself, I was coming up with the worst possible scenarios of how she would respond.

When the dreaded day finally came, everything we discussed left my brain dry and my heart heavy. Kai came over around lunch, and as I led him into the kitchen, he bowed lightly at my mother before quietly sitting across from her at the table. Even before I could take a seat beside him, my mother glared at me, which I knew from experience was because she had not received any notice about Kai passing by. Eluding her eyes, I pulled out the chair closest to Kai and sat down. For a moment, we all sat in silence.

Suffocating from the thick tension, my mother cut the air with a question. "What is this about?"

Shaking in my skin, I knew what words I wanted to say, but nothing came out as rehearsed. With the amount of time I spent going over the step-by-step plan, I was hoping the words would fall into place on their own. "Uh, well . . . I-I'm, we . . .."

"Nila, spit it out already," she crossed her arms in irritation.

Kai grabbed my hand underneath the table. From such a tiny gesture, I was able to calm down enough to pronounce my words properly. "We . . . wanted to sit you down today because . . . we have something important to tell you."

My mother sat tall in her chair with her arms slowly uncrossing. "Yes, what is it?" A look of uncertainty swept over her face as she continued to stare at me. "Is everything alright?"

Not wanting to harbour this guilt any longer, I forgot the plan. "I'm pregnant!"

With a look of complete shock, my mother's nose flared, and her eyes remained unblinking as my word's sunk in. Her jaw dropped. "Pardon, I believe I misheard you?"

Hesitant to repeat it, based on her initial reaction, I shut my eyes as if preparing myself for a slap across the face. "I'm—"

"She's pregnant," Kai said assertively. "She's pregnant with my child, and we have decided to keep the baby."

Without further explanation, my eyes snapped open and I

immediately looked over at Kai. His back was straight against the wooden chair, presenting himself like an adult. With responsibility reflected in his eyes, he was clearly determined to take control of the conversation. Slowly shifting my gaze from Kai to my mother, I saw her mouth shut and her eyes beam with something far worse than anger.

My mother launched forward and slammed her hands down on the table. "PREGNANT! My daughter—PREGNANT? Before finishing college? BEFORE MARRIAGE?" She looked directly at me. "NILA!"

As my mother yelled, I flinched and shut my eyes in fear. Her voice, strong and fierce, travelled straight through me and escaped between the paper-thin walls of the house. Seconds after, Kai released my hand as I heard one of the kitchen chairs screeching across the wooden floor.

"Ms. Kimura," Kai's voice flew straight into my ears. "It takes two people to make a baby; therefore, I am just as much responsible. So, please, don't put all the blame on Nila."

Peeking through my tightly shut eyelids, I saw Kai standing face-to-face, in a war with my mother.

"Mr. Kento," my mother broke first, keeping her voice at the same intense level. "Of course, you're at fault. YOU'RE the cause of all this! I knew I shouldn't have let my daughter get involved with you! I was HIGHLY mistaken by your first appearance, the night you kept my daughter out so late! I should have stuck with my gut! YOU ARE NOTHING BUT A BAD INFLUENCE! I want you to stay the hell away from my daughter—YOU HEAR ME? This relationship ends now!"

Her face was fuming with rage, her ears almost spitting out steam. With the amount of yelling my mother was doing, I was positive the neighbours could hear our entire conversation word-for-word. My mother's head was clouded with emotions, pushing her past the point of reasoning or rationality. She had no clue how loud she was being.

I looked up at Kai with eyes full of regret as I sat in fear, consumed with feelings I didn't understand. Kai kept his composure, with minimal body language expressing the true irritation he felt. The hand closest to me was clenched in a fist, while his eyebrows narrowed in thought. Reaching for his closed fist, I stood to match him.

"Ms. Kimura," he tried again. "I understand you're angry—"

"Angry? How DARE you try to pretend you understand how I'm feeling!"

Kai continued, pretending he was never interrupted. "I've already received lectures from my own parents. I'm sorry if I've disappointed you to the point where you no longer see me as a suitable man for your daughter, but I cannot agree with your decision. Even if you hadn't approved of my relationship with Nila from the beginning, I would have forced my way into your daughter's heart until she gave it to me. I love her, and I will be by her side until I breathe my final breath. I will be a part of my child's life, and Nila's, whether you approve or not. I won't allow my child to have an unreliable, incompetent person as a father." Bowing his head to my mother, he pressed on. "I beg you; please, remain by our sides as we go through this challenging journey."

During Kai's speech, my mother had remained silent. Copying Kai's respectful manner, I also bowed my head. Shortly after, Kai squeezed my hand tighter, then lead us out of the kitchen.

Walking through the hallway, with the front door in sight, my mother finally spoke.

"Do you plan on marrying my daughter, Mr. Kento?"

Kai stopped in his tracks, keeping his head held high as he concentrated. He didn't dare look back into my mother's eyes. "During this time, no," Kai answered. "With the unexpected baby, and the reality of becoming adults quickly hitting us, I'd like to at least have a proper wedding in which we can invite all our family and friends." Turning his head back slightly, Kai spoke over his shoulder. "Do not mistake my words, Ms. Kimura. It may not happen right at this moment, but one day, I *will* marry your daughter. You can count on that."

As I glanced through the arch of the kitchen entryway, I could see my mother fighting the urge to cry as tears formed in her eyes, blankly staring at the two empty chairs in front of her. She was quiet for a moment, then shouted my name multiple times as we walked out. I was heartbroken to leave my mother in such a state as we walked out, but I knew if we had stayed any longer, things would've been worse.

After the conversation with my mother went south, Kai and I went for another long walk to clear our heads and calm down. We both shook nervously as we talked about how differently our parents took the news. Kai offered to put me up for the night, but I knew I couldn't leave my mother alone because I was solely responsible for her well-being until Kenji returned. Even though I was telling Kai I couldn't leave my mother, I also couldn't convince myself to believe my own excuse. I simply didn't want to be separated from him.

Holding Kai's hand, I could tell his unbelievable strength was weakening, while the flame of my sanity was burning brighter.

"Things will be okay, right?" I asked in a hushed voice. "We'll be okay . . . won't we?"

Continuing on the path to nowhere, Kai pressed forward without looking back. "You have my word."

By the time I returned, my mother had locked herself away in her room and refused to come out. She was disappointed in me, and it stung.

Chapter Forty-Two

KAI AND I booked our first ultrasound appointment with Dr. Toma a few days later. The whole time Kai sat in the waiting room, his leg bounced repeatedly. I wasn't sure if he was excited or anxious for the appointment, but there was no way we could turn back. I had been instructed to drink plenty of water to maintain a full bladder for the ultrasound and watching Kai's leg move non-stop was oddly increasing my urge to pee.

Shortly after, Dr. Toma stepped out of her office. We made eye contact and she smiled at me softly.

"Hello, Miss Izawa. Please, come in."

Following Dr. Toma into her office, Kai was the last one to step inside.

"Please shut the door behind you, young man," Dr. Toma said before taking a seat at her desk. "Now, I see you have requested an ultrasound, Miss Izawa. Is your bladder nice and full?"

"Yes, Ma'am," I said nervously, while I stood in front of the desk, trying not to think about it.

"Excellent," she said, flipping through my file. "And this young man beside you, is he the father?"

Kai stood beside me and bowed towards Dr. Toma. "Yes, I am. My name is Kaichi Kento. Please take care of us," he answered in a shaky voice.

"Perfect," Dr. Toma said with a smile. "So, the assumption I am to make is that you have both chosen to keep the child, correct?"

"Yes, Ma'am," we answered simultaneously.

Dr. Toma looked over at Kai. "I am very pleased to meet you, Mr. Kento," she said, closing the folder. "It is during this time that I encourage the fathers to start attending appointments. You see, this is the most important appointment."

"More important than the delivery of the baby?" Kai asked foolishly, with a voice full of nerves.

"Yes, yes, there is that. Would you like to know why, Mr. Kento?"

"Yes, please . . . ."

With a smile, she rose from her chair and made her way to a small closet where she kept her supplies. "This appointment signifies realization and acceptance; that both the mother and father have about bringing a life into this world. Anyone can have a baby, but it takes true consideration and determination for the child's welfare, to become a good parent. Seeing the two of you here today, confirms that." Dr. Toma looked back at me. "Miss Izawa, if you please," she said, handing me a hospital gown.

Taking the gown, I went to change behind the curtain like last time. When I finished, Dr. Toma pointed at the examination bed, a sign for me to get on. With her guidance and Kai's assistance, I sat on the bed.

"Curtain or no curtain, Miss Izawa?"

"No curtain, please."

"As you wish," Dr. Toma answered before turning to Kai. "Mr. Kento, you may pull up a chair if you prefer to sit."

"I'll stand, thank you," Kai answered respectfully.

"They always do," Dr. Toma chuckled as she returned to me. "Are you okay if we proceed with the checkup, Miss Izawa?"

"Yes, Ma'am."

Dr. Toma began the examination. First, she checked my blood pressure and marked it down on her clipboard, then asked me to lie down. Lying on my back, she placed a white sheet on top of my legs before lifting a portion of the gown and applying a cold gel on my stomach. Dr. Toma had set up a large mobile machine with an outdated computer monitor beside the bed. Taking a seat on a stool with wheels, she guided the handpiece, resembling a wand, over my stomach, focusing her attention on the small screen. Kai reached for my hand. The process took a couple of minutes as she clicked a few buttons on the keyboard, making snapping sounds almost like a camera. Just as I thought it was over, she stopped moving the wand and applied more cold gel, then placed it back on my stomach. Trying not to urinate each time she pressed on my stomach was a challenge.

"Congratulations, Miss Izawa, Mr. Kento, you are indeed pregnant," she pointed at a small object moving on the screen. "That small, awkwardly shaped entity there, is your baby, and they have a strong heartbeat. We will not be able to determine the sex until your next visit, usually between sixteen to twenty weeks."

Staring point-blank at the screen, Kai squeezed my hand harder. Shifting my gaze from the monitor up to him, I saw tears had formed in his eyes.

"Wow . . . that's it, right there . . . our baby," Kai said, covering his mouth with his other hand. "This whole experience . . . is insane."

I cried alongside Kai. The image on the monitor shifted back and forth, tightening and releasing, just like a heartbeat.

Dr. Toma gave us a picture from the ultrasound to take home. We booked future appointments, mostly checkups and progression tracking, to make sure everything proceeded normally leading up to my due date. She asked us if we had any questions or concerns that we wanted to address and Kai listed off rapid-fire questions.

The morning sickness finally subsided, leaving me less groggy and more willing to do normal activities. With money saved from my allowance, I bought things for the baby without much thought about the sex. The items I bought were more boy-related, so I took it as a sign. Kai and I decided we didn't want to find out the sex until the birth, which left me excited, but concerned about my spontaneous purchases.

Being pregnant at seventeen, without being married, was definitely still frowned upon within society, especially with the older generation.

It was hard to get sincere support from others without receiving nasty looks from them first. At school, the girls in my classes, who I used to speak leisurely with, had become distant. Having not told anyone for the longest time, as soon as I started to show, a couple of people took a chance to ask if I was pregnant. Since both our families were now aware of my pregnancy, plus a few of our closest friends, there was no harm in letting other people know.

When my midterm exams for first term were over, I was more relieved than happy. Even though I was fully capable of moving around and getting things done on my own, it felt good knowing I was working hard towards something important like education.

I always thought having a baby was supposed to be a joyous experience, but that boat sailed before I could even push it into the water. Kai remained my rock; my main supporter during smooth and rough times. He never wavered from his promise and worked hard to secure the life he envisioned. With only one of us working, Kai went home exhausted each night. He'd found a second job at a convenience store, which had better hourly pay, and worked there strictly on weekends, maintaining his full-time position at the flower shop during weekdays. All money he made was put towards our future, trying to save as much as he could for our baby's arrival. The thought of buying things for ourselves became less important.

The time I needed my mother the most was the time she chose to remain distant. Two weeks passed and my mother never mentioned the pregnancy, she barely spoke to me in general. During this time, my mother had been taking care of her own medications when she could, and tried to properly eat the meals prepared for her. It was harder to face her now more than ever. The guilt I harboured was eating me alive. I knew she was upset and uncertain about the path lying ahead, as was I. I knew she secretly relied on me to live up to all of her expectations, something I could no longer do. She always pushed me harder than Kenji, and now, I felt guilty for how things had turned out.

One day, as I was heading out to pick up the usual groceries, my mother stopped me at the front door. She asked where I was going and I informed her, flashing the list in my hand. Handing it to her, she ripped the piece of lined-paper out of my hands.

"Are you okay to do this on your own?" she asked, her eyes glued to the shopping list.

"What you mean? I've been doing the groceries for a while now. Have I not been doing a good enough job?"

"That's not what I meant, Nila. I mean, are you feeling up to it? Making this trip to the store alone, when one is not pregnant, can be difficult enough. Groceries are heavy."

It was then that I realized my mother was trying to reach out to me in her own, subtle way.

"Yeah, I feel fine."

"That's good," her wrinkled face softened. "Here," she handed the list back.

When I reached for it, she handed me money as well. "What's this for?"

"Use it for the groceries," she said as she walked past me to the kitchen.

Counting the amount, my eyes almost popped. "But this is way too much?" I exclaimed in awe.

"You can keep the change. Think of it as an increase in your allowance."

I recognized what my mother was doing. This was her way of apologizing and wanting to support me. As soon as I came to that conclusion, I broke down in tears. It was easy to tell my mother was disappointed about me getting pregnant, but she was finally able to accept it and that's all I could have asked. Her involvement meant everything to me. It took a giant weight off my chest and released some of the tension lingering in our household.

Kenji returned home after two weeks, but avoided me at all costs. I could only assume he wasn't ready to face me yet, which I respected and understood. The incident at the Kento shop must have been a moment he wasn't proud of. It wasn't until he came home past midnight one night, when our mother was already asleep, that he appeared at my bedroom door.

I was lying in bed, reading one of the borrowed 'new mommy' books from the library close to our house. From my room, I heard the front door unlock. Within a matter of seconds, I heard footsteps come up the stairs. Peering above the lip of my book, I saw a dark figure in my doorway. I had purposely left the door to my room wide open whenever I was inside. This way, if Kenji were to come home and walk by, I could at least see him for a quick second to make sure he looked okay. It was to my surprise that he came to me so easily.

"H-hey," I whispered, as I quickly shut the book and pulled the sheets off me. "E-everything okay?" I sat upright and crossed my legs on the bed.

Kenji looked at me. "Can I come in?"

"Yeah, of course." I swung my legs off the bed, then patted the mattress for him to sit beside me.

Kenji made his way inside and sat on the bed, leaving a distinct gap between us.

"Is there something you need?"

Kenji leaned forward and rested his elbows on top of his knees, twirling his fingers back and forth with connected hands. "There are so many things I need to say. One of them being an apology for disturbing the Kento's shop." As Kenji spoke, he consistently looked at his hands, afraid to waver. "To attack you both like that, in public . . . I was out of line."

To hear my brother being so honest and humble was promising. This conversation was one I had been waiting to have with him.

"We both forgive you. We know you were upset and acting out of anger."

Kenji lifted his head. "I ruined all those plants—I can pay for them!"

"Kenji," I said gently, tugging at his sleeve. "There's no need. Kai and his family aren't expecting you to. I just wish you could've heard the news from me first."

Looking at me with pain-filled eyes, he asked, "How come Kida knew before me?"

"Well, it was a girl thing. I found out I was pregnant the night I slept at her house. I told her not to tell you because I wanted to be the first to do so, but she didn't listen. That big mouth of hers."

"Sorry, really, I am. It's just, how could you let this happen? You're only seventeen."

"I'll be eighteen before the baby is born . . .."

"Nila," Kenji said, unimpressed.

"I know, believe me, I know. But Kai's been great. He's given me the confidence to feel like we can raise this baby . . . together . . . like a family."

He turned his head away from me. "What about Mom?"

"She already knows, I—"

"No," he said sternly. "Not that, her cancer. What about that? Just because you're pregnant doesn't mean her cancer goes away. Don't tell me you've forgotten?"

Kenji's words slapped me across the face. "Of course, I haven't!"

"Then what will you do?" Kenji faced me again. "How will you balance both?"

"I . . . um . . . I'll . . .."

He let out a troubled sigh. "You haven't thought about it at all, have you?"

"I did! I just . . .."

"Do you plan on staying here once the baby is born, or do you plan on leaving? You're already showing. The baby is growing and will be here before we know it. What are you gonna do?"

I was backed into a corner and left without words. Each question Kenji asked, I had no answer to. Our bodies swapped postures. His had become upright and direct, while mine slouched and caved in.

"Like I said, Nila, even though a baby is coming, Mom's cancer is not going away. We don't know what will happen; she may never recover."

With the harsh truth lingering over me, my heart throbbed bitterly in my chest. *May . . . never recover?*

Kenji stood up. "Don't get me wrong, Nila. A baby should be a blessing, especially in this piece of shit family. I'll do anything I can to help you; you're my sister. Our family is small and broken, torn in a million different ways—this baby will definitely bring some good, I truly believe that. But at what cost?"

With those final words, Kenji left my room and went to his, leaving me with a lot to think about. Everything he said replayed in my head, the key points highlighting themselves. Thinking about my brother's concerns kept me up the rest of the night. How could I possibly have answers to questions about an unpredictable future?

Chapter Forty-Three

*E*ACH TIME I looked down, my stomach was bigger. My toes disappeared and when I bent down to grab something, I was unstable, like a tower about to topple over. I sulked daily about how big I was getting when I looked in the mirror, though apparently, I didn't appear as big to others.

Throughout the summer, Kai took some time off so we could try to live the lives of a young, teenage couple. We were even able to catch the annual festival, but when I went to try on my yukata, it no longer fit. Luckily, Mrs. Kento still had a yukata from when she was pregnant with Ryu and lent it to me. When Kai and I arrived, hundreds of people were already walking around, stopping at food and game stalls by the dozen. There were many couples holding hands and laughing as they walked through the festival, enjoying each other's company without a care in the world.

At night, there was a huge fireworks display taking place by the river to conclude the summer festival. Everyone rushed towards the river all at once in order to find good spots for the viewing. Following the herd of people, I pulled Kai along, only to have him yank me back in the opposite direction. When I asked him what was wrong, he simply smiled and told me to follow him. He ended up taking us to a quiet spot on the other side of the river, where a couple of benches were stationed along the bend, away from the crowd. From these benches, you could clearly see the fireworks, along with their reflections on the water—the best seats in the house.

Adding to my summer happiness, my mother finally obtained a sense of self-worth. She got up decently early, for someone who was sick, and did small amounts of housework, along with other tasks she was accustomed to even though we were against it. There were even times she attended her doctor's appointments willingly, alone or with Kenji, urging for me to stay home and concentrate on taking care of myself. My mother seemed to be in higher spirits, finding a drive to keep her going. She lectured me many times on how difficult it would be to raise a child, and all I could do was take note. Deep down, she was still my hard-headed mother. Even though she kept active, she had good and bad days. Some days, she would wake up with a lively colour on her face, while on others, not so much. It was easy to tell when she was in pain, but no matter how severe, she refused to admit it and kept going.

There were still times when the deep conversation I had with Kenji played over and over inside my head. I was frustrated with myself for not having answers for him at the time, but I was even more upset that after two months, I was still at stage one, waiting for a miracle to happen where I could have it all. I realized I had no answers because I was selfishly waiting for someone to hand them to me. I wanted my mother to get better and, like an idiot, I wanted to live a carefree, newlywed life with Kai.

I was afraid to mention my concerns to Kai because he had so much on his plate already. With work and preparing for the baby, I didn't want to put more stress on him. Though, saying that was just an excuse I used to fool myself into thinking everything would gradually get better if I waited it out.

Whenever Kenji and our mother returned from the hospital, I made sure to stay in the loop on how my mother's treatments were progressing. Each time, my mother assured me everything was fine, but unless I heard it from my brother's mouth, I wasn't convinced. Kenji briefly touched base with me as soon as they walked in the door, but it wasn't until we were alone, usually after my mother went to bed, that we discussed things further.

Summer came and went like the wind, leaving no significant mark.

With September in sight, I was nervous about completing my first term of college. Even with my marks submitted, knowing I couldn't go back and change anything, I felt an emptiness inside as I waited for the results.

The final days of August were upon us and it seemed my mother was physically doing much better. She had more good days than bad. According to Kenji, the reports from Dr. Ashima suggested that the cancer had slowly started to admit defeat in response to the chemotherapy and radiation treatments. This delightful news, though a small progression, warmed my heart, melting away some of my worries and anxieties involving her sickness—a wonderful early birthday present.

On the last day of August, Kai and I bumped into my father as we were leaving Kai's house. The last time I spoke with my father properly was on the day of my graduation ceremony; I had been avoiding him since. Immediately, he noticed how oddly round my stomach had gotten and instantly asked the awkward question.

"Nila . . . are you pregnant?"

"She is," Kai answered, bowing in front of my father. "I'm sorry we kept something so big from you. It wasn't our intention to hide anything."

Considering the last time my father and Kai spoke wasn't pleasant, this confrontation was civil and honourable. Following his example, I stood beside Kai and bowed. "Please look after us."

"Nila, I . . .."

Surprisingly, out of all our family members, my father was the one who took the news the best. Lifting my head, I could see his eyes instantly light up, softening to the kind, gentle person I knew he was, before filling with tears.

"Come here," he said, making his way onto the Kento's property.

I broke and fell into my father's arms like an injured child, sobbing uncontrollably. He wasn't mad; in fact, my father congratulated us with open arms. Not feeling backed into a corner, or having to explain what we planed on doing with our futures, like we've had to do with others, gave me a comfort I didn't know I needed. Immediately, I felt lighter.

My father looked to Kai and smiled tenderly before caressing my head as if to let me know everything was going to be okay. As he held me, I could hear him chanting in my ear excitedly. "I'm going to be a Grandpa."

Feeling guilty about the unforgiving words I spoke to him at the café, about having children out of wedlock, I cried and apologized multiple times. He patted my head numerous times until I had no tears left to cry.

"Shh, it's okay, Peaches. It's alright. From now on, I'll always be here when you need me."

Chapter Forty-Four

FALL WAS ROLLING in and my stomach was rolling out; I was in my sixth month. I always looked forward to September because I got to celebrate my birthday. Although Kenji had kept an unpredictable schedule in previous years, he never failed to make an appearance on my birthday. I made an effort to try and treat each year as a blessing, and this year would forever be one.

The night before my birthday, I got myself ready for bed and pulled out another one of the borrowed books from the library about becoming a new mother. The lamp on my nightstand shone brightly on the pages, highlighting each word with just the right amount of light. Unlike most nights, the door to my room was shut. Having everyone from my family safely accounted for, under one roof before bed, made me feel at ease.

My eyes grew heavy as I felt myself drifting between the world of consciousness and dreams. Accepting how tired I was, I welcomed sleep. Right before dozing off, my eyes shot open when I felt a sharp pressure stabbing my stomach. Immediately, I tossed the book to the side and placed my hand over the area. When I did, I realized it wasn't pain. Instead, a remarkable feeling soaked into me.

"Oh!"

Inside my stomach, the baby kicked. I moved my hand around, patiently waiting to feel the baby kick once more. Searching for a few minutes, it happened again. A smile crept onto my face as I continued to rub my stomach in a circular motion.

"Hey, baby, can you hear me? It's me, your Mommy . . .."

Paying attention to my voice, I cringed at how silly I sounded. The more I rubbed my stomach, the more thoughts ran through my head. Was I ready to have a baby? Could I mentally and physically do this? Me?

"When you finally come into this world, I hope you grow to like it . . . I know I did. Your daddy was the reason why I grew to love it so much."

The strokes became smaller until they stopped altogether. With my head slightly lifted so I could look at my stomach, a trail of tears trickled down past my ear and absorbed into my pillow.

"Hey, baby, I hope you grow to love me."

September 8th; my birthday. It fell on a Friday, so Kai and I had made plans to go out for dinner after he was done with work. He messaged me saying the restaurant he chose would be a surprise, but somehow knew it was a place I liked. Kai also said he had something important to discuss with me, so, for the whole day, I was left in suspense. Not wanting to ruin his surprise, I refrained from asking too many questions.

Earlier that day, Kida passed by to spend time with me and gave me a birthday present. Opening her gift, there was a tiny, white long-sleeve onesie for the baby with the words: *'I've got a cool Aunt'* printed on the front, and a yellow stuffed rabbit. With all the names and roles Kida had been giving herself, it would be a miracle if the baby came out and didn't confuse her for the mother. Kida spent most of the morning at my house rubbing and conversing with my stomach, exchanging only a few words with me.

"Hey," she said, turning to face me, putting her obsessive tummy touching to rest. "Have you guys thought about any names yet?"

We were sitting side-by-side on the couch in my living room as the TV played in the background. Folding my hands, I rested them under my baby bump. "We haven't really discussed it . . .."

Kida looked unimpressed as she clicked her tongue. "You don't need to decide on a name yet, but haven't you guys at least talked about some you like?"

"Well, I haven't talked it over with Kai, but I've thought of a boy's name."

Her face perked up. "Ouu, tell me! Tell me!"

A smile brushed my face. "I kind of like the name, 'Souta.'"

Staring at the ceiling in thought, with a waved eyebrow, she asked, "Meaning 'sudden'?"

"Yeah. Well, I mean, he was sort of . . . you know . . . sudden?"

Kida burst out in a fit of laughter. "Oh, man, that's great!"

I joined in the laughter. "It's terrible, I know."

"Every time I call his name, I'll think of this moment and bust a gut from laughing so hard."

With my shoulder, I nudged her, trying to refrain myself from catching her contagious laughter. "Come on, stop."

We spent the rest of the evening coming up with potential baby names and wrote them down. Making a list and dividing the sheet in half between boys and girls, we tried taking the Japanese characters from both Kai's name and mine, mixing them together, but nothing sounded quite right. On the top of the girl's list, Kida wrote her name, circling and underlining it a million times with a pen, stating she had solved my problem.

The whole time we spent chatting away and discussing names, my mother was at the hospital with Kenji for a checkup, giving Kida and I some time to ourselves, like the good old days when we were dumb kids who didn't have a care in the world.

A few hours later, Kai sent me a message saying he had finished work early but needed to prepare a few things before meeting up. Kida did my hair and makeup and helped me pick out a cute outfit from my closet, one that still fit but didn't make me look like a whale. Most of my clothes were either too tight, ugly maternity clothes my mother had given me, or Kenji's old, baggy clothes that were too long for me, but too short for him. After thirty minutes of digging, Kida managed to put a decent outfit together.

As soon as I finished getting ready, my mother and Kenji came home.

When they walked through the door, Kida and I were sitting at the bottom of the stairs putting my shoes on. Putting on a simple pair of shoes became taxing, so whenever someone offered to help, I took advantage of their kindness.

"Are you heading out?" Kenji asked.

"Yeah, I'm meeting up with Kai for dinner."

"Ah, I see . . .," he paused awkwardly. "Hang on a sec."

Kenji quickly ran between Kida and me to make his way up the stairs. You could hear the door to his room swing open with great force as he scattered around. As we waited for him to return, my mother took a few steps forward.

"Nila, here," she said, bending to my level to hand me an envelope with my name on it.

"What is it?"

"Your birthday present."

"Thank you," I said, opening the envelope. Inside was a birthday card filled with money. Overwhelmed by the amount, I hesitated. "This . . . this is too much!"

"It's fine. I know you'll use it wisely," she smiled, standing.

I copied her kind smile. "Thank you, Mom."

Kida placed her arm around my shoulder as a sign of comfort and excitement about the fact that my mother and I were getting along so well. I had been keeping her up to date on our relationship regularly during the difficult times.

All of a sudden, loud footsteps stomped behind us.

"Catch," Kenji said, dropping a small package into my lap from above.

Surprised by the falling package, I was shocked by its texture and weight as it landed. "Oh," I said, squishing the package. "It's soft."

"Open it."

Holding the package with both hands, I began to rip at the edges of the purple wrapping paper. Inside, there was another tiny shirt, very similar to Kida's, but instead this one read: *'I've got the best Uncle.'* I broke out into laughter. "Seriously, you two!"

"I saw the shirt first!" Kida fought, tapping my shoulder like a child who demanded attention. "Kenji also really liked the idea, so he was able to find a matching one."

"She may have seen it first, but mine is way better, because it's from me, and I'm the kid's ACTUAL uncle."

"Whatever!" Kida jumped up and landed into a fighting stance.

As the two of them bickered and teased each other, I couldn't help but let the tears fall.

"Nila, what's wrong, hun?" my mother questioned, carefully kneeling in front of me.

"Nothing," I lifted my head with a smile. "I'm just extremely happy."

My mother leaned in and gave me a hug. "Silly girl."

"Nila," Kenji's voice came from behind me.

"Hmm?" I answered, wiping the tears from my eyes, looking back at him.

"Happy birthday."

With a warm heart, I smiled. "Thanks."

Afterwards, Kida and Kenji went out while my mother and I remained at home. There was an extremely important message I was waiting to receive, so, every two minutes, I checked my phone, in case I had missed it. Kai's message was taking forever to arrive, and my heart wouldn't stop doing somersaults. Unable to sit still, I paced around the house, walking in and out of the same room multiple times. Just watching me was driving my mother crazy.

"Nila, for heaven's sake, sit still would you! You're giving me a headache," she shouted from the living room couch.

"I'm sorry. I'm just so nervous and excited all at the same time! What's taking him so long?" I whined.

"Didn't you say you were meeting up with him at 5:30 p.m.?"

"Yeah . . .."

"It's only a quarter past five, he still has time." My mother shook her head in disbelief. "Give the poor man a break."

Annoyed, I knew she was right. I prepared myself before plopping down on the second last step of the staircase, facing the front door. "Jeez, I can't wait any longer—I'm getting impatient," I whispered under my breath.

Within a matter of minutes, the phone grasped tightly in my hand vibrated; I received a message.

"It's him!"

"Told you," my mother shouted from down the hall.

I opened my inbox to read the message.

[Line Kai]: I'll be there in ten minutes.

"Ten minutes," I groaned again. *These past fifteen minutes were bad enough. I thought he'd be here by now.*

All of a sudden, the doorbell rang.

It can't be . . ..

Reaching for the railing beside me, I pulled myself onto my feet. I walked to the door, turned the knob, and opened it. In front of me was Kai, in semi-formal attire, holding a bouquet of red roses.

"I thought you said ten minutes?"

"That was to get you amped up," he smiled maliciously.

"Idiot."

"So, I guess it worked," Kai smiled dashingly. "These are for you, Milady," he said, handing me the bouquet. "Happy birthday, Nila."

My pout turned into a bright smile as I received the bouquet. Bringing the flowers close to my nose, I could smell their beautiful fragrance. "Thank you, kind Sir."

"Well, then," Kai raised his arm for me to grab onto, "Shall we?"

"We shall, just let me put these in water first," I said, rushing to the kitchen in search of a vase.

After opening a few cupboards, I was able to locate a tall vase and placed the flowers inside before adding water, displaying them beautifully on the counter.

Excitedly making my way back to Kai, who waited patiently at the door, I said goodbye to my mother before leaving. Kai took my hand and led us to the bus stop.

"Whoa, slow down!" I shouted, trying to control his contagious excitement. "I'm pregnant, remember?"

"Right, right, I'm sorry," he apologized profoundly, as he came to a stop. "I'm getting ahead of myself."

Unable to stay mad at such an innocent, good-looking face, I yanked

Kai's arm back and rose to my tippy-toes, placing a kiss on his cheek. "I guess I can forgive you."

He smirked. "Only on the cheek? What is this?" Kai slipped his hand through my hair, grazing my neck with his fingers. "We're far beyond that." With his hand on the nape of my neck, I gave him control, as he guided my face closer to his. Breaking from our tender kiss, he whispered in my ear, "That's how it's done."

Embarrassed by his forwardness, I felt my face becoming hot. "Show off."

He nudged his nose against mine, then pulled back to stand up straight so he could face me properly.

"What?" I asked suspiciously.

"You're absolutely gorgeous."

The heat from my face spread all the way down my neck and rose to my ears. "W-we're going to be late." Breaking eye contact, I buried my face into the fancy pink scarf Kida picked out as part of my outfit.

Kai took my hand with a devilish smile. "Alright, Madam, onward!"

From there, we got on a bus that took us downtown. We got off at the terminal and walked a few blocks until we arrived at a familiar building. It was the small restaurant we ate at during Christmas.

"I knew it," I smiled, looking at him.

"Well, I figured," he said, taking his hand and lifting it above his shoulder as he rubbed the back of his neck, "since we technically had our first date here . . .."

"First date, huh?" I interrupted, bumping him with my hip. "Who said anything about *that* time being a date?"

"Felt pretty *date-like* to me," he said as he leaned over, grinning widely. "It was our first time out together, and even though it started off a bit rocky, I think it ended great. I mean, look at us now."

"I guess you're right," I admitted, sticking out my tongue and scrunching my nose.

"I love when you do that."

"Do what?"

"The thing you do with your nose—it's cute."

"Idiot . . .."

Kai leaned in and kissed me once more. "You love this idiot."

I stayed quiet. Kai didn't seem to notice as he reached for the door of the restaurant and held it open for me. I wanted to openly express my feelings for Kai, like he easily did for me with his romantic and playful gestures.

"You know," I said, pulling him off to the side, away from the door, "this was the place I truly opened up to someone about all the stuff going on in my life."

"Yeah, there's that, too. Man, I can't believe everything that's happened in less than a year. Us meeting, dating, graduating, birthdays, and soon we'll be having a baby. Where has the year gone?"

The joking stopped. As I stared at Kai, I watched the smile on his face melt as he peered up at the sign hanging from the wall.

"Do you regret it?"

Turning back to me, Kai's eyebrows caved. "Regret what?"

"Meeting me . . . ."

"Meeting you?"

Avoiding his intense gaze, I looked down at my stomach. "Mhm, because without me, you could have continued living a carefree life. Hanging out with friends, going to parties . . . working less. We wouldn't have met, and I wouldn't be—"

"Stop," Kai overpowered, his voice hard and strict. "Stop it. I don't want to hear any of that garbage."

"Kai . . .," I looked up, terrified.

"I regret nothing," he said, stepping closer to me. "Nothing involving you comes anywhere near regret. You've made a huge impact on my life, in the most positive way. It's like you gave purpose to my hollow life. After Hatori's death, I was wandering through life recklessly, looking for something to revive me and get me excited again. Then I met you. I only figured out I was lonely once you appeared. You came into my life with beaming attraction, drawing me in. Every time you left my sight, I felt the need to find you. There were so many times you could've told me to 'get lost' or 'go to hell,' but you didn't. Nila, you inspired me to become a better person, one worthy of you and our unborn child."

I was so shocked; I couldn't even cry. Every uncertainty about being with Kai and having his baby, escaped me. "Kai . . . Kai, I . . .."

Before I could formulate a proper sentence, Kai grabbed me, pulling me into his chest. "Everything's alright; you don't have to be afraid anymore. You will always have me. I won't leave you alone."

I sobbed to my heart's content, crying out all the uncertainties I had locked within. I held Kai's shirt with both hands and scrunched it into fists. "I love you," I said in between breaths.

Kissing my forehead, he replied, "I know."

Allowing me a few minutes to calm down, Kai let go, wiping my tears before we entered the restaurant. The waitress told us to follow her to our table and seated us at the same booth from before.

"What luck!" I exclaimed after the waitress walked away.

"Yeah, what a coincidence . . .."

"What's with that sarcastic comment?"

Smiling with a sense of accomplishment, he answered, "I reserved this table in advance."

"They allow reservations at such a small restaurant?"

"Not sure, but I told the girl on the phone that it had to be *this* table."

I couldn't repress my smile. My full heart leapt with excitement.

"I wonder if Ume still works here? Then it'll be a reunion."

With eyes like dangers, I stared at him. "Mmmhm."

"Or not. Jeez, that look could kill someone," he teased.

Once the name *Ume* left Kai's mouth, I couldn't seem to get it out of my mind.

Both of us ordered the same meals as before, unofficially starting a tradition. While waiting for our food, Kai pulled out a thin, square-shaped box from his pocket. The box was wrapped in pretty, pink wrapping paper with a small bow.

"Here," he said, resting the box in the middle of the table.

"A gift? Kai, this is too much. This dinner is more than enough."

"Nonsense, this place is cheap. Even though we dressed up, probably overdoing it, doesn't make it enough for a birthday gift."

"It looks expensive . . .."

"You haven't even opened it yet," he said, pushing it closer to me.

Slowly, I reached for the box and unwrapped it. After removing the wrapping paper, a jewellery box remained in the palm of my hand. "Kai . . .."

"Keep going."

Lifting the lid, something shiny caught my eye. A silver bracelet with a dangling heart charm was inside. My jaw dropped. "It's beautiful!" Removing the bracelet from its packaging, I placed the box on the table before slipping it onto my wrist. "Kai, we should be saving. Not spending your hard-earned money!"

"It's fine; I have enough saved. I'm not that incompetent."

"You have enough?"

"Yeah, plus it was for a special occasion."

I held my negative tongue. "Okay, I believe you. Thank you very much."

Across the table, Kai was already smiling at me dearly. "Happy birthday, Nila."

With such an extravagant gift around my wrist, I couldn't stop smiling each time I looked at it. Shortly after, the server returned with our food and we thanked her kindly. For the rest of the dinner, we reminisced about the last time we were here and talked about the Christmas shopping we did together. The conversation shifted to how Christmas would bring our baby's arrival, given my due date was in December.

"Do you think our baby will be born on Christmas day?" Kai asked anxiously.

"I hope not, a Christmas birthday is terrible! All their friends will be busy each year and will never be able to make it for birthday parties. That time of year is way too chaotic."

"Yeah, you're right. After all, your due date is set for the seventeenth."

"Yep, right in the middle of the month." While I got tense just thinking about a Christmas birth, Kai smiled charmingly at me. "What?"

"It's funny."

"What is . . .?"

"This—us. Talking about our baby's future, even though he or she isn't born yet. It just seems so crazy to me. We don't even know what's going to happen in our own future, let alone the baby's."

"I know what you mean. Try carrying them for nine months, then come talk to me."

Kai chuckled. "I can't even imagine."

We finished our meals around 6:30 p.m. and Kai quickly snatched the bill from the waitress. After Kai finished paying, we gathered our things and made our way to the exit.

"So, are we heading back now?" I asked.

"Nope."

"No?"

"That's right. I still have one more place to take you."

"Another place? Please don't tell me you're spending more money for my birthday," I pleaded.

"Um, yes and no?" he said with a conflicted expression, rocking his head back and forth.

My brow creased. "What does that mean?"

"Just come with me," he said, as he reached for my hand and led me towards the terminal.

"Another surprise?"

Looking back at me, he had a sly grin on his face. "This IS the surprise."

I pondered on ideas of what the surprise could be, after having already received such an expensive bracelet. "Are we taking the bus?"

"Yeah, you shouldn't be on your feet for so long. It'll be too far for you."

"Oh . . . kay," I said cautiously, wondering what else he could possibly have in store for me.

When we reached the station, we jumped on a bus with a scheduled route passing the Kento's shop.

"Are we going to the shop?"

"You'll see when we get there, jeez," he immediately replied. "Stop trying to guess and ruin the surprise."

Rolling my eyes, I slumped down in my seat and folded my arms. "Fine."

I watched countless people hop on and off the bus. When the stop to the flower shop arrived, Kai stood up.

"This is our stop."

"I knew it . . .," I whispered victoriously.

Still holding my hand, Kai took the lead once again, carefully helping me off the bus when I approached its final step.

"So, I was right," I said in high spirits as the bus drove off.

"Maybe, maybe not."

"Hmm . . .."

We continued walking in the direction of the shop, giving me more reason to confirm my suspicions, but as we came across the front door, we passed right by it.

"Sooo, it's not the shop?"

"Patience," he enforced.

Where the hell are we going?

After passing another two store fronts, we came across a wide alleyway in between the tall buildings. The alley was lined with a bunch of flower baskets, which seemed to carry on forever down both sides of the walkway. It was as if every type of flower from the Kento's shop lined the walls of the two buildings, shining in the sun's fair light, making a trail. The flowers blew in the last bits of warm, summer air, as loose petals danced in the gentle breeze before falling peacefully to the ground. All sorts of colours were illuminating from the vibrate path, just like a field of rainbows.

"What's going on?"

"Go ahead and follow it. I'll be right behind you."

I gladly accepted the colourful journey Kai set up for me. Following the flower path, I could see the back of the Kento's shop which could also be accessed by a door from the alleyway, like most other stores in the shopping district. There were a few smaller mom and pop shops in the back, ones secluded from the heavy foot traffic during busy hours. Eventually, the trail of flowers came to an end in front of a narrow building, attached to a small bakery which looked to have been added as an addition. The nameless building was old and rundown, masked in shade from the setting sun, giving the outside a gloomy appearance and a sense of abandonment. The front door and window frames were in desperate need of a fresh coat of paint, while the cement structure needed minor patchwork.

Confused as to why we were here, I took a step closer to the door of the mysterious building. "What is this place?"

Kai took a couple of steps towards me, standing securely against my back like a wall. I could feel his warm breath down the nape of my neck. "Use this." Kai slipped something with an odd texture and shape into the palm of my hand.

I brought my hand closer to eye level to see what I was given. "A key?"

"Use it to open the door."

With puzzling eyes, I turned to face him.

"Nila," he said, lifting his hand and cupping it on top of the one I had holding the key. "Welcome home."

Chapter Forty-Five

MY EIGHTEENTH BIRTHDAY was a day I would treasure for the rest of my life. When Kai presented me with a key to our very own home, my heart did a somersault and everything around me illuminated with bliss. The entire time, Kai had been saving all his money for a place to live in as a family. Not knowing something so materialistic could bring me so much happiness, I could not picture a better place to start out—it was perfect.

Kai told me that a regular customer, from the flower shop, asked to hang a flyer in the window advertising a small apartment for rent. The apartment was attached to this old man's bakery and had been empty for quite some time. The elderly landlord was finding it difficult to maintain the apartment while running the bakery with his wife. Intrigued at the thought of living independently, in a place just behind the shop, Kai proceeded to ask the old man if he could look at it. Kai explained his current situation to the recurring customer and the man was thrilled to hear someone was finally interested in his rental. When Kai went to check it out, he immediately fell in love with its traditional, Japanese style layout. Knowing how badly he wanted the apartment, Kai bargained with the old man to let him buy the apartment portion from him, allowing him to keep his bakery. At first, the elderly man was hesitant to sell his income property, but considering the hardship it would cost him to keep up with maintenance, he agreed to Kai's offer.

Kai had thought of fixing up the place before showing it to me, but with my birthday less than two weeks away at the time, he hadn't been able to do much. When I walked into the apartment for the first time, the inside looked just as rough as the outside, if not worse. Kai took my hand and guided me through the tiny apartment. At the entrance, there was a small foyer to keep our shoes before stepping over the raised, wooden entryway. From the front door, the back door could be seen by looking straight down the narrow hallway. The first room off to the right was a cute, little kitchen with a large window overlooking the front of the building. Further down, the hallway ended and merged into a multipurpose living room, floored with tatami mats. The room was huge, considering the size of the apartment, and had a spacious closet, with original shoji doors, next to a small bathroom off to the left. At the far end of the multipurpose room was a bamboo sliding door leading to the backyard, which was small to match the rest of the apartment, but had the most amazing greenery growing wildly.

With excitement, Kai proceeded to explain the layout he envisioned in his head, using his hands to act out and demonstrate. I had never seen him so enthusiastic. The apartment had potential, and both Kai and I agreed we would fix it up together. It may not have been pretty to look at, but it already felt like home.

He informed me that everyone who was close to us knew about the apartment and his plan to show it to me on my birthday. Kida and Kenji helped keep me busy and away from the shop as much as possible during the weeks before my birthday, giving Kai and Ryu time to prepare the flowers used to line the path.

As soon as I asked about my mother's reaction, he smiled sincerely and said, "She was the first one I spoke with. You should discuss the rest with her."

Not knowing what he meant, I left the conversation for my mother like he said.

After Kai finished giving me the tour of our new apartment, he took me home so I could have a proper talk with my mother. The idea of moving in with Kai was something I couldn't fully wrap my head around. I was so excited; beads of sweat were rolling off me.

"I'm home," I said, walking through the door.

"Welcome home," my mother replied, just louder than a whisper.

Taking a few steps down the hall, I could see her sitting at the kitchen table with two cups. Walking into the kitchen hesitantly, I looked at my mother. In response to my awkward stare, she answered with a strange, tender smile.

"Um, Mo—"

"Have a seat, Nila," she said, continuing to smile. "I made tea for us."

"Al-alright," I answered nervously, sitting down across from her. "How are you feeling?"

As she reached for her cup, she brought it up to her nose and inhaled the steam emanating from it, then took a sip. "Mmm, perfect," she said peacefully.

With my mother being oddly calm, I became skeptical of the tea offering I had stumbled upon. Looking down at the cup in front of me, it seemed like an average cup of ryokucha, but my mother had never smiled at me like that before. As I looked between the cup and my mother's face, not once did her smile waver.

"Something wrong with the tea?"

"No . . . ."

"Then you better drink it while it's hot." She took another sip. "It's the best tea we have in this house."

In that moment, I knew something was up. My mother NEVER used the 'best tea,' unless someone she was trying to impress came over. It was too expensive for everyday consumption. As kids, Kenji and I would steal some of this gyokuro tea and drink it in our rooms.

From where I sat, the strong scent produced by the tea was easy to smell. I felt dumb for not noticing it at first. "Why are we using *this* tea?"

"Because, today's a special day."

"My . . . birthday?"

"That, and the day you start packing."

"Packing?"

My mother looked at me with the same exact smile, one that made its true meaning hard to distinguish. "To move out. You will need to move into a home, one in which you will begin your own family."

My mother's words fell short. They were hard to hear because they were sharp and straight to the point, attacking my heart.

"But I—"

"Nila," before I could finish, she shot me down. Placing her cup on the table, she looked at me. "I know Kai showed you the apartment today, the place you will call home as you live alongside him. It was only a matter of time before this needed to happen. I was well aware of it for the past few weeks."

"Mom . . . ."

My mother's eyes drowned with tears as she struggled to keep her composure. "Eventually, I knew I would have to let you go, like every parent must," she paused with a hazy voice, as she widened her eyes. Trying to hold back the tears, she fluttered her eyelashes to stop them from falling. "I just . . . didn't think it would be so soon. You're so young, I thought I had more time."

Reaching across the table, I placed my hand on top of hers. "I don't have to leave if you don't want me to!" I said in one breath. "I can stay right here! Kai and I can still raise the baby, even if I remain here."

"Nila," she shook her head. "Don't be ridiculous. You can't mistreat Kai that way. Limiting his time with his own child, and you—it simply won't work. With my illness, it is not ideal to raise the baby here. You can't have the best of both worlds, hun. Don't worry about me; I'm fine. Dr. Ashima said I am doing much better, plus Kenji is here when I need him," she winked. "Everything will be fine."

I squeezed her hand tighter. "I'll still be in town, not too far away! Make sure to give me a call anytime you need me, even if it's for something small or stupid!"

My mother chuckled. "Alright."

"I'll pass by every day!"

My mother replied with another smile, this time, one filled with more love and warmth. She turned my hand over, placing hers on top. "I don't want you to constantly worry about me, Nila."

"Mom, I know, but . . . ."

Shaking her head, she pressed on. "I'll beat this cancer; I won't let it win." My mother looked down at our hands, rubbing her thumb back and forth slowly on my palm. "I'm sorry I was so hard on you."

I felt an instant prick at my heart. I could hear the uneasiness and suffering in her voice as her eyes grew sorrowful.

"I always pushed you harder than I did Kenji, and for that, I'm truly sorry. I guess deep down I knew you could handle it, you were strong enough to keep going. I kept pushing you because I wanted you to become stronger, stronger than Kenji—stronger than me. You've always been independent, hardly relying on me for anything, and in that sense, you are a lot like me. I tried my hardest to solely rely on myself, not wanting to owe anyone anything, and look where it got me."

My mother's hand had grown cold in my palm. It was as if the warmth from the tea masked her ice-cold skin. When I stared at our hands, the illusion of ice was noticeable in her white pigmentation.

"After your father left, it was up to me to raise two children alone. I was utterly terrified of screwing up." My mother shook her head rapidly back and forth with her eyes shut as if in disbelief. "Sorry, I never thought I'd be here telling my daughter about my insecurities. How dreadful. I guess being older doesn't always make you wiser."

"No, Mom, it's okay. I'm actually really glad we're having this talk," I said reassuringly.

"It's been a long time coming," she said, finishing my thought.

I smiled. "Yeah."

Removing her hand from mine, she grabbed her tea and took another sip before lowering the cup. "Ultimately, I don't care what this cancer wants. It will not take my life, most certainly not before I meet my first grandchild," she smirked, attempting to lighten the conversation.

"That's right," I giggled in fear, my eyes glossed with tears.

After the heartfelt conversation with my mother, I went to my room to find a few boxes waiting for me. Left on the floor in the middle of my room, I stared down at the pre-labelled, cluster of boxes and immediately broke out in a cold sweat. When I opened a few boxes labelled kitchen and bathroom, I discovered they had already been packed to the brim with items corresponding to the designated room. Seeing fully equipped boxes triggered every emotion other than excitement. Tears overflowed and I sobbed silently in my room as I spun in circles, trying to figure out if what I was doing was the right thing. My young life flashed before my eyes. Everything had changed. Would I ever come back to this room? Overwhelmed, I had no idea where to start.

A couple of days after my birthday, Kai moved into the apartment. Gradually, he brought things over with the help of his brothers. Kai spent the first few weeks in our new home alone. He ran through the apartment, searching for things that needed to be repaired before I moved in. He concerned himself with everything, saying multiple things posed a threat and were potentially dangerous; therefore, babyproofing the entire place like an overprotective maniac. Each night before bed, Kai messaged me with updates on the renovations. He was excited with how everything was coming along. Even though I said I could and wanted to help, Kai didn't want me doing any heavy lifting, or anything at all for that matter. He didn't want me getting hurt, so he temporarily banned me from our new home and put his brothers to work until everything was ready.

During that time, I chose to spend each waking moment with my mother. After she went to bed, I focused on packing in preparation for the big move. With my remaining time at home, Kenji also chose to remain close by. He became interested in all the daily tasks I did for our mother, watching me thoroughly each time I started something, as if I were never coming back. With him constantly around me, my chest ached with guilt. It felt like I was abandoning my mother in her time of need. Even though it was said she was getting better, it pained me each time I reminded myself I was leaving this house.

My first term of college came to an end on the last day of September and I completed each class with a passing score. Unlike high school, I didn't finish with top marks, but there was nothing I could have done to improve towards the end without taking supplementary lessons.

Since the term was over, and Kai finished the renovations, I was finally able to move into the apartment. Kai, Kenji, and Ryu all helped move my stuff, not allowing me to lift a single box like some sort of spoiled princess. Minus my bulky furniture, I only brought a few important things with me at first. Even with my mother's permission, I felt bad leaving my old room at home bare. It pained me to think of my mother seeing an empty room each time she walked to and from her own. The last couple of days I spent at home, my mother seemed to want me gone as soon as possible. She constantly offered to help me pack and kept naming off more stuff for me to bring along, leaving me frantic and perplexed.

With the whole day revolved around moving, things were starting to come together. My smaller furniture pieces had been brought over but still needed to be arranged, like my dresser and bookshelf, while a good portion of the boxes were now unpacked. Without keeping track of time, night crept upon us.

Kai stood up to stretch while looking at the clock on the wall. "Man, I can't believe how late it's gotten."

Following his gaze from where I sat, I looked at the clock. "Yeah, I know. The day just flew by," I said, continuing to unpack items belonging to the kitchen. "Do you work tomorrow?"

"Yeah, sorry. It's Saturday, so I have my part-time. If it was the flower shop, I could've asked my dad for an extra day off."

Shaking my head, I replied, "Don't worry. You can't keep taking days off work. Besides, I still have plenty of boxes to go through, surely enough to keep me busy."

"Alright," he said, smiling excitedly.

"What's with that face?"

"What face?"

"THAT face," I pointed at him. "Such a random, happy-looking smile . . . it's creepy."

Kai walked to me and bent to my level. "I was just thinking. Tonight's the first night we get to spend together . . . alone . . . in our own place . . .," he shied away. "Almost like a newlywed couple."

My chest tightened as Kai brought such a realization to my attention. I couldn't believe after all my preparation for this change, our first night together never once crossed my mind. This was our home now; each night would be just like this one, freedom to act on our own. Immediately, perverted things crossed my mind.

Ahh! Stop! Why is my mind so easily corrupted?

"Well, then," Kai felt the awkward tension and tried to change the topic. "Should we get ready for bed?"

Looking down at my lap, I answered quietly, "Mhm."

Kai was the first to stand, extending a hand to assist me.

"Thanks," I said, taking his hand and rising to my feet.

"Of course."

Adjusting my posture, I yearned for a nice, warm bath. "Would it be okay if I took a bath first?"

"Ah, sure. Let me prepare it for you," Kai insisted, eagerly making his way to the bathroom.

"It's okay; I'm capable of doing it myself."

"I believe you, it's just you'll need to clean it first, which involves a lot of bending over, so it would be better if I did it."

"Alright, thank you. That would be great."

"Yeah," he answered with a smile reaching from ear to ear before running off.

Patiently waiting in the living room—part-time bedroom—for my bath to be poured, I lifted our round chabudai table, which Kai brought over from his old room, onto its side and carefully rolled it. Gently resting it against the wall at the opposite end, I went back to get the zabuton cushions. After tidying up the living room, I went to the closet and rolled out our futon, spreading it across the floor evenly before finishing it off with sheets and two pillows, turning the room into a bedroom. By the time I was done, Kai had finished running my bath.

"It's ready," he called as he walked into the room to get me. As soon as he saw the table up against the wall and the futon spread out on the floor, Kai got extremely upset. "NILA! Why didn't you wait for me before getting this ready?"

"Well, you were working on the bath, so I thought I'd be useful by getting the bed ready."

Kai's eyebrows narrowed. "The table is heavy! What if something were to happen?"

"Kai, calm down," I said sternly, wobbling to my feet. "I am capable of doing simple things like this by myself. I'm pregnant, not disabled."

"Nila, I know, but—"

"Kai, you're being way too protective," I expressed, standing my ground. "I feel like I can't do anything on my own. You won't let me help bring my stuff over; I can't lift a single thing without you breathing down my neck, like my God, Kai, I wasn't even allowed to move into the apartment until you baby-proofed it—the baby isn't even here yet!"

With a look of distress, he sighed heavily and covered his face with both hands. "I'm sorry," he said, talking through his fingers. "I didn't mean to make you feel like that, it's just . . .," he removed his hands, "I've been reading a few books about pregnancy, and babies, and they . . . they all say too much stress and physical activity can cause a miscarriage, and I . . . I wouldn't know what to do if that happened, so I've been trying to keep you from lifting anything heavy."

Kai said everything in one jumbled, out-of-breath sentence, and at parts, I could hear his heart in his throat. Seeing his distraught expression, I walked over to him and hugged him. Looking up, I stole a glance at his face.

"I didn't know you were reading pregnancy books . . . I have been, too."

Kai slowly wrapped his arms around me. "A few months ago, after our first ultrasound appointment with Dr. Toma, I went to the library and checked out a few books. I was starting to freak out. Each day, our baby gets closer to arriving, and I still know nothing. Sure, I've looked after my niece a few times, and I've watched Sosuke and my sister-in-law interact with her, but that doesn't mean I know how to take care of a baby on my own."

I realized then that Kai had the same fears and insecurities as I did, maybe even more. It never dawned on me that there was a possibility I could lose the baby by doing daily tasks. The thought of no longer being pregnant, after so many months of carrying and bonding with the baby, was terrifying. After all this time spent preparing, there was a chance it could disappear, as if nothing were even there to begin with.

"Sorry."

"Hmm?" he mumbled, backing away to see my face. "For what?"

"I didn't realize you were shouldering all this on your own. You could've talked to me, I would've understood, because I feel the same way. It's scary knowing a baby is growing inside of me, and soon, I'll be responsible for a life other than my own. That's why I also went to the library to borrow books on becoming a new mother. Like, what . . . what if our baby doesn't like us? What if I'm a terrible mother? Everything is moving and changing so fast—I'm not ready!"

Kai pulled me in close, squeezing my head in between his arms and chest. "We really are a pair of idiots, huh?"

Comforted by his touch, I buried my face deep into his chest to calm down. "Yeah."

With my bath getting cold, I decided to take it quickly so Kai could have time to take his before bed as well. After we both finished bathing, we got into the futon and laid side-by-side for the first time in our new home. Kai had one arm around my stomach, securing me safely as I laid with my back towards him, keeping my arms bunched and to myself. Shortly after saying goodnight to each other, the room fell silent, but my mind continued to wander, and my heart itched with nervousness. At this rate, it would be impossible to sleep. I chose to have my back against Kai so my anxiety wouldn't shoot through the roof by having his face so close to mine. Obviously, it wasn't working.

"You awake?"

"Yeah," I answered in a whisper.

"Turn and face me."

"Why?" I asked in panic.

"Why? Because I said so," he answered sarcastically.

Rolling my eyes, I flipped over in order to give him a piece of my mind. "Because you said so? Who do you think—" I stopped mid-sentence, as Kai was already smiling at me before I could completely turn over. "What . . .?"

"Can't sleep?"

Hesitant to answer, I looked away. "Maybe . . .."

"Same, I can't sleep either."

"Why's that?"

"Because you make me nervous."

Momentarily lost for words, I looked back. "Me?"

"Yes, you. I mean, I'm nervous, but I'm also excited."

"I guess that's how I'm feeling, too."

Kai smiled again, then reached over to squeeze me tightly, almost suffocating me in his arms. "I can't believe how far we've come."

Settling into his embrace, I loosened up. "Yeah. It's all happening so fast; sometimes, it doesn't feel real." Hugging him with all my might, I got emotional. "You know, I wanted to be found, just like you said. You've opened my world to so much colour, when before, all I could see was grey. That was something only you could do for me."

Kai fell silent.

I can't see his face. Did he fall asleep? "Kai . . .?"

"From yesterday to today, from today to tomorrow, I'm never going to stop adding colour to your world. The same way I'll never stop loving you, Nila."

I could feel my heart pounding in my chest from Kai's fulfilling words. He spoke gracefully, appealing to my ears as if his words were a beautiful song. After that, we continued to hold each other close in blissful silence before drifting off to sleep.

Chapter Forty-Six

"*DADDY.*"

"*Yes, Peaches.*"

"*Why does Daddy call me, 'Peaches'?*"

With a look of enticement, he smiled. "*Why the curiosity?*"

"*'Cause Daddy never calls Kenji, 'Peaches.''*"

"*Hmm, I guess that's true.*" *With a smirk, he reached over and whispered into my ear,* "*You really wanna know?*"

"*Yeah!*"

Grabbing both of my cheeks, he stretched them all sorts of ways. "*It's because when you smile, your cheeks bunch up and become really round.*"

"*Ahh!*" *I giggled, trying to push his hands away.* "*Stop it, Daddy!*"

"*Then, when you laugh, they turn into a lovely shade of pinky-orange,*" *he smiled warmly.* "*And when you get upset, you're like an easily bruised peach. That's why Daddy started calling you, 'Peaches,' because to me, you look like a cute, little peach.*"

Finally getting him off my cheeks, I looked at him. "*You should start calling Kenji, 'Tomato.'*"

Confused, he replied with a laugh. "*Oh, yeah?*"

"*Yeah.*"

"*Why's that?*"

"'Cause when he gets mad, his face turns red like a tomato. Not cute at all."

He burst into an uncontrollable fit of laughter. "We'll see."

The next day, I was awoken by a kiss gently placed on my forehead. Kai was getting ready to leave for work but wanted to say goodbye before heading out. Getting up, I chose to see him off. Once the front door closed, I thought about going back to bed, but I felt energized and ready to start the day.

Still standing by the entrance, I looked at the boxes piled up against the wall. *Right, guess I'll start with these then.*

My morning was booked solid with mountains of boxes to unpack. I had labelled each box with my name and with what items were inside, making things easier to find when placing them in their new homes. I continued with kitchen boxes and worked my way into the bathroom before noon, then took a break to make lunch. After lunch, I continued with the rest of the unpacking, finishing just before 2:00 p.m.

Jeez, I had a lot more stuff than I realized. I don't even remember packing half of this.

Within my boxes were a few books which I placed on the bottom shelf of the tiny bookshelf I brought from home. The bookshelf was in the corner of the living area, sad and practically bare. The books I brought over were some of my favourite reads throughout high school, ones I couldn't leave behind. Reaching for the last pile inside the box, I smiled joyously as I read over the title of each book. When it came to the last one, I held it tightly as I took a seat beside the shelf, leaning my shoulders and back against the wall.

'There's Nothing Wrong with My World'; Dad's all-time favourite read.

Staring at the novel in my hand, a heavy weight pressed down on my heart. I had no intention of opening the cover, but my hands moved on their own. My thumb, placed over the edges, grazed each worn-out page, as my fingers arched the back of the paper copy. At a fast pace, the pages raced before me and a picture flew out, landing on the floor, faced down.

What's this?

Reaching for the picture lying beside me, I grabbed it curiously.

Flipping it over, a familiar memory was exposed. It was a picture of my family, back when Kenji and I were in junior high, during a summer festival. All four of us were wearing traditional outfits.

I . . . remember this day. Looking closely at everyone's faces, a smile illuminated mine. *Kenji fought with Mom because he didn't want to wear the jinbei she picked out for him. What a troublesome kid.*

In the picture, my father stood next to Kenji, wearing a mischievous grin as he ruffled Kenji's hair, probably to make him mad. Beside my father stood my mother, upright with her feet together. She wore a summer yukata, matched with a pair of geta, as she clutched onto her kinchaku with one hand and held my hand with the other, wearing the biggest smile upon her face.

When was it . . .? When was the last time I truly saw my mother smile like this?

Within moments of reminiscing, I could feel myself slipping into a dream state. In an unidentifiable haze, I could vaguely hear a voice calling my name in the background. All of a sudden, in what felt like a surreal dream, there was an annoying nudging motion against my shoulder, followed by a bit of back and forth shaking.

"—la . . . Nila!"

"Hmm?"

"What are you doing, sleeping here against the wall? If you were tired, you should have taken a nap on the futon."

I had fallen asleep beside the bookshelf with my father's favourite book in one hand and my family photo in the other.

"Y-yeah, sorry," I answered, nostalgia lingering in me.

Looking at Kai who knelt beside me, he smiled satisfyingly. "I'm home."

My heart filled with immediate warmth and peace. "Welcome home."

A few hours later, Kai and I began preparing dinner together. Even though basic cooking was something I could do on my own, Kai insisted on helping, just as he did with every other task. When everything was set out on the chabudai, we sat on the zabuton to enjoy our meal as Kai told me about his day at work. From the stories he told, and the way he told them, I could tell he wasn't enjoying his part-time job as much as the shop, but he persevered and continued working hard. Switching the topic to the flower shop, he was proud to say a new customer recently came into the shop and praised the great service she experienced. The customer was thrilled at the huge selection of flowers and was pleased at how knowledgeable Kai was about each flower. It was nice to watch Kai as he shared his pleasant experiences because he seemed so happy telling them. His eyes lit up from excitement as he explained each part, bringing a wholesome smile to my heart.

After dinner, we decided to pull out a deck of cards. Setting up for a simple game of Two-Ten-Jack, Kai fanned out the deck to inspect the cards before shuffling them.

"Hey," he said while dealing.

"Yeah?"

"Do you want a Boy or a Girl?"

Looking at Kai from across the table, I didn't know how to answer. "What brought this on all of a sudden?"

"It's just we haven't really talked about it, y'know? Feels weird not to have had this conversation with you already."

"I know what you mean," I said, relaxing my shoulders. "Personally, I think it's mostly because it's still hard to wrap our heads around it. The baby, our new place—all of it. I know we've had similar talks about how everything is moving quickly, but I still feel that way."

With the last card distributed, Kai repositioned himself across the table from me. "You're absolutely right, so let's have the conversation now."

"Now?"

"I want to know what your preference is; boy or girl, and I want us to come up with names."

Listening at how involved Kai was trying to be, made me really happy. I could tell he was serious about it. "A boy."

Thrown by my answer, Kai put his cards down on the table and leaned back. Stretching out his arms and folding them under his head, he used them as support against the floor. "A boy, huh?"

"Is that weird?"

"It's not weird," he shook his head, tilting it towards the ceiling. "I was just trying to imagine a little boy running around this apartment."

My heart tightened, making a tingling sensation of heat shoot down to my stomach. "Souta . . . ."

Kai's head quickly jerked back at me. "Sorry Nila, what did you say?"

Averting my gaze from his, I looked at the small bookshelf. "Souta . . . for a boy."

Before I could look back at him, Kai was already making his way over to me on his knees. Taking a seat beside me, he crossed his legs. "Meaning 'quick'?"

"More like 'sudden.'"

Kai laughed out loudly. "I get it."

"Do you like it?"

Smiling at me, he grabbed my hand and brought it to his lips. "It's perfect," he said, just before placing a kiss on it. "Just like his mother."

Trying to hide my face, as I was probably blushing, I looked at my stomach. "What if it's a girl though?"

"To tell you the truth, I've never thought about this baby being a boy. Sure, I've thought about having a boy someday in the future, but for some reason, for this one, I just keep thinking Girl."

"Really?" I looked at him with amazement.

"Yeah, I just have this feeling."

"That's funny," I said, slightly giggling.

"Why's *that* so funny?" his eyebrows narrowed.

"Because, I've never thought about us having a girl. I keep thinking Boy."

"No way!" he exclaimed, looking surprised.

"Mhm," I smiled.

"Wow," he let out a trapped sigh. "Hopefully, you're right. It would save me the trouble of chasing away boys."

Poking fun at his overprotectiveness once again, I leaned into him with my shoulder. "What about you, though? Have you thought of any girl names?"

"I have."

With anticipation, I waited for him to continue.

Quickly doing a double take, he asked obliviously, "What?"

"What are the names?" I blurted out. "I thought you would have just said them out loud!"

Laughing with a smile reaching from ear-to-ear, he used both hands to tug at my cheeks. "Relax! I've only thought of one. But you probably won't like it."

Pulling my face away from his grasp, I massaged my cheeks. "Why wouldn't I?"

"Because I was thinking of the name, 'Ume.'"

Taken aback by the name, I looked into Kai's eyes as if to ask why.

"Calm down; I'll tell you my reasoning. Remember when the waitress served us . . . ."

"Ume."

"Yes, Ume—let me finish," he said, patting my head like a child's. "She said her name meant 'Plum,' and for some reason, it stuck with me. On the day of graduation, when your dad showed up, there was one face you made that struck me. After hearing him call you 'Peaches,' like you told me he used to when you were little, your eyes lit up. I've never seen you light up the way you did that day, even though I completely ruined the mood between the two of you afterwards. Instantly, a connection hit me, 'Peaches' and 'Plum.'"

The same tightening from before reoccurred in my chest. *He made the connection . . . for me?*

Tears clouded my vision and slowly trickled down my cheeks, landing on my conveniently round belly.

"Nila?" Kai asked in a panic. "I'm sorry! Did I say something I shouldn't have? Do you hate it that much?"

Shaking my head, a smile formed. "Just the opposite."

Kai bent forward and fell into my lap, laying his head on my legs. "Well, it's just an idea."

Running my fingers through his light-coloured hair, which had grown longer than usual, I replied softly, "Yeah, okay."

Chapter Forty-Seven

 FEW DAYS PASSED, and I was bored being home alone and sitting on my butt all day, watching the time go by. I phoned my mother to let her know I would be coming by for a short visit while Kai was at work. Taking the bus like usual, I arrived at the stop closest to my old house. Not being able to call my old house 'home' anymore, felt empty—like I betrayed it.

At the bus stop, Kenji leaned against the metal pole indicating the scheduled bus route, patiently waiting for my arrival. I stood in the line of people waiting to get off the bus, and when my turn arrived, Kenji was at the end of the steps with an unexpected hand held out to help me down.

"Thanks," I smiled.

"No problem."

Walking side-by-side with my brother seemed so nostalgic. Memories of us walking to and from school graced my mind. It had only been about a week since I had last seen Kenji, but it felt much longer. As we walked back together, we began catching up in each other's lives through small talk. From what Kenji was saying, nothing appeared to be different at home.

Reaching the house, we both walked up the walkway towards the front door where Kenji unlocked it and held it open for me. As I stepped in, my mother's voice was heard from the living room.

"I'm in here."

Slipping off my shoes, I thought it was still appropriate to announce my arrival. "I'm home."

Home? Maybe I should have said 'pardon the intrusion'.

I made my way to the living room to find my mother sitting on the couch, with Kenji following closely behind me. When I entered the room, my mother looked at me with a frail smile.

"Hello, hun, have a seat."

Finding it odd that my mother remained seated to greet me, even as I came into the house, I closely examined her before taking a seat. She appeared thinner and her face had become more caved in. She'd grown paler, almost unrecognizable. In such a short time, her appearance had altered greatly, leaving me disturbed.

She was surrounded by blankets and wore one of Kenji's toques on her head. On her lap was a ball of yarn, along with two knitting needles in her hands.

"Knitting . . .?" I asked, avoiding her sickly frame.

With the same frail smile, a light chuckle came through. "Yes. I've taken up a new hobby, haven't you heard?" my mother said sarcastically. "Since Ashima demands I take it easy, and avoid unnecessary, draining movements, your brother thought knitting would be 'fun.' But, in all honesty, knitting is not for me. With little return, it's too time-consuming for my liking."

With my mother's busy lifestyle before the cancer, I could understand how the simple change in pace was enough to annoy her. Seeing her agitated about something so insignificant, caused me to let out a little laughter.

Across the room, Kenji stood in the arched entryway. "Don't let her fool you. She complains about it, but she's been knitting up a storm, making outfits and all kinds of things for your baby."

Shifting my gaze from Kenji to our mother, I quickly turned back towards her, just in time to watch her blush.

"That's enough," she said, brushing off what he said lightly, turning her attention back to the partially knitted item on her lap. "My grandchild has to wear something warm when he or she comes home from the hospital."

Hearing the clear recognition of her grandchild filled me with incredible bliss. Moments like these made all the hard times worth going through.

As the visit neared its end, Kenji walked me back to the bus stop and waited with me until the bus arrived.

"Her spirits seem to be high; you're doing a good job. Thank you," I said, smiling proudly. "But," I continued, fearfully, "doesn't she seem a bit worn out compared to when I saw her last . . .?"

Taking a deep breath, Kenji looked at me as if he wanted to say something important, but refrained from doing so and just exhaled dramatically instead. "Dr. Ashima said she's doing fine, so she's fine," he said, looking away from me. "Sometimes, you have to get worse before you get better."

"Did Dr. Ashima say that?"

"No, I did. I'm doing the best I can, Nila."

"I know that. I'm not saying you aren't . . .."

"Blood is thicker than water; a family looks after each other, and that's what I'm doing."

"You certainly are," I said, unsure of what Kenji was getting at.

Another month flew by and Kai and I were nicely settled into our home by the end of October. Everything was unpacked and put away as we lived out each day. Bit by bit, we accumulated more items for the baby, and soon, they were casually mixed in with our own things. The tiny apartment managed to get even smaller. Kai's brother, Sosuke, was kind enough to give us an old baby crib, which had been used for Kai's niece, who had since grown out of it. Having the hand-me-down crib helped us out greatly. It felt like things were getting on track and we were finally confident in our preparations.

One day, while Kai was at work, I was at home preparing dinner, carefully arranging the ingredients, when I received a call. After a few rings, I was able to reach my cellphone in time. The call display read: *Kenji*.

"Hey Kenji, how's—"

"Nila," his voice shook as he cut me off, silence shortly following. "I need you to come to the hospital . . .."

Before he could finish, the phone fell out of my hand and landed beside my foot.

No . . ..

Chapter Forty-Eight

HEN KENJI SPOKE those words over the phone, my mind shut off, going completely blank. There were so many unexplainable emotions, I didn't know what or how to feel. Nothing made sense. The static of white noise filled my ears as I ran out of the apartment. Not knowing how I managed, I wound up at the hospital and somehow found myself inside. I passed reception without batting an eye, then rode the elevator to the second floor, presuming it was where I needed to go. Soon enough, my eyes started to hurt. I couldn't remember the last time I blinked, leaving my eyes dry and begging for moisture. The suspense of not knowing my mother's condition was killing me.

Approaching her old room, I found it occupied by a stranger. Gazing upon my left and turning towards my right, I saw no familiar faces. Forced to ask for assistance, I made my way to Dr. Ashima's office to get answers. Once I arrived, I noticed a closed door.

Please be here.

Knocking on the door, I waited a few seconds for a response before knocking again. With no answer, my blood boiled and I found myself aggressively banging on Dr. Ashima's door. From the loud ruckus I was creating, a nurse ran towards me.

"Miss! Excuse me, miss!" the nurse shouted as she approached. "I'm going to have to ask you to please refrain from banging so loudly as it may bother the patients."

"Sorry, um, I'm looking for Dr. Ashima. Is he here?"

"He is, but he's currently with a patient in their room. May I help you with anything?"

The back of my throat was hot, making it hard to swallow. Choking on my own saliva, I managed to respond. "Shino Iz— Kimura, where has she been placed?"

"Are you a relative?"

"She's my mother."

"Oh, yes, I see," the nurse said, changing to a stricter tone. "Actually, that is the patient Dr. Ashima is currently with. Please follow me."

The nurse walked past me and headed down the hall, then waited for me before turning the corner. She took me to the other side of the floor, stopping at the last door at the end of the hallway. Sitting on a chair outside the closed door was Kenji, hunched over with elbows digging into his knees and his face hidden within his palms.

"Your mother's room is here," the nurse stated. "Please come find me if you need anything else. I'll be at the Nurse's Station near the elevator."

As the nurse finished talking, Kenji shot up from the chair. "NILA!"

"Kenji!" I exclaimed, horrified. "What happened to Mom?"

With a pale face, Kenji panicked. "I don't know. I went to check on her and I found her collapsed on the floor in the bathroom and, and—" he tried to finish, but ran out of breath. "She wasn't responding when I called out to her, or when I shook her! So, I called for an ambulance and they came to the house and—everything's just a fuckin' mess, Nila!"

Running to my brother, I wrapped him in my arms and held him as close as I could. Kenji was much taller than me, but soon collapsed to my level, placing all his body weight onto me.

"Shh, it's okay," I said, snapping back into my old, aware self. "I'm here now; it's okay. You did the right thing; calling for help was the right thing to do."

Continuing to comfort my brother to the best of my ability, nurses with machines shuffled in and out of my mother's room.

"They haven't let me in to see her since she left the emergency wing downstairs," Kenji informed, pulling away from me to sit on a chair. "Nila . . .."

"Yeah?"

"She's not gonna beat this, is she?" he asked, looking down in defeat.

Just as I was about to respond, Dr. Ashima stepped out of the room; anguish painted his face. Kenji jumped back up and we both took a step closer to the doctor, seeking answers.

"Dr. Ashima!" Kenji called out loudly. "What's happening with our mom? Why won't they let us see her?"

Standing beside Kenji, I kept quiet, patiently waiting for Dr. Ashima's response.

"Calm down, young man. Take a deep breath," Dr. Ashima directed. Shaking his head in disappointment, he pressed on. "I am sorry. The cancer has spread too far in such a short amount of time. She is at the terminal stage. There is nothing more we can do."

Frozen, I stood and watched the scene unfold in front of me. My heart sank into the pit of my stomach.

"You're sorry . . .?" Kenji asked, rhetorically. "What do YOU mean YOU'RE fuckin' sorry? You said we caught it in time—YOU SAID SHE WAS GETTING BETTER!"

"Son, please, I know this is hard to understand, but she is at stage four. The cancer has spread into her brain and other various areas. Her lungs are also failing. Nothing else can be done, I am sorry."

Kenji brought his hands to his head and ran his fingers through his hair. Tears occupied his eyes as he pleaded, "Don't tell me you're sorry. Just save her! Save my mom!"

Dr. Ashima's face grew full of sadness and regret as he listened to Kenji's plea, unable to fulfil his heart-wrenching request. I could hear everything going on around me, but couldn't speak a single word. My mother wasn't going to die. How could she? She was my mother, the only one I had. She wasn't allowed to die. No matter how many times Dr. Ashima repeated himself, it wouldn't register in my brain.

"How long does she have?" I asked, soullessly.

"It is hard to say," Dr. Ashima answered remorsefully. "With cancer, once it has progressed this far, it could be any moment. She may have a few months, a few weeks . . . or mere days."

"Can we see her?" I asked, my voice hoarse.

"Of course. She is resting now, but you can both go in."

As soon as Dr. Ashima gave the okay, Kenji immediately dashed for the door.

"Before I let you go," he cautioned, placing an arm in front of Kenji to block him. "I need to advise you to refrain from discussing anything that may upset her. She is in a fragile state. Too much negativity could cause her time to come up short. It would be best to allow her to do as she pleases. Allow her to go where she wants, eat what she wants, and see those most important to her before it is too late. Spend as much time as you can with her before her time runs out."

As Dr. Ashima concluded, he released Kenji from his poorly enforced barricade. When Kenji was free to go, he bolted for the door.

"Miss Izawa," Dr. Ashima stopped me before I went in, waiting for the door to shut behind Kenji. "I am truly sorry. Not just as a doctor, but as your mother's coworker and friend. I hope neither you, nor your brother, have blamed yourselves during this ordeal. Unfortunately, she was dealt a crappy hand; there is nothing anyone can do about it at this point."

With Dr. Ashima's sympathy, I bowed my head to hide the tears, painfully walking to the door of my mother's room, alone. Face-to-face with uncertainty, I hesitated before taking a step inside. Thoughts raced through my mind, cluttering it with information I couldn't process or comprehend. I didn't dare think of a future without my mother in it.

I don't get how all this happened so fast. Just a year ago, she was fine, healthy as can be . . .What will I say to her once this door opens?

No longer having to worry about the door, a nurse opened it from inside as she made her way out. "Oh, pardon me," she said, jumping at my presence before carrying on.

When she released the door, it closed slowly, allowing me to catch a glimpse into the room. Half a second was all I needed to photograph the scene of my mother lying in a bed with Kenji standing over her. Taking that first step, I slid the door open to enter. My hands had been clenched for quite some time that my nails stabbed directly into my palms, causing marks I was sure would be permanent. With my breaking heart numbing the pain, for a moment, I couldn't feel a single thing.

My mother was in bed with her eyes shut as she wheezed heavily with the help of a machine, her breathing pattern all out of sorts. She wore a white hospital gown and a knitted hat she must have made to cover her hair loss. Kenji stood beside the bed, holding her hand delicately. Not wanting to wake her, Kenji and I watched her sleep silently for as long as we could until Kenji's phone went off. Quickly reaching for it, he ran out of the room to answer the call and silence the noise. I decided to step in and take his place until he returned. Remembering I had dropped my phone on the floor at home, I realized I hadn't picked it up before dashing off.

I hope Kai hasn't tried to call me. There's no way for him to get a hold of me, and I don't remember his number off by heart.

Not even half a minute went by before Kenji came back into the room.

"Nila, it's for you," Kenji said, handing me his cellphone.

"For me?"

"It's Kai."

"Kai . . .." Reaching for the phone, I took the call into the hall. "Hello?"

"Nila! Hey, is everything alright?" Kai asked frantically. "I tried calling your phone, but you never answered. Then, I came home and found it on the floor in the kitchen. Kenji just told me you guys are at the hospital. What's going on?"

The strength which had held me together moments ago, was gone. Hearing Kai's voice broke me. Tears gushed from my eyes and an obnoxious cry slipped out. Not knowing what to do or how to handle the situation, I fell to my knees and cried into the phone.

"NILA! Is it the baby? Is it your mom? Talk to me! What's going on over there? I'm on my way! Which floor are you on?"

Between all the crying and sobbing, I managed to form a few words. "M-my mom . . . It's bad, Kai. Please, come qu—"

Before the words even left my mouth, Kai shouted, "I'm coming; hold on!"

Hanging up, I felt a burning sensation tightening my chest, and a shattering notion from my heart. A few seconds ago, I was holding together just fine, so why was I like this now? I tried standing, but couldn't get up by myself. Besides being pregnant, my legs wouldn't work; they gave up trying.

Coming out to check on me, Kenji opened the door and saw me on the floor.

"Nila!" he shouted with alarm. "What happened?"

"I'm fine," I said, wiping my tears and swallowing deeply to release the built-up saliva that lingered at the back of my throat. "Just help me up."

I felt off-balanced as Kenji helped me to my feet, so he sat me on one of the chairs in the hallway.

Anxiety swept over him as he bent down in front of me until our eyes were at the same level. "Are you sure you're alright? Why were you on the floor?"

"I'm not sure," I answered honestly. "My legs gave out all of a sudden ...."

"Do you feel okay? How's the baby? Do you feel different? Are you getting sick?"

"Kenji," I grabbed his shoulder. "You're asking too many questions. I'm fine, just a bit tired."

Calming down, Kenji asked another question. "Is Kai coming?"

"Mhm," I answered, rubbing my throat to ease it.

"Good. I'll have him take you home."

"What? I can't go home! Not after the situation with Mom—she needs me here!"

"Nila, you'll just be in the way."

"Kenji!"

"You're no good here if you're gonna be like this. I can't watch over both of you at the same time—it's too much!"

"But I—"

"Nila, stop! Just listen for once, if not to me, then to your own body. Don't put too much stress on yourself. It's not good for you, or the baby."

"Ken—" I tried to speak, only to be interrupted once more.

"Ni—"

"LISTEN TO ME DAMMIT!" I demanded, forcing Kenji to back off. "I'm only going to worry and stress out even more if I go home. My mind will wander, and I'll only start thinking of the worst possible outcomes. Please, I want to stay."

Rubbing the stress off his face, Kenji growled, "Ugh, you're such a pain! Fine. But only if Kai says it's okay. Once he gets here, you're his responsibility." Rising to his feet, Kenji took a seat beside me as he leaned all the way back to rest his head against the wall. "You know," he paused, releasing a heavy sigh as he looked at the ceiling, "lately, you've become more . . . motherly."

Taken by his choice of words, I turned to him. "I have . . .? How?"

"I don't know, you just have. You're always looking out for people, making sure you've done everything you possibly could to help them, even if you haven't looked after yourself first. You're holding it together, though your life's a mess. Mom's do that."

Staring at Kenji, a heartfelt smile crept onto my face and into my heart. These rare, kind words from my brother, were ones to cherish. "Thanks."

"Yeah . . .."

Shortly after, Kai arrived. He met up with us in the hallway as we explained what was going on. We told him everything Dr. Ashima spoke to us about regarding my mother's current state. Kenji left me in Kai's care as he headed back into the room to see if our mother had awoken. Kai took Kenji's place on the chair beside me.

"Nila, I'm so sorry." Kai put his arm around me. "I can't believe this is happening, especially at a time like this."

Sitting in silence, tears dripping from my chin, I held onto Kai for dear life. Not knowing what to say, I sat quietly, crying into the strong arms I knew would protect me. I didn't want to let go, not of him and not of my mother.

Kai and I sat outside the room for quite some time until Kenji came out with empty eyes.

"She's awake."

Looking at Kai with fear, he forced a distracted smile as he helped me to my feet. Following behind me, Kai held my hand firmly as we entered. There was one chair close to the bed where Kai guided me as he stood tall beside me. Kenji was leaning against the wall close to the door, casting his gaze down to his feet with his shoulders slumped and arms crossed.

My mother, frail as can be, laid in bed with eyes half opened as we surrounded her. Just looking at such a skinny, fragile being, broke my heart. This person looked nothing like my mother. She was white, far worse than how she looked just days ago, with no hair left on her head as the knitted hat had been removed. I was amazed at how different she looked in such a short time. Her thin arms and collar bone stuck out—the true appearance of a dying person.

"Ni . . . la," my mother said, faintly.

"I'm here, Mom," I reached out to grab her hand. "I'm right here."

"Mmm . . . that's good," she replied, her eyes trying to focus on my face. "You look lovely, baby."

My throat closed up and my heart stiffened. I could hear the lifelessness in my mother's voice. The only time she used 'baby' when addressing Kenji or I, was when she felt immense sorrow or sadness. The last time I remember her doing so was when my father left.

"How do you feel, Mom?"

"I'm tired, baby . . . so, so tired," she answered as tears fell from her eyes.

"Mom," I pleaded softly. "You can't leave us, okay?"

With a pained smile, she replied, "I'm not going anywhere." Losing her breath, she looked to the plain, white ceiling. "I haven't even met my grandchild yet."

As I rubbed her hand back and forth, I wanted to say something comforting. "Once you're—"

"Nila," my mother talked over me, "I want to go home."

"Mom, I don't know if it's . . .."

"I want to spend the remainder of my time at home."

Looking over at Kenji, our eyes met, both unsure of what to say or do.

"Mom," Kenji took over, "once you're able to breathe without a machine, and Dr. Ashima says it's okay for you to leave, I promise, we'll take you home."

My mother turned her head slowly to face Kenji. She smiled emotionlessly. "That's a good boy."

Kenji didn't respond, not even with a false smile. He continued to stand against the wall, absently looking at her.

"I want to sleep," my mother said, looking at me and Kai. "Kento . . . Kai, can you please take my daughter home."

Not allowing Kai to speak, I burst out, "No! Mom, I'm going to stay here—with you!"

"Don't be ridiculous," my mother replied assertively, pausing to inhale. "You need to be at home in comfort during this period."

"Mom, I'm fi—"

"Your brother will stay with me. That's final," she said dismissively.

"I'll take her home, Ms. Kimura," Kai confirmed.

Not knowing what else to say, and not wanting to cause my mother further pain or distress, I remained silent as Kai helped me up. I gave my mother a gentle hug and placed a kiss on her forehead before heading out the door.

"I'll call you if anything changes," Kenji assured, whispering softly as we left.

Faced with the large, brightly lit, empty hallway, I felt the need to use the washroom before heading home. Kai walked me to the nearest washroom and waited for me outside. When I came out, Kai was no longer waiting for me. Unsure of where he went, I made my way back towards my mother's room to see if he'd returned there. Sure enough, Kai was re-exiting my mother's room, talking with Kenji as they both stepped out in conversation. I couldn't hear what they were saying because they were far, but as I got closer, their conversation quickly ended and Kai started walking towards me, while Kenji went back into the room.

"What was that about?"

"Oh, nothing. I just forgot my phone so I went back to get it."

Finding Kai's response a tad odd, I decided to drop it, saving myself the headache.

"Mommy, can you braid my hair?"

"Right now? Nila, you're going to be late for school if we start now. Why didn't you ask me earlier?" she asked with irritation.

"Mommy was busy with Kenji before . . .."

Pausing to look at the time, she agreed. "Okay, come here."

"Yay!"

"Me too! Me too!" Kenji shouted excitedly, running to the bathroom to follow us.

"Nooo! Kenji's a BOY! Boys CAN'T have braids in their hair!"

His face wrinkled in frustration. "Can so!"

"Nuh-uh!"

"Kenji, hun," Mom interfered, "your hair isn't long enough for a braid."

Kenji started to cry. "Pleeease, Mommy!"

She laughed under her breath. "Maybe we can try for a little one."

Wiping his tears, he smiled as if nothing happened. "Yeah!"

Finishing my braid first, she managed to create a small one at the top of Kenji's head where the longest pieces of hair grew. At the top of his head was a tiny braid sticking straight up to the sky, tied with a little red elastic.

"Yay!" Kenji said, running out of the bathroom to show me. "I have a braid, too!"

"Mine's better."

"Nuh-uh!"

"Yeah-huh!"

"Hurry up you two, or else you're really going to be late!"

"Okay, Mommy!" we replied simultaneously.

Chapter Forty-Nine

THROUGHOUT THE NEXT few days, our mother remained in the hospital and Kenji spent each waking moment and night there, refusing to leave her side. One day, I walked in on Kenji folding more paper cranes as our mother was sleeping. Just like last time, I sat down beside him and silently helped him fold another round of cranes. The following day, I stepped into a room of exploding colour. Cranes were strung together in flocks, hanging from the ceiling and other various places, adding up to two thousand. When I asked Kenji where they all came from, thinking it to be impossible to have folded an extra thousand on his own after I left, he said he had gone home to retrieve the ones stored in the closet, spending the entire night stringing cranes together until dawn.

The day after, Kenji and I sat with Dr. Ashima and asked when we could take our mother home. Unable to give us a concrete answer, he informed us that she wasn't well enough to be functioning on her own, but since we had the monetary accommodations for homecare, we could have the appropriate machines set up. Our mother would need to be under constant supervision if dismissed from the hospital, so we had to make sure we were ready for such a task.

We asked Dr. Ashima his opinion as to what he thought was best, and he restated how precious our mother's remaining time was, so we should do what we felt to be the best for her. Believing my mother would fare better in the comfort of her own home, I negotiated with Kenji, weighing the pros and cons of allowing her to spend her time the way she wanted. At first, Kenji was hesitant. He knew our mother wanted to go home, but was scared to be alone with her if something were to happen. Acknowledging his concerns, I made the choice to move back into the house. Kenji wasn't thrilled about the idea of me returning home, but he knew it would be best to have all the help he could get when the nurse wasn't around. Making his final decision, he agreed to bring her home, but only if she was deemed well enough to transport. On this note, Dr. Ashima agreed to keep our mother in the hospital until all homecare devices were up and running and we felt confident to move her.

Each time I saw my mother, she was worse. I feared she would never make it home. On the day Dr. Ashima had scheduled to discharge my mother from the hospital, her condition became fairly unstable and Kenji lost the ability to hold it together. He refused to bring her home and simply watch her suffer in a place filled with so many memories. He didn't want to associate the house we grew up in with our mother's death.

After that incident, Kenji said our mother never smiled again. No matter how uplifting we tried making things, attempting to convince her she would be able to go home soon, she remained soulless. There were times I couldn't even look at my mother's sickly appearance without breaking down. Her bones protruded as she wilted away to nothing. She complained of pain in areas she couldn't describe, scaring us into calling for help, resulting in the nurses and doctors not being able to help except alter her dosage of pain medication. Spending time with her was heartbreaking and emotionally draining. We all knew, no matter what we did, we could no longer help her recover, only watch fearfully as she slowly deteriorated.

Kenji caught her crying before falling asleep many nights. She must have thought he was already sleeping before exposing such a defenseless side. We couldn't understand her reasoning, but even during all this, our mother refused to show us her vulnerability unless it reached the unbearable extreme where it left her screaming in agony. Visually, everyone could see her struggling, but emotionally, she continued to keep things hidden.

One night, just as I was about to leave my mother's hospital room to head home, Kenji came out into the hall to talk with me privately.

"She'll never make it back home."

"You don't think so?" I asked, pretending to remain hopeful.

"Just look at her, Nila. She keeps getting worse."

Not knowing how to respond, I changed the conversation's direction. "How are you doing?"

"Me?"

"Yeah. You're here, day in and day out, while I get to go home, away from this setting. How are you holding up?"

"Nila, don't worry about me," he said, shaking off my concern.

"I'm being serious," I demanded, staring into his eyes. "Mom's life is not the only one that's important to me. I haven't seen you show much emotion lately; I'm getting worried."

Kenji dropped his gaze. "I don't know how to feel anymore. Kida keeps asking me the same thing," he said with a shaken voice. "Do I cry? Do I smile? Is it okay to constantly feel depressed? Is it okay to laugh with pity? Will any of THAT make me feel better? I don't know."

Stepping towards him, I went in for a hug. "I know what you mean; I feel the exact same way. We're on this path with no direction, no one to help guide us except ourselves. Sometimes, it's hard to communicate these feelings to Kida and Kai."

"Nila . . .."

"Hmm?"

"I think *this* is it."

Frozen, I dared to question. "What is?"

"Mom. I don't think she'll make it past this week."

"What do you mean?" I said, pushing him back. "There's no way it can be that quick!"

He encountered my gaze with distraught eyes. I didn't notice until that moment, but my brother's eyes had huge bags under them. I had been so focused on Kenji's mental state, and our mother's appearance, that I never paid attention to how worn-out my brother had started to look.

"Just go home, Nila."

"Go home? You want me to leave after having a conversation like this?" I raised my voice anxiously. "I won't!"

Kenji shoved me in the direction of the open hallway. "It's too much right now. Please, just go home."

What does he mean, 'too much'? "Kenji!"

"Nila," he said strictly, turning around to walk away from me. "Don't come tomorrow."

I was blown away by his coldness, so I blinked multiple times to refocus my attention. "Are you insane? Of course, I'm coming tomorrow!"

Continuing his way back to the door, he placed one hand on the handle slit and looked down. "No, you're not."

"Why are you saying these things?"

Not meeting my eyes, Kenji answered, confusing me even more. "As my sister, I'm begging you to stay away from the hospital tomorrow. So, please, just do as I say. Don't pry into things further."

With those final words, he stepped into the room, leaving me confused and alone in a place I loathed. My mind raced in different directions, trying to put pieces of an unsolvable puzzle together.

Why tomorrow? And why did he look at me like that?

Not knowing what to do after such an abrupt conversation, I unwillingly did as I was told, leaving the cold, ill-smelling hospital and went home.

That night, I couldn't sleep; the words Kenji lashed out at me kept me up. Trying to figure out what he wasn't telling me, and why, left me with a pounding headache.

Morning took forever to arrive; I had pulled an all-nighter. After tossing and turning most of the night, I had given up on the idea of sleep. Making the littlest of movements so as to not wake Kai, I rose from the futon. Going back to my books, I sat near the shelf and took out my father's favourite novel. I shook it aggressively to make the picture of my family fall out, but nothing was there. Desperately, I searched the area around the bookshelf, but I couldn't find my precious memory anywhere.

I used the wall to help me up and finally came face-to-face with the greatest surprise. Sitting on top of our waist-high bookshelf, was the picture of my family, framed. This was the first picture displayed in our home. While holding the frame, I glanced back at my handsome, sleeping prince.

"Thank you," I whispered, hugging the picture dearly.

"Nila . . .." A familiar voice kept calling out to me in the near distance. "Nila, wake up."

Suddenly opening my eyes, Kai was hovering over me.

"What did I tell you about sleeping in weird places?" he said frantically. "Why can't you sleep on the futon like a normal person? You're going to hurt your back if you sleep like this."

Smiling, I cried out happily, "Thank you."

His eyes softened as he kneeled. "What for?"

"For this," I said, lifting the picture frame. "I love it."

With a sweet smile, he placed a kiss on my forehead. "I found it on the floor. Framing it only seemed right."

Leaning forward, I hugged his neck, releasing my built-up tension in a simple embrace. Warm tears dropped from my face and landed on Kai's shirt, slowly disappearing as they absorbed into the material.

"Now, can you please go back to bed. You must be tired."

I peered up at him. "You knew?"

"How could I not? You moved around all night. I know how restless you must be, but please be careful. When you take care of yourself, you're also taking care of our baby."

"I know. It's just hard to concentrate on myself when I'm feeling like this."

"I believe you." He hesitated. "Am I that unreliable?"

"No, why would you say that?"

"Then, can you try to rely on me a little more? If I can take away at least one of your burdens, please let me."

"Okay."

As I tried to get to my feet, Kai immediately picked me up and princess carried me to the futon. Setting me down carefully, he fell back onto the futon beside me, signaling me to do the same. Once I laid back, he proceeded to cuddle me in his strong, protective arms until I fell asleep.

When I awoke, Kai was nowhere to be found. Even though it was no longer morning, I selfishly expected him to still be beside me. My stomach felt queasier than usual, but after sitting up for a short while, things started to settle. Reaching for my phone, the time read: 2:33 p.m. on Monday, November 2nd.

November already, huh? Where have the days gone?

Taking my time to get up, I made my way into the kitchen. To my surprise, there was a note left on the counter.

Nila,

I hope you had a well-deserved sleep and are now fully rested. I'll be home around 4:00 p.m. from the shop, so, please, wait for me before you leave the apartment. Kenji has requested I keep you away from the hospital until later this evening, so please, follow his orders—I know how you can be. I promise to take you once I get home.

Have a good day.

Love, Kai

Not knowing if I should take the note as a request or an insult, I tossed it aside in anger. This whole ordeal made me feel like an incapable child within an adult situation. No one would tell me what was really going on, as if they had zero confidence that I could handle it, whatever IT was. Every second I spent at home, waiting, was a second wasted because I could have been spending it with my dying mother. Knowing she didn't have much time left, why would Kai and Kenji keep me from seeing her? I had many issues with how they were dealing with things, and it aggravated me down to my core. Yes, I was pregnant, but that didn't mean I couldn't continue living with the hardships of life.

Just over an hour later, I heard the front door unlock and Kai walked in. Closing the door behind him with his foot, he held a giant bouquet of flowers in one arm and a box of miscellaneous objects in the other. Heading towards the entrance to greet him, Kai locked eyes with me as he slipped his shoes off using only his feet.

"I'm home," he said, placing the box down on the raised step of the entryway.

"Welcome home," I said, standing in front of him. "Who are the beautiful flowers for?"

"They're for your mom," Kai smiled, sadly. "I know you have been patiently waiting. Would you like to go and see her now?"

"I made dinner . . .."

"We can always eat it when we get back."

Unsure of the feeling I was getting from Kai, I nodded in agreement.

While making our way to the hospital, an unsettled feeling drifted over me once we arrived. Something about this day wasn't sitting right, but I couldn't place my finger on it. I knew Kenji was indifferent about me coming today, but for Kai to join him, was odd.

We entered the hospital, riding the elevator up like usual. Once Kai and I reached my mother's floor, we got off and walked down the hall; everything was the same so far. When we came to the end of the final strip, Kai took the bouquet of flowers from me and grabbed my hand, bringing me around the corner of the hallway. Quickly looking at him, I didn't have much time to stare because what I saw from my peripherals gained all of my attention. Around the corner, the plain, white hallway was lined with flowers, a familiar scene from a pleasant memory not too long ago. Frozen, I looked down the entire hallway, speechless.

Kai gently tugged on my hand. "This way . . .."

Allowing him to guide me, I ventured my eyes to each side as I walked down a path sprinkled with petals, admiring each flower display I passed. "What is all this?"

"Wait 'til we get there."

Kai left me in suspense, something he was good at. He turned to face me and began walking backwards down the path, locking eyes with me as he held my hand. His eyes were full of love, but also extremely serious in a way I hadn't seen before. The aroma that emanated from the flowers made it feel like spring, as if I were standing in a giant, blooming field.

When I neared the end of the floral path, I wasn't sure if I was feeling excited or scared. The path led straight into my mother's room, where my brother stood at the entrance, comfortably smiling.

Kenji?

At the end, Kai turned to face the front and escorted me into the room, with Kenji following behind us. The hospital room was filled with multiple arrangements from the Kento shop; a spectrum of each colour from the rainbow glowed in the tiny, secluded space from the flowers and cranes above. In the middle of it all was my mother, lying peacefully in bed. Although she was clearly still pale, her complexion beamed radiantly. Walking closer to her, I spun around the room in awe before stopping at the edge of her bed.

"What is all this?" I asked for a second time.

Smiling, my mother adjusted her eyes before licking her dry lips. "Nila," she said, already out of breath, "I'm very proud of you."

Getting a bit choked up, I shook my head. "I don't understand . . . Why are you saying this?"

Kenji walked to the other side of our mother's bed while holding a poorly wrapped box that resembled a gift. Holding onto it securely, he smiled softly. "Turn around, sis."

"Hmm?" I muttered, before looking over my shoulder. Cocking my head, Kai was no longer at eye level. Looking downward, Kai was on one knee. He held out a small box revealing a ring with a sparkle that pierced my heart. Finishing my turn slowly in amazement, my hands covered my mouth as my eyes grew wide. "Kai . . . ."

"Nila, when I met you, I thought you were going to be just some girl who left my life as quickly as she entered . . . ."

"Kai, stop . . . ."

"But, when I saw you for the second time at the karaoke bar, everything changed. Watching you from across the table, an urge came over me where I wanted to annoy the hell outta you. You had this fiery spirit, piquing my interest; I needed to know you, to get closer to you. I obsessed over the need to discover the secrets in those pained eyes of yours. From then on, each time we met, I wanted more from you in ways I didn't know how to achieve. Since the very first day, you have become so heavily entangled in my life, that at times, even now, it's scary. But, without you, I don't know where I'd be. You have saved me numerous times, especially when I was faced with problems or situations my mind chose to avoid. You forced me to face every issue head-on, making me do life-changing things I didn't know I could. For that, I love you. I know our time together has been short, and our relationship is evolving quickly, but I love every part I have discovered about you and I cannot wait to discover more. So," he paused, shaking where he knelt as he looked deep into my eyes, "please consider this ring as a promise, one with the intent of marriage to follow after our lives have settled and we have matured into fine, respectable adults. Nila," he said, taking a massive breath, "will you do me the honour of marrying me?"

Listening to Kai's sonorous voice, my throat closed as if something had gotten lodged in it, while my heart prepared to jump out of my chest at any given second. My mind went hazy, causing tears to spill out as I stared down at the wonderful man before me. It was all too much to take in. No words could describe how remarkably happy I was to have fallen in love with such an incredible person, and to have him love me in return. Thinking back to how fast this year went by, utterly terrified me. I blinked, and somehow, I ended up here in this moment. All the hurdles we jumped over together took a heavy toll on us, but it left my heart smiling.

Speechless once again, I dropped to my knees and helplessly threw myself at Kai. Still managing to keep our balance, I repeatedly nodded my head. "Yes, you idiot!"

Kai's hands shook uncontrollably as he tried to slip the ring onto my finger. Once it was secured, Kai lifted his hand up to my face and kissed my lips like a crazy person, just before burying me deep into his chest. Never having received a hug filled with so much love from someone other than my parents, I remembered my mother and Kenji were watching.

Embarrassed about kissing Kai in front of them, feeling like I might be scolded, I slowly turned around. Making eye contact with my mother, she smiled peacefully as Kai helped me to my feet.

"You both knew?"

Continuing to wear a wholesome smile, my mother responded. "He's a fine, young man," she inhaled excessively. "I am sorry for doubting him."

"Shortly after you guys left the other day, Kai came back and asked Mom and I for your hand in marriage."

Is that when he said he 'forgot' his phone? How slick . . ..

"He said it wouldn't be anytime soon, but . . .," Kenji shrugged.

My lungs pressed forcefully together, threatening to suffocate me.

"He's a great man, Nila. I am sorry I won't be able to see you in your wedding dress," my mother said, coughing aggressively. "Let alone my grandchild."

"Mom! But you said—"

"Here," Kenji shoved the gift into my face from across the bed. "This is from Mom."

"Kenji helped," my mother noted wholeheartedly.

"Not really."

As I reached for the box, I noticed some of Kenji's fingers were wrapped in bandages.

"Kenji, what happ—"

"Just open it," Kenji said forcefully, retracting his hand.

Sitting down on the chair beside the bed, I opened the gift. Inside was a bunch of neutral, handmade baby clothes, including: a couple of outfits, a few hats, and tiny mittens in many colours. Along with all of that, there was a sealed envelope.

"Hats were the easiest to make, that's why there are so many of them," my mother said.

"I think the mitts were easier," Kenji added.

My eyes grew with surprise. "Kenji . . . you helped make these?"

Turning away, Kenji replied, "I had to. Mom said the gift wasn't done, and she's too weak to use her hands."

"Mom," I looked at her. "You . . . can't use your hands?"

My mother's tranquil smile became morbid. "I don't think I will be leaving this hospital," she said, breathless. "I've come to terms with it. It hurts to swallow and I'm constantly tired. I can no longer pretend everything is okay; my body is giving up on me."

435

"MOM! DON'T SAY THAT!" I burst out, tossing the box aside.

"Nila," Kai whispered. "Please . . . ."

"NO! She can't go around saying stuff like that! I see what's happening now—this whole day has been a trap!"

"Nila!" Kenji reinforced. "Calm down."

"Calm down? HOW CAN I CALM DOWN WHEN YOU'VE ALL BROUGHT ME HERE TO TELL ME MOM HAS GIVEN UP!" I looked at Kenji. "And what happened to you? You NEVER gave up on her before! You were ALWAYS the strong one! What happened?" I screamed at the top of my lungs.

Triggered by my words, Kenji glared at me with harsh eyes. "That's enough! You're making this harder on Mom and yourself." Pointing at our mother, Kenji's voice cracked as he continued with rage. "Look at her, Nila. She can barely move—she's dying!"

"Kenji! Nila!" Kai exclaimed, getting in the middle. "You both need to stop!"

Looking past them, I got up from the chair to face my mother. The whole time I was there, my mother never once moved or adjusted herself. Thinking about it with more detail, it was starting to make sense.

"So, that's it. You're just . . . giving up?"

With the most dejected tone I've ever heard from her, she answered with a lack of strength in her voice. "It's time, baby."

'Baby'? "No . . . no! NO! NO! NO!" I broke.

From the beginning, I had known there was something wrong. Kai put so much thought into the proposal, so I should have been overjoyed with warming emotions. Instead, I felt immense heartache as I questioned how much time was left on my mother's mortal clock. It seemed Kai feared losing my mother before properly asking for my hand in marriage, so he did what he felt was best. But how could she come to terms with giving up at a time like this? With everything playing on repeat in my head, my brain had gone numb. It was too much and I didn't want, or know, how to deal with any of it. At the same time, I started feeling nauseous; vomit made its way up, while acid blistered the inside of my throat.

No, not here! Not now!

"Nila?" I could hear Kai's remote voice call out.

Running out of the room to escape for air, I tried my hardest to calm down without initiating an attack. I attempted some breathing exercises but couldn't clear my airway. Before I knew it, I fell to my knees and began to throw up all over myself and the floor, gasping for air any chance I could.

Kai ran after me and took action as he saw me on the floor. Getting down to my level, he started rubbing my back as he called my name over and over. Terror filled his eyes, just like the last time he witnessed me like this. With the disgusting sound of someone throwing up echoing throughout the halls, Kenji ended up following us.

"NILA!" Kenji shouted, also coming to my aid. "HELP! WE NEED HELP OVER HERE!" Kenji screamed at the top of his lungs with one knee down beside me, holding my hair back.

Within seconds, medical personnel flooded the hallway.

"Sir, we're here!" a male wearing some type of medical badge responded, as nurses rushed in behind him. "Can you tell me what happened?"

Flustered, Kenji tried to answer calmly. "I-I don't know!"

Taking over for Kenji, Kai yelled in fear. "SHE'S HAVING A PANIC ATTACK!"

"Sir, calm down," the male medical attendant enforced, speaking to Kai. "The more you two fuss, the worse it will be for her." Turning away, the attendant shouted, "I need a bucket over here!"

Kenji's eyes widened. "She-she's pregnant! She's my sister and she's pregnant!"

"About eight months pregnant!" Kai quickly added in despair.

As soon as the medical attendant looked down and noticed I was pregnant, his eyes changed. "I need someone to check vitals, STAT!" The male attendant said strictly to the small team of nurses, while instructing Kai and Kenji to gently seat me on one of the chairs outside of my mother's room. "The patient is pregnant; signs of respiratory issues and possible high blood pressure are present. I need readings!"

With everything happening in a blur, Kai and Kenji were soon shoved into the crowd. I could no longer see them with all the medical personnel around me. The vomiting had subsided, but my stomach was killing me; thoughts of the baby being in danger crossed my mind, causing me to further panic.

"Miss, look at me," the medical attendant said, guiding my eyes to focus on his face. "My name is Dr. Furukawa and I'm going to help you, but first, I'm going to need you to calm down, okay? If you don't calm down, you could risk hurting the baby or risk going into premature labour. Now, I need you to answer a few questions, okay?"

Staring blankly at Dr. Furukawa, I understood what he was saying, but couldn't respond quick enough.

"Okay?" he repeated once more.

Nodding my head, the doctor's eyes lightened.

"What's your name?"

"Ni—" I cleared my acidic throat. "Nila Izawa."

"Okay, Miss Izawa, are you experiencing any back or stomach pain?"

Nodding quickly, I confirmed. "Yes, a lot of stomach pain."

Mentally analyzing the information, Dr. Furukawa pressed on. "Is it a cramping type pain or more of a sharp pain?"

"It's an intense burning pressure that comes and goes." As those words left my mouth, my stomach pain increased. It was no longer just an upset stomach from throwing up; something else was wrong. The pain shifted to a tightening and squeezing motion as it became aggressively unbearable. "AHH!" I instantly screamed, clenching my stomach and the chair I sat upon.

"NILA!"

I heard Kai's voice shout from the background, but I couldn't see him with the amount of people surrounding me. I was getting claustrophobic. I looked at my feet and saw that a diluted pool of blood had formed. My mind drew blank as I watched the puddle travel down my legs and surround my shoes, completely engulfing theas we walk lip of the thin, white edges.

"Dr. Furukawa, she is reading between moderate and severe hypertension," a nurse informed, removing the cuff from my arm.

"I NEED A WHEELCHAIR OVER HERE!" Dr. Furukawa yelled over his shoulder. "She's going into premature labour, possibly stress-induced!"

My body started shutting down; there were times I even forgot to breathe. It felt like my body was being controlled by everyone except me. I had no idea what was going on or what to do. While being pushed around in a wheelchair, the scenery around me changed rapidly. Everything was a blur; my vision went in and out. The times I tapped back in were the times the pain from my stomach overwhelmed me to the point of tears. Before I knew it, I was lying on a hospital bed of my own, having nurses and medical professionals hooking me up to machines for monitoring.

"She's losing consciousness!" an unfamiliar female voice shouted.

"Sustain it! We need her to stabilize! Set up for a possible Cesarean Section!"

"Yes, Dr. Furukawa!"

"Find out if she has an OB, if so, call them immediately!"

"Yes, doctor!"

Everything turned dark. I could hear voices, but eventually, they all mumbled and mashed together. The pain, once pulsating from my heart, could no longer compare to the one from my stomach. My chest was burned with the strongest of flames. My whole body hurt, an amount of pain I had never experienced, nor wished upon anyone. My insides were exploding; everything was so hot.

I was unable to focus on anything or anyone. In my head, I screamed Kai's name a million times, but feared not even he could hear me. What was this feeling? Why couldn't I scream out loud enough to be heard?

Time slowed until it came to a complete stop. White noise rang through my ears, as if a bomb went off close by, like in a movie. Not really knowing where I was or how much time had passed, the silence was broken with a high-pitched cry.

"Time of birth: 11:52 p.m., weight: 2.22kg. Multiple complications associated with childbirth. Continue to monitor the mother."

Chapter Fifty

I AWOKE TO FIND myself in a hospital room, one similar to my mother's. The room was quiet, sounds of machines beeping were all I could hear. Above me, a rainbow of cranes hung from every inch of the ceiling, twirling back and forth as they danced in the morning sun. Lifting my head, I saw Kai hunched over the bed with his arms resting against me, soundly asleep as he held my hand. Struggling to adjust my body, Kai immediately woke up when I tried to move. Kai's eyes were filled with water as he jumped up and carefully embraced me. Disoriented, I slowly realized the more I tried to move, the more pain I experienced. I had little to no control of my body, paralysis quickly struck me. My nostrils flared as I internally freaked out. Kai tried to calm me down as he explained what happened in mild context. In disbelief, all I could do was cry as my life changed before me. Not sure if the tears I was crying were happy or sad; all my feelings joined into one fixed, unnamable emotion.

I overflowed with joy from the news once Kai confirmed our child was born healthy. When I asked where our baby was, he said the delivery was complicated, so the nurses took our baby to the NICU. Kai said it was complicated because I went into stress-induced labour and didn't dilate properly. Other factors contributed to the complications as well, such as my age and body size; since I was small by nature, labour had been extremely taxing. Kai also informed me Dr. Toma was called into the delivery room to assist shortly after the procedure started. Apparently, after six hours of excruciating labour, longer than what was deemed healthy for the both of us, the doctors decided on a c-section. Kai told me I was in and out of consciousness during the actual delivery process, but honestly, I didn't remember any of the time spent in labour.

Amazed by everything Kai was telling me, for a split second, I had forgotten about my mother. When I inquired about her, Kai fell silent. A cold reality hit me as Kai turned his head. The night a life began was the same night another ended. My mother had passed away minutes after our child was born, right on the floor above me. She was gone, and I hadn't even had the chance to say goodbye.

Chapter Fifty-One

To my precious Nila,

I hope you're reading this letter after I have already passed. I want you to know how proud I am of you, and how proud I have always been of you and your accomplishments. I know I was hard on you and Kenji, but I want you to know my intentions were always good and I had your best interests in mind. I hope the two of you remain the greatest of friends, and the closest of family—no matter what life throws your way. Nila, I love you and your brother very much and I am sorry for keeping my illness a secret from you for as long as I did. I couldn't admit the cancer to myself—let alone my children. I am truly sorry for the hardships I have caused you and Kenji, but I hope you are able to forgive me and move on from this difficult time. I know you can do it, because I know how strong you have become. I may not be around anymore, but I will always protect my babies.

Ps. I hope you enjoyed the baby clothes. I wish I could've seen my grandbaby wear them.

Love, Mom

We can never return to yesterday because we were different people then; therefore, we remain in the present to work towards a fresh tomorrow.

The adults who always used to say, *'Life is too short; it goes by in the blink of an eye,'* could not have been any more accurate. It was as if I had closed my eyes to take a quick nap, only to wake up many years later to find the world around me altered significantly. If someone had told me this is how my young adult life was going to start, I would have thought they were insane. People grow and so does every other living thing, until eventually their time runs out and they pass on. I truly believe every time someone or something dies, a new living thing is born to replace the original—the circle of life.

Dr. Ashima documented my mother's death by saying officially her lungs collapsed, followed by her throat closing, terminating all air passage as if she were suffocated by the cancer itself. Kenji was in the room when she died. He said she looked peaceful, considering the circumstances, but I do believe it to be true. I want to say she purposefully stuck around long enough for her grandchild to be born, making sure everything was okay before passing, but that might just be wishful, spiritual thinking.

Kai and Kenji tried calling each other to inform the other of what was going on at the time, but their calls went straight to voicemail. Deciding to head towards the others' location, they met each other halfway within the hospital halls. Kai said he didn't even have to hear Kenji relay a single word because he already knew the outcome just by the look on his face. Later that day, Kida and the Kentos passed by to see me and the baby, but I don't recall their visits, or much of the entire day.

Once Kai caught me up on everything, he went to find a nurse to let them know I was awake. When I was able to move, Kai took me to the NICU where I met our baby for the first time. I remained in the hospital for four days before being released, only to be faced with my mother's funeral, and the new human life for which I was now responsible.

My mother's funeral, arranged and paid for by my father, took place the day after I was discharged. Distant relatives, friends, and coworkers from the hospital attended. The biggest surprise for Kenji was seeing my father at the funeral. In seeing him for the first time in almost three years, Kenji became irate, and would have caused a scene if it weren't for Kai, who was able to step in and defuse the situation. After the service, my father pulled Kenji aside to speak with him privately, but Kenji walked away from him. It wasn't until a year later, that Kenji took the initiative and reached out to our father to state he could never forget what our father did, but he was ready to try and forgive him in order to move on.

A lot happened the next few years. The two months after giving birth were the worst months of my life. It pained me to admit, but I neglected my child, leaving Kai to practically raise our baby on his own. Each time I would look at our beautiful baby girl, I thought of my mother's death. There wasn't a day that went by where I could look at her with complete bliss, like I felt a mother should, and truly be grateful for her existence. I spent weeks in bed, unable to function. I had many responsibilities, but couldn't manage a single thing on my own. My eyes were bloodshot, but I had no tears left to cry. In this new life, without the love and support of my mother, I was lost.

I honestly believed my mother was forced to give up her life in order for her granddaughter to be born, and this thought sickened me. One saying played in my head in constant repetition: *'A life for a life'*—but why did it have to be hers?

At first, to help me cope, Kai kept telling me: *"Feelings don't die, because we keep feeding them with memories,"* but I had so many memories I still wanted to share with my mother, so I had a hard time accepting his words. You can only try to understand so much until you mentally and emotionally can't anymore. Losing her didn't kill me, but something inside me died that day just the same.

A great deal of time has passed, and those negative emotions I once harboured, are now gone. It's been four years since my mother's passing, but I remember the pain of hearing the news like it was yesterday. She passed away minutes after I gave birth, but it wasn't until the next day that I was informed of her departure—that fact alone killed me. I will forever regret not being able to be by her side during her last moments alive, knowing very well it would have been impossible. When I try to look back, haziness clouds my mind, a faint memory with missing gaps. There was nothing anyone could do to bring my mother back, and I now know that's okay.

People always told me having a baby was the most rewarding thing in life, and the feeling you get when you become a parent is incomparable to anything else. Though it took me longer to get there, they were absolutely right.

"We're late again," I let out a sigh of disappointment as I glared out the car window, annoyed.

"Don't stress so much. It's fine; your dad won't mind if we're a few minutes late."

"But we're ALWAYS late."

"Nila, it's fine." Kai reaches over and places one hand on my leg. "I know you're pregnant, but you're gonna die young if you continue to worry about little things, like fifteen minutes."

"Stop comparing me getting angry, with mood swings from being pregnant. I've had enough of that carefree attitude of yours." Removing his hand in agitation, I point to the windshield. "Can you watch the road, please."

"Yes, Ma'am," he says with a smirk, placing his hand back on the steering wheel.

Within the first year of my mother passing, Kai and I, plus our new little addition, moved out of our small apartment and into my mother's house. In the Will, we never knew she wrote, my mother left the house in my name, as long as I gave shelter to my brother. With a short discussion, and Kenji living with our father being out of the question, we swapped places. Kenji moved into the apartment and we got the house. After settling in, we built a Butsudan altar in memory of my mother, lighting incense with prayer daily. A few years later, Kida moved into the apartment with Kenji.

Last year, after a lengthy engagement, Kai and I finally got married. It was a small wedding with few invitees, but we wouldn't have wanted it any other way. Kida was happy to help plan it, though was upset at the amount of stuff I wanted to leave out. Surprisingly, a few weeks before the wedding, Taki came over unannounced, asking to speak with Kai privately. The two of them went for an hour walk. Once Kai returned, I asked him what Taki wanted so suddenly. He proceeded to tell me that Taki wanted to discuss something which he felt had been weighing on their friendship since before Hatori's passing. The issue was Momiji, and Taki's never-ending feelings towards her. Taki told Kai that he and Momiji had been in close contact recently, and wanted to make sure Kai was okay with it before pursuing things further. Being able to move past such a traumatizing memory, Kai congratulated Taki, telling him it would even be fine if he chose to bring Momiji to the wedding as his date. With both of us in agreement, understanding Momiji was not solely at fault and did not deserve to be hated forever, I was proud we could put the past behind us.

Kai and I had to grow up fast, experiencing many adult situations on our own. Thankfully, we had a lot of help from our families and close friends, making it somehow more manageable than expected.

My life before him was so simple and decided. Kai came into my life with loud footsteps, causing an eruption of new experiences to the modest life I had led. He took charge, guiding me through a world of extreme wonders and distress. There are more times than I can count when I doubted our relationship over the years, but he never let me give up. No matter how many times I pushed him away, or tried dealing with things on my own, Kai made sure to take a step closer. I had been scared to go forward; therefore, it took me forever to move forward.

Also, within the last year, my father-in-law took early retirement and Kai became the sole owner of the flower shop. Ryu, finishing his last year of high school, and Kenji, fresh out of college, started working at the flower shop part-time. Three years back, when I first found out Kenji decided to attend college, another weight lifted from me—I was finally starting to float. Our mother would have been proud. I, on the other hand, never finished my program. I ended up getting a regular office job, with suitable set hours, at a local business here in town. Kai pushes for me to go back to school, but I keep putting it off, not sure how I would handle returning after the many years I've had off.

About ten minutes later, we pull into my father's driveway.

"Practically half an hour late," I hiss in exaggeration as we step out of the car.

"Relax," Kai snaps back. "I said I was sorry for picking you up late from work, didn't I? If it was a problem for your dad, he would have taken her to my parent's house next door. My parents are always looking for excuses to take her."

As we walk around to the front of the car, we meet each other and continue up the driveway.

"I guess you're right."

Kai takes my hand. "No need to guess, we both know I am."

I roll my eyes as I take a step forward. "Idiot."

Kai tugs on my hand, pulling me back towards him. He reaches around to my shoulder and brings me in nice and close to his face, placing a gross, slobbery kiss on my cheek. "You bet I am."

"You're also disgusting," I say, as I wipe the excess saliva off my face.

Walking up to the front door, voices and laughter can be heard coming from around back.

"Seems like they're in the backyard."

"Wouldn't doubt it," Kai agrees. "It's a nice, warm day after all."

Heading around to the side of the house, we face a fence that reaches just past my waist. Kai leads the way, unlatching the gate and holding it open for me to enter ahead of him. The corner of the house blocks us from being seen by those in the backyard. Taking a few steps past the corner, I see my father and daughter happily playing together.

"Be careful!"

"I'm okay; I won't fall Grandpa, promise."

"Oh, really? How are you so sure?"

"Because I've been practising my ball-dance with Daddy."

"Ball-dance? OH! You mean balance."

"Yeah! Daddy holds my hand when I walk on the curbs—but only if I wobble!"

"I see. Well, even though the ledge is small, Grandpa would prefer his Sugar-Plum to be safely on the ground. Here, give Grandpa your hand."

"Ohhh-kaaay . . .."

"Thank you."

"Oh! Oh! Grandpa! Is the paint dry yet?"

"I don't know, let's go find out."

"Yeah!"

Eventually, we're spotted by my father. He stands tall, holding onto my daughter's hand as he spins her around to face us. I lock eyes with my emerald green eyed mini-me.

"Mommy!" She runs towards me at top speed.

"Hi, baby," I say, bending to my knees, bracing myself, and my large stomach, for a strong, running hug.

With a cute little grunt from impact, she looks up at me. "I missed you, Mommy!"

"Only Mommy?" Kai cries childishly. "What about me, Ume?"

"Daddy!" Ume leaves my arms and jumps straight into Kai's. "Where's Hatchi?"

"I had to leave him at home while I picked up Mommy, but you'll see him soon."

"Okay," Ume replies happily.

"How was she?" I ask my father as he approaches us, helping me to my feet.

"She's been fine. Keeping me on my toes as per usual, with all her energy, just like someone else I know," he flashes me a smile.

"I believe it," Kai chimes in. "Hopefully, the next one is less 'spirited.'"

"Hey, a little energy never hurt anyone," I fight in defence.

"Mommy! Mommy!"

I look down at my leg to where Ume is tugging on my skirt. "Yes, baby?"

Her eyes alight with excitement as she continues to tug. "Come see what me and Grandpa Youji made!"

"Okay, okay, show me." I gently remove her hold on my skirt and grab her tiny hand.

"Uncle Yano was helping too, but he left to go to the store with Grandma Chizuko and Aunt Yuki," Ume continues, pulling me along towards my father's shed.

"That was nice of him."

"Yeah!" Her smile is huge.

Ume lets go of my hand and rushes in front of me. Her shoulder length, brown hair whips around in a tangled mess from eagerness.

"Mommy, you gots'ta close your eyes, 'kay? It's a super-prize."

"Oh, I see, a surprise. Alright, I'll keep them shut."

"Promise?"

"Promise."

I keep my eyes shut with one hand on top. Still able to hear everything, I hear her open the shed door before she rustles around with the stuff inside. Ume is never good at being discrete or keeping quiet.

"Ready!" her voice echoes excitedly. "Mommy, you can open your eyes now!"

Removing my hand, I open my eyes to discover something I never thought I'd see again, sitting on a worn-out workbench. Immediately, I shoot a look back at my father who continues to stand tall beside Kai, both facing my direction. As I stare at him, he smiles genuinely, mouthing the words *'I'm sorry'* with tears accumulating in his eyes.

Silently crying over the rebuilt dollhouse my father and daughter worked on together, a gentle hand rests on my shoulder. I look up to see my father now standing next to me.

"A few months ago, your brother Ken paid me a visit. He brought me a smashed-up, pile of wood, which he pushed me into believing was once your dollhouse. He explained what had happened years ago and asked me if I could fix it up for Ume. I didn't ask any questions and got to work on it right away. After all, that was the first thing he's asked of me since even before your mother passed away."

"Dad, I don't even know what to say. I never thought I would see this dollhouse again." Tears further cloud my vision as I stare at it in a different viewpoint. "The colour is different though."

He shakes his head and laughs. "Your daughter wanted a 'pink' house, just like the shirt she was wearing yesterday when we painted it. She seems to have a very complex mind for decision making."

Pleased, I turn and hug my father. "Thank you, for everything."

He soon wraps his arms around me, too. "Anything for you, Peaches."

CPSIA information can be obtained
at www.ICGtesting.com
Printed in the USA
LVHW111324150522
718815LV00004B/587